# MANCHINEEL

By

Daniel E. Harold

Amazing cover by the talented Carleen Lunsford, Hannah Lunsford, and Haden Lunsford

*This book is dedicated to the love of my life, Stephanie, whose hook bridged the gap between generic and unique. I could not have written it without her.*

*To our children, Ryan, Jack, and Layla, make your magic real.*

*Special thank you to my parents, Susie and David, for giving me the keys, and to my father-in-law, Larry, for putting us on the road where this particular story was conceived.*

# ODE TO FAMILY VACATION TIME

## *Chapter One*

*White knuckles.*

*White motherfuckin' knuckles.*

*Barely starting but already white-knucklin'.*

He had been in the car a grand total of twelve minutes, eighteen seconds, and much of that time was actually spent alone outside the car filling up at the gas station. Thomas Preston was already fully tensed. Looking down, he tried to calm himself by joking that he was choking the poor life out of the steering wheel. In reality, he was squeezing it so hard that he felt his palms starting to bruise as the angst enveloped him from the inside out. He started thinking *keep calm and avoid an aneurism.* The more he repeated it, however, the more he thought about having an aneurism and then he started envisioning himself collapsing at the wheel, blood pouring out of his nose, as the car flew off the highway killing him and his family in the process. No matter what he did lately, he could not avoid having morbid thoughts. Now, about to embark on a much-needed vacation with his loved ones, all he could imagine was everyone dying in a horrific accident. *Welcome to my fucked up life* he thought as he turned the car on the main road north to get to the highway.

"Honey, you okay?" Katie Preston's voice called over to her husband from the passenger seat. Her tone seemed part concerned and part distant as she tried to manage their three children in the backseats of the SUV between putting on DVDs in the electronics panel and telling the kids where the snacks were packed. After fifteen years of marriage and eighteen years together in total, Katie knew most of Tom's mannerisms. Although Tom seemed to be in bad shape mentally of late, she did not feel like she had the time to deal with him going through some kind of phase or, dare she think it, the clichéd midlife crisis.

Tom just grunted a little in response to Katie and stared straight ahead. After a difficult year to this point capped off by a whirlwind week at work -- sixty-one-and-a-half *billable* hours total from Sunday through Thursday -- followed by an extra four hours Thursday night helping everyone pack to leave Friday morning, he was exhausted. Physically, emotionally, mentally, he had nothing left to give but the drive up north. Ironically, he wanted some peace and quiet and yet his thoughts were anything but peaceful.

After putting in a romantic comedy for Dawn, their thirteen-year-old daughter in the back seat, and an animated film for Tommy Jr. and Jake, their nine- and five-year-old sons in the row behind them, and then passing out breakfast bars and water bottles to everyone, Katie turned back to Tom. "What's going on with you, Tom? What're you thinking?"

*Oh there's a loaded fucking question,* Tom thought. He didn't want to answer her because he knew that the honest answer could and would lead to an argument, but he'd had enough with lies over the last year. At the same time, staying quiet and ignoring Katie would've started the family vacation off on an even worse note and Katie seemed pretty worn down in her own right. *Just fall on the sword big guy.*

"I'm beyond stressed," Tom replied.

"Yeah, well I'm stressed too," Katie said defensively.

"Hey, I answered your question," Tom snapped back. "If you're going to give me grief every time I answer you truthfully then I may as well not answer you at all."

*Damn that was a good one.* Katie knew it too. *Total zinger her way. Nailed it.*

"You're right Katie said. I know you're stressed. I genuinely appreciate you and how hard you work. I am just stressed out too."

"I know you are, but there is a world of difference between your stress and my stress. I know you work your ass off taking care of the kids and the house. But if you make a mistake, then the worst that happens is we don't have all the ingredients for dinner or one of the kids waits until you pick them up. If I make a mistake, I'm fucked. I could get sued, fired, disbarred. Everybody comes to me expecting me to fix their humpty dumpty. I didn't create their problems but somehow, because they pay my firm, I'm expected to be a magical miracle-worker and fix everything. I know you're stressed, but the kind of stress I have is the medical kind and it's killing me. I'm really feeling it."

It wasn't hyperbole even if it was slightly exaggerated. Tom really was feeling ill from the stress. Every part of his body ached. The other day at the office, a courier, some young kid around twenty-one years old, tapped Tom on the back to tell Tom that he had delivered a package that Tom had ordered him to deliver. Tom literally jumped off the ground when the kid tapped him.

"Or, if I make a mistake," Katie started, "Tommy will get violently ill with missed school time while we end up with huge hospital bills."

"I know," Tom admitted. Tommy was severely allergic to nuts and dairy. Because of that, the family could not go out to eat at more than three or four restaurants and Katie had to cook most of their meals. Not to mention, the allergy-friendly foods were much more expensive than regular groceries. On top of watching out for Tommy, Katie was in charge of scheduling and taking the kids to all of their appointments – the dentist, the orthodontist, music lessons, school sports, the doctor, two different tutors, and dropping off and picking up the kids from friends' houses. It wasn't hard work in and of itself, but taken as a whole, it was constant grinding work each and every day that was enough to drive a person crazy over thirteen years of having kids. Tom knew that. He also knew that Katie had to do all of those things just like he had to work at his office every day from around 9:00 a.m. until 6:30 p.m. and then he usually had varying amounts of work to do at home each night after the kids were in bed. On top of that, he always helped with the laundry and dishes as well as keeping the house clean. It wasn't like he was a deadbeat dad or husband. To the contrary, he worked his ass off at home and at his job. He just needed Katie to understand that his work stress was killing him and, no matter what she said, he didn't think she had the faintest idea of just how hard it was or how real the consequences could be for him and the Preston family financially and professionally if he didn't perform well at work each and every day.

Katie seemed pacified by Tom's acknowledgement of her stress so Tom was happy to let their conversation end.

Back in the day when Katie would ask Tom what he was thinking or how he was feeling, Tom amused himself by thinking of the true answer before answering her with something charming or witty. Like when they were first dating and she'd ask him what he was thinking about, it was taking her to one of the rooms behind the book stacks in the law school library and fucking her brains out. But, instead, he'd say something like "just how lucky I am that we met." He was sincere and Katie loved those responses, but that's what all guys are thinking when they start dating someone special (or anyone for that matter). Shortly after they married and she'd ask him the same type of question, he again amused himself with the thought of a threesome between Katie and one of a million random women. And again, he would tell her something like "just how good we have it" or maybe a sarcastic joke like "are you sure you still wanna be with me?"

But as the years passed, kids came into the picture, work became more challenging, bills got steeper, and the sea of life kept sending stronger and more forceful currents pulling Tom away and down into what felt like an abyss. Tom kept staring down the highway and occupied himself by listing in his head all of the things that were stressing him out. *Let's see: that Fucking Case; working a job that grows worse with each year; paying the mortgage; a job to pay me enough to pay the mortgage; having credit card debt; needing to make repairs around the house, none of which I can afford (we need a new roof, siding, and flashing) and most of which I don't know how to do (like anything other than painting which I don't have time for in any event); having enough epinephrine shots for Tommy in case he eats something with nuts or dairy (thank you Big Pharma for charging a fortune per epinephrine); Dawn becoming a teenager; finding enough quality time to spend with the kids; helping Jake and Tommy with their reading and math; teaching the kids to be more independent; trying to find time to catch up with my college buddies – hey we need to take a road trip and catch a football game. Oh, and Katie, she seems less romantic with each passing day. We haven't been intimate in months. All this and Katie wants to know what's going on with me? What am I thinking? And don't even get me started on that Fucking Case. The world is on my shoulders and I feel like collapsing.*

The last year had been especially difficult and Tom was losing his mind trying to find new ways of hope for his future. The law business sucked and that Fucking Case, also affectionately referred to by Tom behind closed doors as the Bandik Fraud Case that Tom had (hopefully) just finished, pushed him over the edge.

Tom had worked in different fields of law

early in his career. Unable to find a good job offer during law school, Tom started out doing small cases like evictions, defending people against traffic tickets and misdemeanors (mostly DUIs), and some divorces after graduation and passing the bar exam. Basically, he'd take any case he could get to make ends meet. After almost two-and-a-half years of networking with lawyers, judges, and clerks at all of the various legal functions, he received an employment offer from Ames, Strickland & Hardy, the largest bankruptcy law firm in the area. His mentor at the firm, Dean Strickland, had been practicing for nearly forty years and, after all that time, the lessons he conveyed to Tom were anything but comforting or hopeful about the profession.

Strickland's three rules for practicing law were: "One, get the money up front. Two, don't go to jail for your client. And three, get the money up front." Tom hated those rules because they made law seem like a dirty business and yet that was exactly what practicing law was about sometimes. At the end of the day, every single case boiled down to money. No matter who screwed who, no matter how bad of a person a client was dealing with, or, for that matter, no matter how bad of a person the client him or herself was, cases generally settled for less money than was owed being paid, not including all of the costs and fees that had to be paid to the lawyers to get to that point. It was just ridiculous and seemed antithetical to the basic principle of justice. But that's what paid the bills for everyone in the "legal industry" and Tom had five mouths to feed.

Tom also hated Strickland's rules because Strickland himself was always willing to take a case for money and, for his important clients, he was also willing to take his second rule as close to the edge as possible. The Bandik Fraud Case was a prime example. Dean Strickland was retained by his longtime friend, Stellan Bandik, to file for personal bankruptcy in order to avoid business fraud claims being asserted against him by his investors. Strickland assigned the case to Tom even though Bandik was Strickland's close friend.

Stellan Bandik, like Strickland, grew up in a fairly affluent neighborhood. He inherited a large amount of vacant land from his father in an area where real estate development was booming. He could have sold that land for about twelve million dollars to go with the rest of his inheritance but, instead, he wanted to make more money. Tom was never told how much money Bandik inherited from his father, or the value of his father's personal possessions like paintings, old coins, and collector rifles, but he did see that Strickland had set up a number of offshore companies to hold onto assets and bank accounts and the amount total was somewhere in the eight-digit range. It always amazed Tom how the Disease of More universally permeates the lives of all who are blessed and how the disease worsens as the blessings increase.

Rather than use his own wealth to develop the vacant land left by his father, Bandik brought in about twenty individual investors and formed a company with them to develop some of the land into single-home subdivisions and the rest into apartment complexes that the company would own and manage. Bandik, of course, brought in only passive investors and handled all of the day-to-day operations himself. About twice a year, he would send his investors distribution checks for company profits. After two years, the investors had all made their initial investments back and, by year five, they had each made a two hundred percent return on their investments. All seemed great until, by twist of fate or sheer dumb luck, one of the investors discovered some memos on Bandik's desk. Harriet Truman, a recent widow at seventy-four years of age, went to meet with Bandik at his office to let him know that her husband, Earl, had recently passed and to switch Earl's investment interest over to her name. Bandik was outside his office flirting with his new secretary, Robin, when Mrs. Truman looked at the memos which showed nearly twenty million dollars had been diverted to at least half-a-dozen companies affiliated with Bandik and his family. Mrs. Truman was no dummy; in fact, she and

Earl were quite intelligent and shrewd investors, and she smartly pulled out her cellphone and took pictures of the memos on Bandik's desk. When she confronted Bandik and brought his scheme to the other investors' attention, Bandik retained Strickland to file for personal bankruptcy.

By that time, the bulk of Bandik's money had been safely hidden in other companies owned by his wife and children (not including the offshore accounts). Bandik, a man with no scruples, had even asked Tom to shred certain financial statements to keep them from investors. When Tom refused, Strickland had stepped in and told Tom that the documents were not to be disclosed. Tom had protested but, in the end, it was either hide the documents or lose his job. Tom made the "smart" choice and kept the documents hidden in a folder in a secret drawer under his desk. Although the investors and their attorneys always suspected that there was a link between Bandik's family and their missing twenty million dollars, they never got hold of those documents.

In the end, Bandik received his bankruptcy discharge meaning he was cleared of all of his debts. The investors ended up recovering about one million dollars (a mere five percent of what was owed to them) and Ames, Strickland & Hardy received legal fees of nearly two million dollars. *How the hell is that justice?* It was even less just because, of the law firm's two million dollars in fees received, Tom would never see more than a ten or twenty thousand dollar year-end bonus, before taxes, despite all that he had done to get Bandik through bankruptcy. The two million would essentially all go to the named partners, and mostly to Dean Strickland who brought in Bandik and used Tom to do the bankruptcy work and conceal the dirty deals and companies that he set up for Bandik.

The Bandik Fraud Case also tied into Strickland's other lesson for Tom: "You'll win cases you have no business winning, and you'll lose cases you have no business losing. With judges and juries, you never know what will happen." The biggest joke of law was that the law, which is supposed to provide certainty for how to deal with each type of case, was always unpredictable, i.e., uncertain. *As everyone is so fond of typing "WTF?" How can there be justice when the law offers no certainty?* Here was Stellan Bandik walking out of bankruptcy court free and clear of all debts leaving his investors robbed of nineteen million dollars plus costs and legal fees. It was even worse because Bandik actually walked out of bankruptcy court a wealthier man than when he entered. The system really was rigged in favor of those with money and the means to do whatever the hell they wanted.

The cherry on top of Tom's Bandik sundae of excrement was that the sixty-one-and-a-half hours that Tom had put in over the last five days were spent helping Bandik, under Strickland's watchful eye, shuffle his "family" assets around to prevent anyone, particularly Bandik's soon-to-be ex-wife, from ever getting to them. It wasn't that Tom was violating the laws, he was merely using obscurities and loopholes in the laws to move Bandik's assets. And the whole time, Bandik and Strickland constantly let Tom know in no uncertain terms that Tom would be held responsible for any mistakes. After everything that Tom had done for Bandik, Bandik's most memorable line of the week was yesterday evening in Tom's office: "Tom, I'm counting on you. We can't afford to get anything wrong, and I'm holding you responsible for your work and any problems that come up." Never a thank you, never encouragement or gratitude for the remarkable job that Tom had done for him. Just a threat. Not even a veiled or thinly-veiled threat. A mega-millionaire threatening a working man buried in debt. The worst part of that was that Dean Strickland was with Bandik in Tom's office and never said a word in response to Bandik's threat. In fact, Tom was pretty sure that he saw Strickland give him a stern eye as if to say "I'm holding you responsible for everything we forced you to do and the laws we forced you to push to the limit."

Tom was sick of it, and he was sick of waking up every day and going to sleep every night with the pressure of keeping a job that primarily benefitted his boss while missing out on life and needing to make sure that all the bills were paid. Tom knew that he was just like pretty much everyone else in the working world in this regard. He couldn't just stop working without an exit strategy. He needed to keep working to make the money that was needed to cover the ever-increasing bills. So the best he could do right now was take a two-week vacation.

For all his angst, Tom was really looking forward to his vacation. Northern Michigan was gorgeous in the summer. Cold as hell and windy in the winter, but absolutely gorgeous in the warm (sometimes only warmish) summertime. The destination for this vacation was the Lake Superior coastline of the Upper Peninsula with the Pictured Rocks National Lakeshore being the ultimate destination. Spanning 42 miles across the shore of Lake Superior, the world's largest freshwater lake by surface area, Pictured Rocks was among the most beautiful and secluded spots in the United States. Tom had been there twice before -- once on a travel trip through a local camp that he attended as a fifteen-year-old and once with his parents about five years later in the middle of his college years.

*Those cliffs. Those amazing cliffs. And those freaking arches. Get me to those arches.* The thought of Pictured Rocks had been propelling Tom to keep working and make it to Friday morning to begin this vacation. Pictured Rocks is known for the exquisite colors layered along its sandstone cliffs. The cliffs go as high as 200 feet above sea level and the colors can be seen all the way to the lake floor as the water is both clear and pristine shades of blue going from shallow to deep. Over millions of years, the lake had sculpted the cliffs into their current states with layers, caves, and Tom's favorite: arches. Tom's favorite activity of all his camping trips was kayaking through the arches. It was pure adventure and relaxation rolled into his one-person kayak where he could just sit and be at peace by himself for once with no deadlines and no worries while rocking along the water and looking up at the arches.

Tom and Katie were avid campers and hikers growing up. They had gone on a number of camping trips together before having children like Glacier National Park in Montana, Estes National Park in Colorado, Zion National Park in Utah, Mammoth Cave in Kentucky (during tornado season where they had to take cover on two occasions, one of which resulted in their tent being destroyed in the high winds), and the Canadian Rockies at Banff and Jasper National Parks in Alberta, Canada. In one of Tom's most charming displays, he proposed to Katie on the shore of Lake Louise in Banff. He knew that Katie was very particular about her jewelry so, instead of blindly picking out a ring in advance, he surprised her with a special souvenir. Katie, a history fan, major, and teacher (until they started their family), enjoyed collecting fossils during their trips. The Canadian Rockies are known for their ammonites (which look like prehistoric squid with a giant round snail-like shell) that have been opalized in one or more vibrant colors – bright shades of red, yellow, green, blue, and purple (and all of them together if you have enough money to pay for such a rare specimen). Tom had secretly purchased a hand-sized ammonite with the full rainbow of colors, and he presented it to Katie when he got down on his knee. It cost him nearly twelve hundred dollars in American currency at the time but it was well worth it and has always sat over the mantel above the fireplace in their family room as the home's most cherished decoration.

While Tom's thoughts drifted through his visual memories of Pictured Rocks, he thought of all of the stones along Lake Superior and he began to think of the ammonite. With all of the varieties of stones -- iron, agate, quartz, jasper, fossils -- lining the shoreline, Tom thought about all of the possibilities in searching for some new additions to Katie's collection. His mood was picking up— *what the fuck!*

# BUCKHIT LIST

## *Chapter Two*

Alden and Edna Duquette were on their way up I-75 north to Traverse City to celebrate their fifty-year anniversary. The big day had actually been yesterday, but they had leased a lakefront home along Lake Michigan for two weeks for their whole family. Alden, a retired insurance salesman, and Edna, a retired nurse, were racing to reunite with their two daughters, their two sons-in-law, and their five grandchildren. Alden, loving his new royal blue sedan and its V6 engine, whipped around the SUV in front of him with fifty years and one day being what the Good Lord had provided to him. Neither Alden nor Edna ever saw the buck. Unlike like Tom and Katie Preston, they never even saw a flash of anything.

The massive ten-pointer had darted out of the woods right in front of the Prestons' SUV and was caught head-on by the Duquettes' new sedan. Alden and Edna had barely managed to scream when the buck's limp body flew up into the windshield, its antlers piercing Edna through her chest as Alden, succumbing to a massive heart attack, uncontrollably pressed his foot against the accelerator and lost control of the vehicle which went speeding into the downward sloping highway median. The front left tire hit a boulder pointing upward out of the weeds causing the car to flip over and skid on its mangled roof before settling some fifty yards away.

"Hhhhaaawwwww!" Katie's shriek was sheer terror. Never in their eighteen years together had Tom ever heard Katie make any noise even remotely close to that. Katie began crying uncontrollably while trying to reach for her cellphone to dial 9-1-1. Tom, although more stoic than Katie, was making that same noise inside himself and trying to stay composed knowing that he was the one who was ultimately going to have to give the emergency operator directions since navigation and direction were definitely not part of Katie's repertoire. At the same time, the kids, who had all been preoccupied with their movies while simultaneously playing on their tablets (what modern kid can sit through a car ride without at least two forms of screen-time entertainment), all looked through the car windows frantically when they heard the crash combined with their mother's terrified shriek. Even with their headphones on, the sudden noises rocked them out of their electronic stupors.

"Dad, what was that? Mom, what happened? What's going on?" The kids were all concerned and asking the same basic question dozens of different ways. With each passing nanosecond, the kids' voices became more concerned and started to border on hysteria.

"There was a crash," Katie finally answered. "A really bad crash." Katie was doing her best to keep her voice level (calm was not a realistic option) so that her children would settle down a bit as well as her nerves. Her phone dialed through to 9-1-1 and she heard the ring.

"Did someone just die?" Dawn's question was an honest one, but it sent chills down Tom's spine. It put immediate reality into the surreal tragedy that Tom and Katie had just witnessed.

"9-1-1, this is Chris. What is your emergency?"

"C-Chris, my name is Katie Pre-ston. I just witnessed a horrible accident on northbound I-75."

"Where was the accident, ma'am? Do you know the nearest exit, or mile-marker, or city?"

"Tom, where are we at?" Katie handed Tom the phone.

"We're just north of mile marker 124. The accident was maybe about a mile or so further back."

"I got it. In fact, at least two other operators are reporting calls of the same incident."

*Other people are also calling it in. That's somewhat reassuring that some humanity still lives among us.*

The 9-1-1 operator continued, "How bad was the accident, sir?"

Tom hesitated for a second. In law, one always hesitated to think of the best possible answer without giving anything away to the other side. Here, however, was a real-life event and a truthful response was imperative. It wasn't a matter of life and death so much as it was a matter of death. But the emergency responders needed to know so that the right people with the right equipment would know what they were dealing with. At the same time, Tom had his kids in the car and the more they knew, the worse things would be for them. The last thing that Tom wanted was for the moment to scar them for the rest of their lives.

"A car struck a deer. It looked like an older couple in the car. It veered into the median and flipped. It didn't look like they made it." Tom's voice started to trail off in emotion.

"Got it, sir. Thank you for reporting it. We have a large emergency crew en route. You have a safe trip, sir, and don't be afraid to pull over if you need to calm down." The 9-1-1 operator hung up. Maybe it was just another day on the job for him. People calling each day with emergencies no doubt should have conditioned him to some degree. Tom and Katie, on the other hand, had never seen anything like that in their lives. Like other people, they had seen roadkill all over the roads, particularly in the spring and fall as the weather changed. Tom even had the misfortune of running over a hare one evening when it darted into his tire while he was driving home from a late meeting. However, neither Tom nor Katie had ever seen a large animal barreling to its death against a car.

"Tom, I can't believe it. Holy shit." Katie was still crying. The kids all had tears in their eyes as well. Although they hadn't seen the accident (thankfully), they were just responding to the terrible noise and their parents' mournful shock. "I actually saw the deer on their car as it was flipping over. I can't get it out of my head." Katie's tears sped up as she reached for the Kleenex box and grabbed a handful of tissues.

"Is that all you saw?" Tom meant that in a good way.

"What do you mean? Like what I saw – what we saw – was not a huge freaking deal?" Apparently, Katie didn't understand that Tom asked his question in a good way.

"Katie, I saw the whole fucking thing. That's what I meant. I hope you didn't see it all, did you?"

"Oh. No. I didn't."

That was a slight relief for Tom. Katie was much more emotional than him and, while this tragedy would now unfortunately be among their lasting lifetime memories, Katie would at least not have the graphic images that were now etched into Tom's brain. Tom's reflexes caused him to hit the brakes as he saw the flash of the buck run right across the front of his SUV while Katie had apparently started looking out of the SUV's windshield in a forward direction, and probably at all of the children as part of her mama-bear instincts. Tom heard the first *thwack* and saw the deer's body fly up into the windshield. Tom was never a hunter but, as a hiker and animal lover, he could tell that the deer was north of 200 pounds. The sedan's windshield glass obscured most of his view and the sedan was ahead of Tom's SUV but he saw the woman's body push back into the seat as her head went unnaturally to the driver's side and then quickly swung to the door side and fell limp against the window as the car started to veer off the highway. Tom could tell by the deer's head and proximity to the woman's body that it had pierced her with its antlers. As the sedan got further away, Tom could see some blood dribbling from the woman's body onto her door's window. And then, as Katie also saw, the sedan dipped into the median and flipped over with the deer on it. Katie would always assume that the deer was stuck to the car, and maybe in some part that was true, but Tom saw it pierce into the woman. And he wished he could unsee it knowing that the image would haunt and stain his memories forever.

"Oh my God, what the hell happened? I'm freaking out you guys. What happened? We need to know." Dawn was now among the angst-filled and overly-dramatic teenagers but her question and words were legitimate. Tommy and Jake were stone-cold silent and were anxiously waiting for their parents to fill them in. It was a family first that all of the electronics had been paused as the kids sat quietly in their seats. *Why did it have to be death for them to be silent* Tom thought awkwardly to himself.

"A deer just ran out into the highway," Tom started. "We got lucky. It almost hit us. But the car in the lane next to us hit it head-on and flipped into the median." Tom didn't want to have to tell the kids more than a car hit a deer but they were old enough to call him out if they thought he was lying or bending the truth so he offered them the detail of the car flipping over so they would believe him and not press on through their natural curiosity.

"Did they die?" Jake asked. Tom did not want to have to answer that question but he knew it was coming from one of the kids.

"We won't ever know for sure but my guess is that they will be taken to the hospital with some serious injuries." Tom knew it was a lie, but he wanted to leave his children with hope. It was a family vacation after all, and they had their youthful innocence. They really didn't need to know that the couple in the car were definitely dead. On the other hand, Tom's children were pretty smart, and he and Katie wanted to raise them to be intelligent, thoughtful, and honest so Tom continued with his answer. "It looked like the people in the car were an elderly couple. I know it doesn't make it any better, but there were no children or anyone else in the car. Let's just hope that they're okay." Tom was hoping that his children, knowing the human life cycle, would not take the sudden tragedy too hard.

"Maybe we should turn around and check on them," Dawn suggested.

"Yeah," Tommy and Jake echoed.

"We don't need to," Katie chimed in. "9-1-1 said the emergency crews were on their way over and they'll be there before we can turn around and drive back. Plus we'd be unsafe on the highway with cars speeding by."

*Thanks for that save Katie. I love you.*

"There's gotta be something we can do," Dawn persisted.

"Let's say a prayer for them" Katie suggested.

Katie and Tom then led the children in the Lord's Prayer. At the end, they asked that God tend to and heal the couple in the vehicle or accept them into Heaven if they had already passed. Tom then concluded with the prayer that, if the couple had passed, "May their memories be for a blessing." It was a beautiful prayer from the Jewish faith that he learned from his college buddy Mike Gilbert who had taught this to Tom at Mike's father's funeral. The power and beauty in the simplicity of the words had engrained themselves into Tom's faith and he always said them to friends and family during bereavement.

The SUV continued north on I-75 in utter silence for nearly an hour before the kids turned back to their movies and tablets. It wasn't kids being kids, simply the act of young people having thought too much on the recent trauma and desperately needing a diversion. Tom grabbed a few cookies as Katie started reading a new book and eating an apple. Her last tears had dried to her cheeks and the side bin on her door was full of used tissues.

Tom tried think about Lake Superior and Pictured Rocks to return to that happy place in his mind that he had just started visiting before the buck hit. All he could think about, however, was the crash. He replayed the crash in all its gory details about a dozen times. Then his thoughts veered to what the firemen and emergency medical technicians did when they arrived at the scene. He envisioned them using the jaws of life to cut the deer's antlers out of the woman and then cut the couple out of the car. He then envisioned the EMTs placing the couple in separate body bags, hoisting them onto gurneys, and lifting them into the back of an ambulance never to hold each other again. Suddenly, as the ambulance's emergency lights flashed on in his imagination, he envisioned Dean Strickland arriving at the scene only to leave his business card on each of the body bags so the couple's relatives could call him and sue for some imaginary claim. *Shit, maybe that deer was rich. Strickland would sue anything if it could make him money. Maybe the deer was flushed out by a hunter and Strickland would sue the hunter.*

The more Tom thought about Dean Strickland, the more he got back to thinking about his job and Bandik. His grip again started tightening on the steering wheel and his white knuckles returned. They got even whiter as he saw five turkey vultures headed south.

*I hope you've got deer and not some old couple on the menu boys.*

# THE STAIN

## *Chapter Three*

About an hour and-a-half later, Tom turned off at the last rest area before Grayling. The family all needed restrooms, lunch, and a stretch in fresh air. Tom found the closest parking spot to the building and then he and the family shuffled out of the SUV groaning as they stretched. Tom hadn't realized how urgently he needed to urinate until about five minutes before he pulled into the rest area. Of course, he had to help Tommy and Jake first even though his kidneys were bursting.

Tom and the boys waited for Katie and Dawn before leaving the building together. For an early Friday afternoon, the rest area seemed fairly busy with about twenty cars and ten trucks lining both sides of the building parking lot. As the Prestons left the building, Tom looked outside expecting to see people walking dogs and setting up at picnic tables. Instead, he saw a small gathering of gawkers around his SUV.

Tom started walking suspiciously towards the SUV while his family followed carefully behind him. As he started walking through the crowd, he noticed that they were all focused on the driver's side. Tom craned his body over and saw that the side of the SUV was streaked with blood and strands of fur. When Tom purchased the SUV, he specifically chose silver because after years of driving a black car he was tired of having to drive to the car wash, especially in winter, since the dirt and salt on the roads easily stood out on black paint. Now, Tom wished that he had never chosen silver since black would have concealed most of the stain along the car's side.

Tom was trying to think of a plan to get the lunch food out of the SUV and wash the stain off without anyone noticing when Jake suddenly shouted "Oh my God Dad! What is that? How are we gonna get it off?" At that point, all of the gawkers looked at Tom. Katie backed away slowly with the kids.

"You hit a deer, man?" one of the gawkers asked.

"No. It was the car next to us," Tom replied.

"Sure looks like you hit it," the Gawker persisted. The rest of the crowd was now listening intently.

"If I hit it, or if it hit me, don't you think our car would be smashed up or at least dented?"

That seemed to get the gawker and the rest of the crowd thinking. Tom was always amazed by how stupid people could collectively be. And, as he grew irritated, he guessed that there would be more stupid comments to come. People always seemed to push and push for things (information, possessions, whatever) while making a series of assumptions, right or wrong, along the way.

"Did you track the deer down?" another gawker asked.

"Do you see a deer on my car?"

Instead of the crowd realizing the stupidity of the gawker's question, they seemed to be mildly upset with Tom for his snarky response. *This person's the idiot and I'm the asshole?*

At that point, Tom clicked the unlock button on his remote key. The SUV doors clicked and the car lights flashed. Tom started walking forward to get his family's lunch.

"I would have tracked that deer down," the gawker said as if he was either challenging Tom or just not wanting to look like a jackass for asking a stupid question. "That's good meat right there. How far back was it?"

The crowd, which had seemed ready to disperse, now seemed firmly rooted into the concrete intending to hear every word of the dialogue that Tom had been forced into.

"It was about two-and-a-half hours south of here," Tom responded with a tone that was already thickly annoyed and Tom made damned sure that it came across that way. *Take the hint and shut the fuck up stranger.*

"You left a deer to die that far back?" the gawker said exasperated.

At that point, Tom had had enough of everything. He wasn't a large man, normal in height and weight at 5'10" and 190 pounds, but he had an athletic build and he could be intimidating if he wanted to be. "I already told you that it was the car next to me that hit the deer. So go ask them mister loudmouth stranger! They probably won't be able to hear you because they flipped through the median and the emergency crews already got the deer when they pulled its' antlers out of the passenger!" Loud gasps spread throughout the crowd and the gawkers started hustling away. The gawker who had confronted Tom was moving away staring meekly at the ground, but Tom couldn't let it go. "Hey, was that enough for you, man? My family's had a really rough day, but is there anything else or are you done pushing for no logical reason?" Tom could tell that the man was some combination of unhappy and ashamed but Tom wanted to make clear that the man was not welcome near Tom or his family. The man turned and quickly walked away somewhere. At that point, Katie grabbed the kids and took them to the car to get their lunch. They retrieved the food and headed over to a picnic table on the lawn close to the car.

Tom walked back to the mens' room to grab paper towels. He got them wet with warm water and soap and walked back to his car. He started wiping down the driver's side and quickly realized that getting rid of the stain was never going to happen at the current rate. The blood had dried onto the car and acted like a glue for the deer fur. No matter how much water Tom squeezed onto the car from the paper towels, the paper towels were ineffective and shredding as Tom wiped them across the stain. After a few minutes, Tom was ready to just grab a t-shirt from his bag and use it as a rag until the stain came off. Then, a horrible thought overtook him. *Some of this blood, likely most of it, came from that poor old woman. I'm touching her blood and not just some poor deer.*

Suddenly, a bucket full of soapy water and a blue rag was placed on the pavement next to Tom. Tom swung around from his squatted position and saw the rest area custodian.

"This should help," the woman said.

"Thank you so much, ma'am!" Tom could have hugged her.

The portly woman gave Tom a warm a smile in return. "Just drop the bucket off by the door that says 'Employee's Only' inside. I've never seen anything like this, but I've seen plenty of family hardship."

"I truly can't thank you enough. And I

hope your days of family hardship are over forever."

"We all need a hand sometimes. It may not be the hand we imagined, but it helps. I'm good with the family now. Just don't forget to return the bucket," the custodian said as she gave a polite wink and headed off towards the other side of the building.

Feeling somewhat better about humanity, Tom was able to wash the stain off the car in about five minutes. He placed the bloody bucket by the "Employees Only" door inside the building, washed his hands for about five minutes in the mens' room, and then joined his family for lunch. Reaching for his sandwich, he was interrupted by a disturbing question from Tommy.

"Dad, did the deer's antlers really go through the passenger?" Tommy's question, though completely innocent, was filled with dread. Tom had forgotten that the kids and Katie had not seen that and now, because he lost his composure with that ignorant gawker, the truth had come out.

"No, son, I was just angry with that man. I wanted him to leave us alone and stop asking us annoying questions so I made that part up."

"Oh. Good." The little boy seemed relieved but still unsure of something. "Did their car really flip over?"

"Yes, it did." Tom couldn't lie anymore. He was just hoping that Katie and Dawn believed his lie about the antlers. He didn't think that they did. He was right.

The family ate their lunch in silence. When they were finished, they decided to take the short nature hike at the rest area. It was a small trail, maybe a quarter-mile in total distance, but it overlooked a stunning pond. It was a lovely Monet-esque pond that the artist himself might have used as a muse. The dark bluish water was calm and freckled with lily pads complemented by frogs croaking as they basked in the warm sunlight. There was tall grass along the shore right by the trail's overlook and cattails lined the far side of the pond along with a large bolder and the large trunk of a fallen tree. Looking more closely, the Prestons could see fish swimming in the water. It looked like an assortment of blue gills, a few catfish, and many minnows. Looking even more closely, the family could see a leopard frog basking in the grass along the pond's shore while crawfish holes were scattered near the pond's edges.

Dawn also noticed something. Right below the overlook, there was a gigantic water snake with its head resting on the tall grass and its body curled just under the water at the edge of the pond. Its alternating gray and dark gray bands made it easy to identify as a northern watersnake. Katie and Jake feared snakes to the point that the family considered them to have a phobia of snakes ("ophidiophobia" is the term that Tom once found on Google and conveyed it to the family while they were at the zoo one day).

Dawn gently pointed out the snake to the family hoping that its distance, some twelve or so feet below, would not send her mom and brother into panic attacks. "I wonder if it is stalking those frogs. That would just be the perfect complement to everything that's happened so far." Tom could hear the teenage snark in Dawn's voice but her statement was a valid one. After the family watched the snake for another minute or two, it appeared to just be sunning itself but the Prestons each suspected that the snake could strike its next meal in nanoseconds if it wanted. After all, northern watersnakes are known to be aggressive if they feel threatened and can repeatedly bite a threatening hand or take down a prey with one strong bite. Tom recalled golfing with a client, Harvey Reid, who had told him about a watersnake biting his golfing partner on the hand by a water hazard in the middle of a tournament. Harvey said that his partner's hand would not stop bleeding and they both ignorantly thought that the snake was a cottonmouth until another golfer who knew about reptiles informed them at the clubhouse that the massasauga rattlesnake is the only venomous snake in Michigan and that the northern watersnake has an anticoagulant causing bite wounds to bleed a lot.

On the far end of the pond, a mother mallard duck was slowly paddling among the lily pads with her five ducklings. The ducklings were quite small and looked like they had hatched no more than two weeks prior. Katie pointed them out, "Ooh, look at those adorable babies!" The Prestons stared at the ducks listening to the tiny peeps of the ducklings. The scenery was starting to put them at ease, and Tom reached into his pocket for his cellphone to take a picture—

*Snap!*

It was sudden. Too quick to see, but they all heard it. Mother duck was quacking bloody murder flapping her wings wildly and trying to peck at something in the water. Four of her ducklings paddled to shore as fast as their little webbed feet could move them. The snapping turtle must have been waiting in that spot for hours setting up its camouflaged ambush. The duckling's lifeless body sat between its jaws just at the surface of the water.

"Oh my God, we're gone! Now! Everyone get back to the car," Katie firmly ordered.

"This vacation is cursed," Dawn said running back along the trail with her brothers trying to keep up.

"That poor ducky" Jake lamented. "That was so sad."

"I can't believe that just happened," Tommy said. "I can't wait to tell Josh about it when we get home."

"Okay, well that sucked," Tom muttered with sarcastic understatement when they reached the car. The last of the gawkers from earlier looked at the Prestons knowing that something else had just happened. This time, however, everyone kept their distance. No one wanted to be around the seemingly cursed family for fear of catching whatever bad luck was following them around.

As Tom started the engine, he turned to Katie and the kids and said "Guys, we are going to stop in Mackinac City and get some fudge and candy. We all need some good treats to shake this first leg of the trip off." The kids cheered and Katie smiled. There's nothing like Mackinac fudge on a northern Michigan trip. It's practically a requirement. The Prestons had left early enough (about 9:00 a.m.) so that, with the time just past 12:30, they had plenty of time to stop in Mackinac City about an hour away, then maybe one more fun stop, and then make it to their reserved campsite near Whitefish Bay on the Lake Superior coast. It didn't really matter how late they arrived at the campsite because the sun would go down around 10:00 p.m. that far north. An hour of daylight was more than enough time to set up their tent and cook dinner, and the family had plenty of flashlights and lanterns.

# BROKEN POINT STING

## *Chapter Four*

Mackinac City was its usual beautiful, charming, quaint-though-seems-to-be-growing-bigger-every-year self. When Tom exited I-75, he and the family saw the familiar landmarks – the waterslides from the water parks, the downtown shopping area, the old Colonial Michilimackinac, an $18^{th}$-century fort and fur-trading outpost, and, of course, the Mackinac Bridge, which served as the southern, and main, gateway to the Upper Peninsula. Tom followed the signs to the downtown area and managed to find a prime parking spot among the shops. Luck was starting to turn in their favor.

Everyone jumped out of the car, stretched, and started walking around window shopping and keeping an eye out for their favorite place. Tom liked looking at the Native American art pieces in the shops. He was fond of the turquoise- and stone-handled pocket knives. Katie was always keeping her eye out for Petoskey stones, fossilized coral native to Michigan that was beautiful in both its natural and polished states. It was a stone that could not be found anywhere else in the world. Katie, having a few such stones at home in her collection, would never stoop to purchasing what she loved to find, and certainly intended to find on this trip, but she loved looking at them in the stores nonetheless. Dawn seemed focused on sunglasses and new bathing suits. She planned to spend August at the neighborhood pool with her friends before eighth grade. Feeling more and more like the young woman she was, Dawn wanted to shine at the pool and set the stage for a grand entrance in her final year of middle school. Tommy and Jake, meanwhile, were looking at every toy, particularly the cap-guns and cap-grenades. The height of window-shopping came when Jake bolted into a store to show everyone the ultimate novelty item. It was a plastic statue of a man wearing a barrel held up on his shoulders by suspenders. When Jake pulled the barrel down, water spurted out from a little hole where the man's penis would be to look like he was urinating. Jake and Tommy were cracking up and begging Tom and Katie to purchase one. Tom almost caved in. It was pretty damn funny, especially after the morning they had.

About twenty minutes into their window-shopping walk, the Prestons came to their special place: Licoricious. It was not among the original or more well-known fudge shops like Rita's, Murphy's, or McElwain's, but it was a wonderful shop that catered to all of the Prestons. Katie was partial to fudge in more traditional flavors like chocolate, maple, and chocolate-peanut butter. Tom, Dawn, and Jake were partial to fudge in newer flavors like mint chocolate, cookies 'n' cream, and butterscotch. Everyone also loved the chocolate-salted caramel fudge. Tommy, on the other hand, was allergic to the dairy (butter) in fudge but Licoricious was renowned for their allergy-friendly homemade licorice in a variety of flavors like cherry, watermelon, fruit punch, strawberry, raspberry, sour apple, and black licorice. The licorice was custom wrapped by the yard giving the store's namesake a distinct marketing appearance and advantage. Tommy was a licorice enthusiast and, while his family was occupying one of the salesmen behind the counter with their requests to sample each fudge flavor and then choosing their fudge, Tommy got a saleswoman to bag him a yard-long piece of licorice in all but the sour apple and black licorice flavors as Tommy thought they tasted too strong. It was way too much licorice for one boy but Tommy knew that he could play the allergy sympathy card since his parents were getting themselves and everyone else about four pounds of fudge.

Tom paid for the fudge and licorice without thinking too much about the exorbitant cost of glorified, yet delicious, sugar. The family was happy and that was all that mattered at the moment. Tom led everyone back to the car and they hopped in for the final leg of the first day's travel.

Before everyone started diving into their treats, they looked out the windows to the great marvel of the Mackinac Bridge. Tom drove back to I-75 and took it straight to the bridge. Traffic wasn't too bad as the lineup of cars waiting to pay the four-dollar toll was only three deep. Tom made sure to stay to the right. Even though he hated heights, his family was going to love the view from the bridge and the right lane was the best for that. One of the longest bridges in the world, the Mackinac Bridge spans nearly five miles between Michigan's Lower and Upper Peninsulas. Tom paid the toll and drove right onto the bridge with Lake Michigan on the left and Lake Huron on the right. The view was incredible, although Tom did not particularly care for the roughly 200 feet between the bridge and the water at its highest point above sea level.

"Whoa, this is awesome!" Jake cried out.

"No kidding" Tommy shot back sarcastically.

"Just take in the view and enjoy it all" Katie said to preemptively end a sibling war on the bridge. She didn't want Tom to stress out and fly them over the railing.

When the bridge ended, Tom continued north on I-75 heading toward the top of the Upper Peninsula where their campsite by the southern shore of Lake Superior was waiting. Tom hadn't been there in decades but everything seemed vaguely familiar to him. One of Tom's great strengths in life was that he had a photographic memory for the things that interested him. It enabled him to quickly recall and locate documents in his cases at work and, in everyday life, it helped him find the places that he had only been to once or seen on a map without spending time getting directions.

Tom gazed at the clock and saw that the day, still on the earlier side for them, was nevertheless steadily moving on. Nearly 3:30, Tom thought about some of the unique tourist traps coming up. Before he could even contemplate which one might be best to stop at before they got to the campsite, Katie pointed it out.

"Tom, kids, check out the overlook."

Next to the highway but high above it, there was a high cliff overlooking the land. Baring rock on the highway side and surrounded by forest, the cliff looked majestically serene. On the ground and slightly to the side of the cliff was a parking lot with a large store. The store had the large wooden words "COME ON UP" across its roof.

"Let's go do that. Do you guys wanna do

that?" Katie seemed to be suggesting rather than asking.

The kids all eagerly voiced their agreement and Tom took the well-marked (tourism is how the owners survived) exit which conveniently went directly into the parking lot. The Prestons piled out and, while Tom and Katie took a moment to stretch, the kids bolted into the store which, for as big as the building seemed on the outside, appeared much bigger on the inside. Rows of goods of every kind lined the tables and shelves running parallel through the interior of the store. The owners had done a remarkable job of ensuring that every single person who ventured through would not be able to resist making at least one purchase.

"Holy shit Katie, they literally have everything in this place," Tom remarked.

Katie nodded and, in her amazement, she had already started wandering away from Tom who was now taking a mental inventory of everything. There was a food section with the preserved food specialties of northern Michigan like maple syrup (in every size from a small souvenir bottle the size of a finger to one quart), cherry salsa, raw honey, jams from every kind of berry, and bags of homemade baking mixes for pies, breads, and cakes. A bookshelf nearby contained at least 50 different books about the Upper Peninsula, the Great Lakes, ghost stories of northern Michigan, the history of Michigan, mining in Michigan, fossils of Michigan, birds of Michigan, animals of Michigan, shipwrecks of Michigan, and so on. Beyond that, there was a table full of novelty toys where Tommy and Jake were perusing. They were now picking up a plastic bow and dart arrow set and taking turns trying to shoot the arrow at the nearby wall and get it to stick with the suction cup on its head. Tom looked around to see if the store had that same plastic statue of the peeing man under the barrel like in Mackinac City but the store did not carry that. *Well I guess they don't sell everything after all.*

Tom walked over to the next aisle where there were wall and door signs for homes made from wood and other signs made from engraved metal. Some said pleasant things like "Home sweet home." Others were religious like "Christ is king," or simply "Faith heals." Tom gravitated away from them to the humorous signs like "Rules for watching football: 1. Don't talk; 2. Keep the beer cold; 3. Chips, dip, barbecue." Tom could relate to that one. He loved football with a capital L and would have football barbecuing and binge-watching sessions on weekends with his college buddies. Katie, who learned to hate football because it took away Tom's attention for five months out of the year, would always ask him questions or try to strike up conversations right in the middle of the games. One benefit of the games, however, was that Tommy and Jake liked football and watched with Tom which freed up Katie's day. In fact, Tom always did the cooking based on whatever superstition he had with certain foods that he felt would bring his team good luck before each game. While Tom was flipping through the funny signs, he saw a biker couple entering the store from the cliff entrance side and head out the main doors to their motorcycles. The man, large and balding, was wearing a shirt that said "If you can read this the bitch fell off" in large letters across the back. *Classy. But funny. Good stuff.*

Noticing that Katie and the kids were quite content still looking around, Tom meandered over to the counter. The counter was rather large and held an assortment of treasures that included Petoskey stones, arrowheads, agates, northern Michigan copper, gold flakes, necklaces, rings, old coins, and pocket knives. Tom noticed one particular pocket knife about three-and-a-half inches long with turquoise, green, and red stones embedded into the stainless steel handle. He fell in love immediately and broke out his wallet. *Yes sir, they get you every time at these places.* Tom also purchased admission for the family to hike up to the top of the cliff.

"Have you been here before?" the man behind the sales counter asked Tom.

"Sure have, but it was a long time ago," Tom responded pensively. "May have been over twenty years ago." Tom didn't want to pin it down to an exact year. He was just shocked by the amount of time that passed even though it didn't seem like it was all that long ago.

"Where you headed this time?"

"Pictured Rocks."

"Excellent. You guys will have the best time. The weather's been great and it's supposed to stay that way for the next week."

"That's good to hear. I've been looking forward to it for a long time."

"You'll have a great time. Enjoy your hike up the cliff."

"Thanks." Tom walked towards his family to let them know that he bought the tickets for the cliff. Thankfully, the kids were now getting bored of the store and, after a day of mostly sitting in the car, excited to go on the first official hike of the trip. They headed out the side exit toward the cliff and looked up. It didn't seem that tall from the bottom and the kids started running toward the paved walkway that zigzagged up the slope to the clifftop.

"Hey, slow down," Katie called after them. "Wait for us. We need to see you."

Instead of slowing down, the kids just turned and ran back to their parents. They were like hyper puppies that just needed to run and play, especially after sugaring up in Mackinac City.

"Come on guys, we'll walk up together. Mom and I will walk quickly," Tom assured them.

Tom instantly regretted saying that as soon as they started the ascent. It wasn't a long hike by any measure. Not even close to half a mile and the entire path was paved. But it was a steep grade and Tom was now realizing just how out of shape he was. As a kid, he used to run to the top in what seemed like two minutes. Now, he felt like an hour would be more like it as his calves and thighs started to feel the strain. Tom started thinking about how he needed to adjust his weekly schedule to start working out again. He'd gone from a cut young man to a middle-aged dad-body pile of pudge by his standards.

Another thought also occurred to Tom. The hike up seemed really dark. He didn't remember so many trees and shrubs this close to the trail crowding out the sunlight. He also noticed a conspicuous three-leafed plant growing through one of the cracks in the pavement: one asymmetrical leaf at the tip of the stem with two asymmetrical mitten-shaped leaves pointing perpendicularly below. *Hello poison ivy.*

"Guys, stop for a second," Tom called out. "Come here. See this plant? Don't touch it Jake." The five-year-old curiosity caused Jake to thrust his hand toward the plant but Tom caught it early. "This is poison ivy. Notice that all of the leaves are asymmetrical. That means if you fold each leaf in half along its stem, the leaf won't fold evenly. It contains an oil that, if you touch it, will make you itch and break out in a blistery rash for weeks. So know it and, if you see it, stay away from it. This one's growing right on the trail so keep your eyes open for any more. It will ruin your trip up here."

Just as Tom was finishing his little nature education moment, Dawn said "Dad, are all of those plants just outside the fence poison ivy?" The paved path up the cliff was lined on the outside by an old wooden fence. Sure enough, there were hundreds of poison ivy plants sprawled on the ground under and beyond the fence.

"Good eye sweetie. Those are poison ivy plants. Okay, just stay on the path and don't step on any plants."

"This trip, man," Dawn muttered as they continued the upward hike.

"Shush. Don't jinx it Dawn," Katie said. Katie was not a superstitious person but Tom could sense a little trepidation in her voice.

The kids were now walking more slowly and with caution making sure that there were no plants where they were walking. Tom was happy with their slow pace because, not only was there poison ivy, but it seemed like the path hadn't been repaved or repaired in the more than twenty years since Tom had last hiked it. There were many cracks and miniature potholes along the path and stones and fragments from the pavement sat loose on the surface making it somewhat slick. Tom made a mental note to tell the man behind the counter in the store that the owners should at least do something about the poison ivy. It doesn't do for a tourist trap to give its patrons poison ivy rash and ruin their vacations. New pavement would probably be too costly, even if it needed to be done, but the cracks and potholes needed to be repaired. Sprained and broken ankles are also vacation killers.

Five minutes later, the family had made it to the final stretch. At the last zigzag in the path before the final ascent, there was a cement bench with what appeared to be the remains of an ice cream cone from the ice cream cart inside the store slopped near the middle of the bench. Tom was eager to sit but there wasn't enough room for everyone so he just stood and put his hands over his head to catch his breath. Jake and Tommy sat on the bench but kept their distance from the ice cream melt which was attracting flying and crawling bugs of every type.

"Come on guys, let's get to the top," Katie encouraged. "We just have a short climb up the path and we're there."

Dawn started hiking with Katie and Jake, and Tommy walked in front of Tom. They made their way to the top of the cliff which was encircled by a steel railing. The view was breathtaking. They could see for miles out overlooking the highway. Lake Huron was easily in view as was a good portion of the highway coming from the Mackinac Bridge. While the cliff didn't seem that tall from the ground, the view from the top made it feel ten times higher than it looked. They were higher off the ground than the Mackinac Bridge was off the water at its highest point. No other people had been walking up the path either in front of or behind the Prestons so they had the top all to themselves. At first, everyone just enjoyed the view. Dawn and Tommy then started shouting to hear their voices carry. Jake eagerly joined in and, eventually, Katie gave in and started shouting. Tom, wanting to let out all of his tension, joined in. No one, Tom included, had any idea how much stress he was carrying until he let out his shout. It wasn't loud or silly or expressing any freedom or enjoyment. It was downright warlike. Katie and the kids looked over at Tom shocked and slightly afraid.

"Sorry guys, I guess I just needed to let some stress out," he said politely to help soothe them. "Let's take a family picture. We don't have any new ones and this is the perfect spot."

"Oh yeah!" Katie was excited. She loved family pictures and the boys were going to need them for the start of the school year. "Everyone get in front of me and dad."

The kids positioned themselves in front, Dawn in the middle and the boys on opposite sides with Katie and Tom in the back. Tom switched his phone to selfie mode and made sure that he got the view of Lake Huron in the background. He snapped about a dozen pictures and then checked to make sure that he got at least one keeper. There were at least five keepers that Tom could see despite the sunlight darkening the screen. He showed Katie and she was thrilled. Behind them, Dawn was snapping pictures with her phone while Jake and Tommy were looking out holding onto the rail.

*A couple more minutes and then we should hit the road.*

Tom started discussing his ideas for planning the rest of the day with Katie. At first, he didn't notice the crumbling sound. The rust on the middle support beam for the railing crumbled away under the boys' weight and Tom heard the loud snap of the metal. He turned around just in time to see the beam break free from the concrete platform causing the metal railing to bounce up and down yo-yoing from the two rusted but remaining support beams. Tommy fell sideways but landed on the platform. Jake, however, had been placing most of his weight on the railing which was neck-high for the little guy. The broken beam lifted Jake up and his feet skidded off the rust and loose pavement fragments beneath his feet to the point where he was angled towards the gap between the broken beam and the platform. There was nothing but nearly three hundred feet of air and then ground. A terrified Jake reflexively tried to grip the railing for dear life but his hands were too small and the force of everything made it impossible. As Jake was sliding to a deadly freefall, Tom grabbed him around his right armpit and yanked him back. Tom probably could have done it gently but he did it with full force to save his son. There was absolutely no room for guessing or errors. If he had missed in any way, his boy would have fallen to his death. Jake began bawling from fear and the pain of his dad's grab. He clung to his parents, all of them shaking frantically.

*What the fuck is going on. My boy almost died. No fucking way that just happened.*

Tom got up slowly with Jake in his arms. He wasn't going to let go of him for a few more minutes (or at least until carrying him down the path was too much). Katie wiped her eyes as she stroked Jake's forehead with her thumb. The family slowly made their way down the path. To her credit, Dawn was old enough to know not to repeat that the trip was cursed. Rounding the switchback at the cement bench, Tom felt like Jake was gaining weight by the second in Tom's arms. Tom wanted to put him down to walk but Jake still seemed too shaken to move.

"Ow! Ow! Ow!" Tommy was suddenly bent over crying and reaching for his left calf right by the ice cream melt.

"What now?" Tom couldn't see around Jake's head so he swung his body and, along with Katie, noticed the yellow jacket on the back of Tommy's left leg. Its stinger firmly stuck in Tommy's skin, the yellow jacket was flailing around trying to fly away. Tom, still clutching Jake, quickly bent down and ripped the yellow jacket off. Katie then held Tommy upright so Tom could make sure that the stinger was out. It was and only the red blood dot from the sting was left. Tom gave it a strong squeeze to get out any poison and Tommy gave a little squeak of pain, tears flowing down his cheeks.

Dawn couldn't take it anymore. "This trip is totally cursed. I'm outta here. I'll be at the car."

"Just wait for us in the store sweetie," Tom called after her as she bolted down the path. He needed to make sure she was safe and couldn't be abducted by some lunatic in the parking lot the way this trip was going. Besides, he wanted to give the place's owner a few suggestions, from his lawyerly perspective.

The family continued their descent.

*Of course it was Tommy who got stung.*

Tom didn't want to bring it up but Tommy was the family klutz. He was a human lightning rod for accidents. He had been leaning on the rail at the clifftop with Jake and he was always tripping or falling over something. He was the clumsy child with allergies and –

*Oh shit. No he isn't. He can't be. Oh ferfucksakes.*

Katie heard it too as she was escorting

Tommy down the path. Tommy was wheezing heavily. And starting to cough and make choking noises in his throat.

"Oh shit," Tom and Katie blurted in unison.

They looked at Tommy's calf and it was red and swelling. Tom didn't wait for anything. "Jakie, stay here with Mommy and Tommy okay?" Anaphylactic shock was nothing to mess around with. Time was of the essence.

Tom put the boy down and ran like hell to the car. Out of shape or not, his adrenaline was rushing and the path was all downhill. He ran through the store like a missile straight to his car. He unlocked the doors and grabbed the first aid kit in the glove compartment. He slammed the door shut and locked the car as he ran back through the store and up the path. At no time did Tom remember that Dawn was in the store. He didn't hear her shouting "Oh my God, what now?" as he ran through the store or asking him what happened while he was at the car. He barely noticed her as he locked the car and ran back up the path.

Katie was nervously sitting with Jake next to her and Tommy on her lap. Tom flopped down and unzipped the first aid kit. His hands were sweating profusely. He reached for the epinephrine case, opened it, and injected it into Tommy's thigh. Tommy winced and cried but his anaphylaxis quickly subsided.

When Tom saw that Tommy was pulling through and breathing comfortably, he started to notice the sweat dripping down his body from every pore. His polo clung to his stomach with a large sweat streak in a crescent shape around the top while the polo's neckline and armpits were completely soaked through. He was panting heavily and, although he tried to raise his hands above his head to stretch his lungs like his high school football trainers had taught him back in the day, he was too tired and sore to get his hands above his shoulders. His hamstrings and quads were throbbing, his lower back ached, and his lungs were burning.

"You are my hero, honey," Katie called over encouragingly. She was cuddling Jake on her left arm and Tommy on her right. Her eyes were large and bloodshot and she looked like she couldn't move.

A whole cadre of people came up the path to check on the Prestons. They were led by the man behind the counter who had sold Tom the pocket knife.

"You folks alright?"

Tom, who was slumped over with his hands above his knees looked over and gave the man (and effectively the cadre) a summary of what had transpired -- the broken railing, Jake's near-death fall, and the bee sting. People in the group were making gasping noises and shocked expressions. Normally, Tom would have been amused by the variety of shocked expressions among different people but he was completely indifferent at the moment. The “oh my goshes,” “no ways,” “sweet Jesuses,” “whoas,” and “for reals” didn’t register with him in the slightest. At the end of his summary, the man from the counter picked up a walkie-talkie that was clipped to his belt buckle and spoke into it.

“Gerry, I need you ASAP at the path. There’s a family in need of assistance.”

Not more than two minutes later, a fairly tall man, about 6’1”, approached the man and the Prestons.

“Hello folks, I’m Gerald Tiebolt. I run this place. It seems you’ve had some real trouble for which I sincerely apologize.”

The man behind the counter gave Gerald a quick summary of Tom’s summary. Gerald removed his cap, a firm 101st Airborne hat, and ran his hand from his forehead to the back of his head and started scratching the back of his neck.

“Folks, there aren’t enough words to express my apologies. I don’t know what to say.” Gerald looked down at Katie and the boys and noticed the used epinephrine syringe lying on the ground by its opened container. “Look, why don’t you come down to my office so you can rest for as long as you like.”

“We need to get our sons checked out at a hospital to make sure they’re okay.” Even in his fatigue, Tom was able to get out his firm, skeptical lawyer voice. On top of wanting to make sure that Tommy was alright, Jake hadn't said a word or really moved since the railing broke and Tom was secretly worried that he might be in shock.

"Yes sir," Gerald said with a tip of his hat. "You've all been through heck at what's supposed to be a great attraction. Just please give me the chance to do right by you and at least get you energized for the trip over to the hospital. It won't take long but the nearest hospital's in Sault Sainte Marie. It's about an hour away and I assume that the kids could at least enjoy some pick-me-ups."

Gerald extended a hand to help Katie up from the path along with Jake and Tommy. Tom, although in pain, picked Tommy up in his arms and walked down the path with him. Katie carried Jake, and Dawn trailed behind. Gerald and the man from the counter walked with them pace for pace. "Let's just take it nice and easy folks," Gerald said in a soothing tone.

When they got to the store, Gerald held the door open and said magic words that all tourists wish they would hear from a roadside store. "Kids, please help yourselves to anything you want. Sir, ma'am," he continued looking at Tom and Katie, "please help yourselves to any food and drinks for the ride and any hospital stay."

Tom's heart rose when he saw Tommy and Jake come to life when they heard they could have anything they wanted. They didn't run, but they started walking slowly together towards the toys. Dawn was not as excited. Her emotions were racing all over the place and she was intent on just grabbing a new pair of sunglasses. "Guys, don't be greedy," Tom called after Tommy and Jake "just get one thing each."

"Nonsense," Gerald called after the boys "I know you should listen to your father, but how about three items each?"

Tom took no offense to being contradicted by a stranger, especially when he heard Jake and Tommy exclaim "yeah!" with two little fist-bumps. "Okay, fine guys, you can take three each like Mr. Tiebolt said. Remember to say thank you."

Tom looked nervously at Katie for a second expecting a moment of awkward silence between them and Gerald. Fortunately, Gerald seemed genuinely intent on doing the right thing and making the Prestons comfortable. Gerald politely asked for their names and then began talking to them about what happened. He seemed like a homely Yooper (Michigan slang for someone from the Upper Peninsula). He was wearing a pair of comfortable black work shoes, blue jeans and a short-sleeve black button down shirt with the top two buttons open. Tom couldn't tell if he had a custom belt buckle under his shirt, but he had a custom necklace with an unusual design. Rather than a bear claw or a crystal or some stone and metal art, there was a tree with an infinity design carved in its trunk. It seemed like every Yooper had some unique trinket in his or her wardrobe. Tom thought that Gerald looked to be in his mid- to late forties. His face showed no wrinkles and his hairline was immaculate with straight black hair, on the longer side, weaving around his ears and hanging down covering half his neck.

"Look Mr. and Mrs. Preston, I've been running this place for thirty-five years. We've never had anything like this happen. I am so sorry. I'm glad, at least, that I was here. I have managers so I'm only here a few times a month. I wouldn't call that a lucky break by any means, but at least I can help you as much as possible. I'm going to refund you the money for the hike obviously, and I saw that you had to use an epinephrine shot. I know that the manufacturer charges about $600 for them now. I insist on reimbursing you for that as well and your hospital bill. Here's my card. You call me with the invoice and I'll pay it, no questions asked. I mean it. I just feel awful."

Whenever Tom's college buddies asked why there were so many lawsuits, Tom explained that a lot of lawsuits had to do with the fact that the person who screwed up refused to own up to his or her mistake so the person who was hurt would have no choice to sue followed by having no desire afterwards to walk away from the lawsuit. Tom would often say that many lawsuits would never be brought if the wrongdoer had simply done that most basic thing which parents tell their children as babies: "Say you're sorry and do the right thing." And here was this stranger doing exactly the right thing. Tom wasn't going to sue him anyway (the thought never even crossed his mind), but the day's events could certainly give rise to a lawsuit. *Hey kids, politicians, people of Earth, here is your reminder. Apologize and do the right thing.*

"Thank you," Tom said. "We appreciate that."

"Think nothing of it. Please go help yourselves and the kids. I'll be right back." Gerald headed towards an office near the side door at the back of the store building.

Tom and Katie walked over to the kids. Dawn has holding the sunglasses that she picked out along with a book about ghost stories of the Upper Peninsula. Tom looked at the book and raised his eyebrows. "It fits with the tone of the trip, Dad," Dawn said preemptively figuring, correctly, that Tom was going to question her choice. *Snarky and right as usual today.* Katie avoided the subject and preempted conversation by turning to the boys and asking them to show her what they picked from the store. They had each selected cap gun revolvers, small amethyst geodes, and whoopee cushions. *Nothing says classy like fake farts.*

Tom and Katie pretended to be excited about the boys' choices (the geodes at least were a great choice that the boys would have forever) and led the kids over to the food and drinks. Tom and Katie each grabbed a bottle of water and the kids all went with pop since their parents never let them drink any at home. Everyone grabbed a bag of chips except for Tommy. He actually got a bag of local taffy after Katie read the ingredients and saw that there were no ingredients to which Tommy was allergic. The family walked over to the counter and placed their items on top. Not one minute later, Gerald came walking briskly from his office with some customized canvass bags in his hand.

"Here you go Mr. Preston."

"Thank you Mr. Tiebolt. We sincerely appreciate everything."

"My pleasure, sir. Here let me bag these items for you." Gerald started placing each child's items in separate bags. He then place all of the food items in a bad and the drinks in another bag. "Thank you all for choosing to come here today. I wish it could have been perfect for you and I truly hope you come again. We're going to fix the railing and give it an upgrade. Please drive safe and have a wonderful rest of your stay up here."

The kids each took turns saying "Thank

you" and Katie did as well plus "We appreciate how you handled this."

Tom unlocked the car and watched them head over to it. "Look Mr. Tiebolt, thank you for stepping up."

"Don't mention it Mr. Preston," Gerald interrupted "it's the least I can do."

"I came here as a kid and, while today wasn't so great, I do hope to come back again."

"Please do. That would be wonderful."

"35 years you've been running this place?"

"Yes sir!"

"You look like you must've started as a kid."

"No, I'm much older than that," Gerald said with a disbelieving laugh. "Just clean living up here sir."

Gerald extended his hand and gave Tom a firm shake. He then turned and walked back into the store. Tom headed over to the SUV. *I wish I could age like that.*

# NORTHBOUND AND DOWN

## *Chapter Five*

Their little excursion had cost nearly two hours. It would be around 6:30 p.m. by the time they expected to arrive at the hospital in Sault Sainte Marie.

"I think we'll have to find a hotel to stay for the night," Tom said to Katie.

Katie had just finished loading a comedy into the DVD player to keep the kids distracted and in a good mood. "Yeah, I think it'll be fine. Hopefully there will be some with vacancies near the Soo Locks. We can have a leisurely day there before heading up to the Whitefish Bay campground."

The Soo Locks are the locks at Sault Sainte Marie that allow ships to travel between Lake Superior and the lower Great Lakes. Tom and Katie had both been there to watch them as kids and had been debating about whether they'd take the kids (and themselves) to see the locks during their trip. Their answer was now presented to them with the boys needing medical attention. Tom was glad to hear Katie agreeable on the hotel. Katie hated -- no she abhorred -- hotels. She would rather sleep outside near a swamp than in a bedroom that strangers had been sleeping in for however many years. Between Katie holding up and Gerald Tiebolt behaving in such a gentlemanly fashion, Tom was able to hold up himself. He was completely fatigued and stressed, but not overwhelmed by the stress like he might have otherwise been. Or so he thought.

Unfortunately, Katie needed to think about things out loud and with an immediate sense of urgency. It was her way of dealing with most stress, planning, and making sure that she didn't forget to do something. Tom, in contrast, needed peace-and-quiet time to recharge his batteries. He was hoping to have twenty or thirty minutes of just silent listening to the movie playing in the backseat before he and Katie would discuss their plans.

"We're going to have to get another epinephrine syringe. Hopefully there are some decent hotel rooms we can get. And find restaurants that are allergy-friendly. Hopefully Jake doesn't need any real medical attention. He was kind of holding his arm that you yanked."

*Yeah, thanks for just jumping right into the*

*honey-do list honey. And that's a real bitchy way of saying you hurt our son by saving his life because you sure as hell didn't save him. Why do you always say things in such horrible ways instead of thinking through your word choices?*

"Yeah, I was really trying to dislocate Jake's shoulder when I grabbed him in a fraction of a second to save his life," Tom snapped.

"What? What are you . . . oh, I didn't mean you hurt him on purpose," Katie mustered.

"How about just ending your sentence with Jake's arm seems sore. Leave it at that. I saved his life. Me. Not you. You don't just blurt words out that sound accusatory. I do everything for those kids. I just ran my out-of-shape ass at Olympic speed to save Tommy after saving Jake. I'm there for them all the time and that's how you talk to me going through your list not even three minutes into a one-hour drive after what we just went through? Look, I've had it. I need some quiet time. We are *not* having a conversation. You can start Googling your list and planning on your own. I'm done. Just don't talk to me for thirty minutes."

Tom was choking the life out of the steering wheel. His knuckles were bright white and his teeth were clenched. Katie really hadn't said anything bad or meant anything accusatory but she saw that it was apparently Tom's last straw. More than that, Tom had never snapped at her like that in all their years together. She could tell that his stress from work and everything else had taken him to a dark place that she had never noticed before. Katie pulled out her phone to start looking for hotel rooms, epinephrine, and restaurants. She checked on Tom several times over the next few minutes and saw that he was still steamed so she kept all the information that she found to herself and typed it on the memo pad on her phone.

About a half mile ahead, the Prestons' SUV came upon a bobtailing Peterbilt big rig. It instantly caught Tom and Katie's attention. The big rig without a trailer looked like some kind of a war relic. It was the oldest-looking truck that they had ever seen with beaten-up brown paint showing flaking and cracking all over the frame. Tom passed it as quickly as he could and kept up that speed until the truck was a dot on his rearview mirror. He let out a sigh of relief as the truck took the exit that they just passed to one of the small towns along the way.

Katie continued looking up information on her phone and the kids were enjoying their pops and chips watching the movie. Tom had even heard them laughing at some of the funnier lines.

*Bing! Bing! Bing! Bing! Bing!*

The warning lights on the SUV's dashboard all starting going off. Everyone jumped. Tom was hoping that there was just an electrical glitch as opposed to an engine issue. His knuckles grew ever whiter as he held his breath praying that the car would keep driving. Within seconds, however, he closed his eyes heavily as the car started to sputter. Tom saw an exit up ahead and used the car's momentum to get off the highway and pull over into an open space on the shoulder of the road. All of the electronics in the car had shut off and, as the car lost all inertia, it stopped with a ghostly silence.

The kids, having been through an emotional roller coaster all day, were freaking out asking what was happening in full alarm.

"Daddy, what's going on?"

"Is the car dead?"

"Where are we going?"

"Why is the car making those sounds?"

"Why are we leaving the road?"

Tom's stress turned instantly into a panicked fear. There were no food or gas or attraction signs posted at the exit. It was just one of many exits that went to a road used by however few local residents there were and nothing more. At the moment, there was no one and nothing around. Tom whipped out his cellphone but noticed that it was not getting any reception.

"Katie, is your phone getting reception?"

"No. Dawn, check your phone. Is it getting reception?"

"No mom."

Tom, sitting upright, took a deep breath.

"Look, the car just broke down. I have no idea what happened. Frankly, I've never been in a car when this happened. Wherever we are, we're not getting cellphone reception. I'm going to check the glove compartment for a map."

Fortunately, Tom and Katie always made sure to bring maps of where they were traveling. Part of it was being old-school since they grew up using maps to travel and hike. The other part was to have an emergency backup in case it was needed, like now. Tom showed Katie where he thought they were and it seemed to both of them that the only likely place to find help would be at the previous exit where the old truck had left the highway. That exit, from Tom's memory, seemed to have a sign with a gas station and local restaurant on it.

"Okay, let's wait a few minutes to see if the car starts or if we can get service on our phones," Katie suggested.

"Good idea," Tom replied. "Don't worry guys, we'll get through this."

Ten minutes later, Tom tried the ignition with no luck. Not even so much as one dashboard light came on and the engine made no noise whatsoever. Tom, Katie, and Dawn had all turned off their phones. When they turned them back on after the car failed to start they all saw that there was still no service.

"Well, we're going to have to walk about a mile back to the last exit guys," Tom said in a serious but somber voice. "We're going to be walking along the highway so you need to just stay in a single-file line behind me. Mommy will be walking at the back so she can see you all. Maybe we'll get lucky and a police car will drive by. If not, there's a gas station and restaurant at the next exit. I know we're all tired and it might feel like a long walk but it should only take us maybe twenty minutes or so. Just stay together. I'll put the rest of our drinks and some food in my backpack to take with us."

Tom hopped out of the car and retrieved his backpack from the back. He made sure to double-check that his compass and gadget knife were still there along with everyone's flashlights. He emptied the two books that he packed for the trip and then filled the backpack with the two water bottles and remnants of the kids' pops. He grabbed what was left of the cookies, the kids' chips, taffy and licorice for Tommy, and the bag of apples that Katie had put in their cooler for lunch that day but that they had forgotten to eat at the rest area. He then grabbed a phone charger.

"Okay guys, I've got everything. Oh, Katie, will you get the map please."

"Yes, here it is."

They started walking single-file towards the highway. Tom had put on a brave show for Katie and the kids. He suspected Katie was trying to keep her emotions in check after he snapped at her, but he was going crazy on the inside. For the first time in his adult life, Tom Preston was terrified. He was fairly certain that he had never been this scared in his entire life and was now thinking that the whole trip had been a series of bad omens leading up to this situation. They needed help. Tommy and Jake needed medical attention. They were about to walk on the side of a highway with a 75-miles-per-hour speed limit. What if someone got struck by a car? What if there was no gas station or restaurant at the next exit or what if they were closed? What if some psychopathic serial killer picked them up? Were they going to end up in a well? In a ditch? In some foreign country?

Tom's mind was wandering into scarier and darker thoughts when he and the others heard the sound of a vehicle coming towards them. Tom's heart was racing as he turned to see if the sound was really a vehicle and, if it was, who was inside of it. At first, Tom saw nothing but the sound was getting closer. He then saw the vehicle approaching from the east. It was another silver SUV that looked to be a about a ten-year-old model. The silhouettes of two people in the front seats were coming into view. As the vehicle drove closer, Tom saw that they were two fully bearded middle-aged men in dark button-down shirts with sunglasses. Tom's heart jumped as the vehicle approached them and slowed down as it turned eastward towards them. The passenger's window scrolled down and the man in the shotgun seat removed his sunglasses. A pair of bright blue eyes beamed at Tom.

"Broke down?"

"Yes, sir," Tom responded. He tried to sound confident and protective in case the men had any bad intentions.

"Where're you headed?"

"Up to the next exit," Tom didn't want to give them any more information.

The driver then leaned forward around blue eyes and said "That ain't a safe plan. We'll get Ollie to come by and get you fixed up."

"Who's Ollie?"

"He's our town mechanic. He can pretty much fix anything. We'll go get him."

Before Tom or Katie could say anything, the men drove back the way they came.

"Was that lucky or should we be worried," Katie said to Tom.

"I was just wondering the same thing," Tom said back. "Do we have a better choice?"

At that question, Tom, Katie, and Dawn all checked their cellphones. Still no reception. They all looked at each other knowing that there really was no other choice but a long highway walk with no guarantee of finding help versus someone named Ollie who supposedly could fix pretty much anything.

"Alright, let's wait a little bit for this

Ollie. If it takes too long or we don't like this Ollie, we'll just head back to the last exit," Tom said.

"That's about the only choice we have," Katie said.

"Yeah," Dawn agreed.

"I've gotta pee," Jake called out.

Tommy was already relieving himself in a nearby bush."

"Let's go pee by your brother Jakey," Tom said.

Katie and Dawn walked over to a nearby tree and went behind it to relieve themselves.

Five minutes after the Prestons had regrouped by their car, they heard the sounds of vehicles coming up the road from the east. Out in front was the silver SUV and behind it was a blue tow truck. The vehicles passed by the Prestons and then u-turned with the silver SUV pulling over on the shoulder behind the Prestons' car with the tow truck pulling over on the shoulder in front of the Prestons' car and then backing up to within five feet of the front bumper. The tow truck driver stepped out of his car first and made the short walk over to the Prestons. He looked over each of them and then extended a hand towards Tom while flashing a homely smile.

"Hello sir, ma'am, kiddos, I'm Oliver Gustafson. People call me Ollie. It's a common nickname, but I'm pretty sure that I was the original Ollie so just remember that I'm the unique one," he said with a wink in the kids' direction.

Tom extended his hand and shook Ollie's. "Good to meet you sir. Thank you for driving over. I'm Tom Preston. This is my wife Katie, our daughter Dawn, and our sons Tommy and Jake."

"You mind if I take a look at your car," Ollie asked as a formality.

"Please do, sir," Tom responded in kind.

"It's just Ollie, but you can write Oliver on the check," Ollie chuckled back. He walked over to the Prestons' SUV, opened the driver-side door, and flipped open the hood.

"Hey Tom, would you mind trying to start your car? I need to get a look at her," Ollie called out.

"You bet," Tom said hustling over to the driver's seat. He inserted the key into the ignition switch and turned it. Absolutely nothing happened. Ollie shook his head and wiped his sweating forehead with a dirty old hat that had been placed in the back pocket of his dirt-stained jeans. He walked back to his tow truck and lifted a small device out of the side compartment by the driver's side door. Tom took a look at it and saw that it was a battery tester. Ollie placed it on the Prestons' car battery and grimaced. "Tom, does your car have gas?" Ollie asked without looking up.

"Sure does Ollie. I filled up in Mackinac City before we left. It should be about 85% full."

Ollie stepped out from under the hood and leaned sideways towards the two men in the silver SUV. "It's a no go. The thing's completely dead."

The two men looked up and nodded. They started to exit the SUV and head over. Tom's fear level rose realizing that his family was now surrounded by three fit-looking middle-aged men. They were completely at the mercy of these strangers who could basically do anything they wanted to the Prestons. Tom didn't want to think about it but his mind was racing with horrific fear-driven images.

"What do you think is wrong with the car Ollie?" Tom asked hoping that the men were genuinely interested in helping and trying to keep the conversation on the car and nothing more.

"It's tough to say for certain," Ollie replied. "I checked your battery and it has a full charge. If it has gas like you say, then I suspect that the car's alternator or electrical system, or some combination, are fried and that's why nothing's happening when you turn the key."

The two men from the silver SUV had reached Ollie and the Prestons in the middle of Ollie's preliminary diagnosis. Ollie gave them a quick nod and said "These are the Prestons. This is Tom and Katie and their children, Dawn, Tommy and Jake." Then Ollie continued speaking, "In order to know for sure, I'm going to need to get your car back to my shop and run diagnostics on it and, if that doesn't work, start going through each and every part until I find the issue or issues."

"When you say electrical system, you mean the car's computer chips that control the car's electronics?" Katie asked.

"Yeah. You have a new car and newer cars basically run like computers with gas," Ollie replied.

That sounded right to Tom and familiar to Katie. They had good friends, the Tiptons, who were car enthusiasts. The Tiptons lived for the annual Dream Cruise north and south along Woodward Avenue during the third weekend of August where people lined up and drove their old cars to the tunes of their time along the main road from Detroit. The Tiptons loved walking around and looking at the classic cars and would even dare to drive the hours-long drive along approximately seven bumper-to-bumper miles on Woodward Avenue in their 1967 Corvette. One of the things that the Tiptons had mentioned as a concern was that preserving the old classics was going to be difficult in the future because parts were all shifting to computers.

"How far away is your shop Ollie, and how long do you think it will take?" Tom asked.

"My shop's back in town and it will probably take me a few hours. I don't mind working late tonight but I'm going to get dinner because it is getting late and it'll probably take a couple-a hours to do a thorough inspection."

The Prestons all winced when they heard this. Their minds were all concerned with where they were going to get food and shelter in the middle of nowhere.

"Don't fret folks," the silver SUV driver spoke out. "My name is Edward Stanton and this is my brother Herman. We've taken the liberty of making some arrangements to accommodate your circumstance if that is acceptable to you. Deacon Forsythe of our congregation and his wife have offered to put you up for as long as you need. I know this situation is not ideal and you're probably tired and, dare I say, scared? But I promise you that Ollie is a genius mechanic. No vehicle has defeated him yet. Our town is a magical place. A good, clean, wholesome northern Michigan town. The hospitality will also help make up for this inconvenience and I'm sure this part of your trip will be something that you'll never forget."

At that point, Tom felt Katie's gaze. She was just as unsure as he was, but what real choice did they have? Tom didn't want to incite a conflict and, knowing that there was no other real option, he responded with a "Thank you all. Edward, Herman, Ollie, we really appreciate this. We're grateful for your help."

"Let Herman and I grab your belongings. It looks like you have some camping gear but you'll just need your clothing and any other personal items that you want to keep by you."

Tom escorted the Stantons over to his vehicle and started picking up each person's clothing bags. Tom kept his backpack on him and Katie grabbed her purse. The kids each grabbed their backpacks that had their tablets, toys, and books that they had packed for the trip. Edward and Herman put all of the items, with the exception of Katie's purse, into the back of their silver SUV. Herman then walked over to Ollie who had already mounted the Prestons' car onto his tow truck. Ollie told Herman that the car was secure and Herman hopped into the tow truck's passenger seat.

Edward invited Tom into the shotgun seat of his SUV and then held the door open for Katie and the kids to squeeze into the back. The back felt bigger than it looked and, although it was a squeeze, it wasn't too bad.

"How far away is town?" Tom asked Edward as Edward started the engine.

"It's about an hour, give or take," Edward responded.

Tom suddenly got nervous and seemed to pop up. Katie and the kids noticed, and so did Edward.

"Relax Tom. Me, Herman, and Ollie were fishing in the creek about 20 minutes east of the highway. We have a nice hunting and fishing property. We keep our gear in our cabin there and we had finished for the day. Ollie was actually putting the fishing gear away since it was his turn today and Herman and I drove ahead to town. Lucky for you, we came across you."

"I'm sorry," Tom said solemnly. "You caught me. I was suspicious when you said the town was further than your drive back with Ollie seemed to take."

"Don't worry Tom. Your thinking was logical. I would have thought the same thing myself in your shoes."

Tom now seemed to relax a little and wanted to ease the conversation for everyone's benefit. "What is the name of your town, Edward?"

"Manchineel."

# MANCHINEEL

## *Chapter Six*

Tom's furrowed eyebrows said it all.

"Never heard of Manchineel I take it," Edward said with a smirk.

"No, sir," Tom replied.

"We're a small town. A very small town. Population of 68. Unlike most towns up here, we have no roots in mining, logging, fur-trading, tourism, or being a military outpost. Just a bunch of folks like our ancestors who wanted our own place away from everything else. It's special to us but not really special for anyone else."

"I'm sure it's lovely," Katie said hopefully.

"Well it is to us, and it's ours," Edward said back with a wink.

"Are there any restaurants or shops in Manchineel?" Dawn asked.

"Afraid not," Edward replied. "There are restaurants and shops in some of the nearby towns. We go to them when we need provisions or just for excursions. Manchineel is really our home."

"What about Ollie's shop?" Tom was wondering the same thing as Dawn. He was proud of her inquisitive mind and her boldness in asking the question. He beamed with pride inside at the person she was becoming.

"Ollie's place is nearby in McIntosh," Edward replied. "We do, however, have a storehouse in town. It's not a store per se. We all put extra goods in there for the rest of the town in case anyone needs them."

"So it's like a community you have?" Dawn asked in follow-up.

"Sure. That's what a town is young lady. A community. At least that's what it's supposed to be," Edward responded. "Isn't where you live like a community with people taking care of each other?"

"Somewhat, but not really I guess," Dawn responded.

"Where do you live?" Edward asked. The question was innocuous but it still made Tom and Katie uncomfortable having strangers know their personal information.

"We live in the Metro Detroit area," Katie jumped in.

"So you live with thousands of people in your community and you have some friends and neighbors that you can count on but most of those thousands of people go on with their separate lives, right?"

"Yeah, I guess," Dawn responded.

"Up here, we don't have as many people and conditions can get rough in the winter so we really have to be a community and look after each other. In fact, that's what most of us live here for. It's our lifestyle choice."

"Is anyone in town a doctor?" Katie asked. Getting Jake and Tommy examined was still among their top priorities right after surviving this ordeal and before having the car fixed.

"Yes ma'am. We are fortunate and have a doctor who lives in town and helps take care of us. Dr. Arbour. Do you need a doctor?"

"We do. Our sons need to be examined. Tommy was stung by a yellow jacket and had an anaphylactic reaction. Jake nearly fell off a cliff and hurt his arm socket." Katie was very careful in phrasing Jake's potential injury after Tom's outburst which seemed like months ago at that point.

"You folks sound like you had one crazy day."

"We sure did," Jake blurted out. "We heard a car hit a deer. Dad saw all of it and I think Mom saw some."

"Whoa, that sounds terrible –"

"Yeah, and blood and fur splashed all over the side of our car," Tommy interrupted.

Tom didn't want to hear about the deer but the boys were perfectly in their right to tell their rescuer about their crazy day. It happened after all. It was the truth. Tom just let the conversation continue while rubbing his forehead.

"That sounds like a *horrible* accident," Edward said with emphasis so the boys would feel his interest in their story in response to their excitement.

"And we know that the deer died," Jake continued "but we don't know what happened to the people in the car."

"We're pretty sure they died. Dad said their car flipped over in the median," Tommy added.

"So much life lost in one crazy accident," Edward responded sympathetically. "We see and hear about deer accidents all the time up here. I myself haven't seen one or been a part of one, but I have had a few near misses where deer just jumped out right in front of my car."

"The deer did the same to us and we just barely missed it," Tom chimed in.

"The loss of life is the most tragic loss there can be. What could have been but for one decision."

None of the Prestons had any idea what that meant and none of them felt inclined to ask Edward. He was their host taking them to an unknown small town to stay with some strangers in their home until their SUV was fixed. Edward was entitled to say and feel whatever he wanted.

Edward continued driving west. Half an

hour into the drive, Ollie's tow truck turned northwest on a diagonally interesting county road. Edward followed. Tom noticed that there were no homes or structures of any kind along the road. It was mostly thick brush and trees along the road with an occasional clearing or pond. Ten minutes later, the road started to become bumpy as pavement became dirt.

*Holy shit, he's taking us to some ghost town-like place in the middle of nowhere.*

Tom, a claustrophobe, was starting to panic. He grabbed the handle on the door and started to squeeze. "How close are we?"

"About twenty minutes. Not much out here is paved or maintained well. It's mostly a snowmobile route in the winter. Don't worry though, the town'll pick up your spirits."

Tom looked over at Katie to give him courage. The beauty in having a family was the ability to draw strength from them just being part of you. Katie looked back at Tom and gave a reserved smile. She then gave each child a pat on the shoulder to reassure them. The thick brush and trees lining the road blocked out much of the sunlight and made it appear like they were traveling down the abandoned road as night was setting in.

Fifteen minutes later, the bouncing grew weaker as dirt gave way to gravel which then gave way to pavement. At the same time, the brush and trees lining the road gradually thinned letting in more light.

*Thank God.*

Tom noticed something unusual as the trip became a little more comfortable. Normally after a bumpy ride, he had to urinate. His middle-aged bladder was easily shaken. However, after all of the sweat of the day, he felt his body dehydrating. "Edward, do you mind if we have some of our drinks?"

"Help yourselves."

Tom asked Katie to get him his water and the kids likewise asked for their pops. Katie passed out the drinks. The kids emptied their bottles quickly while Tom and Katie drank over half of their water bottles.

"Drink up," Edward encouraged. "You guys will have earned it when all is said and done." Here again the Prestons had no idea what Edward meant and none of them felt like it was their place to ask.

Minutes later, the ever-thinning bushes and trees made way for brush. The sunlight was still bright and now filled the entire road. Tom, already feeling better from the water and less claustrophobic, began entertaining the thought of feeling relaxed. The road started to take on a steep incline at which point Tom started leaning towards anxiety. He was about ready to panic when he saw that the road ahead had a dog-leg turn which Ollie passed by, continuing on the road, while Edward made the turn. They were now alone with Edward going to some tiny town they never heard of. However, the scales of Tom's internal debate switched towards feeling relaxed as the dog-leg turned into a giant clearing. The windshield revealed a quaint little town sitting just below the hill that they had apparently driven up. There was no welcome sign or town sign saying Manchineel. There were no signs of any kind. There was only beauty.

"Welcome to Manchineel," Edward announced.

The town was situated in a clearing about the size of 200-plus acres and surrounded by rolling hills and thick forest. Looking at the town as they made the descent down the road, Tom noticed about three dozen buildings, most looking like old-fashioned colonial homes, sprawled around the perimeter of the town, except for the back-third of the area. There was also a water tower set on the edge of the far woods. The road divided into a track shape connecting all of the buildings. The homes looked immaculate -- the exteriors were white bricks with stained wood doors and shudders. All of the homes had at least one stone chimney and some appeared to have two. The homes also seemed to have white garages with driveways and walkways to both a side door and the front door.

Immaculate as the homes looked, what made Manchineel stand out was the scenery and the landscaping. Where the road and buildings stopped, there was a pristine blue lake right in the middle of the town going all the way into the back third of the land. And, where the lake ended on the far side of Manchineel, the land started to rise into a small hill overlooking the town from the back. Paths along both sides of the lake led to the top of the hill where a large building sat with what appeared to be a small waterfall coming out from beneath it and down the hill into the lake. The building was extremely unusual and unlike any building that Tom had ever seen before. The portion of the building facing them with the waterfall looked like a modern-day greenhouse with magnificently tall and wide windows forming a semicircle overlooking the water while, at the roof, curved windows formed a skylight crown over that part of the building. In contrast, the back portion of the building looked like an old museum or church with beautiful stone architecture. Like the rest of Manchineel, the building was accentuated by the most exquisite landscaping Tom had ever seen or could have ever imagined. While there were indeed areas of lawn that were well-mowed and bright green, there were countless varieties of ground cover, bushes, shrubs, small trees, and flowers, all over Manchineel. They came in seemingly every color of the rainbow. There was no symmetry or pattern to any of the landscaping, it was just that all of the vegetation appeared diverse, healthy, and well-maintained.

"This is gorgeous!" Katie exclaimed amidst the "whoas" and "holy shmolies" coming from the kids.

"Thank you," Edward said appreciatively. "We're mighty proud of this town that we built for ourselves."

"Only 68 people live here and maintain this?" Tom asked in amazement.

"Yessir" Edward chuckled.

"What's the name of the lake?" Dawn asked.

"You know what? We never really named it. I guess if it had to have a name we would probably just call it Manchineel Lake or The Lake," Edward said matter-of-factly.

"You guys should call it Fish Lake or Frog Lake," Jake suggested.

"Or Bright Blue Lake or Blue Glass Lake," Tommy joined in the suggestion pool.

"Those sound like good names. We'll think about," Edward said with a smirk.

As Edward drove into Manchineel, the Prestons looked out the windows in awe. Pictured Rocks National Shoreline was undoubtedly the prized scenery of their trip, but now Manchineel's beauty was calling to them as it was unparalleled in beauty to any other places that they had ever been. They could all easily imagine themselves vacationing there. Katie, who had always wanted to stay at a bed-and-breakfast with Tom, was secretly wondering if there was a bed-and-breakfast anywhere in the Upper Peninsula that could compete with Manchineel. In fact, neither Tom nor Katie could think of such a beautiful town or scenery in any of the coffee table books, *National Geographic* magazine photographs, or pictures posted on the Internet. This town in which they were now stranded was the most beautiful area they had ever seen.

"Maybe this is lucky after all," Katie said. "Although we really don't want to impose on you or the Deacon or anyone here," she added in case her statement offended Edward.

"No imposition at all Katie," Edward responded. "You're our guest. Welcome to the UP (Upper Peninsula to the layperson). We help one another out, especially in times of distress."

Edward slowed the SUV and pulled into the driveway of the home closest to the lake on the far side of town. "We have arrived at Deacon Forsythe's home. Hop on out."

The Prestons climbed out of the SUV and gave their bodies some quick stretches. Edward did the same while loudly cracking his neck and jaws. "Long day for me, longer day for you," Edward said while leading them along the stone walkway to Deacon Forsythe's door. It was not a standard-sized door but, rather, an extra wide door about 50% larger than a regular door and easily ten feet tall. It was made out of what appeared to be solid oak wood and stained a rich maple brown. About six-and-a-half feet up in the middle of the door there was a large black metal door knocker in the shape of what appeared to be an apple with the handle protruding out of both sides. Edward lifted the handle and gave a few heavy knocks. The Prestons could hear the metallic knocks echoing inside the house.

Edward and the Prestons just stood there on the porch for what seemed like a full minute. For the Prestons, the silence was becoming awkward. Edward, however, seemed unconcerned and just stood by the door. About thirty seconds later, the Prestons heard the sound of heavy footsteps heading closer to the door until they stopped. Five seconds later, the door opened. A black-haired giant of a man, about six-and-a-half feet tall with a large frame carrying at least 250 muscular pounds, pushed the door aside and stepped down onto the porch where he was now only just naturally towering above the Prestons. His hair was perfectly combed, parted on the side, and had the look of being firmly greased in place. He was wearing black pants with a dark gray sweater vest over a long-sleeve button-down crimson shirt. He had a square jaw and stern look on his face as he stood erect with a perfect posture.

"Welcome and good evening my friends. I am Deacon Jonathan Forsythe. I've heard that your car broke down and that Oliver is taking it to his shop to get fixed. In the meantime, we've made arrangements for you to stay here as our guests given the circumstances. Please come on in and make yourselves at home."

Tom, craning his neck upward, extended his hand and received the firmest-gripped handshake of his life from the Deacon. "Tom Preston," he said trying not to make an inflection from the force of the handshake. "Thank you, sir, so much for your hospitality. We really appreciate it. This is my wife, Katie, and our children, Dawn, Tommy, and Jake."

"Again, welcome everyone," the Deacon said stepping into his home and pulling the door fully open. "Please come in. Edward, would you please bring the Prestons' belongings?"

"Already on it Deacon," Edward said while walking toward the silver SUV.

Edward quickly returned holding all of the Prestons' bags in his two very strong arms without a hint of any deep breaths nor any sweat beads along his bearded face. The entrance to the Deacon's home was rather spacious and covered with a large red Persian rug. The floor, which seemed to run throughout the house, was a rich maple brown wood that appeared to match the door. The Prestons had just finished removing their shoes when Edward had returned and placed their bags gently in the center of the rug.

"Here are your belongings folks," Edward said to the Prestons. He then turned to the Deacon who had remained standing to the side of the entrance holding the door open. "The Prestons are going to need Dr. Arbour to take a look at their sons. I'm sure they'll tell you all about it. My cellphone isn't getting any reception for some reason. It stopped working right around the time I called you from my car before we picked up the Prestons. I'm going to swing by Dr. Arbour's home and ask him to pay a visit."

"Excellent, Edward," the Deacon replied. "That will be much appreciated."

"It would, sir," Tom chimed in. He wanted to make sure that the Deacon knew his family was grateful for everything and not looking to take advantage.

With that, Edward nodded at the Deacon and headed out to his car.

The Deacon then closed the door and it seemed like there was about to be an awkward silence as the Prestons and the Deacon were gauging each other.

"We've been unable to get cellphone reception as well," Tom said preemptively to avoid an uncomfortable silence.

"I haven't checked our phones recently," the Deacon replied. "The cellphone tower near McIntosh is probably down. It happens from time to time."

# DEACON FORSYTHE

## *Chapter Seven*

"We haven't had guests in ages so please forgive my stiffness," the Deacon said trying to sound disarming despite his firm tone and titanic appearance. "Why don't you please come join me and meet my wife, Maryanna, in our parlor."

Deacon Forsythe led the Prestons down the hallway on the unhinged side of the door to a parlor in the back of the house. Tom and Katie both noticed that they had passed a number of rooms on their way to the parlor. The Deacon's house was definitely not an open-concept buildout as there seemed to be multiple enclosed rooms throughout the house. The interior also seemed to be vastly larger than the exterior indicated.

The hallway ended at a large room in the back of the house. It occupied most (or maybe all, but the Prestons could not tell) of the back of the house and there were large bay windows across the back wall overlooking the lake and the greenhouse-like building. In front of the windows there were two enormous matching antique couches made of hardwood with ornate floral patterns along the legs, bases, armrests, and tops. The cushions were made of soft yet thick fuchsia velvet outlined with gold trim. In front of the sofas were two matching antique wood tables, and there were four matching antique armchairs, two at the end of each table on opposite sides of the room, apparently for hosts to sit and speak to guests on either of the couches. Tom didn't notice any artwork on the walls, which were painted dark red, like garnet. There were, however, decorative hardwood columns along the walls on the non-window sides of the room. Ornate black metal sconces were mounted on the walls in between each of the wooden panels matching the door knocker with what appeared to be an apple in the middle with floral patterns filling in the remainder of the metal. It was still light outside and, with the bay windows, Deacon Forsythe did not need to turn on the sconce lights.

"Please have a seat and make yourselves comfortable," the Deacon implored the Prestons.

There was enough room for all of them to fit comfortably on one couch.

"Thank you," Tom and Katie responded.

"The couch is so comfortable," Katie

went on.

"We do love spending time in here," the Deacon said courteously.

"Well hello new family!" A cheery-looking woman came walking into the parlor from a door concealed among the wooden panels on the opposite side of the parlor that the Prestons had entered with the Deacon. She was a tall woman, almost six-feet tall, with an athletic frame and wavy black hair that was just a touch lighter than the Deacon's. The woman was rolling a cart behind her with crystal pitchers of iced tea and lemonade on top and a large tray of chocolate chip cookies and empty glasses on the middle tray along with a pile of red napkins and small white china plates outlined with metallic silver.

"Ah, snack time," the Deacon said cheerfully. "This is my wife, Maryanna. Maryanna, these are the Prestons." The Deacon escorted his wife along the couch starting with Tom and, as he introduced each of the Prestons to his wife, she gave them a very warm, firm handshake.

"Welcome to our home," Maryanna said after the greetings were complete. "I'm sure you've had quite a long day. We haven't had guests in quite a while and I'm sure you've never had a situation like this," her voice was quite endearing. "I've baked some fresh cookies for you, and please help yourselves to some lemonade or iced tea. Dinner won't be ready for about another hour so please don't be shy."

"Thank you so much, but please don't go to any trouble on our account," Katie said. "We feel bad imposing on you like this."

"Oh, nonsense," Maryanna shot back with a smile. "We're happy to have you for as long as you need. Oliver is a great mechanic, but breaking down in these parts can also take some extra time to fix. You just never know. Hopefully we'll hear back from Ollie tonight on his prognosis. In the meantime, let me get you all started."

Maryanna poured a tall glass of lemonade for each of the children and placed them on the table. She then placed two cookies on each of three plates and put them in front of the children.

"Oh, no thank you, ma'am," Tommy said tepidly. "I'm allergic to dairy."

"Well that is just so unfair for a child to not be able to eat these cookies. Is there any kind of treat that maybe I can get for you?" Maryanna inquired.

"Well, I still have some licorice in my backpack," Tommy replied.

"I'll go get it for you if that's okay with your parents," the Deacon volunteered. "I just need to know which backpack it is."

"Of course," Tom said permissively. "It's the red and black one."

The Deacon exited the room while Maryanna turned her attention to Tom and Katie.

"What can I get for the two of you?"

"I would love some iced tea and cookies, please," Katie said.

"That sounds great. May I have that too, please," Tom followed.

"Of course." Maryanna poured two tall glasses of iced tea and placed them in front of Tom and Katie. She then gave each of them a plate with two of her cookies.

Although Tom joined in, he kept thinking *did they drug the food or beverages? I don't want to seem rude but I will not eat or drink anything until I see that my family is safe or the Deacon and his wife drink and eat. I'm not waking up on some operating table getting my kidneys removed or looking at my family's cadavers.*

Deacon Forsythe returned with Tommy's backpack and lifted it over to Tommy on the couch with a long hand that looked like a tree branch with its enormous reach.

"Thank you, sir," Tommy said gratefully. He opened the zipper enthusiastically and started picking through the flavors. Having settled on fruit punch, he pulled out the packaged yard.

"Oh my gosh, is that licorice?" Maryanna excitedly asked hoping to quell any disappointment that Tommy may still have about the cookies.

"Yes, ma'am. It's my favorite!" Tommy responded enthusiastically. "Would you like to try some?"

"Er, well, uh, how can I refuse that offer," Maryanna answered.

Tommy, as only a nine-year-old would do, pulled off a small piece (hey, he only got this licorice maybe once a year) and handed it to Maryanna. She timidly took the piece and looked at the Deacon who was giving her a stern look.

"Thank you, Tommy," she said as she popped it in her mouth and swallowed. Suddenly, she let out a slight gag and began coughing. "I-i wen- d-o-wn w-ong," she managed to say before going into a coughing fit. To Katie, it seemed to have gotten stuck in her throat or caused a reaction much like Tommy would have if he ate something that had an ingredient to which he was allergic.

The Deacon poured a glass of iced tea and gave it to her. She took a few small sips and the coughing subsided. She cleared her throat and then seemed fine.

"Are you alright?" Katie was concerned.

"I'm fine, thank you. I haven't had licorice in quite a while."

Seeing that Maryanna had some iced tea, Tom took a sip from his glass.

The Preston children were leaning over the couch eating the chocolate chip cookies and licorice and drinking their lemonades. Katie began to eat a cookie while Tom just held his glass secretly trying to make sure that his family wasn't being drugged. He noticed the Deacon and Maryanna just staring over all of them as the moment seemed to be culminating in the proverbial awkward silence.

Fortunately, the silence was quickly broken by Jake. "Do you wanna hear what happened to us today?" he asked the Forsythes.

"We sure do, young man," the Deacon said. His voice, though still somewhat firm and monotonous, tried to make a pleasant intonation. "However, let's save that for a suppertime conversation. We've invited a few of our neighbors over to meet you and help us give you a more proper introduction to Manchineel. In the meantime, just enjoy your snacks and rest up."

"Who's coming?" Jake asked, one of the many blessings of children being that they can often ask prying questions out of innocence that adults otherwise feel unable to ask.

The Deacon pursed his lips and raised his eyebrows a bit in surprise but he quickly composed himself. "We've asked Reverend Jacobson and his wife to join us. You can think of him sort of like our town figurehead and she is the first lady. Deacon Thornhill and his wife will also join us. You can think of him as our assistant mayor. After supper, hopefully Oliver Gustafson will stop by to let us know about your vehicle."

"What is your position?" Dawn asked.

"You can think of me like the town chief of public welfare," the Deacon replied dryly.

"Is that the town church up on the hill overlooking the lake?" Tom asked pointing to the greenhouse building.

"In a manner of speaking," the Deacon answered cryptically. "It's really our Sacrarium and we generally refer to it among outsiders as our temple."

"What is your denomination?" Tom wondered.

"That's the thing. We don't have one that is defined by any modern sect or convention. We practice Judeo-Christian values in line with the religions' history."

"That's fascinating. Katie is an avid history buff and I used to be a good student of history until I got into the workforce."

"Well Katie, the Deacon said, we'll have to talk history at some point. We in Manchineel are very fond of that subject."

*Clack! Clack! Clack!*

The Deacon was cut off by the metallic sound of the door knocker which echoed throughout the house.

"That might be Dr. Arbour," Maryanna guessed and rose to go answer the door.

The Deacon watched her leave the room and then stayed focused on the empty doorway until he saw Maryanna return with a shorter man, about five-foot-eight in height, with brass-framed glasses and a slender frame. He had a full head of bushy brown hair and bright hazel-green eyes.

"Hello, Deacon," he said as he entered the room. He then focused his gaze on the Prestons. "Ah, you obviously must be the Preston family that I have been told about. A bee sting and a sore arm, have we?" His voice was confident and his words flowed easily from his lips unlike the Deacon.

"Yes, Dr. Arbour?" Tom said rising and extending his hand.

"No, I'm Dr. Arbour and you're Tom Preston," Dr. Arbour said with light sarcasm and a swift laugh. "Sorry, Tom. I don't ever get to use that joke so I had to do it. I can see the Deacon shaking his head, but you only live once after all." Dr. Arbour then shook Tom's hand firmly to convey that, joke aside, he was a competent doctor and ready to do his job. He then turned to Katie, "And you must be Katie Preston. Pleasure to meet you."

Doctor Arbour then turned to the children. "Okay, Dawn, it's nice to meet you. Would you mind just moving over to the next couch so I can examine your brothers? Tom and Katie, why don't you stand behind me as well." Dr. Arbour then placed his medical bag on the ground next to the table and sat right on the table facing the two boys on the couch. "Alright, which one of you is the bee sting boy?"

Tommy raised his hand, "I am."

"And you are Tommy or Jake?"

"Tommy."

"Alright Tommy. Show me where you were stung."

Tommy pointed to the back of his left leg.

Dr. Arbour lifted Tommy's leg gently and had him roll over onto his stomach. "Well, I see the mark where you were stung. Mom and dad did a good job of getting the stinger out." Dr. Arbour then turned to Tom and Katie and winked. He then asked them, "Tommy had an anaphylactic reaction?"

"Yes," they simultaneously answered. "We gave him an epinephrine injection," Tom added.

"Alright. Has Tommy had any symptoms since the epinephrine injection, like dizziness, nausea, shortness of breath, choking, coughing, wheezing, anything bad or unusual like that?"

Tom, Katie, and Tommy all shook their heads and said "No."

"Here's what I'm going to do," Dr. Arbour started. He opened his medical bag on the floor next to the table. Reaching in, he grabbed a glass jar full of a white cream. He opened the jar and began rubbing the cream on and around the sting mark.

"That doesn't hurt at all," Tommy said in brave boy scout-like tone.

"Good. It shouldn't," Dr. Arbour interjected. "This is a very mild cream made of coconut oil and lavender oil. It will heal the sting mark within two or three days, at the latest. I am going to put a large bandage over it so that Tommy doesn't wipe it off accidentally as kids tend to do. Now, Tom and Katie, you've seen that we have a tremendous amount of flowers in Manchineel. Do you have another epinephrine syringe?"

They both shook their heads "No."

Dr. Arbour reached into his medical bag and produced an epinephrine syringe. "Here you go."

"Oh my goodness, thank you!" Katie choked up and a tear protruded from her right eye as she reached for the epinephrine. Tom tried to not get emotional and simply squeezed Katie's hand.

"Okay Tommy, off you go," Dr. Arbour said in a happy mission-accomplished tone. "Now on to you Jake. Show me which arm hurts."

Jake raised his right arm towards the doctor.

"Jake, I know you're a strong boy, but I need you to do me a favor okay?"

"Okay."

"Just relax all of the muscles in your arm and let me move it around. I am also going to give you some light squeezes. Relax and breathe easy and, this is the important part, tell me if anything I do hurts you, okay?"

"Okay."

Dr. Arbour then began moving Jake's arm

and squeezing it from the wrist to the shoulder blade. So far so good as Jake didn't make any noise or flash any discomfort. Dr. Arbour then lifted Jake's arm over his (Dr. Arbour's) shoulder while maneuvering it around in a circular motion. Jake let out a little peep. Dr. Arbour then began pressing and squeezing around the back of the shoulder. When he reached the small part where Jake's armpit began, Jake let out the same little peep as he winced.

"How bad did that hurt Jake?" Dr. Arbour asked.

"A little."

"Are you sure it was a little and not a lot?" the doctor followed-up.

"Yes."

"Okay, Jake. I'm all done. Thank you. I think, at worst, it might be a mild sprain of the shoulder right by the armpit. It should be completely healed within a week. He should just make sure to take it easy and not use that right arm to lift anything heavy, including himself like hanging from a tree branch or something, and no throwing a ball or frisbee. That shoulder needs to rest. Do you understand Jake?"

"Yes, I do," the little boy dutifully responded.

"Well then, my work is done here. I'll follow up with you tomorrow since I assume you will still be here. In the meantime, I leave you to your gracious hosts." With that, Dr. Arbour stood up and turned fully towards the adults. "If there are any issues please have the Forsythes call on me" he said to Tom and Katie.

"We will doctor," Tom said heartily. "What do we owe you?"

Deacon Forsythe raised an eyebrow while Dr. Arbour took a little step back and pursed his lips as if he were thinking deeply about the matter of his compensation, but not in a serious manner.

"You owe me nothing. Let's call it a firm handshake," Dr. Arbour said quickly exchanging handshakes with Tom and Katie. "I'll leave it to the Deacon to explain our philosophies here as your host but you are our guests under very difficult circumstances. It wouldn't feel right charging for this courtesy visit."

"We can't thank you enough," Tom said gratefully.

"Your presence here is gratitude enough," Dr. Arbour said as he exited the room with Maryanna trailing behind him.

Like Edward, Dr. Arbour had a weird way with words. But the town's beauty and hospitality had really started to win Tom over. He could sense that in Katie and the children as well. Maybe this would become a main part of the vacation instead of a crazy and initially scary blip on what had started off as a cursed trip.

"You're all being so wonderful to us," Katie exclaimed to Deacon Forsythe as they remained in the parlor.

"It's not often we have guests and we do like to practice good values," the Deacon responded. "Why don't you finish up your snacks and I'll show you to your rooms."

"That would be wonderful," Tom said. "I could use a catnap before dinner."

"I'm sure you could," the Deacon sympathetically responded.

When the children finished their cookies and lemonade, the Deacon instructed the Prestons to leave their glasses and plates for Maryanna to clean up. He then escorted the Prestons back to the front of the house where the Prestons each grabbed their backpacks while the Deacon insisted on carrying their larger bags -- one with Tom's and Katie's clothing and toiletries, a separate such bag for Dawn, and a third such bag for the boys. He led them up a winding wooden staircase that started at the edge of the entrance and extended to an upper level with vaulted ceilings. It had the same look and décor as the downstairs portion of the house that they had already seen – a maple brown wooden floor with wooden panels along the walls and garnet paint. The upstairs was comprised of a large hallway with what appeared to be six doors. The Deacon led the Prestons to the far end.

The Deacon stopped at the second-to-last door on the right side of the hallway. "Tom and Katie, this will be your room." He opened the door into a beautiful room with maple brown baseboard and crown molding running across the walls along with matching chair railing. Instead of garnet, the walls were painted a midnight blue.

"This is lovely," Katie said.

The Deacon placed Tom's and Katie's bag inside the room and allowed them to place their backpacks and Katie's purse right beside it before moving on to the next room which was the last room on that side of the hallway. The Deacon opened the door to a spacious bathroom which was comprised of white marble and porcelain. The bathroom had the appearance of a regal Victorian bathroom with gold-plated spouts on the sink and bathtub faucets and handles as well as the toilet handle. There appeared to be a curtain and track that encircled the bathtub, which had a shower spout mounted with the bathtub faucet.

"This is the bathroom for you and the children. Unfortunately, our town is in the middle of a public works project with the water tower so the sink and bathtub-slash-shower do not work. Here are some cases of bottled water for you to use for rinsing and washing. The septic system still works though so there are no issues with the toilets."

The Deacon then closed the door and turned to the room on the opposite side of the hallway. He opened the door and announced the obvious as he set the childrens' bags down, "This will be the childrens' room. The boys will have to share the bed and I brought in a mattress for your daughter." The room was just as exquisite as Tom's and Katie's room but with a light pink paint.

The kids stormed the room and began looking around and marking their territories with their bags and backpacks.

"Make yourselves at home. I'm going to help Maryanna and I will come get you when supper is ready," the Deacon said.

"Again, thank you so much for everything," Tom expressed as the Deacon began his turn to leave.

The Deacon slightly bowed and tried to form his lips into a smile. He was certainly polite but the Prestons could tell that warmth was not his strongest suit.

# WELCOME PARTY

## *Chapter Eight*

As soon as Tom and Katie got the children situated in their room, Tom headed to the bathroom and relieved himself while feeling relieved by the act itself after feeling so dehydrated on their way to Manchineel. Afterwards, Tom went straight to the bed in his room and laid down for that catnap he had talked about.

*The family needs me to be alert. Quick nap. Don't crash.*

Nearly forty minutes later, Tom heard the sound of Katie unzipping their bag. He bolted upright.

"How long was I out?"

"Not long. Dinner is supposed to be ready in twenty minutes or so. I couldn't sleep so, instead, I was taking turns playing our travel-sized board games with the boys. Our phones are still not getting reception but they are charging. I'm going to start washing up and getting ready for dinner."

"Okay. I'm going to check on the kids."

"I was just there. They're fine."

Tom rubbed his eyes. He slowly sat up and let out a gigantic yawn. He then hopped out of bed and did a full body stretch letting out a hefty grunt as his muscles loosened and his shoulder joints and knuckles cracked.

*Man, every year there are more cracks and they get louder.*

Tom shuffled out of the room and across the hallway. He opened the door and walked in on the children relaxing. Jake and Tommy were sprawled across their queen-size bed playing games on their tablets. Dawn was lying on her mattress in the corner and reading a book. Besides being intelligent and inquisitive, Dawn was an avid reader like her mother. Tom used to enjoy reading as well but that is all he did every day as a lawyer so reading was at the bottom of his to-do list during non-working hours.

"What're you reading sweetie?"

"The ghost story book that I picked out at the store today."

"Don't you think we've had enough crazy stories on this trip so far?"

Dawn gave him that 'give-me-a-break-dad look' and rolled her eyes. "This is the perfect setting for reading this book. There are some really incredible stories in here."

"Oh yeah, like what?"

"Well, I haven't read very far yet. I'm only

in the middle of the second story. The first story was about a haunted hunting cabin where the ghost of a hunter who was accidentally shot and killed by another hunter eighty years ago is said to live and protect it as his territory. Five years ago, a film crew that was making a documentary on ghosts actually recorded audio of the hunter's ghost saying things and they also got video footage showing that the cabin had been rearranged after they left it one day. The video showed the ghost had set a spring-gun to shoot anyone who walked into the cabin because the ghost believed they were invading his territory. Before the film crew had left, they intentionally left the gun in the cabin but removed all of the bullets to see what would happen. When they walked in the next day, the gun somehow got a bullet and shot the cameraman. The crew evacuated him but, when they went to show the footage to the local sheriff, the film was gone. The ghost must've taken it out of the camera."

"That's an interesting story," Tom lied, not believing a word of the tale. "What's the second one about?"

"I'm just at the beginning, but it's set on a freighter and there is a major storm heading in."

"That sounds like a great book."

"It really is. The foreword said that there are dozens of confirmed unexplained occurrences here in the Upper Peninsula. There were even whole towns and colonial-era armies that disappeared up here without a trace."

"No kidding."

"I'm getting hungry. Do you think dinner will be ready soon."

"Based on what the Deacon told us it should be ready in about fifteen minutes. Mom's washing up and getting ready."

"I'm gonna join her and change too. I feel gross."

"Go ahead but you're fine."

Dawn got up with the book and walked into her parents' room to see what Katie was going to wear for dinner. The boys, meanwhile, hadn't looked up from their tablets. Tom just stared at them to see if they would even notice him. They didn't. He then headed back to his room where Katie was now telling Dawn that, since they were on a camping trip, the nicest outfit she had was a pair of khaki shorts and a powder blue collared shirt and that there was no need for Dawn to change since she was just a child and had nothing nicer to wear than what she was already wearing. Tom's nicest outfit was a pair of blue cargo shorts with a burgundy polo which he began changing into when Dawn turned her head in a dad-you're-embarrassing-me motion. Tom left with his toiletry bag while Katie and Dawn continued talking. He washed his face and hands with a water bottle, reapplied his deodorant, brushed his teeth and combed his thinning light brown hair.

*Never in a million years would I have imagined how this day would end.*

As Tom shuffled out of the bathroom, he saw the Deacon walking down the hallway towards him.

"Tom, supper's almost ready and the other guests have arrived. Please come with me and we'll join everyone in the dining room."

"Wonderful. Thank you."

Katie and Dawn heard the Deacon and came out of the room. Tom went to grab the boys who were still buried in their tablets.

The Deacon led the Prestons down the stairs and, at the bottom, took them in the opposite direction of the hallway to the parlor. This side of the Deacon's house was more open. There appeared to be a closet and two rooms whose doors were closed followed by two maple brown doors with elaborate black metal triangular designs running horizontally along the outer edges like pointing daggers or arrowheads across the wood. The doors were completely open and facing inward forming an entrance to a magnificently long room with wood columns along the walls and the same metal sconces with apples and floral patterns in between them. The walls were painted in the same garnet as the parlor and the rest of the house but this room was regal. Instead of just being vaulted, the ceiling was arched with two giant crystal chandeliers hanging over an enormous carved wood table that ran along the length of the room and looked to be able to comfortably seat twenty people. In the middle of the room on the far side, there was an enormous stone fireplace with a few interesting-looking trinkets on an ornately carved maple brown mantel. Above the mantel, there was a giant painting of a robust tree with a solitary bright yellow apple on a branch on one side. There were a number of other paintings throughout the room of beautiful landscapes with flowering trees and bushes. The table, covered with a gold-colored tablecloth, had eleven place settings of white china plates with gold trim, antique-looking silverware, and crystal glasses and pitchers full of water.

"This room is breathtaking," Katie blurted out. "I've never seen anything like it."

"I'm glad you like it," the Deacon said. "Let me introduce you to our other guests, the people who I spoke of at the parlor with Dr. Arbour."

Tom and Katie had been so preoccupied with the room that they hadn't noticed the four people who had been standing on the far side of the room and were now approaching them.

"These are the Prestons. Tom, Katie, and their children, Dawn, Tommy, and Jake," the Deacon announced to the four as they walked up to the Prestons.

"This is Reverend Caleb Jacobson and his wife Molly," the Deacon said formally as he stepped aside to allow the two to shake hands with the Prestons and exchange greetings. "And this is Deacon James Thornhill and his wife Patricia," the Deacon continued as another round of handshakes and greetings was exchanged. "Please make yourselves at home while I go help Maryanna with supper." Deacon Forsythe then left the room through an open doorway at the far end of the room.

"Could you have ever imagined that this is how your day would end?" Reverend Jacobson asked the Prestons in a pleasant ice-breaking tone. He was a tall man, just over six feet, with a very slender frame and gentle jaw line despite a very firm-looking chin. He had very unique eyes that, at first seemed gray, but were really a faint blue the longer that Tom stared at them. He had thick black hair combed slightly up and back and, although it was beginning to gray, nevertheless seemed youthful. The Reverend appeared to be no more than perhaps mid-fifties and he seemed very energetic.

Tom gave a brief laugh and responded "No, sir. We packed up for a two-week vacation. We have a full-sized spare tire, maps, cellphones, a first-aid kit, and here we are after a full car shutdown."

*Now here comes the predictable "we can't always plan for everything" cliché from the Reverend and then something about God's will.*

"It's ironic how planning for emergencies

seems to invite them," Deacon Thornhill said bluntly.

"Sure is," the Reverend agreed as their statements caught Tom by surprise.

Deacon Thornhill was a bull of a man. He had cropped black and gray hair with the darkest brown eyes that Tom had ever seen. He wasn't particularly tall, just slightly under six feet, but he had the thick frame of a football linebacker. He seemed to be in his mid to upper fifties and, although he had no wrinkles, his face showed some slight scarring along his left check and the side of his left eye. His mouth seemed to be pleasantly shaped with the corners turned up as opposed to a frowning position but it was concealed by a very firm salt-and-pepper goatee giving the man a very serious and tough appearance. He certainly would not seem an approachable person if Tom had just seen him walking down a street somewhere, and Tom might run for his life if he saw a man like that in an alley.

"Mhhmm, sure does" Patricia nodded with tight lips. The expression that couples start to look alike after they've been together for a while certainly applied to the Thornhills. Patricia looked very similar to her husband James with the exception of the scars and goatee. She was almost his height and thickly built with a remarkably pretty face except for her crooked nose.

"Well, let's not dwell too much on exigencies. The table of our situation has been set, double entendre intended," the Reverend said taking over the conversation with a broad smile. "Please have a seat," he said directing Tom and Katie to sit facing the fireplace while flanked by the children. Dawn sat next to Katie on the right with an empty chair followed by the head chair. Tom sat on Katie's left with the boys to his left. The Jacobsons took their seats directly opposite Tom and Katie and the Thornhills sat to their left.

"So what do you think about our little town?" the Reverend asked.

"Honestly, it is truly beautiful," Tom said.

"It might be the most beautiful town we've ever seen, live or in a photo or video," Katie added.

"Thank you. And Tom, you don't have to preface a sentence with 'honestly.' We hear that a lot from Lower Peninsula folk who drive up from their cities. Maybe that's a way of life down there that you need to embellish or, dare I say lie, to endear people to you or make yourself heard or believed or get a deal done or whatever, but we take people at their word up here. It's all honesty because without honesty it would be dishonesty."

"I apologize," Tom began sheepishly "I didn't mean --"

"Oh, we know what you meant," the Reverend said dismissively. "I just want you to know that you should feel at home here. There is no need for you to feel that you have to say or do anything extraordinary just because of your circumstances. After all, the Bible commands us to welcome guests for we are all essentially neighbors."

"We truly, um, I mean, we greatly appreciate that Reverend Jacobson," Tom said in an effort to seem less like the slow student being tutored by the teacher that he felt he was at the moment.

The Reverend returned the statement with a grateful grin and turned to the children. "What do you children think of Manchineel so far?"

"It's beautiful, like my parents said," Dawn replied. She wasn't quite ready to join an adult conversation and she was growing very tired from the combination of the long day and hunger pains for non-dessert food.

"I think it's very pretty," Jake said, not really interested in the question as his five-year old mind was fixated on the ornate silverware before him. He had never seen silverware with silver handles and gold tips and it was the coolest thing in the world to him at the moment.

"I think Jake likes the silverware, don't you?" Molly Jacobson asked sitting almost across from him. She was a radiant woman who, probably close in age to the Reverend, looked a good ten years younger. Her brown shoulder-length hair framed her round face with big brown eyes, a perfect nose and perfect lips that were not too thick or thin. She looked like she should have been in beauty pageants throughout her life.

Jake's cheeks turned slightly red. "Yes I do," he answered in a shy quiet voice.

"They are lovely. I am quite fond of them myself which is why I like to visit often for tea," Molly said to Jake with the warmth of an aunt talking to her nephew.

"They are antiques. They've been in my family for over 400 years," Maryanna Forsythe said as she walked through the doorway carrying a large silver platter of turkey. "Most everything in our house is a family heirloom," she said placing the platter in the middle of the table. The Deacon walked in behind her rolling the cart from the parlor. She reached down and pulled out a silver gravy boat on a silver platter that she placed on the table next to the turkey platter. The Deacon then passed her a large silver bowl of stuffing which she placed on the table while the Deacon placed a silver bowl of mashed sweet potatoes on the table. Finally, he placed a bowl of very small hard boiled eggs on the table.

"Maryanna, you always outdo yourself," the Reverend proclaimed while inhaling loudly through his nose as if taking in the amazing smell of dinner, minus the eggs.

Tom saw the boys ready to jump at the

food but gave them a subtle "hold it" hand signal under the table to wait. Out of the corner of his right eye, he saw Katie do the same to Dawn.

Maryanna took her seat next to Dawn without placing a napkin across her lap as if she was not yet ready to eat. Deacon Forsythe sat at the head of the table and bowed his head as he closed his eyes and clasped his hands in prayer. The Jacobsons and Thornhills joined immediately and Tom and Katie signaled their children to do the same. Tom and Katie, although people of faith who were raising their children to have faith, were not religiously observant. They never prayed before meals except on Easter, Christmas, and Thanksgiving. Fortunately, between those prayers and some of the movies that the children had seen, they knew to assume the prayer position instead of causing a scene by asking what everyone was doing and why they had to join in.

"Our *Lord,* who art in heaven, hallowed be *Thy* name. We thank *You* for this bounty that *You* have placed before us. And we give humble thanks for our guests whom *You* have delivered safely to us that we may perpetuate and prosper in their blessings. May you keep them safe in *Your* eternal bond as you have kept us. *Amen.*"

"Amen," everyone joined in unison.

*Not sure what the heck that meant, but it sounded positive, I think.*

"Here, let me serve you," Maryanna said

rising and moving between Tom and Katie.

She had Tom pass the boys' plates and filled them with turkey, gravy, sweet potatoes, and stuffing. She then did the same for Dawn and finally Tom and Katie who noticed that Maryanna had served over half of the food to their family. "Please eat up," Maryanna ordered as she sat down.

Thereafter, Molly Jacobson put a little of each food on her plate and the Reverend's plate along with several of the eggs while then passing the food to Patricia who did the same for herself and her husband. The Deacon then did the same for himself and Maryanna while instructing Maryanna to put the remainder of the turkey, stuffing, and sweet potatoes between Tom and Katie.

"Tom, Katie, children, please don't be shy. You must be hungry so eat up and help yourselves to more. We've already had a bit to eat before you arrived so we won't be eating anything more," the Deacon implored as Maryanna returned to her seat.

The Prestons gave in to their hunger and weariness from the day and dove right into their food which, regardless of their hunger, tasted delicious. It was a savory way to end the day. The Reverend and Deacons sat in silence with their wives allowing the Prestons to eat in peace while occasionally swallowing some pieces of turkey or an egg. After several minutes had passed and the Prestons looked to be finishing up their firsts and taking second helpings of dinner, the Forsythes, Jacobsons, and Thornhills began conversations amongst each other about different goings-on in the town. Tom and Katie didn't understand much of what was being said but they heard the word jubilee a few times.

"The Garden of Eden!" Tommy suddenly blurted out.

Everyone in the room sat silent and stared at Tommy in puzzled suspense.

"The Reverend asked what we thought about the town and I never answered. We learned about the Garden of Eden at Sunday School last year. All of the plants and trees and flowers and lake make the town look like the Garden of Eden," Tommy explained.

The Reverend gave an open-mouthed 'I-am-in-shock' look to Tommy and then gave him a proud smile. "Tommy that is a wonderful compliment to our town, and a great observation." The Reverend then focused on Tom and Katie, "'Out of the *mouth of babes* and sucklings hast thou ordained strength,' Psalms 8:2. We really have been blessed by your presence. We have actually tried to model Manchineel into our sort of Garden of Eden." The Reverend looked like he wasn't quite sure where to go and the Prestons noticed that the others were looking at the Reverend wondering where he was going with his speech.

"How did Manchineel come about," Tom asked trying to facilitate the conversation and also learn how this small beautiful place came to be to satisfy his own curiosity.

"Yes, thank you Tom. That's a helpful way to get me started. Are you a lawyer by chance?"

"I am."

"Well that figures in you helping to facilitate a discussion starting point for me. And, while we're on the subject, what do you do Katie?"

"I currently work at home but I was a high school history teacher and I'll begin substitute teaching this year now that all of my children will be in school fulltime, and then hopefully get offered a fulltime position next year."

"First of all, good for both of you to raise your children. Forgive me for budding in and seeming judgmental but there is nothing better for a child than being raised by his or her parents as opposed to day care. Family is everything. You know, I had a good feeling about you when we met. Now, as far as history, I think you'll really appreciate the story of our town. Believe it or not, Manchineel is older than the United States."

*If I don't get to say "Honestly" to start a sentence, why should you start a sentence with "Believe it or not," wait -- older than the United States?*

"Yes, older than the United States," the Reverend repeated as if he had read Tom's mind. Over 100 years older. It was founded in 1674 as a new home for western Europeans, mostly from Britain and some from other northern countries, who wanted freedom from various government regimes. They were fortunate to have amassed some considerable wealth and were able to purchase three armed vessels and two additional vessels to assist in transporting themselves, supplies, and as many of their possessions as they could hold which they used to travel to the so-called New World at the time. Now Katie, pop quiz: who was the first to explore and settle the Upper Peninsula, outside of the Native American tribes?"

"It was the French. I believe it was Étienne Brûlé who began exploring Michigan in 1620 and the first permanent settlement was established in Sault Sainte Marie in 1668," Katie responded sounding slightly unsure at first but fully confident as she proceeded to answer realizing that, despite her years away from teaching to raise the children, she had retained a great deal of information.

"Bravo!" the Reverend exclaimed. "Well done. Most people wouldn't have gotten that answer, let alone the additional information that you provided. You must be a great teacher. So back to Manchineel, our ancestors obtained a copy of the French maps of their territory in what is now Canada and Michigan and noticed the Upper Peninsula surrounded by the

Great Lakes. Relying upon nothing more than intuition and geography, they decided that the Upper Peninsula would be the ideal location to begin anew with complete freedom. They also knew at the time that travel would be long and rigorous.

"They set sail across the Atlantic in 1672 and then proceeded down the St. Lawrence River. Katie, do you know why they stopped after passing through Quebec City?"

"Well not all of the Great Lakes had been connected to make them navigable and there were rapids, I think?"

"Right on Katie! The Lachine Rapids at Montreal prevented the ships from getting through. Now, our ancestors were not French but they spoke the language and sailed French flags to avoid any trouble. They passed by Quebec City and they landed before they reached Montreal. Between their hired ship crews and a little-known local Native American tribe, the Korbani, they moved all of their possessions to Manchineel over two long years. They even stripped most of the wood from the ships, much of which is still in our homes to this day. Can you imagine that process?

"Fortunately, again, our ancestors' wealth allowed for that to happen. They had hired over 150 crewmen to man the ships and then transport them through the land, and they purchased wagons and horses in Montreal. The

Korbani tribe had been virtually wiped out between the French, Algonquins, and Iroquois. Our ancestors' offer of cookware that they could use and trinkets that they could trade, along with muskets and the protection of being part of the entourage moving to Manchineel, was an offer they couldn't refuse.

"After two long years, Manchineel had officially been established. Obviously, we made substantial improvements over the centuries, but that is how the town came to be. It survived the French and it survived the British. We, all 68 of us residents, are the heirs of the founders of Manchineel. Over the generations, those who chose to stay or return to take over their family home have preserved and upgraded the town."

"That is remarkable!" Katie exclaimed. "The beauty and the history of this place is overwhelming."

"We overheard you discussing something about a jubilee while we were eating," Tom pried.

"Yes, there is a connection. When the town was established, it was just before the summer solstice. By coincidence, the summer solstice was taking place during a full moon which is practically a once-in-a-lifetime event as it happens about every 70 years. Our ancestors held what we refer to as the Grand Jubilee on that full-moon summer solstice for themselves, the crewmen, and the Korbani to officially commemorate the establishment of Manchineel and as a thanksgiving of sorts to those who had helped them relocate and build this new free home."

"What happened to the crewmen and the Korbani?" Katie interrupted. She was genuinely engrossed in the story of Manchineel.

"Well, no one really knows. Our ancestors never kept in touch with them, but they heard stories and rumors. It was believed that the crewmen, with their newfound money for their years of work, settled into various parts of Quebec City and Montreal. Although they were not French, they paid no allegiance to Britain and their money was very much welcomed. The Korbani were rumored to have used the goods and weapons that they received to form a lasting truce with the Ojibwe and eventually were merged into the tribe."

"I have to admit," Katie started "that we weren't going to have campfire stories quite that good on our vacation. Thank you for sharing that with us."

"We grew up with the story so it's become stale for us, but to hear it with new folks is refreshing," Deacon Thornhill joined in the dialogue. "It reminds us of how unique this town is."

"Amen," the Reverend said in agreement. "Now, to continue with the answer to Tom's question about a jubilee, we are planning a fifth anniversary Grand Jubilee on this coming Sunday – in two days' time – during the full moon and just before the summer solstice which will be on Wednesday and coincide with the last night of the full moon. It will be only the fifth time in the town's history that the summer solstice will occur during a full moon. In years past, we wouldn't do all that much to celebrate Manchineel's anniversary. We'd do things like a town-wide barbeque or fireworks or some combination of the two. Then, about five years ago, we decided to throw annual jubilees and invite the neighboring town of McIntosh to join us. They have a reeve, their small-town version of a mayor, with whom I have become friends and, with their town really starting to boom, it is a nice way for us neighbors to get to know each other in a casual and non-commercial, non-touristy context. We barbeque, exchange home-grown crops – herbs, berries, vegetables, – crafts, the works. And we of course have a band and fireworks. So I guess in that context, our Grand Jubilee this year will be a double five-year anniversary in terms of the summer solstice and celebrating with McIntosh."

"Do the citizens of Manchineel do anything special or unique just to you for the Grand Jubilee?" Katie asked. It was a basic question that naturally arose from what the Reverend had been describing but Patricia shot a look at Katie as if to say "How dare you ask, it's none of your business." At the same time, the Forsythes and Molly all tensed as they looked at the Reverend in seeming wonderment over how he would answer that question.

"Well, Katie, we do have a special ceremony planned. We'll be following the ceremony laid out by our ancestors that we obtained from the town archives. It's really a very sacred ceremony to us because it was the very one which our ancestors created. We'll also be reading some scripture and sharing a variety of family histories from Europe through the present. But these are things that we feel protective of and would rather not share them with the outside world."

"Oh, I completely understand," Katie said slightly embarrassed. "I didn't mean to pry into your town affairs--"

"Don't fret on it," the Reverend quickly cut in. "It was a natural question to ask. We're fairly open here in Manchineel but we do hold our traditions and ceremonies sacred. I don't know if or how much Deacon or Mrs. Forsythe explained to you about our religion but we really don't have one that is defined by modern conventions. Our Judeo-Christian beliefs and practices relate to the beginning of the Bible which, as you must know, the Torah-slash-Old Testament predates recorded history by thousands of years. Very few, if any, religious denominations have practices based upon a complete combination of the customs and rituals predating the Exodus to the very beginning of time itself as recorded in the Torah-slash-Old Testament, the laws given during and after the Exodus with the Jewish faith taking root, and the laws of Christianity that arose later as it splintered off from Judaism following Jesus Christ. Anyway, I don't mean to bore you or sound cryptic but our religious practices and their preservation is what led our ancestors to take their own exodus out of Europe and found Manchineel. They had no interest in growing this religious practice of ours or seeking to convert others. They passed it down to us and we continue in their faith."

"The Garden of Eden is from the beginning of time in the Old Testament," Tom pointed out.

"Well, Tommy didn't fall far from his parents' apple tree," the Reverend cleverly said in follow-up. "I'll bet you're a great lawyer with your listening skills and intellect."

"I wish I were," Tom humbly responded to the compliment. "But speaking of apple trees, that is a beautiful painting over the mantelpiece Deacon Forsythe and Maryanna."

Tom's initial impression of the painting was magnified after facing it throughout dinner. Although the painting was simplistic in its substance, a tree with a solitary bright yellow apple on a branch, it was a masterpiece. It was an oil painting with magnificent detail. The daylight and shading were painted to perfection. The bark lines and curvatures around the trunk and branches of the tree combined with the stems, veins, curvatures, and points of the leaves, which included several rich shades of green ranging from light to dark, made it appear like a photograph of an actual tree. The apple was painted to scale and, despite the vibrant yellow, looked real enough to pick through the canvass.

The Deacon and Maryanna gave Tom appreciative nods.

"Well that tree is part of the Garden of Eden," the Reverend said in a 'gotcha' tone. "We all know the story of creation and the Garden of Eden, right? Tommy, you started this off with your description of our town. What do you know about the Garden of Eden?"

Feeling all-important, Tommy straightened up in his chair. "God created the Garden of Eden and put Adam there and then created Eve from Adam's rib. And there were two special trees in the Garden of Eden and God told them not to eat the fruit from those trees. But they ate fruit from the tree of knowledge and God threw them out of the Garden."

"Excellent job young man!" the Reverend exclaimed. "God created two trees in the middle of the Garden of Eden: the tree of knowledge between good and evil and the tree of life. Eve was approached by a serpent, the shrewdest of the wild beasts that God had created, who asked if it was true that she and Adam could not eat the fruit of those two trees. Eve replied that it was true and that God told them that they would die if they ate the fruit. The serpent responded that they would not die. Rather, God knew that eating the fruit would open their eyes and make them like divine beings who know good and bad. Eve then took fruit from the tree of knowledge and ate it. She then gave some to Adam who also ate it. God punished them and cast them out of the Garden of Eden.

"God punished the serpent and said it would always crawl on its belly and live on the ground like a snake. And god punished Adam and Eve. First Adam would toil all the days of his life and Eve would endure the pain of childbirth and they would both return to the dust from which they were made," Dawn chimed in very much interested in making a point. "And God told Eve that Adam, who blamed her for the fruit which he ate, would rule over her and women have been subjugated because of that and it needs to stop."

The Reverend and Deacons froze with puzzled looks on their faces. Tom and Katie froze awaiting their hosts' reactions.

"I like her!" Patricia shouted out with glee.

"Amen sister," Molly followed suit.

Tom and Katie let out sighs of relief although the Forsythes seemed like statues sitting in their chairs and not particularly caring for the conversation.

"Okay, young lady, I won't disagree with you there," the Reverend said politely to Dawn. "And don't worry because that is not where I am going with this long explanation over the painting. The painting is the tree of life. It was painted by one of our residents, Lilith Townsend, and given to the Forsythes as a wedding gift, I believe?"

"Yes it was," Deacon Forsythe confirmed.

"I still have a sharp memory," the Reverend said with amusement. "The tree of life symbolizes the choice that could have been versus the choice that was made. Had Adam and Eve eaten from the tree of life, people would live forever. Instead, people have the power of knowledge of good and evil. So it is important to make the right decisions because we know what is right from wrong. I guess there is my evening sermon," the Reverend concluded with a cheerful grin. "Tom, Katie, your children are wonderful. Things here can get monotonous so I appreciate having some children here to involve again."

"There aren't any children in Manchineel?" Tom asked.

"Not for a few years. They're all grown and off to college or living adult lives now."

"Well, Molly and I will take Dawn if you want," Patricia jokingly said to Tom and Katie.

"Well then, I guess Deacon Thornhill and

I will have to take Tommy and Jake," the Reverend added playfully.

"Well you can have them," Tom joked in response.

"Not our babies," Katie said while pretend-hitting Tom in the arm.

Everyone at the table had a good laugh. Even Deacon Forsythe and Maryanna cracked some smiles and a few small laughs.

"So Reverend," Tom began as the laughter waned, "what is it that people do here in Manchineel?"

"Well, that's a fairly broad question Tom. Some of us are what you might call retired. Others work in nearby towns either owning or tending to shops. Myself and the Deacons, well, we grew up in the same area and served in the military. You can tell by my physique that I was a chaplain and the Deacons were highly decorated soldiers. We moved back here when it came time to retire."

At that moment, the echo of the door knocker rang throughout the dining room. Deacon Forsythe quickly rose from his chair and returned a short time later with Oliver Gustafson.

"Evenin' Reverend, Mrs. Jacobson, Maryanna, Deacon Thornhill, Mrs. Thornill. Evenin' Tom and Katie." As he spoke, Oliver was clutching his grease-stained hat in his hands. "I've come to report on the Prestons' vehicle."

"Please have a seat," Deacon Forsythe invited.

"Thank you Deacon," Oliver said taking a seat next to the Reverend across from Tom. "It's one of those good news – bad news situations folks. The good news is that your car's electronics look to be okay. It took me a while but I checked the wiring and the microprocessors and everything seems to be in order. The bad news is twofold. First, my old battery tester that I had in my tow truck is broken. I didn't know it at the time but I used my new tester at the shop when I saw that the electronics in your car were okay and your car battery is completely dead. Second, your alternator is dead as well. I have a new battery for you but it's going to take until Monday to get a new alternator."

"There's no way we could get a tow from you to Sault Sainte Marie or any other city tomorrow?" Tom asked. He knew it might come across as ungrateful or pushy but he really didn't want to spend a three-day weekend in a small town with seemingly nothing to do by way of entertainment. One thing the Prestons had noticed was that the Forsythes did not seem to own any television sets.

"Afraid not. I have a prior commitment tomorrow and every shop I know is closed on the weekends. There's also another complication as you have probably already been made aware. We're not getting any cellphone reception here. The cellphone tower in McIntosh is still down so I can't even get any calls out."

"Alright," Tom said feeling like there was no choice but to cave into the circumstances. "What'll the repairs run us?"

"No charge for the tow. Hundred dollars for the battery, I won't charge labor on that, and the cost of an alternator for your vehicle with labor will be $750."

"Okay, we accept. And thank you for helping us out Mr. Gustafson."

"Call me Ollie, remember? You're welcome Tom."

Maryanna, who had disappeared shortly after Ollie's arrival, returned with a tray of her chocolate chip cookies which she offered to the Preston children. "Don't forget to have a Friday night snack before bedtime."

"Lucky children," Molly chimed in. "Maryanna's cookies are the best."

The children nodded in agreement and thanked Maryanna profusely while helping themselves to two apiece.

"Deacon Forsythe, the Prestons are welcome to stay with Molly and me if need be," the Reverend offered.

"That won't be necessary," the Deacon responded with a pleasant grin towards the Prestons. "We have plenty of room and would enjoy the company."

"Again, thank you all so much for your warmth and hospitality," Katie said gratefully.

"We appreciate it so much and don't know where we'd be without you right now."

"You and your family are in great hands," the Reverend said encouragingly. "It probably seemed like 'The Vertigo Zone' at first but I'm sure this will be the most memorable part of your vacation."

"What's 'The Vertigo Zone?'" Dawn asked.

"It was a television series that had different kinds of themed episodes like science fiction, fantasy, suspense, thriller, horror that always had some kind of unexpected spooky twist," the Reverend explained.

"Do you have episodes that we could watch at some point this weekend?" Dawn asked in follow-up as the series seemed right up her alley.

"Unfortunately we don't. It was a series that started running over 50 years ago. We do have a television, not modern by your standards, with some VHS tapes of movies – they're PG rated movies Tom and Katie – that you are welcome to watch."

"Okay, thank you," Dawn unenthusiastically responded. She was only into PG-13 and R-rated movies since turning thirteen, and she preferred to play games on her tablet and phone and re-watch the same two R-rated movies that she downloaded to her tablet rather than watch some goody-two-shoes movies at a reverend's house.

"I get it," the Reverend replied. "The weekend will fly by and you'll be back to cellphones and Internet in no time."

"Yeah, I have to tell all of my friends about this and how our day was like an episode of The Vertigo Zone," Dawn said.

"By all means, tell us about your day," the Reverend enthusiastically invited.

Dawn began telling the story of the day's catastrophic events with Tom and Katie chiming in to flesh out some of the details (except for the antlers stabbing the old woman).

"That is definitely a remarkable story," Deacon Thornhill said after the Prestons had finished. "I've never heard of a trip quite like that."

"Heavens no," the Reverend said in amazement. "No matter how things have played out in the past and no matter how well we plan for the future, there is no telling how a day will play out when you wake up in the morning."

"Amen honey," Molly said.

From the corner of his eye, Tom saw Ollie scratch his head in disbelief while Patricia and the Forsythes simply stared at the Prestons with sympathy. The Prestons' story seemed to resonate with their hosts.

Afterwards, some brief small talk was exchanged and the dinner party started to break up just before sunset as it was nearly a quarter-to-ten. Tom and Katie and their children shook hands with the Jacobsons, Thornhills and Ollie as they left the dining room and showed themselves out.

"May we help with the cleanup?" Tom asked the Forsythes.

"Absolutely not," Maryanna said with a mocking frown. "You're our guests."

"The children have been yawning for a little while. Why don't you take them up for bed," the Deacon suggested. "Maryanna and I usually sleep in on Saturday so please do the same if you wish."

"Thank you again Deacon and Mrs. Forsythe for everything. We are so grateful to you," Tom said with Katie in tow as they led the children upstairs. The children, completely exhausted, brushed their teeth, used the bathroom and passed out within ten minutes as the irony of the moment dawned on Tom. *Maybe we should go through major crises every day to get the kids to go to sleep right when we tell them.*

# THE VERTIGO ZONE

## *Chapter Nine*

Ollie came running up to the Forsythes' door with a package. The alternator had arrived early. Tom was standing next to Ollie in Ollie's garage looking down under the hood as Ollie installed the new alternator. The engine roared to life and Tom felt a deep sense of relief. He took a deep breath knowing that his family could leave and continue on their trip. Tom hopped behind the steering wheel and headed to Manchineel to pick up his family. Just as he pulled into the Forsythes' driveway, he saw that everyone was inside the house looking out a window and pointing at a giant beehive on the ground in between two hydrangeas. Tom opened his door and jumped out to find a way to get his family into the vehicle without Tommy getting another bee sting. As soon as his feet hit the ground, he heard a loud hissing sound. Looking around, he saw a deer antler firmly lodged in the tire which was getting flatter by the second as the air was leaking out. The hissing continued and then everything went dark and then light.

*Pssssss psssssssss.*

*Waayyaaa.*

*Kuup psssss.*

"Please, Tom, wake up," Katie was now forcefully nudging Tom by the shoulder. "Tom, wake up. Please, are you awake?"

"Yeah, I'm up. I'm up."

Tom was a night owl and, while he needed to be at his office no earlier than 9:00 a.m. on most days, he needed every bit of his sleep. It was a pet peeve of his when Katie or the children woke him up before his alarm clock went off. Tom rolled over ready to give Katie a very irritated response to whatever needed his attention. And then he saw the dark bags under her eyes and the palpable worry not just on her face but emanating from her entire body.

"What is it?" Tom said hoping for something that was fixable.

"I can't find the children," Katie said in a panic.

"Wait. What?" Tom asked springing up and reaching for his shorts.

"I can't find the children. I looked in their room and the bathroom. I can't find them." Katie's voice was getting weaker.

"Maybe they went downstairs to the parlor or to the dining room with Maryanna?" Katie didn't respond. She was starting to hyperventilate. Instead, she pulled Tom by the arm into the hallway to the doorway of the childrens' room. Katie was always driving Tom crazy with little things that she could easily figure out for herself without having to call and bother him at work, like what to say in an email to one of the children's teachers if there was a problem in class, or what to bake Tommy to eat at a friend's birthday party due to his allergies, or which day she was going to schedule doctors' appointments. Right now, Katie's demeanor had Tom on the brink of terrified.

As Tom walked through the doorway, the brink of terrified became a full-on panic at what he saw. Or, rather, what he didn't see. The boys' bed was perfectly made and their clothing bag and backpacks were missing. Dawn's mattress was gone and her bag and backpack were also missing. Tom ran into the room and opened the closet doors to emptiness. He opened every drawer in the room – nightstand, dresser, desk – and there was nothing there. Tom ran to the bathroom and the only items in there were Tom's and Katie's toiletries.

"Oh my God! What the hell is going on? What the fuck is going on? Maybe the Forsythes' moved them or something," Tom was hoping that there was some logical explanation running frantically in circles between the rooms and the bathroom.

"Wait," Tom stood upright and paused.

"Our phones. Get our phones and call Dawn."

Tom and Katie ran back to their room and grabbed their phones from the chargers.

"Shit! I'm still not getting any service. You?" Tom asked Katie.

"No! Oh my God, holy fuck no!"

They both dialed Dawn's cellphone anyway but there was no connection. The service was still down.

"Let's text her," Katie suggested next.

They both tried to send texts to Dawn but nothing was going through.

Tom led Katie in another circle between the rooms and bathroom while they both repeatedly tried to call and text Dawn to no avail. Seeing nothing and no evidence of their children and having no service whatsoever, Tom grabbed Katie's hand and led her down the hallway, down the stairs, and straight to the dining room. The room was completely empty. The wooden table stood bare, no tablecloth or candlesticks or bowls or plates. Just a long antique hand-carved wooden table. Tom and Katie walked towards the far end and began to smell food. They passed through the doorway which led straight into a kitchen. For as big of a home as the Forsythes appeared to have, the kitchen was relatively small. True to the house décor, there were brown maple wooden cabinets with black metal handles. The countertops were made of stone and the stove, oven, and refrigerator were smaller than the average appliances which perhaps made sense with only the Deacon and Maryanna living there. To the side of the sink there was a pan and a cookie sheet drying on a towel. The kitchen smelled wonderful but Tom and Katie only wanted the scent to find the Forsythes. They followed it through a passageway at the end which was the open parlor door.

Tom and Katie hurried through and saw the Deacon sitting on a chair next to Maryanna talking peacefully and enjoying what appeared to be tea while looking out at the Sacrarium. When they saw Tom and Katie, they turned pleasantly towards them.

"Good morning friends," the Deacon said in a welcoming voice that was strange to them in its warmth.

"How did you two sleep?" Maryanna asked. "We haven't had guests in ages. I hope the bed was comfortable."

"Have you seen our children?" Katie asked in desperation.

"Children?" the Deacon asked looking puzzled.

"Where are the children?" Tom asked annoyed.

"We don't have any children," Maryanna answered. "The Deacon and I had wanted children but unfortunately we were never able to have any."

"No. Our children. Have you seen mine

and Tom's children?" Katie asked in frustration.

"I don't understand," Maryanna began, "What children are you talking about?"

Katie froze in panicked disbelief. The blood drained from her face as she was contemplating what to say or do.

"Our children," Tom persisted. "Our thirteen-year-old daughter Dawn. Our nine-year-old son Tommy. Our five-year-old son Jake."

"Tom, I don't mean to sound rude but did you and Katie take any narcotics or alcohol or medication before you went to sleep last night?" the Deacon asked.

"Of course not," Tom said indignantly.

"I know that Maryanna and I do not imbibe and there is no liquor in our home."

"We don't either," Tom said defiantly. "Now where are our kids!"

"Wait, wait, wait," Maryanna said patiently. "Let's calm down. Come on over and have some breakfast. I made it specially for you. You had such a rough day yesterday with your car and coming here that I wanted to start you off right today. You'll have a pleasant weekend stay here and Ollie should get you going by some point on Monday."

In their hustle and exchange with their hosts, Tom and Katie hadn't noticed the breakfast platter of bacon, scrambled eggs, and biscuits that Maryanna had placed on the table behind two china plates accompanied by cloth napkins and the silver and gold silverware that the kids loved looking at last night. There was also a kettle of hot water and box of tea bags alongside two teacups and saucers matching the ones that the Forsythes were using.

"I can't sit," Katie said almost crying. "I need my children. I need my babies."

"Come on, have something to drink or eat," the Deacon said as he got up to escort Tom and Katie to the couch and help themselves to the breakfast on the table. "It will calm your nerves."

"But we -- "

"I'll tell you what, we'll talk about children and anything else that you wish to discuss after you've had some tea and a bit to eat," the Deacon said politely while cutting off Tom and using his enormous body frame to send a foreboding message to suggest that the Prestons take him up on his offer. With slight hesitation, Tom gently grabbed Katie by her elbow and escorted her to the couch as the Deacon hovered behind them.

*I get it. Sit the fuck down and do as you're told so I don't escalate whatever the fuck it is that's going on here. Wait, we can't eat or drink. What if the food is drugged? Or the tea is drugged? Or both? There's no fucking way. We're going to end up on slabs being tortured with our fingernails ripped out and they're going to strip us and rape us with everything from people to objects and they're going to chop us into pieces and ship our organs out to hospitals or some criminal gang on the black market. Where are our kids? What the fuck have they done with our babies? What is that guideline? The first 48 hours are the most critical to find missing children before the chances of finding them go way the hell down. I need a weapon. Where's my knife? Why the fuck did I not get a concealed pistol license? Nobody wants one until you need a gun and by then you're already fucked. We are so fucked!*

"Tom, I can see you're thinking of many horrible things. I don't know what's gotten into you folks but we had a great time yesterday. Maryanna and I have no ill intentions towards you. Here, see?"

At that point, the Deacon removed his teacup from its saucer and helped himself to a strip of bacon, a biscuit, and some eggs. He then poured some hot water from the kettle into his teacup. Quickly, the Deacon broke the bacon strip in half while grabbing some scrambled eggs and a piece of the biscuit. He put them all in his mouth and gulped them down. Then he chased it with some hot water. Maryanna, looking hurt by the Prestons' distrust did the same.

"Okay, see, there is nothing wrong with the food or water," the Deacon said in an I-told-you-so tone. "Everything is perfectly safe. You are in absolutely no danger. Now, please, eat your breakfast. My mother always said that a person cannot properly function without breakfast."

Tom and Katie did as they were effectively ordered by their hosts. They each filled their plates with the food and poured themselves tea. They moved slowly and didn't eat or drink much. In the five or so minutes that it took them for breakfast, Tom felt that he had aged five years while wondering how all the joys in life seem to last only a second while the horrors, however shorter in duration, seem to last forever.

"Okay. We did as we were told," Katie said coldly. "Now we are going to discuss our children."

"I don't even know where to begin," Maryanna said with a concerned look. "I honestly don't know what you are talking about."

"May we speak with the Reverend?" Tom inquired.

"Of course you may," the Deacon said. "You don't have to ask our permission for anything Tom. You're our guests. This is your home for the weekend. I was actually going to take the morning off given our late night but we can absolutely go to the Reverend."

"With all due respect Deacon, I just meant for myself and Katie to speak with the Reverend. I don't mean to offend you. It's just my preference."

"No offense taken, Tom. I just meant that we would take you to him. He's giving a late morning sermon so we'll take you over and you and Katie can speak privately with him after the service has concluded. I apologize that Maryanna and I don't have any clothes in your sizes, but please give us some time to get ready and we'll take you over."

"Thank you," Tom said as only a lawyer can where it comes across as genuinely polite but really means *I don't fucking trust you*.

"So you do services on Saturday mornings?" Tom asked the Deacon feigning interest in the religious practices of Manchineel.

"Not usually," the Deacon responded. "But this week, with the Grand Jubilee, we are holding a short service outside today which you are absolutely welcome to attend. Tomorrow there will be a lengthy service at the Sacrarium which, I apologize, you will not be permitted to attend as that is only for the Manchineel faithful."

Maryanna stacked the plates on the platter and took them to the kitchen. Deacon Forsythe grabbed the tea kettle and asked Tom and Katie to please help with the tea cups and saucers. He then escorted Tom and Katie up the stairs while Maryanna remained in the kitchen to clean. Tom and Katie, who had been wearing a combination of clothing for sleep and for being out in public quickly changed into clean shorts, collared shirts, socks, and shoes.

"Wait, I have an idea," Tom said to Katie.

"Let's show them the videos and pictures of the children from our phones."

*Oh no. No. No, no, no, no, no, no nooooo!*

"My gallery is empty," Tom said mortified.

*Oh no. How in the fuck is this possible?*

"My entire contact list has been wiped clean."

*There's got to be something left. They can't have taken every digital footprint off this phone.*

"My email folders have been deleted. I mean, the whole fucking folders. There are no email folders on my phone. Oh shit, they took the downloads too. This phone is practically blank."

"Mine too," Katie said weakly while uncontrollably shaking as tears and snot were now pouring towards her mouth.

*This is crazy horror movie shit right here. Don't say it or Katie will have a heart attack. We have to find the kids. Toughen up and start figuring it out.*

An idea occurred to Tom and he then moved quietly towards the door and waited.

"What are you planning?" Katie asked frailly.

"Follow me after Maryanna goes to change."

Three minutes later, they heard Maryanna's footsteps and saw her enter her room and close the door.

"Now," Tom turned to Katie. "Move fast and be quiet."

They went down the stairs perfectly – fast and without so much as a creak in the stairs. There was something to be said for the way old homes were constructed. At the bottom of the stairs, Tom turned towards the dining room side of the house and went straight for the two rooms, or at least the two doors to whatever, that were closed last night and remained closed that morning. He tried opening each door but they were locked. He then led Katie to the other side of the house where the hallway led to the parlor. Tom tried opening each of the doors along the hallway to no avail. Everything was locked.

"Tom, Katie, we're ready to go now," they heard the Deacon calling from the entranceway.

Tom and Katie hurried to the entranceway where the Forsythes were standing in very formal attire. The Deacon was wearing a plain black suit with a white shirt and crisp royal blue tie with a silver chain coming down from his collar behind his tie. From the side, it appeared to be a cross, however, when the Deacon shifted his weight, Tom saw that it was a tree. Maryanna was wearing a royal blue shirt with a black dress and black sport coat. Her hair was in a bun and she had a silver pin on the collar of her shirt that also appeared to be a tree but it was concealed by the collar on her sport coat.

"We were just taking a look at the lake and the temple," Katie said.

*And the Forsythes are both looking at us calling bullshit.*

"Good," Maryanna said in what Tom perceived as slightly disingenuous. "You really will like it here. Did you see if the Reverend had started the service yet?"

"Um, a, yeah it looked like he had," Katie said sheepishly although even in her embarrassment she couldn't blush in the panic of not knowing where her babies were.

*And the Forsythes are definitely calling bullshit.*

"Well then, let's head over," the Deacon implored opening the door and then following everyone out. He and Maryanna led Tom and Katie around their home to the open side of the lake where the town's folk had gathered in seats set up around a podium near the lakeshore where Reverend Jacobson was speaking.

*At least Katie guessed the correct answer to Maryanna's question. We need this day to end with our children in our arms. Please God.*

# THE SERVICE

## *Chapter Ten*

The Forsythes led the Prestons to the congregation of townies. Molly Jacobson, Deacon Thornhill, and Patricia Thornhill were seated front and center. Four of the town's folk seated closest to them on the side where the Forsythes and Prestons were approaching got up and moved towards the back. The Prestons had not heard any of what the Reverend had been saying up to that point. They simply observed everyone in church attire and the Reverend standing up speaking from his podium holding a book that appeared to be very old based on the thick yellowed pages and cover which was made of a dark brown leather with metal engravings along with what appeared to be gemstones set into the metal. Neither Tom nor Katie could make out the design between the glare from the sun and the Reverend's hand which concealed much of the cover. None of the town's folk were holding prayer books and there were no carts or tables with any prayer books or scriptures for the service.

As soon as the Prestons sat down next to the Forsythes, Reverend Jacobson paused. He was standing majestically next to the lakeshore in a black suit with a white shirt and bright green tie. Around his shoulders was a shiny silk scarf that started out as a deep brown at the ends and gradually changed into a lustrous bright green from above his chest and around the back of his neck. Upon closer look, Tom noticed that the scarf looked like two trees growing up and joining as one.

"My friends," the Reverend began after his pause, "I am pleased to introduce you to our guests for the weekend, Tom and Katie Preston--"

"And our children, Dawn, Tommy, and Jake," Katie indignantly interrupted.

The Reverend raised his head back and furrowed his eyebrows in surprise but then continued a second later. "As some of you may have heard, their car broke down and they will be staying with the Forsythes until Oliver Gustafson can get it fixed. Please help us in welcoming them to Manchineel and we are very glad to have them join us here this morning. And now let us continue. Divine are the brave."

"Divine are the brave," the town's folk repeated in unison.

"Divine are the bold," the Reverend then

said.

"Divine are the bold," the town's folk again repeated in unison.

"In God's image were we created and in God's image have we proceeded," the Reverend continued.

"In God's image were we created and in God's image have we proceeded," the town's folk repeated.

"Nearly 350 years ago, the founders of Manchineel marked the town's foundation with a Grand Jubilee on the summer solstice which coincided with the full moon. Roughly seventy years later, that Grand Jubilee was again celebrated, as it was roughly seventy years afterwards, and again nearly seventy years after that. Now, nearly seventy years later, we mark the fifth full moon summer solstice anniversary Jubilee of Manchineel. This is a blessed occasion. From torment and oppression came the freedom of Manchineel for us to enjoy and celebrate. On this Grand Jubilee, we pray that Manchineel will continue to be this way forever."

A round of "Amens" rang out from the town's folk.

"Last night, Molly and I, along with the Forsythes and the Thornhills, had the privilege of dining with our guests, the Prestons, and we discussed the story of the Garden of Eden. As I left it last night, the basic message that is always taught from the story is that humans took the power to be divine by eating from the tree of knowledge which gave them the power to determine what is right and what is wrong. Indeed, the moral of the story of the Garden of Eden that is taught to the youngest students and all the way on up to those in adult education is to make good decisions because that is the power given to us from the tree of knowledge of good and bad.

"But here's the issue. Humans were created in God's image. Yes we, each one of us, was created in God's image. And yet, after the Garden of Eden, God saw what was described as humanity's wickedness on Earth and how every plan devised by people was nothing but evil all the time. Genesis, Chapter 6. So God flooded the Earth saving only Noah and his family. Genesis, Chapter 7. But then, when God saw their descendants building the great city and tower of Babel, he confounded them with different languages and scattered them over the Earth. Genesis, Chapter 11. And afterwards is a history of humanity mixing advancements with wickedness. The crimes and wars and greed perpetuated by man from the beginning of time continue to exist in proportion to modern times alongside humanity's scientific achievements. All the while, humans are created in God's image and, at the time when humanity pursued the ultimate accomplishment in Babel, God put an end to it.

"So what are we to make of all of this? If humans are created in God's image and act wickedly is that not in the Divine's image? If humans unite and grow, we are then divided and again thrust into wickedness. The Catch-22.

"The truth as we know, my friends, is that the moral of the story of the Garden of Eden is wrong. The serpent made a mistake. Adam and Eve made a mistake. The fruit from the tree of life was the true fruit of divinity. Had the serpent led Eve to the apples of the tree of life, the power of everlasting life would have been bestowed upon humanity and, in that divinity, humanity would not have a need for wickedness. Nor would humanity have a need to unite and pursue scientific advancements and achievements over the status quo in the name of discovery and prolonging life. It is mortality that causes people to act out of wicked motivations – greed, envy, fear. It is mortality that causes people to never be content with the status quo. Immortality is the cure. Immortality was the cure. And in that moment upon which the entire future of humanity rested, the serpent and the first man and the first woman chose wrong. Just imagine the world, imagine the universe, if that mistake had never been made. That is a monumental task so let us take a few moments of silence for contemplation on this."

The town's folk all sat in silence, some with their eyes closed absorbing the Reverend's words, and others who bore deliberate gazes of deep thought.

After several minutes, the Reverend continued with the service as he and the townsfolk exchanged a few responsive prayers along with several songs that sounded like Latin and came across more like incantations than prayers. When the last song was finished, the townsfolk all rose from their seats and stood at attention. The Reverend then gave a deliberate and powerful stare across them with the following: "From the apple comes life eternal."

"From the apple comes life eternal," the congregation replied.

"We will hold the remainder of our Grand Jubilee ceremony tomorrow morning in the Sacrarium" the Reverend announced. "The Marshes have graciously invited us over to their home for late morning tea and snacks. Please bring your chairs over as we will set up in their backyard. Please enjoy this day and the gifts that it has brought us," nodding oddly at Tom and Katie.

The town's folk began folding their chairs and carrying them to the fifth home from the Forsythes. Tom and Katie intercepted Reverend Jacobson as he was heading towards his wife.

"Where are our children?" Katie asked him in a half-screaming panic. "Where are Dawn, Tommy, and Jake?"

The Reverend took a half-step backwards

and gave Katie another perplexed glance. "What children?"

"You know goddamned well what children!" Tom had lost his patience. "Our children. The ones you met last night at dinner. The ones whom you spoke so highly of. The ones to whom you gave your pseudo-sermon last night." Tom looked like he was simultaneously on the verge of throwing punches in rage and breaking down into a crying fit.

Deacon Forsythe stepped his massive body in between Tom and the Reverend as if to signal that Tom was out of line and needed to tone it down.

"Molly, you must have noticed where our children went or at least know where our children went," Katie said noticing that Tom was being shut down in his efforts. "I'm begging you, as a mother, to tell me where my babies are." Tears were flowing down her cheeks.

"Sweetie, you must be confused. We never met your children. You are here without them. Edward drove you and Tom into town and dropped you off at the Forsythes."

"Please don't be upset," Patricia Thornhill chimed in, "your children must be at home with their grandparents perhaps, or a babysitter. You can go see them once your car is fixed."

"Oh my God this isn't happening! This can't be happening!" Katie shouted in anguish.

The townsfolk turned to watch the scene

from afar with looks of genuine surprise and amazement.

Tom positioned his body to place Katie behind him in a protected spot as he began to squat in a defensive posture wondering what his next move should be. In his periphery he caught a glimpse of Edward Stanton walking with his brother Herman and two women who looked to be their wives. There was no sense in fighting the Reverend, especially with the two large Deacons right there, and there was no sense talking to any of the Jacobsons, Forsythes, or Thornhills who were clearly engaged in some kind of nefarious plot. They had not drugged Tom or Katie. Tom and Katie remembered every detail of yesterday. Tom and Katie were not crazy and they were not imagining things. Something evil was at play.

Grabbing Katie by the hand, Tom ran to the Stantons.

"Edward, Herman, please help us," Tom said panting heavily.

"Please," Katie begged as new tears welled in her eyes.

"So this is the couple that you guys helped yesterday," one of the Stanton wives said pleasantly.

"Along with our children," Katie snapped.

The Stanton wife looked towards her sister-in-law with an eye-roll to which the sister-in-law gave a soft chuckle as the two of them walked away.

"Dawn, Tommy, and Jake," Katie shouted towards the women as they walked away.

"Of course we'll help," Edward said in a concerned voice. "What can we do for you?"

"Our children are missing," Tom said trying to sound calm amid a breaking voice. "Do you know what happened to them? Do you know where they are? Please tell us."

"You got me folks," Edward said in a friendly voice holding his hands up in surrender.

Tom and Katie both felt a sense of hope welling up inside.

"I honestly don't know how to respond," Edward began. "Look, I really like you folks. You seem like sincerely decent and upstanding people and I don't want to upset you. I heard you call out names of people, I guess you said your children, during the service and it caught me off guard. I realize you had a rough day yesterday with your car breaking down in a strange and barely-populated area, but I can't tell you about your children because I never met your children."

Katie gave a loud gasp and began saying "No, no, no," aimlessly while fully bawling. Her tears flowed uncontrollably as she clutched her fists to her face.

"What the fuck are you talking about?" Tom shouted at Edward. "How dare you! Whatever game you are playing at I promise it will be your endgame!"

"I knew that's how you'd respond," Edward said keeping himself collected and lowering his voice submissively. "I didn't want to upset you. I don't know what else to tell you. There were no children with you yesterday. There were no children who got in my car with you yesterday. There are no children in Manchineel."

At that particular moment, the wind seemed to be completely sucked out of the Prestons' sails. Tom had no idea of what to do next. Katie had slunk to the ground in a heap of tears and snot and drool. Tom's father had a famous saying that "Hope is the seed of all things good," but there was none left in Tom. It wasn't rock bottom. It was worse, an abyss of utter hopelessness and darkness.

Suddenly, as Tom was staring lifelessly in Edward's general direction he saw something peculiar. It seemed like Herman was secretly trying to signal him while Edward was staring down at Katie as if wondering what, if anything, he could do to get away from the scene. Herman was squinting his eyes purposefully at Tom and subtly lifting his hands above his waist as if to say 'Relax. I'll help you out. Just act cool.'

*Please God, let it be so. Help us.*

"Hey Edward," Herman called over to his brother, "how about bringing over some refreshments for our guests."

"You really think they want some iced tea

right now in their condition Herm?" Edward sarcastically asked.

"Look, it might help calm their nerves. Come on, be polite."

"Fine," Edward shot back. "But I'll be quick so don't you be getting any ideas Herm."

As he took his leave, Edward shot Herman a noticeable warning glare. Edward then began the process of completing the short walk to the Marshes' backyard, dropping off his chair and grabbing some iced tea for the Prestons.

"Alright, listen up," Herman said in a dead serious tone to Tom at which point Katie also perked up a bit to listen. "We don't have time so I can't repeat myself. I don't know where your children are but I do know that they are unharmed. Don't ask me how I know, but it is a fact you must accept. We have blood oaths here among our townsfolk and my life will be forfeit if they find out I gave you any help. We have to get you to McIntosh for help. Edward is going fishing later this afternoon and our wives are going over to play cards with the neighbors. Come to my house at one o'clock. It's the first house on the left as you enter Manchineel. I'll go tell Deacon Forsythe that you're coming over to look through my collectibles. I'm known for them – old coins, old toys, antique weapons – cool stuff. Anyway, you need to–"

"Herm, what are you talking about," Edward said in an accusatory tone as he walked up and cut his brother's speech short.

"My antiques collection which makes yours look like child's play, uh, oops, sorry Tom. No pun intended."

"Fine," Tom said back.

Edward handed the glasses of iced tea to the Prestons who pretended to be grateful and drink. At least now they had something to move on.

# EMBOLDENED

## *Chapter Eleven*

The Stantons headed over towards their wives who had set up their chairs with a small knot of people in the Marshes' backyard. Tom and Katie sat where they were taking occasional sips of their drinks without saying anything to each other. There was no real-life experience, no conversation, no book, no movie, no anecdote that could have prepared them for that day. And there was nothing to be said between them at that point. Their babies were gone and they were stranded among 68 strangers, 67 of whom had been lying to them as part of some sinister evil scheme that was being kept from them. As the minutes passed, they became more anxious worrying about the time and the probability of finding their children who had now been missing for hours. The fact that Tom and Katie had no clue as to when their children went missing only made the panicked anxiety worse.

"Katie, the only play we have right now is

to do what Herman told us and meet him at one o'clock at his house," Tom finally said. Both of them knew he was pretending to be strong and sound confident and hopeful because, at that moment, there was nothing else that they could think of doing.

"Yeah, I got it," Katie said reassuringly.

"I have an idea," Tom continued and kept his voice as soft as audible for only Katie's ears. "Sometimes, when I don't know how to get information in a lawsuit from a witness during a deposition, I just act in a way that is completely unexpected to trip them up and reveal information that they are trying to conceal. Make sense?"

Katie nodded yes.

Tom was specifically recalling a case where a client of his had been ripped off by a partner who embezzled about two million dollars from their joint business over the course of five years. Since the embezzling partner was the one who maintained and kept the company books, neither Tom nor his client could initially find a link between the embezzling partner and the missing money. But, as luck would have it, Tom was at his client's office at the joint business one day when the embezzling partner's rather attractive wife pulled up in a brand-new luxury convertible. The next week when Tom deposed the embezzling partner, who was rather unattractive and obese, Tom decided to change his approach. Instead of being the courteous professional that he had always been with the embezzling partner's attorney, which the embezzling partner had seen during the course of the lawsuit, Tom laced into the man over his wife and asked question after question insinuating that she had taken the money and that he was going to include her in the lawsuit with claims for fraudulent transfers. Tom had rightly guessed that the man valued his wife above all else and Tom's belligerence took the man by surprise. He ended up confessing on the spot to embezzling the money and the case settled with Tom's client receiving full ownership of the joint business which had a net worth of nearly five million dollars. Of course, the equity partners of Tom's firm never factored that huge settlement or the firm's substantial attorney fees of over two hundred fifty thousand dollars into Tom's annual bonus.

"Alright, here's my plan Katie. We need to go over to the Reverend and Deacons and let them know that we're okay. Don't look happy – I know that won't be a problem for either of us – but I don't want them to think that we're acting and then get all suspicious. Just leave the conversation leads and crazy shit up to me and play along. While we're with them, we need to take photos and videos of them from as many angles as possible to record their faces and the town. Once we get to McIntosh with Herman we'll get help and use the photos and videos to identify the people and the town. You on board?"

Katie shook her head in the affirmative.

"I have my cellphone on me. Do you have yours?"

Katie again nodded in the affirmative.

Tom pressed his feet into the ground, leaned forward, and lifted himself up. He then held out his free hand and helped Katie up. They walked over to the Marshes' backyard and saw the townsfolk seated in various groups around the yard talking with each other. Nothing looked unusual or out of place. Tom located the Jacobsons who were still with the Forsythes and Thornhills. Their small group was in the far corner of the Marshes' backyard so Tom led Katie past the rest of the townsfolk who all seemed to casually look at them as they walked by in curious hunger for more information about their guests.

When Tom and Katie reached the Jacobson-Forsythe-Thornhill knot he turned to the Reverend and cleared his throat to signal that he had something to say. The knot turned towards Tom as he cleared his through again to calm his nerves. "Reverend Jacobson, Molly, Deacon Forsythe, Maryanna, Deacon Thornhill, Patricia, I'm sorry that we got off to such a weird start today. This whole ordeal with our car and being in a new place with new people has really frazzled us. We feel terribly for interrupting your service and even worse for our outbursts and vulgar language."

"Tom, I appreciate that," the Reverend said. "Our imaginations sometimes get the best, or worst I should say, of us."

"Look, you folks from the cities and suburbs need to learn to relax and enjoy life," Deacon Thornhill chimed in. "You need to learn to slow down and enjoy the good things like nature and peace and quiet."

"You're right and I hope to fully learn that lesson before work finishes me off," Tom said with a sigh. "And Deacon Forsythe and Maryanna, we want to apologize to you most of all. You took us -- strangers -- into your home and have cared for us like visiting relatives. We can't thank you enough. Please accept our apologies."

"Of course we do," Deacon Forsythe said looking awkwardly surprised, almost taken aback.

"Don't worry about anything," Maryanna said, her voice scratching.

"What did you think of the service?" Molly asked.

"I don't know that I'm in a position to opine on your faith," Tom started.

"Oh, don't be so humble," Molly said. "I want to know your opinion. You're not sitting in judgment on us just by giving your opinion."

"Alright. As a lawyer, I appreciate logic. We're trained to follow logic. And, in all honesty

-- yes I just used that phrase Reverend -- I follow the logic in the Reverend's sermon or whatever you call that speech. I think life is a giant Catch-22."

"How so?" the Reverend and the Deacons testily asked almost in unison.

*Oh, you wanna test me? I'll play that game with y'all any day.*

"Start with my job for instance. I'm measured by how much money the firm generates from a client. Not whether the client is right or wrong and not how well I represent the client and do my job, just how much money I can get the client to pay to the firm. The client could be lying through his or her teeth and, as long as he or she pays the bills in full, the firm is perfectly happy to let that continue.

"As for the court system, either you go through it with nothing but uncertainty or you take matters into your own hands and end up in jail. The courts have no consistency in who wins or loses a lawsuit. Each judge is burdened with a full docket of hundreds of cases a year. They have small budgets and their clerks are not all lawyers. Most are mere law students or people who don't have the professional training or important life experiences necessary to sit in judgment on anyone else. They get the facts of cases mixed up every day and they also get the applicable laws wrong too. And they couldn't care less about correcting mistakes when those mistakes are brought to light. The state judges only care about their elections and the federal judges only care about the interests of whichever political affiliation got them their seat on the bench. And yet this is the system that is in charge of our justice. We are supposed to rely upon this flawed system to take care of us because we are not allowed to take justice into our own hands.

"Look at the world as a whole. The more money and power that one person has, the less money and power that another person has. Humanity and our way of life is, at its core, a competition. It's Darwin's natural selection at work. Survival of the fittest. If I want to succeed, others must fail to some degree. I mean, it starts as kids. The strongest and most confident kids are followed by the weaker ones, the smartest kids get the best grades, the best athletes get the best spots on teams, and so on. That is inherently human nature. So forget about the knowledge of right and wrong, the law of life is competition, not some peaceful state of co-existence."

The Reverend, the Deacons, and their wives were all standing in a state of silent surprise and, it appeared, admiration for what Tom had just said. Katie seemed to share in that sentiment.

*Take that fuckers. I heard where you're coming from and I get it. It doesn't make you right but fucking chew on that until we can get the fuck outa here.*

"Hey, honey," Tom turned to Katie "we haven't taken any pictures yet. How about we take a group selfie with our gracious hosts."

Reverend Jacobson began to gesture and say something in protest over pictures but Tom, ignoring him as he quickly raised and extended his phone, grabbed Katie around the waist and began snapping pictures.

"We're not used to having our pictures taken," the Reverend finally managed to say with palpable discomfort.

"It's no big deal," Tom said dismissively. "Katie, get a few of me with everyone. I want to show our friends back home."

Tom maneuvered among the Reverend, the Deacons, and their wives as Katie snapped almost two dozen photos while recording the whole time. Afterwards, she and Tom took selfies by themselves making sure to get the town from all angles with as many of the townsfolk in the background as possible. At one point, Katie started to smirk. As distraught and afraid as she was, Tom's idea was a damned good one. None of the townsfolk knew how to handle the situation and they were all looking on in great discomfort over their little photography session.

"Say, when do you think the cellphone reception will be up and running Reverend?" Tom asked.

“We’re not sure yet. If it doesn’t come back at some point today, hopefully Ollie will have some updates at least when he gets back from McIntosh,” the Reverend replied.

“So that’s where his prior commitment was,” Tom said rhetorically. “Maybe he’ll have some updates for us about our car.”

“Um, yeah. Perhaps he will,” the Reverend said. Tom couldn’t help but notice that the Reverend seemed caught off guard by giving away Ollie’s whereabouts when Ollie only said last evening that he had a prior commitment that day. Perhaps there was something useful in the knowledge that Ollie’s prior commitment was in McIntosh.

“Deacon Forsythe,” Tom said turning to the large man, “is it alright if Katie and I go and introduce ourselves to everyone else since we’ll be around for another couple days?”

“Well of course, but we’ll take you around,” Maryanna responded. “Come on, follow me,” she said taking Katie by the arm while Tom and the Deacon followed them.

For the next thirty minutes or so, Maryanna and the Deacon introduced Tom and Katie to the townsfolk going from knot to knot. The small talk exchanged was fairly redundant but Tom was doing his best to try and feel for information and keep the Deacon off guard. During the first set of introductions, Tom had asked the people how far away McIntosh was and they told him about ten miles. Tom asked the next group where the next-nearest town was after McIntosh and was informed that it was probably Quincy some twenty-five miles away. On a whim, Tom asked the next group how big Manchineel was in terms of the city limits. He noticed the Deacon become visibly frustrated at the question as well as the answer which surprised Tom. The Manchineel city limits extended five miles out in all directions. When Tom asked a follow-up question about who actually owned all of that land, the Deacon cut off everyone else and gruffly answered that it belonged to the town. He and Maryanna then ushered Tom and Katie to the next group of people which included the Stantons.

Tom didn't want to continue his act in front of the Stantons to prevent the Deacon from catching onto the plan with Herman so he scaled back the boldness. The Deacon, to Tom's surprise, let go of his frustration and started the next round of introductions on a more cheery note.

"Edward and Herman Stanton," the Deacon pronounced loudly with enthusiasm, "I believe you know our guests Tom and Katie Preston quite well."

"Sure do Deacon," Edward replied. "And this is my wife Lucinda."

Lucinda stepped up to the Prestons to greet them each with a firm handshake. Like Edward, she had strikingly dark blue eyes and deep black hair. Unlike Edward whose words came across with sincerity and kindness, her voice radiated with a level of abrasiveness and a general distrust of the two guests. Nevertheless she put on her best smile, pretentious as it felt, and offered to provide any help that the Prestons needed.

Next up, Herman brought his wife forward. "This is my wife Marjorie," he said to Katie and Tom. Marjorie seemed like a much softer and kinder version of Lucinda with softer brown eyes and lighter hair. Her smile was much warmer and she gave Tom and Katie a very friendly handshake and greeting.

"How long have you been married?" Katie asked them.

*Apparently you didn't get the memo to not ask any questions of substance to the Stantons. Get your answer and stop.*

"Um, why we've been married thirty years," Marjorie slowly answered.

"Thirty years! You must have met when you were children," Katie said in amazement. The Stantons, all of them, looked to be about Tom and Katie's age, certainly no older than mid-forties.

"You're too kind," Marjorie responded with a dismissive flip of her hand.

*That question caught you off guard, didn't it? Why would it? Herman and Marjorie are both blushing. Well, Katie started this show.*

"Edward and Lucinda, how long have you been married?" Tom asked.

"Coming up on thirty-five years," Edward responded.

"You must've also met as children," Katie said.

"Yes, yes we did," Lucinda curtly answered.

"Hey Deacon, how long have you --"

"Forty years," the Deacon responded without waiting for Tom to finish his question. The Deacon now seemed impatient and upset with the Prestons' apparent testiness.

*Switch gears now. Don't overdo it.*

"Herman, earlier you were telling me about your antiques collection," Tom said to change the subject and put them on track for the planned afternoon visit.

"Yes, it really is world class. I think you'll enjoy it and it will be a good way to pass some time here and free up the Forsythes to plan some of the Grand Jubilee events and ceremonies with the Reverend. What do you say Deacon, shall we have the Prestons come by at, say, one o'clock this afternoon?"

The Deacon looked satisfied with that idea and turned to Maryanna for confirmation. She gave him an approving nod so he turned back to Herman and said "Of course. That will work just fine. Just make sure to have them back by supper."

*Who the fuck do you think you are? You sound like our parents. Our freaky evil parents who stole our children. Wait. Stop it. Tom, keep your fucking mouth shut. The Deacon agreed to the plan. It's going to happen just as long as you keep your big goddamned mouth shut.*

"Hey Edward, Marjorie, Lucinda, would you like to help me entertain the Prestons while I show them my antique collection?" Herman asked the others.

*What the hell? You're going to sabotage our plan.*

"Heck no, Herm, I've seen that collection a million times," Edward huffed. "I'm going fishing."

"Marjorie and I are playing cards," came Lucinda's response. "No offense Tom and Katie but we see that collection practically every single day. We can't handle the same objects and speeches again," she said with a weird smile and, despite her statement of no offense, her words were said in a fairly blunt and rude tone.

"Fine, suit yourselves," Herman said with a slight smile out of the corner of his mouth.

Some small talk was then made amongst everyone and the Deacon led Tom and Katie to meet the second-to-last knot of townsfolk after confirming the one o'clock time with Herman. The Deacon and Maryanna proceeded to make the usual introductions of Tom and Katie to everyone followed by the exchange of welcoming pleasantries. Tom, emboldened by the recent interactions and the one o'clock appointment with Herman Stanton, turned to the new knot of townsfolk and asked them how long they had each lived in Manchineel. Their responses to this basic question, however, were a curious stuttering before they eventually agreed that they had grown up near Manchineel going there often as kids before taking ownership of their homes with each of the three couples varying their answers between ten and twenty years. Tom tucked that information away with the other mental notes that he had made from the previous information that he had been given by the townsfolk.

Upon being escorted to the final knot of townsfolk, a small group of two couples, Tom and Katie had trouble keeping up their act as they gazed into the hazel-green eyes of Dr. Arbour. The man, a professed doctor no less, who had been so warm, charming, and generous with them and their children the previous evening, was now acting as if he had never met the Prestons in his life. It took every ounce of restraint for Tom not to punch him right in his faking throat. Even the Stantons, despite their participation in the town's evil plot, didn't pretend that they had never met Tom or Katie. Fortunately, Katie came to her senses after watching Tom tensing-up while noticing in her periphery that the Deacon and Maryanna were unsure of how to begin this last round of introductions based upon Dr. Arbour's visit the previous evening.

"Hello everyone," Katie began as she cleared a nervous blockage from her throat. "We haven't had the pleasure of meeting you yet. I'm Katie Preston and this is my husband Tom."

"I'm Dennison Arbour and this is my wife Ginnifer. Over here are our friends Reginald and Stefania Balkman."

"Would you happen to know if there is a doctor in town? I seem to have tweaked my back when our car broke down."

Katie suddenly perked up at Tom's question which seemed to go directly against their tactic of being clever but unassuming.

"Actually Tom, I am a doctor," Dr. Arbour tersely responded. "I mean, I practice locally at this point in my life. Closed my office in the Lower Peninsula and moved up here where I check in on the townsfolk and people in the area in need of check-ups or basic, low-level medical care."

"Would you mind checking my back out at some point? I think I just pulled a muscle but, when I turn, there is a sharp pain that feels like it could be something more than just a pull."

"Of course. Come by my house anytime you want this afternoon and I'll be happy to take a look at your back."

"Maybe you could rub some of that coconut oil and lavender cream on my back," Tom said while directing a stern gave directly into Dr. Arbour's eyes.

At that point, everyone in the group felt the tension and escalation emanating from Tom. The Deacon and Maryanna strategically moved between Tom and Dr. Arbour without trying to make a scene.

"Why don't we return to see the Reverend and Molly," Maryanna suggested. Everyone could tell the fakeness in her tone and that her real intention was to break up Tom's attempt to antagonize Dr. Arbour. Tom, in particular, was not going to have any of it. He had already figured that he and Katie had extracted as much information as they probably could have extracted under the circumstances, and he wanted to send the message to the townsfolk that he and Katie could stand up for themselves. Refusing to leave on Maryanna's terms, Tom then raised his watch to his face. It was almost 11:30.

"Deacon, Maryanna, would you mind if Katie and I head back to wash up and rest?" Tom asked his bedeviled hosts as if Maryanna had not said anything.

"No, of course not," the Deacon replied trying not to sound perplexed.

"Help yourselves to anything you want from the kitchen," Maryanna added, clearing her throat as she was clearly puzzled by Tom's behavior.

"Thank you," Katie said pretending to return the courtesy. She then followed Tom back to the Forsythes.

Once they were out of earshot of their hosts Katie turned to Tom. "What do we do now?"

"We just stay in our room until we go to Herman's. We don't know who or what we're dealing with and Herman's the only real option so we can't screw it up. By the way, did you notice that something didn't quite add up?"

Katie shot him a look of death and he realized his mistake.

"You know what I mean, honey. And besides the uncomfortable answers to our easy questions. I only counted 66 people. There's supposed to be 68."

"Ollie wasn't there and said he had obligations today," Katie reminded him.

"Yeah, but that still leaves one person unaccounted for."

At that point, they arrived at the Forsythes. What once felt like a glorified bed and breakfast now felt like a jail. And even though they had what normally would feel like a short amount of time until meeting up with Herman, an hour-and-a-half felt like days to Tom and Katie. The loneliness and isolation made the reality of their missing children sting all the more at their hearts and they just spent several minutes changing positions and staring into the empty bedroom where their children had stayed last night.

"I keep hoping that we'll hear them through the quiet," Katie whispered.

"Me too."

"There's no evidence of them anywhere. What are we going to do in McIntosh?"

"We'll file a claim with local law enforcement and show them the pictures and video you took. Hopefully their phone lines will be up. We won't leave until we get help."

Tom's voice trailed off at that point. The realization that they had to find some kind of local law enforcement and get help was easy in principal but how exactly were they going to do it? McIntosh seemed like a small town and the local sheriff or deputies could be further away. Time was wasting and Tom could feel his heart beating fast and loud with anxiety.

"Hey Katie," Tom said suddenly. "There *is* something from the kids left behind."

"What?" Katie asked in confusion.

"Dawn's book. That ghost stories book she picked up at the store."

"Great. What'll we do with that?"

"Look, it's here. It's hers. We're going to find them. We're not going anywhere until we do. It's a sign."

"It could be a bad sign."

"It could be a good sign too."

"I just want to go to Herman's now."

"I know."

They sat in silence on the edge of the bed for a few minutes until Tom, always needing to be active, reached over for the book. Only ten minutes had passed since they arrived in their room and it felt like time was moving through molasses. He needed a distraction.

*You're fucked up, dude. Your children have been stolen and you're reading about ghost stories. Balls of steel or new low? Survey says . . . who the fuck cares. Need to pass the time. Seriously though, this is sick.*

Tom began reading the first story about the haunted hunting cabin that Dawn had been telling him about. In a strange way it gave him comfort to be reading the very story over which he and Dawn had bonded last night. But at the same time, it was disquieting to be reading that type of story at the moment. It seemed like the wrong topic.

*Wake up. This isn't a ghost story. Check the table of contents. See if you can find something on point.*

*How would something be on point in this case?*

*Look, you never thought in a million years that you would be where you are right now. True?*

*True.*

*So what the fuck does it matter if you try to find something that seems crazy. This whole situ-*

*ation is insane.*

Tom flipped back to the table of contents which listed the stories with one-sentence summaries. He was looking for story titles and summaries that implicated disappearances or missing persons. He found a couple of candidates and began reading the first one. Tom was surprised by the quality of the writing and the apparent detail given in the story. It was almost like a historical fiction. No wonder Dawn was so interested in reading it. Although the story didn't do much but entertain him for nearly an hour, that was important time for Tom to kill. Katie had been crying silently for much of the time and pacing around the childrens' empty room. Tom got up and walked over to hold her for a few minutes but Katie needed to pace. He went back to the book and continued with the next story. As he got further in, something struck him and Katie looked on as Tom was flipping around between different pages in the book. One thing that Katie had always marveled about with Tom was his photographic memory and ability to put puzzles together – real puzzles as well as cases where the facts were being concealed from his clients. She had seen him do it while working on cases at home late at night and she was curious whether this was Tom actually thinking he had found something or whether it was just Tom hoping to find something. She didn't have time to ask.

"We're back!" came the Deacon's echo from the front door.

"We're upstairs," Katie called out. Tom was so wrapped up in the book that the Deacon's call sent him jumping off the bed.

They heard the Deacon's heavy footsteps coming up the stairs and then closing in on them from the hallway.

*Those ominous sounds from his footsteps should be a story of their own.*

With that thought, the Deacon's footsteps stopped as the giant man appeared right in the middle of the doorway. Only at that moment did Tom fully comprehend just how much damage a man of his size could do to them. He practically filled the doorframe as he gazed down on them with his huge hands and full, muscular build.

*Teddy Roosevelt would love the Deacon as his campaign mascot. He is the embodiment of walk softly and carry a big stick.*

"It's getting close to one o'clock," the Deacon said. "You should probably head over to visit with Herman Stanton."

"Are you going to head over with us or should we just walk alone?" Tom asked. It seemed like a stupid thing for a grown man to ask another grown man but Tom was curious how the Deacon would respond after the morning's questions.

"You're grown adults. You don't need a

chaperone," the Deacon said with a cackle. "I assume Herman told you where he lives?"

"Yes sir," Tom replied.

"Alright. Enjoy your visit. Herman has quite the collection of trinkets. I know his family complains about them because he is always talking about them and showing them off but I assure you that all of his other visitors have come away with very lasting memories of their visit. And no, Tom, you don't have to return at any particular time."

Tom couldn't tell if that was sarcasm or friendly banter or disdain. For all of his attempts to throw the Deacon off that morning, the Deacon was in his head.

# MAKING ROUNDS

*Chapter Twelve*

Ten miles away, the town of McIntosh was bustling under the warm summer sun. So many of the small towns in Michigan that began under one circumstance or another over the course of more than two hundred years had faded into ghost-town status as the finances dried up and the populations dwindled to abandonment. Like them, McIntosh was now at the crossroads of time having both an aged founding generation and a decent contingent of teens and young adults representing the town's third generation. McIntosh, however, had a stable financial situation which looked poised to at least remain at a sustainable level if not grow significantly within the next decade.

Loosely formed in 1970 by a group of fledgling farmers looking for cheap land off the beaten path, McIntosh was prime fertile real estate. Slightly over one thousand acres nestled among hilly terrain with several intersecting streams, McIntosh could easily have been among the Upper Peninsula's hidden gem destinations for tourists but for the fact that the farmers, for the most part, led a quiet and unassuming existence. It was only within the last few years that there was a push from within the town to try to generate more tourism and business to keep that third generation at home and allow the town to thrive. Specifically, while most of the farmers continued to shop their crops to local businesses and chains operating in the Upper Peninsula, a small contingent of farms and the town's stores, restaurant, and trio of bed-and-breakfasts were essentially trying to work as a McIntosh chamber of commerce by reaching out for tourists through Internet advertising and online sales offerings. The local chief of police, who also served as the town reeve and whom the residents affectionately referred to as "Chief" or "Reeve," had successfully lobbied the county to construct a small administrative building by the county road that ran closest to the town which the townsfolk hoped would give McIntosh a presence on the map.

Curtis (Curt) Maybin was having a fantastic day. Approaching twenty-seven years of age, he had been sworn in as a deputy of McIntosh less than a year ago and was looking forward to the upcoming Grand Jubilee in Manchineel. Curt was born and raised in McIntosh where his family co-owned the Haverhill Honeybee Farm which was founded by his maternal grandfather Owen Haverhill. Curt became somewhat of a local celebrity when he walked on to the hockey team at Lake Superior State University where he graduated with a major in criminal justice. After graduation and not being particularly fond of bees or the honey business, Curt spent the next four years working as an officer of the Lake Superior State University public safety department before reaching out to the Chief who finally agreed to take on a deputy to help him manage the McIntosh town affairs.

Feeling in his prime like a big fish in a small pond, Curt beamed with pride and hope inside his freshly-pressed uniform as he chauffeured the Chief around McIntosh in his squad car. The two of them were making rounds to check up on their constituents while the Reeve was also helping people get organized for the Grand Jubilee the following evening. As a deputy, Curt didn't have many quality opportunities to hang out with any of the local women and he was looking to make a good impression on all of the women who were in the eighteen-to-early-twenties range in anticipation of being able to socialize with them at the Grand Jubilee. For all of his accomplishments in college and early on in the workforce, Curt was a late bloomer, social-wise, who was now intensely looking for a romantic relationship.

Curt and the Chief had started off their

day by meeting up at the administration building, which they commonly referred to as their "police station." Occasionally, the Chief would muse about how all administration buildings and courthouses feel like police stations. Curt didn't see it that way but he couldn't argue with the Chief's logic since all of those places have jails inside of them or nearby. Heck, they even had a small jail cell fifteen feet from the station's entrance door and the Chief, who was also the reeve, was a uniformed officer even when he was only acting in an administrative capacity running McIntosh.

"Your turn to drive rook," the Chief said to Curt as they headed towards their squad cars parked out in front of the station.

"Pleasure Chief," Curt responded. He didn't mind being the rookie or treated as such. Curt had latched onto the Chief as a mentor and role model where he envisioned himself taking over for the Chief down the road after the Chief retired. Curt didn't spend much time with his family since he avoided the bee farming business. They weren't estranged and Curt certainly wasn't a black sheep but his interests fell outside of bees and farming which is mostly what the rest of the family focused on, and Curt was happy being taken under the Chief's wing. Getting behind the wheel of his almost-new squad car, Curt pressed the ignition switch and headed into McIntosh to begin their rounds in what was considered the downtown area.

The first stop was Ollie's Garage which was positioned on the far left as the road wound into McIntosh. Curt had grown friendly with the proprietor, Oliver Gustafson, and hopped out of his car to say hello after noticing that Ollie was walking around inside even though it was a Saturday. The two of them had a pleasant conversation while the Chief waited in the squad car.

When Curt returned a few minutes later, he drove the squad car to the right where the real downtown area sat: a small crossroad with five businesses bordered by a wooden sidewalk and four lampposts situated at each of the inside corners. Curt parked the squad car off to the far left side of the crossroad as he and the Chief made their way around.

The first store was Ted Husker's souvenir shop which Ted decided to name "Ted's" as opposed to something along the lines of "Ted's Souvenirs" or "McIntosh Souvenir Shoppe," or something cute and witty to attract patrons -- anything other than a man's common name which said nothing about the store's business. Ted was a unique guy that way. He always seemed to come up with bland or generic ideas (many in McIntosh simply referred to them as stupid ideas) and yet Ted always seemed to make out okay. Occasionally at the tavern behind the restaurant, Ted would recount his favorite success stories of how bizarre ideas made millions of dollars. His favorite success story was about the pet rocks from the mid-1970s and which Ted still made and sold in his store. Most people would never spend money on a rock with glued-on eyes and hair and a painted face but, when they turned into tourists, somehow they saw a treasure in that. Ted was never sophisticated enough to realize the compulsion of materialism in people on an academic level, but he just had a way of selling trinkets that, in the scheme of life, seemed useless.

When Curt entered "Ted's" with the Chief, Ted was in the process of opening a thick shipping box on his counter.

"Mornin' Chief. Mornin' Curt. How're ya doin' today?"

"Doing great. How are you sir?" Curt asked politely.

"Same." Ted's wild hazel eyes were facing Curt and the Chief from above his bushy beard but it was obvious that his mind was distracted.

"Whatcha got there?" the Chief asked pointing to the open box on Ted's counter.

"My next new item, Chief," Ted proudly responded. He then reached into the box and pulled out two large clear bags full of small furry items in virtually every color. "Rabbits-feet keychains," Ted announced as he held the bags up for the two men to view.

"Rabbits-feet keychains?" the Chief asked with a hint of sarcasm. "Didn't those go out of style in the '80s?"

"I didn't know they were ever in style," Curt said incredulously.

"Are you going to bring some of those to your booth at the Grand Jubilee tomorrow?" the Chief inquired.

"Sure am. You know, rabbits feet're lucky and I'm fairly certain that these are gonna sell like hotcakes this summer," Ted said in a matter-of-factly tone that was also full of confidence.

"I don't understand how the feet of a cut-up animal can be lucky," Curt chimed in confused.

"Just watch and see," Ted challenged. "Startin' tomorra night, these're gonna bring a whole lotta luck my way."

Curt and the Chief said their goodbyes to Ted and closed the door behind them as they exited the store.

"You think those rabbits-feet are going to be Ted's next crazy successful idea?" Curt asked the Chief.

"I don't think Ted's going to have any luck with those tomorrow night," the Chief responded tersely and opened the door to Miss Maisy's Market.

Curt fluffed and straightened his hair as they entered the market. Kristie Dorbert, the daughter of Miss Maisy, was working at the checkout register. Twenty-three years old, Kristie was a plain beauty. She rarely wore makeup and never needed it as she, like her mom, had a perpetually youthful and pretty look to complement her petite figure even if she wasn't considered a "hottie" by modern standards. Of all of the women in McIntosh, Curt was most interested in dating Kristie. She, like Curt, was more on the shy side while still knowing how to have fun without being reckless. All too often, Curt would hear police reports about bored teens in the Upper Peninsula who got drunk, high, or both, and had a fatal crash. Kristie definitely was not prone to that type of craziness although she was known to hang out in the tavern with friends or head out to Marquette every so often for an evening at a club or a girls' weekend with those same friends and a few other friends she made while attending Northern Michigan University.

"Good morning Kristie," Curt said in a slightly cracking voice.

"Hi Curt." Kristie seemed interested in Curt as well, although she was playing coy.

"I'll leave you two alone," the Chief said slyly as he walked towards the back of the market to speak to Maisy about the Grand Jubilee. Maisy was hunched over placing some new items on the shelf and, as she saw the Chief heading over, she held up one of the bottles. It was a new company featuring organic jams without any corn syrup or added sugar. The Chief feigned interest and then asked Maisy if she had received and delivered all of the hot dogs, hamburgers, buns, beef ribs, vegetables and beverages over to Reverend Jacobson in Manchineel to which she nodded in the affirmative and then thanked the Chief profusely, yet again, for all of the business that came her way from the Grand Jubilee. The annual jubilees with Manchineel were definitely a major financial boon for Maisy and her family, and she wanted that to continue every year by making sure that the Chief and Reverend Jacobson knew just how grateful she was for the opportunity and business.

In the meantime, Curt and Kristie were making awkward flirty small-talk. Eventually, they agreed to meet up at the Grand Jubilee and walk around together. Curt was unable to drive Kristie to the event because the Chief had ordered him to stay at the police station until at least a couple of hours after the Grand Jubilee started just to make sure that McIntosh wasn't left unattended for too long since most of the residents would be in Manchineel.

As the Chief bid farewell to Maisy, he motioned for Curt that it was time to move on. Curt leaned in to Kristie and they exchanged a hug which quickly went from nervous to bliss. Emboldened, Curt leaned in and kissed her soft cheek before heading out the door with all the confidence in the world. From that moment, he knew that seeing the rest of the young women in McIntosh would be for show -- a mere chance to check out some eye candy or boost his self-esteem, -- because he believed that his heart was with Kristie.

"You got a spring in your step now rook," the Chief teased as he walked up the street with Curt.

"Yes sir!" Curt responded enthusiastically.

"Young love," the Chief shot back.

Curt just gave the Chief a pat on his shoulder. He was truly happy and felt no shame or need to hide the great thing that had just happened. He beamed with pride knowing that he had seized the moment.

"We'll skip Rusty's," the Chief said as they passed Rusty's Inn which was both a restaurant and a tavern. The restaurant was situated in the front section of the building and had a family picnic feel to it with checkered red and white tablecloths draped over thick wooden tables with thick wooden chairs. The tavern was located in the back section and had the look and feel of a hunting cabin as it was lined with dozens of antlers from deer, moose, and elk accompanied by fifty or so small taxidermied animals that the owner, Rusty Hawkins, had hunted near McIntosh. Being a crop-farming community, the residents of McIntosh were in a perpetual battle with deer, groundhogs, cottontails, chipmunks, raccoons, and squirrels over their crops and gardens so everyone loved Rusty's taxidermy collection which was comprised entirely of these nuisance pests. Everyone loved when Rusty put little Santa hats on all of the animals during Christmastime and then put little American flag hats on the animals for the Fourth of July.

Curt and the Chief were regulars at Rusty's and would eventually head back there for a late lunch or early dinner, depending on how the rest of their day played out. Rusty, however, had no role to play in the Grand Jubilee (he was anxious to have a night off to allow someone else to handle the cooking and catering) so the Chief and Curt took a pass on his establishment for the moment.

The next stop was the Haverhill Honeybee Farm store which was Curt's family's business. His grandparents, Abigail and Owen Haverhill, were among the founding farmers of McIntosh and had left Haverhill Honeybee Farm to their daughter, Curt's mother Lianne (who married Anthony Maybin), and their son, Curt's uncle Dwight (who married Miss Maisy's sister Annette). With seven children between them, Curt being the second-youngest, the family business was crowded at the top which was fine because the business was ready to grow. The farm already boasted an apiary with two hundred hives which were cared for by the Haverhills, Maybins, and their hired hands from among McIntosh's residents.

The shelves of the store were stocked

with jars of honey, honeycombs, beeswax, and royal jelly. In the middle of the shelves, a high-standing open rack held different versions of manufactured beehives that tourists could purchase and place around their homes to try and attract bees and create bee farms of their own. The store walls were decorated with old beehives and, encased in front of the counter, was the very first queen bee that Owen Haverhill had placed into his first beehive.

"How you doing Cliff?" Curt said to his cousin behind the counter.

'Er, uh, fine," Cliff stumbled as he looked up from the comic book he was reading. "How goes it cuz? How ya doin' Chief?"

Cliff Haverhill, at seventeen years old, was the youngest of the grandchildren by a good margin. His conception was definitely an accident and he was known to the family, and to the McInstosh community at large, as an accident waiting to happen. As a young boy and even to the present day, Cliff could not be trusted to safely manage or handle the bees, and every attempt of his resulted in bee stings despite supposedly having properly affixed his protective gear. Cliff was just one of those people who could trip on air.

Although Cliff was minding a store surrounded by breakables, it really was the safest place for him because, unfortunately, Cliff was also cursed with being a magnet for trouble.

The famous story about Cliff was that he had been bitten by a massasauga rattlesnake when he was eleven while playing in his parents' garden even though no one had ever seen a rattlesnake within the McIntosh town limits. But that was Cliff: snake-bitten. Curt also suspected that Cliff was becoming a pothead and, while that might be concerning to Curt if Cliff was still that way in his mid-twenties, Curt sympathized with the fact that Cliff really couldn't do many other things as a klutz and lightning rod in a farming community.

"We're fine, *bud*," the Chief responded. Cliff took it as a sign of the Chief liking him. Curt knew from the Chief's long pause and intonation on the word "bud" that the Chief was making a subtle reference to Cliff's reefer habit.

"What're you and your friends up to tonight?" the Chief pressed.

"No plans. If anything, we'll just hang out Chief. Nothing crazy, I swear." Cliff's response sounded as unsure as it was fake. He had scored an ounce of quality cannabis from a dealer friend near Quincy and invited his local group of friends and some of their friends to share joints with him later that night. After all, there really weren't a whole lot of entertainment options for the late-teens and early-twenties kids in a small town.

"Alright. We'll believe you," Curt said trying to take the heat off his little cousin. "How is everyone coming along for the Grand Jubilee?"

"Everything's all set and done. We've got jars of everything all packed up in the back of the store along with some of our new beehives in case the Manchineel folks want farms of their own. With all the flowers and flowering plants there, I'd think that would be easy for them to do. Anyway, between the drive and loading and unloading everything, it shouldn't take us an hour to get our stand set up and running."

"Good to hear. Our family really moves that business like clockwork, don't they?"

"Sure d-"

"Just don't go getting into any trouble tonight," the Chief interrupted the teen. "You know how trouble comes looking for you Cliff. Be careful young man." The Chief then abruptly left the store and headed to the last one.

"What's with him?" an incredulous Cliff asked his big cousin.

"I'm not sure. He's probably just stressed over the Grand Jubilee since he's in charge on the McIntosh end. He's the one on call tonight and he definitely doesn't want to be woken up in the middle of the night to deal with any problems." When Curt saw that his words made sense to Cliff, he then joked, "either that or the Chief doesn't like you."

Cliff gave a short laugh and fist-bumped his cousin as Curt stepped out of the store starting to think that the Chief really didn't like Cliff.

Hopefully, that would pass in time.

The last store on the street was Claudette's Antiques owned by Rod and Diane Denisson. The store was named after Rod's mother, Louise, who always wanted a daughter named Claudette (at least the middle name since Claudette was so old-fashioned) after her mother who died young from cancer. Unfortunately, Louise only had one child but she would call Rod Claudette every time that Rod did something without her approval. It became a running joke in the family so Rod and Diane named the store Claudette's Antiques in Louise's tribute for which Louise was always grateful, and she frequently worked or loitered around the store just to be with the family in the store she loved.

At the moment of the Chief's arrival with Curt, Rod and Diane were driving southwest to a multiple-home estate auction that was being held in Edenberg, a few towns over from Quincy. As always, the Denissons were on the hunt for valuable antiques that they could pick up on the cheap and sell in their store, both physically and on the Internet, for a considerable profit. Their daughters, Jennifer, nineteen, and Rachel, seventeen, were taking care of the store in their absence.

"Good morning young ladies," the Chief said politely with a tip of his head.

"G'mornin' Chief," they responded.

"Good morning," Curt greeted as he

walked in behind the Chief.

"Hi Curt," Rachel answered. She knew that her sister had her eyes on Ricky DeWeis, a fellow teen in McIntosh, but Rachel liked older men and she had something of a crush on Curt. Mindful of the age difference between them and the commencement of his courtship with Kristie, Curt kept his distance from Rachel while smiling to be polite.

"Your parents out treasure hunting?" the Chief inquired.

"Sure are," Jennifer responded. "They probably won't be back until suppertime. Anything you need from them? Our cell phone reception's been out today, but we can try to reach them."

"No. I just heard they were planning on having a booth at the Grand Jubilee. Are they all set?"

"Pretty sure they are. I think they were just planning on bringing their best antiques. I think I saw a tiffany lamp, some beaded purses from the 1920s and some expensive-looking glass vases packed away in the back. You know those Manchineel folks. They have very expensive taste."

"Sure do," Curt echoed his agreement.

"Elegance is eternal. Why not have quality things that last?" the Chief asked rhetorically.

Before the conversation could continue,

the Chief heard his name being called from outside. When he looked through the store's windows, he saw Ernie Fitzgibbons calling loudly for him and walking their way. Ernie ran one of the three bed-and-breakfasts, and the Chief could see that the owners of the other two, Beverly Dowd and Sanford Williams, were walking briskly behind Ernie trying to keep up with him.

"Chief? Could we have a word?" the Chief could hear Ernie loud and clear as he slowly propped the door open to walk outside but Ernie was already close to the doorway and just walked in across the Chief followed by Beverly and Sanford.

"Chief?" Ernie began again, "those friends of yours who booked our bed-and-breakfasts for the weekend haven't arrived yet. They were supposed to come here yesterday afternoon. Are they still coming?" Ernie was referring to the Chief's friends, three couples, who had each booked the weekend at one of the three bed-and-breakfasts. "I've tried calling them. We've all tried calling them. Repeatedly. There's no reception. Do you know what's going on with the reception? Have you talked with your friends? Do you know where they're at? Are they still coming?"

The Chief closed his eyes and swung his head around in a slow circle while taking in a deep long breath and then slowly, deliberately exhaling. He was trying to send a message to Ernie to calm down while simultaneously keeping himself collected. Of all the people in McIntosh, the Chief found Ernie to be the most annoying. In fact, the Chief pretty much despised Ernie who had made a decent living as a carpenter before moving to McIntosh at the age of forty-one following his divorce. Ernie had an obsessively compulsive personality which frequently created extra work for the Chief who by now completely understood why Ernie's wife left him. Last week alone, Ernie called the Chief about some of the teens setting off fireworks late at night -- a group that had included Jennifer and Rachel Denisson, along with R.J. McRae, Stephen Thompkins, Maya Clovis, and Fabian Telli who were working as farmhands for the Haverhill farm that summer. While many in McIntosh woke up early to work the farms, everyone was fairly laid-back. Nobody gave two shits about teens setting off fireworks over empty spaces, let alone enough to call the Chief at midnight, except for Ernie Fucking Fitzgibbons. The week before that, Ernie had asked the Chief about water well regulations because he thought that the well on Roy and Adelle Sweeney's pumpkin farm was not properly secured. After the Chief had listened to Ernie's complaint, reviewed the regulations, and inspected the well (a waste of five hours), it had been the Chief's greatest pleasure at the time to tell Ernie just how wrong he was. Rather than apologizing to all involved,

Ernie just repeated his accusation that the well seemed unsecure which permanently drew the Chief's ire. It also seemed that the Sweeneys, who were an unusual and mysterious family to begin with, were plotting out some form of revenge against Ernie for starting what, in their minds, was a feud.

"Ernie, my friends called me yesterday afternoon and said they were stuck in Mackinac City with car trouble but that the mechanic promised that they would be up here by sometime tomorrow since he promised to work today to get the vehicle fixed. They said they tried reaching you but you were probably busy calling them on redial so they couldn't get through –"

"Or maybe you couldn't hear your phone over the sound of our fireworks," Rachel blurted out, interrupting the Chief's sarcasm with her own barb. She was still sore over Ernie squealing on them and, even though the Chief never punished the teens (the Chief had actually joined them to set off the last fireworks), Rachel needed to goad Ernie as a matter of principle.

Curt audibly giggled which he tried to hide by turning his head and cupping his mouth. The Chief, however, just looked right into Ernie's eyes and let out a short chuckle. "She burned you there, Ern."

"Look Ernie," the Chief continued after a brief pause to compose himself and return to professionalism, "I know that your business is important to you. It's important to all of you," the Chief said looking at Beverly and Sanford as well. "I know that my friends have booked your establishments for the whole weekend and, if they don't pay each of you for the whole weekend, then I will guarantee the difference so you won't lose any money. Sound fair?"

Beverly and Sanford happily nodded in the affirmative and then thanked the Chief. Ernie, however, just couldn't let things go that quickly. "But Chief, how come your friends haven't called us. We've been cooped up for the last twenty-four hours waiting for them. It's so inconsiderate of–"

"Ernie, let me just stop you before you say something about my friends that I may not want to hear. You know that the cellphone reception's been screwy the last twenty-four hours, right?"

Ernie nodded. He'd been in enough altercations with the Chief recently and was smart enough to know that the Chief didn't like him anymore. He could tell by the Chief's toughening voice that the Chief was ending their conversation then and there, and on the Chief's terms.

"Ernie, I told you everything I know and you're getting paid in full. It's done, okay?"

"Yeah Chief. Thanks for your time." Ernie showed himself out of the store and held the door for Beverly and Sanford who each shook the Chief's hand in gratitude as they left.

"Next he'll be complaining about all of the animals making noise at night," Rachel mocked as the door slammed.

"He's a piece of work alright," Curt chimed in. "But he sure can build." Trying to avoid further gossip about a resident, Curt wanted to remind everyone about Ernie's one true virtue: he was a skilled carpenter and construction guy, and he did great work for the people in McIntosh. Early that spring, Ernie repaired major portions of the sidewalk that had been damaged by years of use and the harsh winter. Ernie's bed-and-breakfast was also picturesque to the point that Ted Husker had used it for a stack of postcards he was selling at his store. Using six-inch wide dark wood panels to frame the doors and windows and a roof that curved and rounded over to the exterior walls instead of running straight and hanging over the outer walls like virtually all of the homes in the country, Ernie created a gingerbread house-looking bed-and-breakfast. To add to its uniqueness, Ernie painted the exterior yellow and surrounded the house and windows with only variations of flowering perennial plants that alternated flowering over the months from May through September to give the constant illusion of candy growing around his gingerbread house.

Jealous of the results of Ernie's handiwork, Beverly and Sanford had hired Ernie to fix up their places and, to his credit, Ernie did a magnificent job. Beverly's bed-and-breakfast was painted a welcoming soft green to complement Ernie's yellow home, and Ernie had built her a round-the-house upgraded porch with custom rockers to provide magnificent sitting areas and views from every angle. Sanford's home had been a small five-room cape cod to which Ernie added three more rooms as well as an upgraded outdoor porch and a screened-in porch. Ernie then finished the job by painting Sanford's home a soft welcoming blue to give the bed-and-breakfasts a collective charm that was doing a steady job of drawing tourists into the town.

"Well, if your friends won't be up here until tomorrow, business is going to be slow today," Jennifer said disappointed. One constant of bed-and-breakfast guests was that they all made their way into Claudette's Antiques and usually purchased at least one item.

"Maybe slow. But better slow than dead," the Chief said cheerfully. "I think Ernie's far enough away now Curt, let's head out to the farms and see how they're coming along for tomorrow."

Curt and the Chief exchanged brief goodbyes with the two sisters and headed back to the squad car where Curt drove up the road and past the bed-and-breakfasts towards the farms. Along the way, they stopped at the homes of four residents who had also signed up for tents to showcase various crafts at the Grand Jubilee.

Dorothy Schlotten made wind chimes and birdhouses, Samuel Borden made wooden recorders and pan flutes, Nathaniel Stein was a talented oil painter, and Debra Kozlowski made quilts. After pleasant conversations with each one of them, the two officers headed towards the main farms of McIntosh.

The smaller farms which were spread out along the way had a nice selection of crops, mainly vegetables, and some of the farmers would bring some specialty dishes of theirs to the Grand Jubilee (Carlota Libum's carrot cake was a delicacy not to be missed), but the Chief felt no need to check in with them since only one of them had signed up for a tent of their own. The lone exception, Beanie and Morty Clovis, had a nursery for flowering plants. The Chief thought they were crazy for having a tent at every jubilee with Manchineel since Manchineel was covered in flowering plants. When Curt double-checked whether the Chief wanted to visit the Clovis,' the Chief responded "No. They're out of their minds. Trying to sell flowers in Manchineel is like trying to sell meat to a butcher."

"That's an odd comparison," Curt quipped. "More like trying to sell candy to a candy maker?"

"Whatever makes you comfortable," the Chief snickered.

Curt rolled his eyes and shook his head

at the Chief while continuing up the road which opened up to a view of McIntosh's four main farms: the Haverhill Honeybee Farm, the Burles' tea farm, the DeWeis' cherry and blueberry farm, and the Sweeney's pumpkin farm, roughly laid out in that order as they reached out to the McIntosh town limits. On the hill at the northernmost point of McIntosh sat the town's border and cemetery with twenty-six tombstones and counting since 1973 when one of the founding farmers' five children, Todd Sweeney, was the first of the townsfolk to perish when his tractor flipped into a ditch and crushed him into the muddy ground.

Having already visited with Cliff at the Haverhill family store, Curt drove straight to the Burles' tea farm, U.P. Organic Tea. Jim Burle was a master of puns who loved to "pun"ish people with his incessant jokes at Rusty's tavern. Sophie Burle was a marketing wiz who felt like the name would catch on with their target market and serve to attract tourists up north while also drawing traffic on the Internet. She was right on all counts.

The Burles were relative newcomers to McInstosh, having arrived just over fifteen years beforehand from the grindstone of professional life in Metro Detroit. In fact, the Burles were the primary driving force for McIntosh's attempts to attract more tourism and business while modernizing to keep the third and future generations in town.

Sophie had been a slave to the marketing industry where working overtime was the norm, as was watching the parade of men leapfrogging her for promotion after promotion. She'd work nine to ten hours a day at the office plus two to three hours at home on some additional work one of her male supervisors had given her only to then pretentiously thank her while promoting other men within her team that hardly worked at all. Jim had become a jaded lawyer who grew tired of clients trying to have him fix their mistakes and judges who did not care enough to ensure justice in every case. Exhausted and overworked, Jim and Sophie took the bold step of saving enough money over an intense three-year period and selling their house to buy farmland in McIntosh. Their efforts were all the more ambitious because they had just had a daughter, Toby, and were busy raising Toby and paying for Toby's daycare while working around the clock. Fortunately, Toby was too young to remember the countless hours that she was stuck away from her parents.

The U.P. Organic Tea farm was a unique farm in that it organically grew a variety of plants for tea. Jim and Sophie had always enjoyed tea, especially during the rare quiet moments that they could spend together during their long workweeks, and they were health-conscious to boot so the idea for an organic tea farm was something that they readily agreed upon. The farm utilized a combination of outdoor fields for native plants and plants that could persist through Michigan winters as well as greenhouses to grow tropical plants and plants needed for year-round sales. Over the years, their business had grown and the crops included spearmint, peppermint, cinnamon, hibiscus, apples, raspberries, cherries, chamomile, lemons, and many others.

Curt pulled up to the Burles' parking lot which was an elongated cleared patch about the size of a regulation basketball court covered in crushed limestones. The Burles had done a magnificent job with the property. Their home, a modest tudor, was off to the far right of the parking lot entrance pushed up against the property's boundary so as to maximize the functional space for their farming operation. Just in front of the middle of the parking lot was the Burles' tea store which was filled with two dozen different flavors of homegrown organic tea, tea sets, tea pots, metal filters, saucers, and, Jim's favorite, a coffee table book about tea (he never shut up about how "pun"ny that was).

Over to the left of the parking lot was a warehouse-looking building which was where the Burles dried and sorted their crops to place in the various tea tins and prepare orders for shipping. Beyond that were three greenhouses spread among fields of outdoor crops being tended to by Toby, who was now eighteen, and the six farmhands whom the Burles had hired for the summer, a mix of local high school-aged and college bound kids looking to make some money.

The Chief and Curt found Jim and Sophie inside the store setting items aside for the Grand Jubilee. The parties were having a pleasant conversation when Jim mentioned in the passing that he and Sophie were thinking about renaming the business to Celebritea Organics.

"Is that a pun or is it a real business idea of yours," the Chief asked noting the confused look on Sophie's face which suggested that her husband was making a bad joke. Seeing that Jim was struggling for a witty answer, the Chief turned to him and said, "Why don't you sleep on it. If that really is the right thing for your business, it'll come to you like a snap." With that, the Chief said goodbye as he and Curt took their exit hearing Jim mumble something silly and incoherent about how sleeping on tea would be uncomfortable. The Chief just let out a deep breath and quietly said, "That man just can't stop himself."

"He's a nice man, Chief," Curt said diplomatically.

"All of his efforts to modernize the town's business and bring in more tourists just draw too much attention to us. We don't need the world's problems out here and the fact that Jim can't stop himself isn't going to help."

Curt just nodded and hopped in the car. It was the first time that he ever truly disagreed with the Chief as he, among the third/young generation of McIntosh hoping for a bright future, was greatly in favor of modernizing and growing the town.

"Let's head over to the DeWeis farm," the Chief ordered. "Maybe we'll get there for 'Pie Time.'" Pie Time was a DeWeis tradition dating back to when Earl and Maude DeWeis helped found McIntosh. Instead of lunchtime during the summer, the DeWeises had Pie Time to recharge their batteries with a variety of cherry and blueberry pies or tarts which they served a la mode on hot days, although that day did not qualify as particularly hot.

Sure enough, the DeWeises and their farmhands were all seated at three picnic tables by the main house when the squad car pulled up. Ricky, Earl and Maude's nineteen-year-old grandson, lifted his head and waved them over. Despite still being a teenager and getting into the usual trouble, Ricky was among the more intelligent and perceptive people in town. He was also fairly strong and responsible, all traits which made him among the Chief's favorites.

"Welcome Chief," Ricky's father Clinton called out. "Hi Curt. You guys here checkin' up on us for the Grand Jubilee? We're all set and ready for it. Come on over and join us."

"We were hoping you'd offer," the Chief

said with a grin.

Plates of fresh blueberry and cherry pie slices were passed to each officer as they took seats among the group.

"Anything new we should be aware of?" the Chief asked Clinton.

"Things here are good, we can't complain. You guys may want to check up on ol' Sweeney though."

The Sweeneys were a reclusive group that rarely mingled with the town folk. They grew their pumpkins and sold them in the fall before hunkering down even more for winter. It was rare to sight any Sweeney by him- or herself and, even when they were out in public, they tended to cling to each other.

"What's going on up there?"

"They're just sitting on their pumpkin patches without really keeping the land clear of weeds and vermin. It's going to start causing a pest boom with all of the nuisance animals making their way to our crops soon."

"Actually, Patrick and I were out that way yesterday evening hunting rodents and we didn't see any more animals than usual," Ricky said joining the discussion and nodding towards Patrick McRae, his childhood buddy who was working on the DeWeis farm that summer.

"Maybe the Sweeneys are catching and eating the animals," Patrick mused. After all, he, like the others, could easily see the Sweeneys gorging themselves on raccoons and squirrels and groundhogs.

"The Sweeneys seem like they're a generation or two away from becoming incestuous cannibals like in the horror movies," Ricky mocked despite the scolding look that Clinton shot his way for gossiping about a neighbor. After the Chief and Curt visited the Sweeneys following Pie Time with the DeWeises, both officers couldn't help but think that Ricky's perception was dead on, if not optimistic about thinking it would take the Sweeneys that long.

# DAUNTED

## *Chapter Thirteen*

Tom and Katie walked down the street and headed over to Herman's house. Strangely, the street was devoid of all life even though Tom had assumed that he would feel like they were being watched the entire time. Instead, it was as if he and Katie could have gone streaking through the street shrieking at the tops of their lungs and no one would be around to take notice. All the same, Tom led Katie at a brisk pace trying to get to Herman's as soon as possible. Looking ahead, Tom saw the first house on the left entering Manchineel. They were almost at their destination.

Walking up to Herman's house, Tom and Katie noticed that it was constructed with the same basic architectural design as the Forsythe's home. The major exception was that, instead of large columns up to the roof, the front porch was enclosed like a cape cod with a beautiful outdoor sitting room. Tom assumed that Marjorie was a Holly Homemaker type from the immaculate look of the porch with little wicker tables holding antique vases containing fresh flowers and chairs covered with flower-patterned cushions.

Tom stepped up onto the porch with Katie in tow and leaned into the door to lift the door knocker. As he put his weight on the knocker, the door slid open.

*And every horror movie that was ever made has started with this cliché. Do not say anything to Katie. She knows, and she's on the edge.*

Tom didn't know what to expect but every single muscle in his body clenched as the door opened.

"Get in! Quickly! Quiet!"

Tom easily cleared four inches with his jump. Katie gasped and knocked into Tom hard on his way down. They were so startled they barely noticed Herman moving towards the doorway and pulling them in with a swift closing of his door.

"We're here like you said." Tom was breathing heavy from the scare and now defensive as to why Herman had called out to them in such a startling manner.

"I know that," Herman responded in an irritated and nervous voice. "I told you that my life would be forfeit if I am caught helping you. I'm wound up in knots too. Did anyone follow you or watch you on the way over?"

"I didn't notice anyone," Tom responded honestly.

"What now?" Katie asked Herman.

"Now, we look at my collection of antiques for a while. If my car leaves town right away, everyone will assume that I betrayed them and left with you. Also, if people ask you – and the Forsythes will certainly ask you – about my collection, you are going to need to have seen it to answer their questions with details. Otherwise, they'll suspect something is up. We'll wait about an hour or so to be safe."

Herman noticed Katie starting to shake her head from side to side and tear up.

"Katie, I know you need to get to your children," Herman said sympathetically "but this is the only way that that can happen. The townsfolk are smart. They're sophisticated. Look, let's not beat around the bush: This is a matter of life and death. For all of us now."

"Why are you helping us?" Katie asked now covered in tears.

"This town is my family. But families have disagreements. I have a different set of morals and values when it comes to this."

"When it comes to what? What is this?" Tom asked hoping to get the answer to the million dollar question of what was happening and why.

"That I can't tell you," Herman said firmly. "That is the one and only ground rule between us. As long as your children are safe – and I assure you again that they are – I can't tell you for everyone's safety. My safety, your safety, and your childrens' safety. Do you understand?"

"Yes," said Tom even though he was not satisfied with Herman's position or explanation in the least.

"Katie, I need to hear that you understand too," Herman said in a stern voice to her.

"I understand," Katie nodded wiping her eyes.

"Alright, since we're going to be here for a little while, can I make you comfortable with something to eat or drink?"

"No thank you," Tom said. The day's events had left him without an appetite.

"Me neither," Katie said feeling the same way.

"Come with me please."

Herman led Tom and Katie to the left of his home's entranceway. The entire left side of the house was one giant room that easily looked to be fifteen hundred square feet with a twelve-foot ceiling. There was only one window in the entire room and it was located in the middle of the outside wall and covered by maroon velvet drapes. The main lighting for the room was supplied by three chandeliers that were evenly spaced along the middle of the ceiling. The lighting from the chandeliers was supplemented by twenty sconces that were evenly spread on the wooden walls around the room. It was the same maple brown wood that adorned the Forsythes' house.

Directly below the two chandeliers on either side of the room were circular sofas covered in the same maroon velvet fabric as the window drapes. Below the chandelier in the middle of the room was an enormous piece of wooden furniture that was five feet tall. It appeared to have a glass top like a display case that was about a foot deep. Tom and Katie were not yet close enough to specifically see the items that were in the case. Below the case area there appeared to be shelves containing objects in the corners of the furniture piece while the sides appeared to contain numerous drawers.

Along the walls there were some display cases and pieces of furniture that appeared to be used for storage. There were also a multitude of weapons, helmets, armor, and items on display which Tom either could not see clearly or recognize. On the far end of the room, there were some pieces of equipment that Tom could also not make out, although their outlines reminded him of a museum.

"It's a lot to take in," Edward's voice rang out with pride. "Let me give you the grand tour." Edward then nudged Tom and Katie into the room by their elbows and began the tour in the middle of the wall on the entrance side of the room opposite the lone window.

The wall was covered with antique shields. They looked to be authentic artifacts and they dragged Tom into an old world. Herman's room in the middle of Nowhere, Michigan in the Upper Peninsula was every bit the museum that any history museum anywhere in the United States could be. Tom couldn't help but marvel at the shields and then, with each passing gaze around the room, see just how much variety and authenticity there was in this collection. At the same time, Tom's heart was heavy with guilt. Their children were taken and must be terrified and yet Tom and Katie were being treated to probably one of the better collections of ancient weaponry in the country.

"On the bottom of the wall here are my scuta," Edward said pointing to two enormous and slightly curved shields that were each about four feet tall based on the floor and resting against the wall. "This scutum here," Edward said pointing to the one on his left, "was used by the Romans when they conquered Jerusalem. The one on the right was used by the Romans in the Punic Wars. Above them on the left, that bronze circular shield, is ancient Greek. The soldiers would cluster them together and stick out their spears in a formation called a phalanx. On the opposite side of that, that wooden shield with the steel circle in the middle is a Viking shield. Above it is a Hun shield from Hannibal's army. Next to that is a Mongol shield from Genghis Khan's horde. Over here, I'm sure you can tell by the trademark red cross, is a Templar knight's shield. Then scattered among them are various medieval shields from Western Europe."

"What about those two shields that you have set up sort of in the center of everything?" Tom inquired.

"Thank you for asking that, Tom," Herman said graciously. "Those shields are mine and Edward's. We're brothers but we broke from family tradition and each created our own coat of arms. Edward was kind enough to sell me his old shield.

Katie, though paying slight attention to Herman, was not really focusing on anything in the room. Tom, however, was fixated on the shields.

"Which one is yours?" Tom inquired.

"The one on the left," Herman proudly responded.

Tom looked over it. It was a pentagonal curved shield about 36 inches in height with a wide top, straight sides, and then two lines curving into a point at the bottom. Herman looked to be in his late forties and yet the shield looked every bit as old and dented as some of the medieval shields hanging beside it. In the middle, there was a large painted face divided into four quadrants. The right side of the face had a troll-like complexion with a crown placed on its forehead while the left side of the face had a human-like complexion with a jester's hat above it.

"What's the symbolism or meaning of your coat of arms?" Tom was curious.

"Well, it symbolizes a man's ability to be that which he chooses at any particular moment. He can be evil, royal, a clown, or average. And they're not mutually exclusive. Man can be all or any combination of those things at any moment."

"How'd you get it to look so authentic with the aging and dents?" Tom followed up.

"Skilled craftsmanship," Herman boasted.

Tom then glanced over at Edward's shield. It was identical in shape to Herman's shield but the coat of arms was much different. In the middle was a very graphic painting of a human skull. It was not bland or plain like the skull on a pirate flag. This skull was pointed forward with the eye sockets, nostrils, jawbones, mandible, and teeth all shaded to give it a three-dimensional appearance. The shading above the eye sockets gave the skull an angry appearance.

"What's the meaning of Edward's coat of arms?" Tom asked.

"Back in the day, Edward was really a bloodthirsty SOB. His coat of arms was all about his aggression and putting fear into his enemies."

"Enemies?" Katie chimed in curious that maybe there was a link to her children there.

"I mean metaphorically. Edward wanted

his shield to let people he didn't like know that he was not someone they should provoke or stand against."

*What the fuck is he talking about? Who here in the Upper Peninsula is going around with a real shield and coat of arms? What people in the Upper Peninsula are worrying about provocation or standing up against others?*

"What did he change his coat of arms to?" Tom wondered aloud.

"He, uh, I guess had some kind of epiphany and went for the life route instead of death. He sold me this and bought a new shieeee—"

Time froze as Tom stared at the metallic needle sticking into Herman's neck with small red feathery tufts protruding from the back. As Tom spun in the direction that the dart was angled towards, he saw Katie's body falling limp to the ground. He then heard the thud from Herman's body hitting the ground. In his periphery, Tom saw Edward heading right at him mouthing the words "get him already" to some unseen person as Tom's neck suddenly stung from an acute pinch an inch below his ear. As the pinched area began to burn, a warm haze set over Tom's eyes and mind.

It was pitch black. His head ached. At first, his eyes would not open. No, they could not open. No, there was something wrapped tightly around his head. Tom was coming into consciousness realizing that he was blindfolded. He made a move to pull off the blindfold only to realize that his hands were strapped down to wooden boards. It felt like he was sitting in some kind of wooden chair. It had a flat bottom and, along with the headache, Tom's consciousness made him acutely aware of how sore his backside was from being on the chair. Strangely, his legs were dangling in the air. They were asleep from poor circulation but Tom could feel them dangling freely with only a board extending from the back of his knees to the top third of his calves behind his legs. He started moving his legs around to get his blood circulating and help his sore bottom. The more his legs moved, however, the more concerned Tom grew as he could not feel any legs to the chair.

*Scream for help! Wait. Don't scream. Don't draw attention to yourself. Try and see if you can loosen the blindfold or the wrist straps.*

Tom began shaking his head. To his surprise, his headache started to fade. Unfortunately, the blindfold was tightly secured around his head and would not budge. He then began a series of futile efforts to try to loosen the restraints around his wrists. At first he tried to wiggle his fingers up to the restraints but they were securely fastened facing down on the wooden boards. He then tried twisting his wrists around to test for any weakness or looseness in the restraints. There wasn't any. For all intents and purposes, he was completely immobilized.

"Katie?" Tom whispered. "Katie, are you here?"

No response.

"Katie?" he tried again. "Katie, are you here. Honey, wake up. Katie? Katie, can you hear me?"

Again, there was no response.

At that moment in the darkness, Tom was enveloped in fear -- fear for his children, fear for his wife, and fear for himself. He wondered in the darkness if he was scheduled for a torturous and painful death, if his children had met all forms of horrible fates, and what horrible fate had befallen Katie. Would he be strapped in this position until the discomfort of the chair became painfully unbearable? Would his fingernails and toenails be ripped off? Or screwed down? Or ripped off and screwed down? Would the people of Manchineel take a drill and start drilling holes in his body? Would they use a saw on him? Would they cut off his limbs? Disembowel him? Cut out his tongue? Gouge his eyes? Douse him with gasoline and set him on fire? Get him wet and electrocute him? Had any horror story ever come up with something as fucked up and unimaginable as what the Prestons were going through? Was Katie being tortured? What would happen to her? Was she being gang-raped by the townsfolk?

*Don't fucking go there. Don't you dare fucking go there Tom. And don't think about the children. Be strong for your babies. Remember the macho lines from the war moves. "Suck it up," "no retreat," "everybody fights, nobody quits," "we all go home together."*

Tom then tried to switch gears and debated whether mental anguish was worse than physical pain. Sometimes he thought that it might be. Other times he changed his mind. In the meantime, Tom lost track of time sitting there with only morbid thoughts for company. How long had he been awake he wondered. A few minutes? Was it hours? He then started thinking about one of life's many cruel twists: a treasured memory feels that it lasts but a moment while a bad memory feels like an eternity. And there in eternity Tom awaited his fate.

He didn't know how long he had been in the darkness. As whatever increments of time passed, Tom's body felt worse and worse. The discomfort of the chair was now outright pain in his backside. His lower back was on fire and his thighs were cramped from the weight of his legs. Tom wondered how much longer he could exist in this state.

"He's probably going to start telling us that he came here with his wife" a voice rang out.

"Hah! Yeah, he'll probably give us that

same speech like with the children," another voice said.

"Where are my children?" another voice mocked. "Where is my wife?"

Tom remained silent. Aside from the fact that there was nothing to say that seemed helpful to him, the cruel words just spoken left him in petrified silence.

"What's that lawyer man? I've never heard a lawyer at a loss for words," the first voice said. It was a familiar voice.

"Edward?" Tom asked. His voice was weak and scratchy.

Suddenly, there was pressure on the lower part of Tom's forehead between his eyes as his blindfold was ripped off. There was white light everywhere. Tom squinted in its brightness as he tried to get his bearings. A dark shape started coming into view and, as Tom's eyes adjusted and focused, Edward's steel-blue eyes were pointed right into Tom's in a death-stare; his glower was all business. Tom looked down in submission.

"You and Herman have been naughty, haven't you?" a familiar voice behind Edward said after a brief pause.

Tom looked over in the direction of the voice and saw Reverend Jacobson standing to Tom's left behind Edward Stanton. Tom then glanced over to his right and saw Deacon Thornhill. The Reverend looked smugly pleasant but

Deacon Thornhill wore the same killer look as Edward. The men all seemed shorter than before until Tom looked down and realized that he was in a chair-like device that had him lofted almost four feet off the ground. Quickly, Tom scanned the room more thoroughly. It looked like an old cellar with heavy stone and mortar walls. There was a black curtain that appeared to run along the side of the room on Tom's left from where the Reverend was standing. Edward was standing face-to-face looking slightly up at Tom while the Deacon was standing near a corner next to a sconce along the wall facing Tom. Along the wall beside the Deacon were dozens of objects that Tom quickly recognized as tools. Not just any tools. Tools he had seen in history books and articles on the Internet. There were knives, hooks, hammers, chisels, pliers, and saws in different shapes and sizes. Tom also noticed a cat o' nine tails and a bull whip among them as well as a few round objects that looked like different types of pears of anguish.

Tom's breathing sped up as his heart was beating so fast and loud it felt like it was pounding out of his chest. Beads of sweat began to drip down his forehead and neck, and his shirt began to reveal the sweat protruding from his armpits and stomach. He tried not to give into his instincts but his fear overwhelmed his senses and he began looking frantically around the room trying to gauge his captors' intentions. The Reverend and his men, however, just remained silent with the Reverend continuing his smug look and the Deacon and Edward maintaining their death-stares.

*They have no pity or compassion. They are going to mess with you before they even begin to bring the pain.*

Finally, the Reverend gave a quick nod in the Deacon's direction. Deacon Thornhill then placed a thick hand on the sconce above him and pulled it down like a lever. Once the sconce was positioned near ninety degrees, the portion of the wall between the sconce and the Reverend spun around to reveal Katie blindfolded and bound to the same chair-like device as her husband. She appeared to still be unconscious from the dart. Tom simultaneously reveled in the joy of knowing that she was alive and seemingly not yet harmed while realizing that they were now together in this torture chamber.

"Please don't hurt her," Tom pleaded. "I will cooperate. I will do anything you want." He knew how pathetic and cliché that sounded but there was no choice. It was his wife.

No response came from the Reverend or his men making the situation feel continuously more torturous and evil.

After a few minutes passed, Edward walked over to Katie and ripped off her blindfold. Katie began stirring and eventually began squinting her eyes as she adjusted to the light and her new state of consciousness. Tom watched helplessly as he saw Katie processing their surroundings and began to mumble something when the Reverend cut her off.

"Tisk, tisk, tisk," the Reverend said in his smug authoritarian tone. "Tom, Katie, you have betrayed our trust. So here's what we're going to do. I'm going to give you a brief lecture to set you straight. And I must warn you right here and now that, if I can't get through to you with my words, then I will get through to you with the implements on that wall. Now I'm hoping that I can get through my lecture without any interruptions from you, otherwise we'll have to gag you. Nod if you understand and agree."

Tom and Katie both nodded.

"Good. Excellent. I know you both have a great many questions for us and, as you know, we in Manchineel strive to be gracious hosts. In that vein, I am going to answer a few of the questions that I know you must have. First, where are you? You're in Edward Stanton's basement. We saw you admiring the shields in Herman Stanton's home. You no doubt saw that, while Herman is somewhat of a multifaceted philosopher, Edward is, shall we say, all business. Make no mistake about it, Edward can be a stone-cold killer and this is his lair of crafts. Take, for instance, the devices on which you sit. Edward custom-made these devices. Not for you, just his attempt to improve upon interrogation techniques. If you look at each other, underneath your chairs is a Spanish donkey. Those metal triangular points on adjustable stands are the items to which I am referring. During the Spanish Inquisition, many people were placed naked atop a Spanish donkey and then painfully slid down to their gruesome deaths as they were cleaved and split open by the combination of the device and their weight. Your seats may feel uncomfortable as they are perfectly flat and you may feel a noticeable crack down the middle of each seat which exists because the seats are comprised of two hinged boards locked in the flat position. Edward has conveniently rigged a lever to the seat so that, when the lever is flipped, the boards will fall and the person in the seat will land on the Spanish donkey which Edward can make as high or low off the ground as the chair allows.

"How was that explanation, Edward?"

"Pretty good this time Reverend," Edward proudly responded.

*How many times have you fucking done this?*

"Wonderful. Now Tom, Katie, before you go getting all frightened, you'll notice that you each have your clothes on. It is not our intention to torture you. At least for the time being. We simply want you to choose to remain cooperative. The next question that I will answer for you is what are you doing here? A picture is worth a thousand words."

With that, Edward Stanton pulled down the black curtain. Behind it was an empty wall lined with several sconces. At the far end of the wall there appeared to be a stairwell leading to the main level of Edward Stanton's house. Tom also noticed a couple of tables and a rack near that end as he craned his neck. On the portion of the wall between where Tom and Katie were being held was a large metallic device that Tom instantly recognized as an iron maiden. Inside the iron maiden was yet another horrific site. Herman Stanton was bound into the back end. His body was wrapped in what looked like a beige canvass fabric with leather straps buckled tight around his body at the shoulders, chest, waist, thighs, and legs. Adjustable metal rods were holding Herman in place.

Herman's mouth was gagged with a large cloth strip framed in leather that covered his entire mouth and went all the way up to his nostrils. A large gash with blood sat above Herman's right eye and his hair was wet with sweat. He looked dazed, yet terrified, from the combination of the dart and the apparent beating that he had been given by his brother and their comrades.

The door to the iron maiden was all the way open revealing dozens of sharp spikes to Tom and Katie. The spikes were twice the width of the door so that, when the iron maiden was closed, the spikes would penetrate the victim being restrained in the far end. The bottom of the door had five large holes bored in it. Tom had no idea what the purpose of the holes was but assumed that it was probably to ensure that the victim died of the spikes and not suffocation.

"Herman here inexplicably tried to betray us, his fellow townsfolk, and his family. I don't know if he told you the penalty for such a thing although, knowing Herman, he probably told you something like his life would be forfeit. See, we don't have many rules in Manchineel, but the ones that we have are serious and the consequences for violating them are severe. I am not here to tell you the rules. That is not your place to know or mine to tell. I, no we, need to know that you understand the principle that our rules must be followed. Do you understand?"

Tom and Katie again nodded in their duress.

"Excellent. Deacon Thornhill, are you ready?" the Reverend asked.

*No. They're not serious. They can't!*

Tom and Katie eyed Deacon Thornhill walking slowly over to the Reverend. Edward in the meantime had walked over to Herman and was whispering what seemed like a great number of things to him while holding his brother at the ribs in a semi-embrace. Herman was crying as he leaned into his brother and listened to his brother's words.

"Please no!" Katie begged.

"Uh, Katie, you nodded your agreement," the Reverend said curtly. "Don't make us gag you or worse. Tom, you don't have anything to say, do you?"

Tom shook his head from side to side.

"Good," the Reverend said annoyed.

When Edward was finished with his final words and embrace with his brother, he stepped away. Deacon Thornhill didn't hesitate. He quickly swung the door closed as Tom watched Herman try to scream as his eyes opened wide before the door cut off his light and slammed shut. The slamming mostly muted the sounds of the spikes piercing Herman's body and what appeared to be the last noise of Herman Stanton – a stifled scream. The Deacon then flipped a latch on the door to lock it shut. Within a few seconds, bright red blood poured out of the bottom of the iron maiden spreading around the base of the torture device and across the pavement on the floor.

*And that's what the holes at the bottom of the door were for. To show the victim's blood and make sure they bleed to death. And scare the ever-loving shit out of those who are forced to watch the execution.*

Tom waited for another period of uncomfortable silence but there was none.

Without hesitating or pausing in reverent silence for the deceased, his fellow townie and constituent, Reverend Jacobson reached into his coat pocket and pulled out two cellphones. "I do believe these are yours," he said to Tom and Katie in a mocking tone. The Reverend then walked over to Tom and unbuckled the strap around Tom's left wrist. He then roughly placed Tom's cellphone in Tom's hand. The Reverend then walked over to Katie and did the same for her.

"You thought that it was witty taking pictures and videos of us, our constituents, and our town, didn't you?" the Reverend said like a teacher scolding his class. "It's okay, you can verbally answer that question."

Tom paused briefly wondering whether saying anything would be an invitation to more horror, this time with Tom and Katie as the actual victims. Katie seemed to be thinking the same thing. After a few seconds, Tom noticed that the Reverend was growing impatient and beginning to look angry.

"Yes Reverend," Tom responded meekly.

"Katie?" the Reverend said looking her dead in the eyes.

"Yes Reverend" she responded softly, almost in a whisper.

"Unlock your phones right now," the Reverend ordered.

Quickly, Tom and Katie unlocked their phones.

"Now, open your camera files," the Reverend ordered next. "Feel free to scroll through them."

Tom pressed his thumb on the camera folder. He saw the pictures and videos that he and Katie had taken of the Reverend, the Deacons, Maryanna, Molly, Patricia, Edward and Herman Stanton, and all of the people and geography of Manchineel. At the end, Tom's eyes teared up as the final picture was of Dawn, Tommy and Jake. He looked up and assumed that Katie was looking at it as well because tears were flowing down her cheeks.

Lost in nostalgia, Tom jolted when his phone vibrated and the screen started flashing red. The spontaneous force of his jolt pulled a muscle in his lower back but he was lost in the moment. The pictures and videos in his folder were being cascaded in columns across his screen. Hoping that he hadn't pushed anything, Tom lifted his thumb and extended it as far as it would go from the screen while moving his fingertips to the bare edges of the phone case. The movement on the screen seemed to stop and Tom was about to close out of the folder when the pictures suddenly began disappearing, one at a time in rapid succession. Tom frantically searched the room to see if anyone was using a computer. There were no electronics in sight.

*How the fuck are they hacking into our phones again?*

Tom looked over at Katie who looked

completely lost in her phone trying to process what was happening. When she finally saw the picture of their children being deleted for the second time, Tom knew it because she looked up at him with a sad helplessness.

As hard as it was for him to do, Tom stared at Katie trying to offer a stoic image for emotional support. Soon, his phone screen flashed a bright light and Tom saw that the entire phone had been reset. There was no need to scroll through the screens. Tom could already tell that his and Katie's personalized files and downloads had been deleted, most likely shredded and unrecoverable -- disappeared into cyber trash the way his children had been taken from them. He just hoped that somehow, someway, his children could be recovered unlike his files.

*Those fuckers deleted everything. Goddamned monsters! How could they get into our phones? Wait, they said that the cellphone tower in McIntosh was down. They've been hacking us this entire time! They targeted us! Where the fuck did this come from? The whole town must be in on it. How do we find where they are hacking into us? We can call for help if we can shut the hacker down. How are we going to get out of this?*

"Now where are those children you keep talking about?" Deacon Thornhill taunted. He was now pacing the area between Tom and Katie. "From here on out, you keep your traps shut. Do you get me?"

Tom and Katie nodded frantically.

"We didn't want it to come to this," the Reverend said with a scold.

"But you can see that we don't much care that it did," Deacon Thornhill spat.

"You all have caused me a great deal of pain and anguish today," Edward sneered.

"Tom, Katie, I trust that this ends your escapades and that we won't have to worry about you leaving Manchineel?" the Reverend asked going back and forth between them and looking right into their pupils.

Tom and Katie gave a final round of submissive nods.

"Alright. Deacon, would you kindly release our guests? We'll escort you back to the Forsythes' home where you will stay until called upon. Edward, please lead the way."

Tom leaned over to make a controlled fall off of the chair. His ass and legs felt numb and his back felt weak and sore. He tried stretching his body but he started feeling pain from the pulled back muscle such that he could only muster some minor stretches that felt like they were bringing more pain than relief. Tom then shuffled over to Katie and helped her down. He noticed and felt that her shirt was soaked in sweat just like his own. They leaned into each other and walked side by side between their escorts to the stairwell. As they walked up the stairwell, Tom could see sunlight coming into the house. Despite their long ordeal, there was still sunlight outside. Tom didn't know whether that was a good thing.

At the top of the stairwell, they were turned left into a hallway area that opened into the front hall of Edward's home. Walking through the area, Tom glanced over and saw a living room through an open entryway to the left. There was a shield hanging from the far wall facing him. Tom wondered whether that was the new shield that Edward acquired after selling his old shield to Herman. The coat of arms was too far to see but Tom saw what appeared to be a tree with what looked like two circles next to each other in the trunk. It looked familiar but Tom was unable to focus on it as Deacon Thornhill was firmly moving him along with his hand on Tom's back.

"Monsters! How could you? How you could you do this? I'll kill you! Do you hear me? I'll kill you!"

All of the men and Katie jumped as Marjorie Stanton, Herman's now widow, burst through the front door just as they were about to open it. Marjorie's eyes were crazed as she lunged at Tom and Katie. Both the Deacon and Edward tried to restrain her but her adrenaline busted her through them.

"Sweetie, no! I'm so sorry!" Lucinda had followed Marjorie into her house trying the impossible task of soothing her sister-in-law.

"No!" Marjorie bellowed. "You caused this! This is all your fault and on your conscience! You'll burn for this. Hell is coming for you!" Inconsolable and adrenalized, Marjorie momentarily eluded the Deacon and Edward as they struggled to grab her from behind. She violently snatched Tom by the front of his shirt ripping it at the collar. Her hands then grasped Tom more firmly after the Deacon and Edward wrapped their hands around her waist to pull her away. Just then, Marjorie's right hand swiftly went down and across the front of Tom's shorts and he felt a solid object being placed in his left front pocket.

"No! I'll kill you! I'll kill you! You caused this!" Marjorie screamed as Edward and Lucinda dragged her into the living room.

Lucinda embraced Marjorie in an affectionate hug saying words of encouragement and soothing. She then turned to the Reverend and said "We'll be okay here."

"Very well," the Reverend replied.

The Reverend nodded to Deacon Thornhill who pointed to the door as his order to Tom and Katie to exit first. On their way out, Tom and Katie saw Edward walk up behind a sobbing Marjorie and shoot her in the back of the head with a small handgun. They both gave involuntary jumps and screams as they watched and heard the blast along with the blood spurting out from Marjorie's head as her body crumpled to the floor. Deacon Thornhill just pushed them through the doorway and told them to remain silent.

The Reverend moved to the front of the group as Deacon Thornhill walked closely behind Tom and Katie. There was no surprise where they were heading. The only surprise would be in how Deacon Forsythe would greet them.

# GETTING THE MESSAGE

*Chapter Fourteen*

There was no silent moment of waiting in fear. The giant man was standing in his doorway with his folded leather belt in one hand. He was wearing a sleeveless undershirt tucked into black workpants. With his free hand, he slid his thumb to the top of his belt and pushed in with his hand. He then pulled the belt with both hands making a loud snap like a whip. Tom flinched as Katie muttered "Oh God" under her breath. The giant man's lips were tensed shut as his nostrils flared and his eyes burned through them.

"We've retrieved your houseguests," Reverend Jacobson called out as they approached the door.

"You might want to keep them on a short leash," Deacon Thornhill said smartly.

Deacon Forsythe didn't pay them any attention. Instead, he began putting his belt on through his belt loops and then buckling it, all while staring right into Tom's and Katie's eyes. Tom and Katie instinctively and submissively looked downward but the giant Deacon wasn't having any of it. He reached out with his thick arms and grabbed their shirts tight around the necks. Tom and Katie could hear and feel the fabric of their shirts ripping in his grasp at the necks and under the armpits. Without so much as a heavy breath, Deacon Forsythe lifted Tom and Katie off the ground until they were eye-to-eye with him, trembling and at his mercy.

"Do not ever make a jackass of me again!"

With that, he dropped Tom and Katie who landed roughly on the porch.

"Now get up and get in here. And you will stay in here. Maryanna fixed you supper. You can change and wash yourselves later."

"Tom and Katie, I strongly urge you to do as your host has commanded," Reverend Jacobson said forebodingly. "I've never seen him react to something upsetting so well. He was very close with Herman Stanton and Maryanna was very close with Marjorie."

"We're all close here," Deacon Thornhill interrupted. "We don't take kindly to the breaking of blood oaths and we don't take kindly to strangers – guests – who cause such sin. You had best mind yourselves and behave for the Forsythes or you will find that the next time we'll help ourselves to the instruments in Edward Stanton's home."

"Alright, alright. That's enough James. I think our dear Prestons have gotten the point, no pun intended to Herman. I'm sure they'll be on their best behavior from now on. Won't you?"

"Yes Reverend."

"Yes sir."

The Deacons and the Reverend took a quick pause at the Prestons' silence signifying the sound of their defeat. They seemed satisfied and, with that, Reverend Jacobson and Deacon Thornhill left the premises. Deacon Forsythe stepped back from the doorway and escorted Tom and Katie into his magnificent dining room where Maryanna had left two plates of food for them with some chicken, potatoes, and carrots. There were two glasses and a pitcher of water.

Tom pulled a chair back for Katie and pushed it to the table as she sat. He then sat next to her and the two of them ate in silence. Their ordeal had left them hungry and thirsty but they took no joy in their meal as shock, fear, and sorrow were all they could taste.

After finishing their meal, Tom and Katie noticed that Deacon Forsythe had disappeared somewhere and Maryanna was nowhere to be seen. Not wanting to do anything further that might upset their hosts, they took their plates, silverware, glasses and the water pitcher to the kitchen. Tom turned a handle on the sink faucet to begin washing the dishes but there was no water. He tried the other handle but, again, there was no water.

"Where do they get their water from?" Tom wondered aloud to Katie.

"From bottles," Maryanna said from behind them as she walked into the kitchen startling Tom and Katie whose hearts were already on the edge from the weekend's events. "Remember, we are still working out the issues with our water tower. Marjorie and Herman Stanton were dear friends. I'll come to forgive you in time. In the meantime, upstairs with you. The Deacon needs his space from you tonight so please stay in your quarters. Do you understand?"

"Yes ma'am."

"Of course."

"Good. Now go."

Tom and Katie walked slowly down the main hall, up the stairs, and down the hall to their room. It seemed odd to Tom that he found comfort in the fact that, after their shitstorm of a day, their room was untouched.

"Tom, what do we do now?"

"I think they're using our cellphones to track us."

"Do you think they implanted tracking devices in us?"

"Maybe. At this point, we can't rule anything out."

Tom undressed and had Katie check his body for any small cuts while he ran his hands over every part of his body to feel for any bumps.

Katie then undressed and had Tom check her while she felt for any bumps. It seemed as if their bodies were untouched although there were no guarantees.

"It's probably just our cellphones," Tom hoped when they were done.

"Sure," Katie said trying to reassure them both.

"Look, the truth is that we would die for our children," Tom began. "We need to find them and figure out what the fuck is going on. If they're tracking us through our cellphones, we need to leave them here in this room so that the Deacon and Maryanna and whoever is doing the monitoring here doesn't think that we have left the room. We'll keep our phones on their chargers tonight and we'll leave late when the Forsythes and the rest of this fucking town from hell should be asleep."

"Okay. But how are we going to get away?" Katie asked.

Tom reached his left hand into the left front pocket of his shorts and pulled out a set of keys that Marjorie Stanton had placed there before her execution.

"Marjorie Stanton placed these in my pocket when she went into what turned out to be a phony tirade before they shot her. This is our lifeline out of here. We'll wait until everyone is asleep and then we'll sneak out and go to the Stantons' house. We'll take their car and drive to that town, McIntosh. We'll get help."

"Wait, Marjorie left you that keyring?" Katie asked incredulously.

"Yeah. I felt her put it in my pocket. We thought she was threatening to kill us and trying to hurt me but she was actually trying to finish what her husband started or get revenge on the townsfolk, or both. Either way, she left us this lifeline."

"What an incredible sacrifice from complete strangers," Katie leaned into Tom and they embraced for a long time. Tears drained from both of their eyes reflecting on the Stantons' sacrifice and the fact that they had now just witnessed their first murders to go along with the elderly couple that they had witnessed being killed in the accident with the deer.

After several long reflective minutes, Tom plugged their cellphones into their chargers and noticed that it was approaching 9:30. There would be daylight for just over an hour and they would have to wait until sometime past midnight before they could sneak away.

"Katie, you can go ahead and sleep for a bit. It's just past nine o'clock."

"Just make sure you don't fall asleep," Katie warned as she hopped up on the bed. "If you want to switch, wake me up." With that said, Katie was fast asleep minutes later.

Tom, meanwhile, had picked up Dawn's book and continued reading. None of the stories isappearances seemed to match up with tuation and the more Tom read, the more he felt silly thinking that a fiction book of ghost stories somehow would yield a clue to the complete nightmare real-life scenario they were facing. As interesting as the stories were, Tom felt more and more stupid as he continued reading. At least it helped him pass the time and shift his focus from his deplorable status quo.

"Katie, wake up," he whispered gently at her.

Katie was fast asleep.

"Katie, wake up," Tom whispered more loudly while nudging Katie's shoulder.

She rolled over and opened her eyes. "Let's go. I'm ready."

Katie was usually the late sleeper and always had trouble waking up. This was one of the few times, short of family vacations to places like Disneyworld, where Katie woke up anxious to get going. Tom didn't blame her one bit and never even thought to make a smart-ass comment about it. They were on the most serious of missions and, after what they had witnessed that afternoon, the consequences for failure would be dire.

"What time is it?" Katie whispered.

Tom put his finger up across his lips signaling her that they shouldn't talk. He then lifted up his cellphone and pushed the button.

The time 1:23 AM came up and Katie nodded. She grabbed a sweatshirt as did Tom and they headed towards the door.

Carefully, Tom turned the doorknob and, when it could go no further, he slowly but firmly swung the door open so that it would not make a sound. He and Katie shuffled into the hallway and he closed the door trying not to make any noise as the door came to rest in its frame and the latch bolt closed into place. Unfortunately, the latch bolt was not positioned correctly and they heard a loud click as it came to rest in its proper position. Tom and Katie crouched down and stayed still for five minutes waiting to make sure that the noise didn't rouse the Forsythes. Without seeing any light or hearing any noise coming from the Forsythes' room at the beginning of the hallway, Tom and Katie moved slowly and quietly to the stairwell. They tiptoed down the stairs holding the railing for support and finally made it to the front door. Tom unlocked it as quietly as he could, both of them cringing each time a noise rang out from the metal on the deadbolt, handle, and latch. Once the door was unlocked and the bolt was completely retracted, Tom swung the front door open. He and Katie walked out and he swung the door quietly into place, this time waiting and firmly pressing the door into the frame before releasing the door handle.

They made sure to walk, and not run,

across the lawns to keep as silent as possible. Although they had no flashlights with them since those would have only served to awaken the wicked townsfolk and tip off their whereabouts, Tom and Katie had a stroke of luck in that the waxing gibbous moon provided more than sufficient lighting to move around outside. Especially up north where there was no light pollution, the moon was almost better than having a flashlight. It certainly covered the entire area instead of one particular trajectory covered by a beam. At the same time, the moon seemed perilous in failing to provide them with cover of darkness as they moved about their prison grounds, far from their prison cell.

When they reached the Stantons' house (*the ex-Stanton's house*), Tom grabbed the keyring from his pocket. There were five keys on it. He picked a key that looked most like a house key and tried the door.

*Success!*

Tom pressed the latch lever on the handle and the door opened. He led Katie inside and then they both froze in the entranceway trying to let their eyes adjust to the darkness. The *ex*-Stantons' home did not have many windows and so the moonlight only penetrated in a few select areas. After a few moments, they continued into Herman's collection room and began walking towards the end hoping that the archway there would lead to the garage which the Prestons had seen was on that side of the house as they had walked up to the porch. Tom could make out the outlines of the shields, spears, armor, helmets, swords, and other items around the walls and in the room but there was only scant light coming in from the lone window. He slowly walked over to it holding Katie's hand and they each pulled the curtains in opposite directions to let in the moonlight.

Tom didn't recognize the sound that came out of his mouth as he choked on his fear. It sounded like a gargled scream. He bit down hard on his lower lip to keep from letting the noise leave the area and, more critically, the house. Katie had jumped up and, luckily, her shriek came out as if she had laryngitis. Her only fortuitous moment of the day was that all of her previous crying and terrified shrieks had drained most of the strength from her larynx. She fell into Tom covering her mouth in horror.

Two skeletons hung on each side of the window. They had been hidden behind the curtains only now they were dangling in front of Tom and Katie, the movement of the curtains leading them into a sordid dance guided by the wires wrapped around their necks. Had they just been mere skeletons, the fright might have died down like a Halloween decoration exposed to the light, but the skeletons were still covered in some bare flesh and muscles clinging to the exposed bones. The skulls were the worst as the eye sockets, nostrils, and teeth were perfectly exposed but surrounded by significant amounts of flesh and bone between them. Blood was covering the exposed tissue and bones, and some of it still appeared wet and fresh with the occasional drip on the floor below the curtains. The word "TRAITORS" was spelled in thick blood across the window and, below it, a tree with two circles side-by-side, was also painted in blood.

"Edward Stanton's coat of arms," Tom grunted. "That's his calling card Katie."

"They're watching us," Katie said shaking.

"We can't be sure."

"Well then whose benefit is this message for?"

Tom bowed his head in fearful recognition of the fact that Katie had a valid point; she was probably right. They were the only outsiders in Manchineel and this gruesome display didn't seem to serve any purpose other than a warning to outsiders. There didn't seem to be much sense in Edward sending a message to his murdered brother and sister-in-law.

"Maybe they are watching, but we know that we have to do this. We don't really have a choice. I guess that's a rhetorical statement."

Katie nodded and they both leaned on each other and quickly left the room with their newfound moonlight lighting up the archway at the end of the room. As they walked through it, they saw from the remaining moonlight a door to their left which appeared to be near where the garage seemed to be located from the outside of the house. Tom turned the knob and, as he had hoped, it was in fact the door to the Stantons' garage. Inside, Tom and Katie could see some large shelves lining both sides of the garage with the outlines of garbage cans and some tools along the back wall. In the middle, there was a dark sedan – their escape ticket. Katie saw the sedan and headed straight for it.

"Hold on a second," Tom whispered. "I don't know if we can prevent the interior car lights, but let's make sure the headlights are off."

He and Katie walked over to the driver-side door and opened it. The interior lights turned on and Tom played with the dashboard panel until he was able to spot the headlight switch and turn it from automatic to off. He did not want to spend time using the keys to turn the car's power on and find the menu to turn off the interior lights. The more time they spent in Manchineel, the greater the danger to them and, potentially, the recovery of their children.

"I'm going to release the latch from the garage opener so that I can open the garage door by hand," Tom said next. "It'll make a noise but we don't want the garage opener lighting this place up and it'll make lots of noise anyway. When I lift the garage, you hop in the car and shut the door as quietly as possible and start the car, okay?"

Katie nodded in agreement and Tom handed her the keys with the car key pointing out for her.

Tom slowly and silently pulled down on the latch to the garage opener and released it. He then cautiously walked to the garage door and lifted it up slowly and steadily until it was open enough to stay up on its own while allowing enough space to get the car out. Katie had opened the door and started the ignition while pulling the door up to the car and then forcing it into the locked position so as not to make any real sound from the door being shut. Tom jumped into the driver's seat and pulled the car through the garage without fully shutting his door. After clearing the garage, Tom quickly jumped out and brought the garage door back down slowly and quietly before getting back in the car and closing the door the same way that Katie did in the hope that no one heard them or saw the interior car lights for the brief period they were on.

Tom put the car in drive and slowly headed down the short driveway and out of Manchineel. The moonlight was sufficient but Tom needed to focus all of his attention on driving.

"Katie, look around. Do you see any lights turning on or any movement anywhere in the town?"

Katie surveyed the entire town until Tom had gotten far enough away that she couldn't see it any more. "I didn't see anything," she reported back.

"Good. Hopefully we're in the clear now. Maybe getting to McIntosh isn't the best solution. Maybe we should drive to the nearest big city like Marquette or whatever big city is between McIntosh and Marquette. Shit, we won't really know where to go. We don't have our phones or any maps or GPS devices."

"But Herman told us that we needed to get to McIntosh. Maybe we should just do that. I mean, he and Marjorie died for us. They were murdered." Katie stopped speaking as she choked up.

Tom thought long and hard about what to do. "Let's just see about McIntosh first since that's the nearest city or town or whatever it is."

Four sudden beeps from the car amidst their ghostly silence sent the Prestons airborne only to be restrained by their seatbelts.

"What the fuck!" Tom spat out as intense pain shot through his back. "Oh, shit, it's the gas. The car is almost out of gas, honey. Perfect fucking complement to this trip."

"Is your back okay?" Katie could hear audible pain in Tom's voice. The sudden jump against the seatbelt from the car beeping had enflamed the pulled muscle in Tom's back. Katie felt like she had tweaked her back muscles in the process as well.

"I'll be fine. I guess this is karma for lying to Dr. Arbour earlier today about pulling a muscle in my back," Tom said with a disgusted sarcastic grunt.

"I guess we really are going to be stuck with McIntosh unless they have a gas station," Katie replied with a manic laugh. She felt Tom starting to lose his composure and knew that he hadn't slept back at the Forsythes. She was hoping to keep him calm so that they could make it safely to get the help that they needed or whatever they could get in McIntosh.

"Just stay alert and let me know if you want me to drive," Katie said while gently rubbing the back of Tom's neck.

"I will. That feels better. Thank you. The townsfolk said that McIntosh is only about ten miles away so the drive shouldn't take long. Just help me by keeping an eye out behind us to make sure that we aren't being followed."

"Oh shit, I will," Katie dutifully responded.

They drove on guided by the moonlight and, when they hit the fork in the road, Tom turned to head in the opposite direction from where they had come to Manchineel. It was the same direction that Oliver Gustafson had towed their car. What had seemed like a remarkable act of compassion and charity hardly more than one day ago now seemed like the first act of an unspeakable horror story where they had unknowingly been cast as the stars. Driving down the road with nothing more than the moonlight and the ominous silhouettes of the surrounding trees and bushes, Tom couldn't escape his awful feeling that their ordeal was far from over and that the worst was yet to come. It was an obvious and easy feeling to have given their missing children, but something else seemed off. He couldn't quite figure it out, but he felt like there were clues around them that they just hadn't or weren't noticing.

As a litigator, Tom was trained to pick up on clues and use them to solve the puzzles presented in each case. In cases about missing money, he'd look at tax returns to trace assets. He'd look at bank statements, checks, accounting spreadsheets, and financial statements that had been provided to banks to trace money. In cases that concerned ownership of assets, he'd check with the county and municipal clerks' offices as well as the state corporation files. He would look through all of the documents produced in every case to verify facts and piece the documents together to figure out what happened and then tell the true story to the judge or jury. Tom proudly called it mosaic intelligence, a term that he had picked up dealing with a case that involved several government contracts that his clients had entered into with the

United States Department of Defense.

So far, the mosaic in this nightmare involved three stolen children and a town of secretive and evil people who had a torture chamber and murdered two of their own for offering nothing more than minimal help to the Prestons to save their children. Of course it was bad and of course it had to get worse. Tom cringed thinking just how much worse it could possibly get. He looked over at Katie who was still periodically rubbing the back of his neck and gently placed his hand on her thigh.

"Nothing to do but go forward, huh?" he said to her.

"And no one's been following us," she said in response and then, after a short pause, "I love you."

"I love you too."

The car continued along the road for several minutes when the brush along the side of the road opened up and Tom and Katie could make out the silhouettes of structures a few hundred yards ahead. As they continued forward, they saw the outline of something that looked like a sign near the side of the road. Tom stopped the car and briefly turned on the headlights to get a clear look at the object. It was in fact a large wooden hand-painted sign that said "Welcome to McIntosh" in bold cursive letters. Below that, the sign read "Established 1970" with "Population 452" underneath.

“Probably a quaint little town but not what we need right now,” Tom muttered.

The gas alarm went off again as Tom turned off the headlights sending them both into their seatbelts for a second time.

“And the shitstorm saga continues,” Katie muttered in follow-up.

# MCINTOSH IN THE MOONLIGHT

## *Chapter Fifteen*

Small-town boredom was a constant for the teens growing up in McIntosh. It was especially frustrating for the young adults who returned from college to work the farms that summer since they had grown accustomed to having entertainment options on or near their campuses. In McIntosh, the nearest movie theater alone was forty minutes away. That night, however, Cliff Haverhill had delivered with a big assist from the covert efforts of Kristie Dorbert who had left five cases of beer that she had secretly sold to Patrick McRae by the back door of Miss Maisy's Market. Kristie had originally planned on joining the group but worried about how one Deputy Curt Maybin might perceive such a thing given their burgeoning relationship.

The kids were partying under the moonlight near the four lampposts of the so-called downtown McIntosh toking the quality joints that Cliff had prepared from his freshly purchased weed while swigging their beers. It was practically the only fun thing for them to do in McIntosh, but it was in fact a fun thing to do. Figuring that the Chief and Curt had made rounds earlier that day and were getting rested for the Grand Jubilee, the kids felt safe partying right in the middle of the downtown area as opposed to risking getting caught in or near their parents' homes. The night had been filled with stories, laughter, and, above all, heavy flirting with the teenage hormones in full bloom.

Toby Burle and Ricky DeWeis were cuddled up together sitting on the edge of the sidewalk in front of Rusty's Inn, further away from the rest of the group and the light of the lampposts to give themselves some privacy. Occasionally, Jennifer Denisson would cast an envious glance at them from in front of Ted's where she was sitting with her sister, Rachel, Patrick McRae and his younger brother R.J., Stephen Thompkins, Maya Clovis, and Fabian Telli. Fortunately, Jennifer couldn't see Toby's and Ricky's faces in the shadow of the night and, with the weed and beer steering her mind into a state of calm, she started feeling like maybe Fabian was attractive in his own right. In the meantime, Rachel was keying in on Patrick, a twenty-year-old junior at Northern Michigan University. As Rachel scooted closer towards

Patrick, Stephen had his arm wrapped around Maya and the two exchanged brief kisses every few minutes.

Nearby but closer to Miss Daisy's Market, Cliff was toking up a fresh round of joints with Vic and Dominique Dowd, Marcus and Michael Williams, Tammy Doyle, Cyndi Grimes, and Dana Port. Half-baked, they went from laughing hysterically to becoming paranoid and quieting down every time they heard a howl or screech from the surrounding nature to laughing hysterically at the fact that they got startled. Ricky and Patrick occasionally messed with them by taking turns clanking small rocks off the lampposts and store signs to create new rounds of paranoia and laugh attacks. After about the thirteenth time that happened, Cliff had had enough.

"Hey, what gives, man? Cut it out!"

"Just having fun with you guys, man," Ricky answered followed by Patrick smugly repeating "Just having fun with you guys, man."

After a short pause, Cliff doubled over with laughter and the whole group burst into deep belly laughs.

Suddenly, Ricky shot up from the sidewalk. "Hey, what's that noise?"

"Joke's over. Quit messing with us," Marcus Williams said while still laughing a bit.

"I'm not joking. I heard a noise," Ricky insisted.

"What noise did you hear?" Toby asked with some concern. The kids all knew the area well and there was nothing remotely frightening about it. At the same time, Toby had pretty much grown up with Ricky and had never known him to get spooked.

"I swear I heard a noise like a car rolling in."

"You're paranoid," Jennifer said, her high state mixed with vindictiveness against Ricky for choosing Toby over her.

"Yeah, man, like there's nothing around here," Vic piped in with his eyes half-squinted.

"Wait, I hear it too," Patrick said.

The group got quiet and listened. From out in the distance they heard the sound of tires rumbling along the road heading into McIntosh.

"Do you see anything, man?" Cliff asked.

"I don't see a damn thing," Ricky responded. "But it might be the Chief's or Curt's patrol car with the headlights turned off so they can bust us. I didn't think they'd be working tonight. Let's get out of here."

"And go where?" Cyndi asked.

"We can go to my parents' farm," Toby suggested.

"Good idea, man" Cliff slurred, stoned out of his mind.

"Just make sure you turn off your headlights," Ricky said authoritatively. "If they see our headlights, they'll know where we are and we'll be busted."

The teens quickly secured their beer and joints, jumped into the five cars and trucks that they arrived in, and Ricky, Patrick, Michael, Tammy, and Stephen, the five oldest ones deemed the most sober among their stoned and inebriated peers, drove away from the lit downtown area toward the Burles' farm.

Under normal circumstances, Tom would have wanted to put the car in park and step outside to examine the town before driving in so that he could have an idea as to how the town was arranged and where he should head. With the gas running so low, however, Tom didn't want to risk the car stalling out atop the hill leading into town and sticking them with the difficult task of trying to hide the car while moving around the town.

As they started down the hill, Tom made out what appeared to be four streetlamps and a center crossroads with a few buildings on some of the sides almost forming the shape of an asymmetrical plus sign. On the fringes of that area was a stand-alone building and, beyond it, there appeared to be some scattered structures that resembled homes. Out in the distance, there appeared to be some farmlands. Tom could not make out the silhouettes of any livestock and assumed that maybe the farms were crop farms. There also appeared to be a grouping of carved stones up near a far hill that Tom speculated might be a cemetery.

Tom drove towards the center crossroads hoping that maybe someone would be around or that, perhaps, he could find some business that might be helpful when the sun came up. He worried that driving too close to the homes might alert the homeowners and, in this location, they would probably be armed and not too welcoming of strangers past two o'clock in the morning. In any event, he and Katie really had no plan so it seemed that the smartest and safest course of action was to head to the center of town, familiarize themselves with what they could, and then hope for the best at daylight.

"Tom, do you see Ollie's garage?" Katie asked.

*How'd you miss the obvious you old fart? I must be getting tired. Of course, we need to find Ollie's garage and get our car. That's step one. Step up your game Tom. Stay alert.*

"I think I saw it," Tom responded and headed towards the stand-alone building.

As the car pulled up alongside the building, Tom and Katie saw an old sign reflecting the words "Ollie's Garage" in the moonlight.

"Wow, Ollie's garage is in fact named Ollie's Garage," Tom said in mock amusement.

"Do you think Ollie's sleeping inside?" Katie asked.

"We have to assume that he is, but I don't

care one way or the other," Tom responded. "It's life or death for us and the kids from here on out."

Tom turned off the engine and they both exited the car as quietly as they had entered it.

Ollie's Garage was an older-looking building that seemed to be well maintained. While the exterior cinder blocks had a fresh coat of paint, Tom could make out cracks from the hot-and-cold of the Michigan seasons. The roof was fairly new and the business sign must have been recently painted as it stood out brightly in the moonlight with the words "Ollie's Garage" in bright red paint. On the left side of the building, there was a glass entrance door and what looked like a waiting area and cashier counter from what Tom could see through the two windows just to the left of the door. On the right side of the building, there were two tall and wide garage doors, however, unlike most mechanic garages that Tom had seen, the doors had no windows. It also looked like they could use a fresh coat of paint. The exterior of the building appeared to be painted in a light gray while the garage doors had been painted white and were showing a number of scratches, cracks, dirt, and chipped paint. Tom assumed that Ollie needed two garage spaces in order to house his tow truck and whatever car he was working on at a given moment. Tom further assumed that, in a place like this, Ollie wouldn't be servicing more than one car at any particular time.

Tom and Katie approached the front door and Tom gave it a firm pull. The door didn't budge and Tom could see that it was locked with a deadbolt. He walked over to the windows and tried looking through them from every angle attempting to see if their car was inside but it was too dark within the building and he could only make out a pile of tires, some chairs, and a cash register on the counter.

"Let's go around the back," he said quietly to Katie.

She walked up to him and they rounded the corners together to the back of the building. The back wall was merely a plain extension of the building's façade with light gray cinder blocks lining its entirety with the exception of one brown door in the middle. However, there were a few items at the back of the building that caught the Prestons' attention.

First, there was a separate garage behind the building. It was nearly twice the length of Ollie's Garage, and Tom could not imagine what Ollie could possibly need such a building for unless he was using it to store things like a decent-sized boat and snowmobiles.

In addition to its size, the building had a satellite dish mounted to the far corner of its roof. It was not the small variety dish that people used for satellite television but, rather, something that looked about three times the size. At that moment, the thought hit Tom and he needed to share it.

"Didn't they tell us in Manchineel that the cellphone tower was out in McIntosh?"

"They did. They absolutely said that when our cellphones weren't working."

"I didn't notice a cellphone tower anywhere in the area when we were driving in. But it's dark so I could have easily missed it."

"Why would there be a satellite dish this big on Ollie's?"

"I have no idea. Let's check it out and see if there are any wires or a way in."

Tom and Katie walked over to the corner. They couldn't see any cables but they did see a brown door that matched the one behind the main building of Ollie's Garage. They also saw what appeared to be a back-road entrance to this separate garage which exited to a different road rather than the main road into McIntosh.

Tom grabbed the doorknob and tried to twist it while giving a hard pull. Nothing happened as the door was locked and bolted.

"I don't know how we're going to get in here," he said in frustration. "We might have to break glass to get into Ollie's Garage instead and see if we can find anything in there." His energy was starting to wane and the lack of sleep was now overtaking the adrenaline from sneaking out of Manchineel and driving to McIntosh.

"Try the keys," Katie said pointing to

Tom's pocket.

"Okay," he said cynically "but I doubt they'll work."

"Maybe they won't. But Marjorie gave you the keys to their car for a reason. She knew that we would drive it here and come to Ollie's Garage. They were friends and did things together so maybe the Stantons have keys to this place and Marjorie made sure to give them to you. I mean, it was the last thing she did before she was murdered. She basically sacrificed herself to get us here. Why would she leave us locked out."

Tom gave her a grateful nod and rub on the shoulder. It made perfect sense. There were three keys on Marjorie's keyring in addition to the Stantons' house key and car key. There was no reason for Marjorie to not give them keys to Ollie's if she had them.

Tom pulled out the keyring from his pocket and began to appreciate the value of moonlight all the more. It enabled him to shuffle through the keys and segregate the house key and car key from the other three. Tom picked the first of the three remaining keys and slipped it in the lock. It went all the way into the keyhole and turned all the way in Tom's grasp. Tom then quickly removed the key and used it to unlock the bolt. Then he turned the nob and carefully pulled the door open entering first and then holding the door for Katie. The place was pitch black inside confirming what Tom had noticed on the outside – no windows.

"We can turn on the lights in here. There aren't any windows," he whispered as Katie remained slightly behind him holding the door open for the moonlight.

"What if Ollie's here?" she asked.

"We'll have to beat him down," Tom said. "We'll have to force him into telling us where the kids are and the only way that can happen is if he's our prisoner."

"I think I see a light switch," Katie said pointing to the wall behind Tom.

Tom turned around and brushed it with his hand. "It is a light switch. Go ahead and close the door behind you so that no one around sees the lights."

Katie closed the door quietly so that only a slight click echoed through the large garage space.

"I'm going to flick the switch on the count of three. If we see Ollie, I'll attack him and you find something that we can use against him like a tool or board of wood. He'll still be disoriented from sleep. Ready?"

Katie nodded. Both of their hearts were beating loudly.

"One, two, three."

Tom flipped the light switch and three fluorescent lights along the center of the ceiling turned on illuminating the garage. There was no sign of Ollie. It was just as bad. Maybe worse.

Filling out the bulk of the elongated garage was an old brown beat-up looking Peterbilt truck. It had to be the very one that Tom and Katie saw and passed on I-75. No other truck that they had ever seen looked like it.

"No fucking way! That's that creepy big rig that we passed on Friday," the shock in Tom's voice resonated throughout the space.

"Don't yell. What if Ollie is sleeping inside?" Katie glanced around nervously.

Tom ran over to the driver side door and swung it open. He then quickly jumped into the cabin and Katie anxiously waited for him to give her some kind of positive signal.

"Katie, get in here," Tom called out a minute later. "Even after everything else, you're not going to believe this shit. Oh my fucking god."

Katie hopped up into the cabin and gave a loud sigh after she had a moment to take everything in. There was a loft above the seats with a twin bed that, luckily, was unoccupied. The cabin behind the seats and below the loft, however, had a shelf running across its sides with a leather chair like someone was running an office from back there. The shelving contained a lot of computer equipment and a couple of cameras and camcorders. Tom wasn't much of a technology guy but he could make out two sophisticated laptops and what appeared to be two additional hard drives.

"What is all of this equipment for?" Tom wondered aloud. "What does all of this mean?"

Katie wasn't thinking to herself about what to do next or what the truck meant. Unlike Tom, whom countless friends and lawyers referred to as a Luddite, Katie was fairly proficient with computers and technology. She grabbed both laptops and flipped them open. She pushed the power buttons and waited for them to start up hoping that either there was no login required or that the passwords would be easy enough for her to crack.

"Great idea," Tom encouraged.

"Tom, try looking at the videos and photos on the camera and camcorder. Hopefully the memory cards are still in them."

"I'll try."

"Don't try, just do," she said back with a witty wink.

*I love it when you channel your inner general.* In that moment, Tom remembered just how special she was and why he had to be with her forever. Ninety percent of the time, Tom's kids, job, financial stress, professional stress, family stress, and day-to-day stress consumed his existence. But ten percent of the time, things were truly great and, every so often like now, Katie would do something remarkable that just made Tom realize how incredible things could be. He was a passionate guy and those gestures went a long way towards fulfilling his needs.

Tom picked up the camera and instantly found the next clues before Katie could begin with the computer login screens.

"Oh my god!" Tom couldn't contain his emotions.

Katie ran over as Tom showed her the first picture that came up. It was the Prestons – all five of them – on the side of the I-75 exit after their car had broken down. Tom scrolled backwards and the next picture was of the Prestons inside their car just before it broke down. Tom scrolled backwards again and there was a similar picture, and then another one. As Tom continued to scroll through the memory card, the background scenery continued to change all the way until Tom could make out the stop at the cliff tourist stop. The last picture on the camera was of the Prestons getting into their car before leaving the parking lot.

"They were following us since we left that stop," Katie said with the horrific realization that they had been targeted and stalked.

"Those fuckers. I guess there truly isn't a safe place in the world anymore."

*Was there ever such a thing as a truly safe place? You always hear about the 'good old days,' yet you hear about all of the horrors of history and how people were always afraid to report the bad things that happened for fear of reprisals. Maybe that is human nature. Now you just sound like Reverend Fuckface. Just shut up and focus on getting the kids back.*

"Let's check the camcorder," Katie said reaching for the device. She turned on the power and realized that there was only one video on there after attempting to scroll through the memory card. She took a deep breath and pushed the play button. The video started with movement down a corridor. It was dark at first and there were no people in the frame. Suddenly, lights from sconces lining the corridor turned on and Tom and Katie could tell that the corridor was the Forsythes' upstairs hallway. The video continued moving down the hallway until it came to a doorway on the end. A gloved hand reached out to turn the doorknob and open the door. Inside the room, the video first showed Dawn sleeping on her mattress on the floor. It then swung over to show Tommy and Jake sleeping in the bed. The video moved closer in on Dawn as a gloved hand reached out with a white cloth. It placed the cloth over Dawn's mouth and nose and she seemed to momentarily struggle before going limp into some sort of unconscious state. The video then turned to the boys just as a pair of gloved hands with similar cloths moved from their faces and out of the frame. Just like Dawn, the boys were in a state of unconsciousness. The video then showed cloaked and hooded figures with what appeared to be masks, almost like snouts of some sort protruding outwards from under the hoods, move over to the children and pick them up. The video ended there.

Katie hit the play button a few more times and tried checking the menu for more videos but there were none. Both Katie and Tom had tears streaming down their cheeks. There was nothing that needed to be said between them about what they had just seen. They were on a real life treasure hunt where the hidden treasure was their children. No words could do their mission justice.

"Are you ready to try the computers or should we check Ollie's Garage?" Tom asked following their shared silence.

"I'm ready," Katie said through a sniffle. She took a deep breath and said "I think I will try the same passwords on each computer in case one works for one but not the other. It might save time and the computers seem similar to each other. Hopefully I'll get lucky." She took another two deep breaths and turned to the login screens. The first login screen had "Ollie" as its user ID and the second had "Oliver" which further confirmed to Katie that using the same passwords might be a smart approach.

"Gustafson," she typed into the password boxes.

Both screens flashed the message of a login error.

"Manchineel," she typed next.

Login error again.

Pausing for a moment, Katie typed "Preston."

Login error.

"Maybe we should just check Ollie's Garage instead," Tom suggested. "The passwords probably have different capital letters and numbers and characters like an ampersand or asterisk or any of the other symbols."

Suddenly the computer screens flashed bright red and began beeping loudly in alarm as if the volume was on the highest level. Tom and Katie jumped in shock and then desperately reached for the laptops to pull out the batteries and force them to shut off. Before they could, however, the computers became silent. One second later, a skull with two swords crossed behind it appeared on each of the screens. Tom and Katie looked on in terror as the following words appeared in black font on each screen below the skulls: "You have been caught trespassing on a private computer. The owners have been notified and you are now one step closer to death. They are coming for you and there is nowhere you can run. There is nowhere you can hide from them. You should have stayed at the house!"

Both Tom and Katie began hyperventilating and choking on fear. They were caught somewhere between having an adrenaline boost to sprint a mile and paralysis. Doom was closing in on them and, as their minds started spinning out a series of horrific scenarios, the skulls animatedly opened their mouths and began laughing. The computer volumes again sounded as if they were at the maximum levels and, this time, Tom and Katie managed to take out the batteries to shut off the shrieking computers.

Tom, picturing someone running into the garage, turning the lights out, and chloroforming them while they were blind in the dark, grabbed Katie by the arm and quickly dragged her out of the truck and out of the garage. He hurried her over to the back wall of Ollie's Garage by the brown door and said "We need to find gas and fill up the car. We have to get the fuck out of here and get help right fucking now!"

Ricky led the caravan of cars and trucks through the moonlight to the Burles' U.P. Organic Tea farm, a name that made him chuckle every time he saw it. Toby didn't want her parents to wake up so she had Ricky lead the caravan to the far left end of the parking lot which was furthest away from her house. Ricky and the others parked and Toby led them into the warehouse building. For being a crop-intensive business, the inside of the warehouse, which served as a drying and sorting facility for the Burles' tea crops, was well-maintained and kept in pristine condition. The Burles were careful to prevent cross-contamination of crops and kept each of the different varieties of crops in separate bins. Even the tea mixes using multiple different crops were kept in the back of the facility in separate and conspicuously-marked bins to ensure that the teas were correctly packaged and sold. Perhaps most impressive was the fact that, despite all of the dried and drying crops, the floor appeared immaculately spotless. The Burles had quite the impressive operation.

"My parents would kill me if they knew we were in here right now," Toby said. "Let's wait a few minutes and make sure that the car has left before we go outside and finish."

"Yeah, I'll go stand watch outside," Ricky volunteered.

"Cliff, don't light up in here," Toby shouted. "Put that goddammed joint away or I'll throw you out. You know this is our livelihood."

"Sorry," Cliff said apologetically. He was too drunk and high to muster anything else at the moment but, growing up in McIntosh, he knew what Toby meant and that she was right.

Ricky stepped outside and was followed by Jennifer, Patrick, Tammy, and Michael. They looked around in the moonlight but couldn't see anything other than the farm and the dark silhouettes coming from the faint light from the streetlamps at the McIntosh crossroads. They didn't hear anything other than leaves rustling in the occasional breeze.

"It's always so beautiful up here," Tammy said to the group. "Without the light pollution you can see thousands of stars."

"Yeah. And maybe the Northern Lights will come out," Michael said hopefully.

"It's wrong," Ricky said in all seriousness staring off into the distance. "This is wrong. Something's not right here."

"Oh my god, you're right!" Jennifer exclaimed in alarm. Despite her not-so-secret crush on Ricky, Jennifer was not agreeing with him to gain his favor. She knew exactly what he was thinking and she started getting nervous.

"What do you mean? What's going on?" Tammy asked.

"It's not what's going on. It's what isn't going on that's wrong," Ricky cryptically responded.

"And what's that? Or isn't that" Tammy asked impatiently.

"There's no sound. No crickets, no bugs, no wolf or coyote howls, no owls, no frogs, no nothing," Ricky said.

"I've never heard it this quiet," Jennifer added. "Especially under a bright moon. Not ever."

"Maybe there's some bears out nearby," Patrick said venturing an explanation.

From far away out in the fields, the group heard a rustling that, at first, sounded like a stronger breeze blowing through the plants. The rustling, however, didn't stop and seemed to be getting louder and coming from multiple directions with each passing second.

"Get inside right now!" Ricky ordered.

The group ran into the sorting building and Ricky locked and bolted the door behind them. "Lock and bolt the back door right now Toby!" he called across to her.

"What's going on?" she asked.

"Just do it! There's things out there!"

Toby ran to the back door and quickly turned the lock and bolted it. As Toby was locking the door, Ricky flicked on the lights.

"What're you doing, Ricky?" Cliff asked.

"There's things out there, man. It was dead silent. I mean dead silent. No animals. No nothing. And then all of a sudden we heard rustling coming from everywhere getting closer."

"We have to call for help then. Just in case," Toby had never known Ricky to panic. He was always the hard worker and voice of reason. Seeing Ricky this way was a first for her and she was growing from scared to terrified as Ricky's alert level was on the rise.

"Definitely," Ricky responded. "Good idea. Jennifer, call the Chief's office."

"What if it was nothing?" Jennifer asked.

"It doesn't matter. We can't fuck around with what we just heard. Call now please. Toby, call your folks and I'll call mine. Cliff, if you can pull it together, call your parents."

The teens pulled out their phones.

"What the fuck!" Ricky shouted. His phone was dead even though he knew it was almost fully charged.

"My phone's dead!" Toby called out in a panic.

"Mine too!" Jennifer said trembling.

The other kids pulled out their phones and each phone was dead. All of them shared the information and then started loudly asking in their confusion what they needed to do next even though no one really had any ideas.

Suddenly, the phones all turned on and vibrated loudly in their hands. The screens then simultaneously flashed bright red as the phones rang out in the sound of an alarm at the highest volume. Shrieks started emanating from the group and, a few second later, a skull with cross-swords behind it outlined in black appeared in the middle of their screens. Amidst the new shrieks and cries and "what the fucks?" from around the room, the skull's jaws became animated and began a ferocious high-pitched laughing.

Tom fumbled through the keys on the key ring separating out the three keys that he had already used – the Stantons' house, the Stantons' car, and Ollie's back garage. His hands were trembling making the task all the more difficult. He took a deep breath and managed a firm grip on the fourth key and put it in the door lock. Again, luck with the keys was on the Prestons' side as the doorknob unlocked. Tom then quickly removed the key and inserted it into the bolt lock and unlocked that as well. He then pulled the door open and quickly hopped inside with Katie. The interior section where they were had no windows and the room was pitch black.

"What do we do? Can we afford to turn on lights?" Katie asked in a voice dripping with palpable fear.

"We have no choice. My hand is on the light switch. As soon as I turn on the lights, just stay by me and we'll figure it out."

Without hesitating, Tom flicked on the lights illuminating the interior of Ollie's Garage. He and Katie glanced around frantically and surveyed the interior for Ollie or signs of anyone else. Fortunately, there were none, at least for the time being. Looking over to their left, Tom saw Ollie's tow truck parked in the far garage space next to the exterior wall. To its right and practically in front of them, their SUV was parked in the first garage space next to the office area.

Despite her overwhelming fear, Katie immediately ran over to the windows when she saw blinds hanging over them and pulled them down to block out most of the light being emitted by the interior lights. While Katie was doing that, Tom noticed a black car cover along the back wall as well as a tool box. He grabbed the car cover along with two flathead screwdrivers and a hammer from the tool box and ran over to the front door which was all glass and not covered by anything. Quickly, Tom slid one of the waiting area chairs under the door and then, raising the car cover to the drywall above the door, he hammered the first screwdriver through the car cover above the left side of the door. He then did the same above the right side. The hammering made some slight noise but it was not nearly as concerning as the people closing in on them any moment. At least for the moment, most of the light inside the garage had been blocked from shining outside.

"Good thinking," Tom said encouragingly.

"We're still a good team," Katie said.

They exchanged brief looks of admiration and then returned to the garage area.

In between the office area and the garage space where their SUV was parked, there was a wall that went halfway between the side of the garage door and the garage's back wall as a sort of mini-divider. Five large shelves were spaced above and along the wall in one stack of two and one stack of three. Below them, a desk was pressed up against the wall. There was a large hard drive in the chair space below the desk, and the desk itself had two large computer monitors hooked up to the hard drive along with a keyboard and wireless mouse. The shelves held what appeared to be some sound equipment, headphones, a few small devices that appeared to be microphones, and several mini video recording devices attached to wires that looked like they were used for surveillance.

"No time to check the computer and we won't know the password," Katie said rhetorically.

"Yeah, let's just see if we can find our keys and start the car."

"You go do that. I have another idea." Katie saw the look of concern in Tom's eyes. "Don't worry, I'm staying here," she said reassuringly. As Tom turned to look for their car keys, Katie rain over to the computer equipment. Her idea was *they can't get to us with this equipment if they don't have any power.* Moving quickly, Katie began removing the laptop batteries as well as all of the power cords for the hard drives, monitors, and other electronic devices. Of course, Katie also realized that the computer equipment in the old brown big rig was still operational but it was too late to go back and get it. Besides, she still held out hope that taking the power out of this computer equipment might prevent the evil people from tracking their SUV.

In his periphery, Tom watched Katie go to work as he opened his driver's side door and looked for his keys. They were not on his seat but, fortunately, they were folded in above the car visor. Katie was still working on the power cords which raised the idea in Tom's mind that the Manchineelians might be tracking them. He quickly exited the SUV and grabbed a phillips head screwdriver and a thick flathead screwdriver which he used to remove the vehicle's navigation and control system. He then quickly popped the hood and looked for anything blinking or that looked like a tracking device. He did not see anything unusual and knew there was no time to waste so he shut the hood, cringing at the sound which was louder than he anticipated. He then slid under the car and did a brief check for blinking or anything unusual and, again, saw nothing in the few seconds he looked. He then sprung up and saw Katie approaching with the batteries and cords in her hands. He opened the back door and she threw them in and then ran around Tom to open the shotgun door and get in her seat.

Tom took his seat and inserted the key into the ignition switch. He pleadingly uttered the words "Please God," and turned the key while clenching his eyes shut. The sound of the engine purring to life brought a huge breath and sigh of relief from deep within his lungs. As he then put his hands on the gear shift to put the SUV in reverse, he realized that the garage door was still shut. He jumped out and ran to the garage door looking around frantically until he saw the door button which, immediately as he pushed it down, caused the door to lift up. The noise resonated throughout the garage and sent Tom to his seat even faster than he imagined he could move. He put the car in reverse before even securing his door and didn't buckle his seat belt until he had cleared the garage, put it in drive, and remembered to turn off his headlights. A quick look at the dashboard reminded him to check the gas tank. Fortunately, it was almost three-quarters full. That would be enough to get them pretty much anywhere with an open police station.

"Should we try that back route behind the second garage since those Manchineel fucks will probably be along the other road? Although they could be anywhere."

"Yeah. Let's try that back route since we know they will come from the other route no matter what."

Tom took the back route and they were on their way into yet another great unknown.

Life in McIntosh had been the most peaceful existence that Sophie and Jim Burle had ever known or could have ever imagined. It was the perfect place to raise their daughter Toby among a true community of neighbors. In fifteen years of living in McIntosh, they had never locked their doors or worried about strangers. In fact, they made it a point never to lock their doors in homage to the sanctity of their peaceful home.

Watching Toby mature into a young woman, they trusted her to make good decisions based on the values and morals with which they raised her. They also knew that, like all teens and young adults, she was going to party with her friends. Heck, they spent their teen and young adult years smoking pot and drinking with their friends – they still indulged as adults, – so they were fully aware of what Toby and her friends were probably going to be up to before they headed upstairs and went to bed. Saturday nights were always great nights because Sundays allowed them some extra sleep and unwinding from the long week behind and the long week ahead on the farm.

At no time did Sophie or Jim hear their front door open and, if they had, they would have assumed that it was Toby. At no time did they hear any of the footsteps walking up their stairs or entering their bedroom. In an instant, they each simultaneously felt strong hands grabbing them around their chins and the backs of their necks. They had no time to move, panic, scream, or even think as their necks were broken with forceful and vicious flicks of their chins to the side just past their shoulders.

The skull's laughing stopped and the seventeen cellphones began to vibrate again. This time, however, the vibrating rang out like a rhythmic alarm: *beep – beep – be – be – beep*. It repeated several times, *beep – beep – be – be – beep*. After several iterations, words hissed out at full volume chanting in rhythm to the vibrations: *"you're – all – go-nna – die, you're – all – go-nna – die, you're – all – go-nna – die."*

Holding their cellphones in terror-stricken disbelief, the seventeen kids frantically looked around at each other as if begging someone to come forward and declare that the whole thing was a nasty prank. At the very least, they were hoping that someone, Ricky or Patrick in particular, would take command and lead them out of whatever fucking dread was descending upon them. The group, which had been full of stories, laughter, desires, weed, and beer not thirty minutes earlier, was reduced to a bunch of petrified mannequins panting and whimpering.

*You're – all – go-nna – die. You're – all – go-nna – die.*

Outside, the sound of rustling in the nearby crops grew louder and louder by the second. Whoever was out there was coming right for the sorting building. By the sounds of the rustling, it would be thirty seconds at most before the rustling would stop because the crop fields ended about thirty yards from the building. At that point, it would take only a few seconds for whoever was out there to reach the building. Storm doors and stormproof windows were all that stood between the young adults and their threatened deaths.

*You're – all – go-nna – die. You're – all – go-nna – die.*

Snapping out of his frightened trance, Ricky ran over to Toby and placed himself between her and the nearest window. The others naturally moved towards them to form a large cluster. The middle of the sorting room was lined with tables where individual crops had been separated or, in some cases grouped, according to the flavor of tea being canned. Cyndi, Maya, Stephen and Vic had already made their way in between the tables and were hunching over ready to dive for cover. Patrick, Tammy, Fabian, Michael, and R.J. had been carrying pocket knives that they had used in the fields earlier that day. They held them up in front of their bodies towards nothing in particular hoping that the knives might ward off whatever it was that was coming for them even though the short blades looked like splinters of futility in the horror of the moment.

*You're – all – go-nna – die. You're – all – go-nna – die.*

In desperation, Ricky ran over to the nearest wall and lunged for a walking stick that Toby's father occasionally used while hiking around the farm. It was leaning against the wall along with Toby's mother's hiking stick which Ricky grabbed and tossed over to Toby before returning to where she was standing.

*You're – all – go-nna – die. You're – all – go-nna – die.*

"Grab anything you can use to defend

yourselves!" Ricky ordered the group.

Being among those who didn't have pocket knives on them, Cliff, Marcus, Jennifer, Michael and Rachel managed to grab scissors, hand shovels, and two pairs of hedge-clippers, but that was the extent of usable objects in the building for self-defense.

"Oh shit, man, this is real," Cliff muttered in disbelief, his whole body shaking as his left foot slipped on the little yellow puddle of urine that he had made on the floor through his soaking wet jeans and shoes.

"Right about now I wish we had a cattle farm so that we had better tools to defend ourselves," Toby almost cried to Ricky.

"I think this is about to become a slaughterhouse," Ricky said boldly.

A few of the teens reacted courageously with "damn rights" and "we'll show 'ems." Toby, however, knew Ricky. He was deflecting his true feelings and fear of how the night was going to end for them, not the intruders.

*You're – all – go-nna – die. You're – all – go-nna – die.*

The rustling outside in the crops transformed in an instant to the sound of dozens of footsteps crunching on the limestone-covered ground around the building and heading directly towards them. With the lights on in the building for their own safety in case anyone or anything got inside, the kids were blind to who was charging them. But they all knew above their pounding heartbeats, welling tears, and panicked breathing that they were about to find out.

The six windows that spanned along opposite walls of the building, three on each side, shattered inward from the force of softball-sized steel balls. At least two of the balls had lighted wicks emitting smoke as they crashed through the windows and landed on the floor. One of the balls came in at an angle striking Patrick in the head with a sickening thump. His body collapsed to the floor following the force of the metal ball where a dent around his right temple and ear had caved in the side of his head. The area around the dent was a sickly dark-bluish gray color amidst blood pouring out from his ear-hole, nostrils and mouth. His right eye had been pooped out of the socket and was dangling down by the attached nerves onto the floor where it slowly danced in the growing pool of blood.

Glancing over at Patrick's lifeless body, the kids got their first glimpse of a murder victim, and a most grotesque one at that. Shrieks and screams filled the room as R.J. gagged and ran over to his fallen brother. Most of the others collapsed to the floor begging in tears for their parents or offering surrender.

Ricky held firm with Toby behind him. The rustling and the footsteps had come so fast. Whoever was coming to kill them should have broken into the building by now. The thought struck him: *They're still messing with us. The cellphones weren't enough. They wanted us to see Patrick dead on the ground and break our will to defend ourselves even more. Soften us up more. Another second and we won't even be able to see them through the smoke.*

Without hesitating, Ricky ran over to the nearest window and raised his walking stick at the ready-to-swing position like a baseball batter ready to swing at an incoming pitch. As soon as he heard something near the window, he swung the stick at full force and connected with the upper torso area of a hooded figure clad in a black robe as the intruder was jumping through the shattered window. The figure let out a hiss of air and pain while the walking stick's momentum pushed it back through the window frame where it fell to the ground outside the building.

From his periphery, Ricky could tell that no one else had reacted the way that he had as hooded and black-robed figures jumped through the other five windows. They all seemed to be wearing masks that looked like they had protruding snouts, perhaps like the skulls of a dinosaur or small alligator. The smoke was filling the room and visibility was rapidly disappearing. Hearing two loud bangs coming from opposite ends of the building, Ricky knew that the intruders had also just broken down the doors.

If there was any chance for him and Toby, it was through the window. He looked at her and pointed his head at the window. She nodded her understanding and, without hesitating, he jumped through the window with his walking stick out in front. Toby, with the smoke closing in around her and deafened by the surrounding screams, jumped through the window and tripped into the ground as she landed awkwardly on top of her mother's walking stick which pressed into her wrist and ribs. It hurt her a great deal but there was no time for her pain. She knew that they had to run away as fast as they could.

Rolling over and using her non-injured hand to help her get to her knees, Toby's eyes bulged as she began to gag and hyperventilate. The intruders had copied Ricky's strategy. The intruder that had been struck by Ricky was standing hunched over near the window frame panting and coughing with his hands on his knees above his long black robe which bore some tatters along the left shoulder and side marking where the man had hit the ground after being struck by the walking stick. A second intruder had been waiting outside either to stand guard or jump through the window after the first intruder. Apparently, after watching Ricky connect with his accomplice, he had waited for Ricky to jump out of the building and run away. There was no further investigation that

Toby needed to form or confirm this conclusion. Ricky was slumped over on his knees in between the two intruders with a large knife that looked like some kind of dagger protruding from his stomach. Ricky's eyes were drooped in defeat. He had no energy left and no ability to protect Toby. Even worse, he had no hope for either of them.

"P- p- p- lee -ees," he began, panting heavily with his last breaths pleading weakly to at least protect Toby, "l- l- l- ee- v- h- er 'lone."

From inside the sorting building, Ricky and Toby heard the bloodcurdling screams of their friends. Smoke was exiting from the empty window frames and nothing inside could be seen except for the shadowy movements of the intruders. As the seconds passed, the teens' dying shrieks and gags grew softer until there was nothing left but an eerie dead silence.

Toby cast a longing last look at Ricky. He gave her a meek smile and tried to pucker his mouth as if to blow her one last kiss. When the first intruder finally walked over to him with his dagger in position, Ricky glanced up at his assailant and Toby noticed the unbridled fear in Ricky's eyes as his mouth opened wide in fright. Toby then instinctively looked up at the second intruder and she immediately noticed what caught Ricky's attention. Fortunately, their confusion and horror had acted like anesthesia. Neither of them felt much pain when the intruders' twin daggers fatally plunged through their necks.

# ESCAPE

## *Chapter Sixteen*

The Prestons' frantic drive out of McIntosh had the added fret of using the moonlight to navigate a road that was little more than a poorly paved trail bordered by dense brush and trees. Tom found himself reaching for his headlights at least a dozen times after near collisions with trees and definite collisions with some bushes and a few baby trees that undoubtedly must have left dents along the front bumper and sides of the SUV. Each time that happened, Tom reminded himself to slow down because the noise might alert the Manchineel crazies and the headlights would certainly pinpoint their location.

"What time is it?" he asked Katie.

"Just past 3:30."

"Have you noticed anyone following or anything like that?"

"No, but we have to keep the headlights off. Just go slow." On any other day, Tom would have thought this was just the usual kind of patronizing that he would get from Katie about how to do everything that he did and that he was obligated to do for the family which drove him crazy (and it was even worse when Katie's mother did it). In fact, it had recently become a hot-button issue for them to start fighting. In this instance, however, he knew that Katie's words were said soothingly to comfort him and, on some level, herself as well.

Leaving McIntosh felt like retreat. They were supposed to find the clues and help that they needed in McIntosh and, yet, they had found only a handful of clues with no signs whatsoever of where their children were taken or where they were at the present. Furthermore, they had not found any help whatsoever in McIntosh. Their lone accomplishments of finding the truck, garage, photos, and videos of their children, along with getting their SUV back and stealing some power cords, added up to jack squat. They had nothing. They were losing and now they were retreating which affronted every fiber of Tom's competitive nature.

Minutes later, Tom felt the heaviness of his need to sleep weighing on his eyelids. He started blinking slowly and heavily and, as the SUV swerved into another bush, a much bigger bush than the previous ones, Katie loudly said "Tom, let me drive."

"Okay. That's probably a good idea."

Tom started to slow the SUV to park it and switch places when he noticed a large clearing about fifty yards ahead with what seemed like an intersecting road.

"Wait a second," he said "is that a road up there?"

Katie looked ahead and said "it's definitely a road. A used road. I can see the yellow lines running along the middle."

Tom gently pressed the accelerator and crept up towards the road. He wanted to get his bearings while making sure that there was no one and no cars around from Manchineel. About twenty yards from the road, the SUV was into the cleared area enough that Tom could get a panoramic view of the night sky which, fortunately for them, was still not cloudy. Tom opened the sunroof and popped his head out. Katie leaned in towards him and asked what he was doing.

"I figure that the nearest big city is probably Marquette. Based on where I think Manchineel and McIntosh are, it is probably northwest from here. So I'm trying to find the North Star."

"How do you do that?"

"My dad taught me. He always used to drill it in my head on hikes growing up: 'Find Polaris Tommy,'" he said in a low-toned voice mimicking his father's. "You know the Big Dipper, right?"

"Of course I do."

"Alright. There it is up over there where I'm pointing. Do you see it?"

"Oh yeah. It's surreal. I haven't really bothered to look at it over the years and yet now we need it and it is still beautiful."

"Yeah, we should write a book called 'Our Surreal Nightmare' when we get out of this with our children. And we will get out of this with our children." He and Katie then exchanged a long deep stare into each other's eyes. They needed that moment of pseudo-levity. That was one part of their relationship that truly made them strong together, their shared characteristic of easing the tension from life's surreal union of horror and beauty with a joke or sarcasm. They had even once written a poem together in college about how life is a surreal mirror reflecting love, good, beauty, horror, and evil and how people never know which side anyone or anything is ever truly on as the mirror spins through space.

"Anyway," Tom said snapping back to attention, "look at the two stars at the bottom of the Big Dipper forming the far bottom and top end of the spoon. Make a line from those two stars and it points to the North Star. There it is. Do you see it?"

"I see it," Katie exclaimed with some genuine excitement. She then lowered her head downward upset with herself. Tom knew why.

"Don't feel guilty. Neither of us is excited or having fun without our babies. We're fighting Katie," he finished as he gave her a comforting wink. She kissed his hand in gratitude as he leaned back into his seat and buckled up.

"That way's north and the road seems to be north-southish so we're going north."

Tom pressed the accelerator and turned north as their path intersected with the new road. He sped up to about 40 miles-per-hour which was as fast as he felt comfortable driving without his headlights using only the moonlight and North Star as his guides for fear that a car of unfriendlies might be in the area or drive by at some point. The new road and North Star break had given him a second wind.

Dozens of thoughts danced in his head and he needed to process them. Maybe they held more clues for the whereabouts of his children. Maybe they were somehow connected. Maybe they were merely mental gibberish. But they needed to be processed. It was how Tom functioned and, after the last nearly 48 hours since they woke up for their family retreat up north, Tom needed this exercise.

"Katie, we've got to start putting this case together so we can try to figure out why the children were taken and that might help us find them," he said with his newfound energy.

"It's not a *case* Tom," Katie said annoyed. Katie's demeanor had instantly changed from caring and hopeful to distant and irritable. Despite the moment of levity that she and Tom had just shared, the fatigue and stress now seemed to be wearing on her and she was losing her energy and patience.

"I know. I didn't mean a *law* case. I meant a mystery case that needs to be solved. The only way we're going to have any chance at solving it is if we hash everything out. Maybe we'll come up with some ideas."

"Oh, that makes sense. Alright then." Tom heard the patronizing and sarcastic tone in her voice. *Here it comes*, he thought. "Well, let's see Tom, we were on the family trip from hell when our car broke the fuck down. We were taken to an old town no one's ever heard of called Manchineel with a creepy reverend and two psychotic deacons, one of whom is our jailer. For that matter, the whole fucking town is full of our jailers. They stole our children, pretended it never happened, and then basically tortured us while killing the only two decent people in that God-forsaken town who tried to help us. Oh yeah, and then we had to sneak out and see a video of our children being kidnapped after which a hacker threatened to murder us after we discovered that he was the one who hacked into our car and shut it down. How was that Tom? Did that hash everything out for you Tom? Is it all a neatly packaged case for you to present to the judge and jury Tom!"

Tom's blood was starting to boil as it always did when Katie added to his daily stress and pressure with her inability to not drag him into every single one of her daily events and feelings. This time was particularly egregious because he was with her every step of the way, physically and emotionally, and none of this was his fault yet she felt that venting her frustration on him was somehow an appropriate action to take either to make herself feel better or put the blame squarely on his shoulders. Gripping the steering wheel tighter than ever, he prepared to lash out at her when thoughts started jelling in his mind.

"Wait a minute. What about the Garden of Eden?"

"Now you're going to fucking patronize *me* Tom!"

"Shut the fuck up Katie! Listen up for once instead of always making me have to live and feel everything inside of you! For once in your life be stoic and keep it to yourself and stop putting your shit on me, especially because you don't fucking ever listen to what I have to say. And I have something important to go over with you. Can you calm down now so that we can talk about this?" he asked lightening up on his tone.

"Fine. Go ahead," she said unremorsefully.

"When we arrived in Manchineel, it looked like the Garden of Eden. That's what Tommy called it and spoke about with the Reverend."

"Yeah. So?"

"How many animals have you seen up here?" Tom paused as he waited to see if Katie would start to grasp what he was wondering about. She seemed to be thinking about something although she seemed unimpressed so Tom continued. "We're in the middle of the Upper Peninsula, the hotbed of wildlife in the Great Lakes State. We were in the most beautiful town imaginable full of exquisite flora and fauna, and I haven't seen one damn animal. No deer, no moose, no raccoons, no porcupines, no squirrels, no chipmunks, no bears. Hell, I haven't even seen so much as an ant or a ladybug. Have you?"

As if sprung awake, Katie suddenly looked over at Tom and placed her left hand over her mouth as she gasped. "Oh my God, you're right! That whole town is covered in beautiful trees, bushes, flowers, and not one animal. I haven't even seen any birds, let alone heard any chirping. If any one of those houses was ours, we'd have dozens of animals and birds around it."

"Yeah. I didn't even think about that, but you're right. No birds. No animal sounds of any kinds. We didn't even hear crickets chirping at night."

"What do you think that means?"

"No idea yet. Let's just keep going and see what comes up from everything."

"Okay. That makes sense. What else is on

your mind?"

"Well, the Reverend told us that Manchineel was founded in 1674, right?"

"Right. I definitely remember him saying that."

"When we drove into McIntosh, I saw an old cemetery out in the distance."

"And?" Katie was starting to use her irritable tone again.

"According to the Reverend, Manchineel is older than the United States. It's over 340 years old. Did you see a cemetery in Manchineel?"

Katie took a deep breath and a brief pause. She turned to Tom and put her hand firmly on his chest, "I'm so sorry, honey. This is getting to me. I know it's the same with you and I shouldn't always force my feelings and everything on you. It's just my way. I see what you were getting at before. I'm sorry."

He picked her hand up and kissed it. "Apology accepted."

"So, what do you think? Everyone in Manchineel looks relatively young. Is it really an old town?"

"I don't know anything one way or the other. But we have to keep looking at the pieces to solve this puzzle. No animals. No cemetery. No known age of the town."

"They have that once-beautiful but now creepy Sacrarium, as they call it, above the lake.

And they are going to have a service there tomorrow – I mean technically later this Sunday morning – in honor of the Grand Jubilee, right?"

"That's right."

"And, in addition to our three missing children, we can report to the police that they murdered two of their fellow townsfolk, a husband and wife, whose supposed sin was trying to do the right thing and help us find our children."

"Damn right." With that, Tom felt more comfortable on the road. Despite its many hills, Tom had grown used to its rhythm of ups and downs and slight bends. He pushed down harder on the accelerator to get to the police in Marquette as soon as possible.

"Anything else you can think of?" Katie asked now understanding the usefulness of Tom's method of hashing out details and facts.

"I feel like we've seen some things that we're just not putting together. I mean, it just feels in my gut like we've already seen what we needed to see in order to figure out what is really going on."

"What if maybe we're overthinking this and we're just in some child-trafficking ring of the north." Katie paused and then busted out into tears. "I can't believe I just said that."

Her words pained Tom too and cast doubt on everything he had been contemplating and hoping would come to fruition. The odds were that Katie might be right and their 48-hour window to locate their children was closing fast. Tom began to tear up as he pressed down harder on the accelerator. "That might be. We can hash things out all night, but it's all futile unless we can get to the police right away. What time is it?"

"About 4:15."

"So we've been driving about 45 minutes from McIntosh. We should be getting close to something soon."

Speeding along the northbound road, Tom heard the wind begin to pick up. He looked up at the sky to see if there were any clouds but it was all clear. Just a sparkling pre-summer sky unblemished by light pollution which, on any other night, might seem beautiful beyond imagination. Tonight, they merely accentuated the hopelessness of finding the children among an infinite sea of possibilities, any one of which could be a starting point, dead end, or no point at all. The wind picked up some more and Tom again looked up to see whether any clouds were overhead. No clouds appeared but another loud gust of wind picked up.

"You hear that wind Katie? It sounds like it might start to rain."

Just then, red and blue lights flashed behind their car as headlights, on bright, flicked on. The police cruiser behind them had been the wind sound as it had sped up to them from behind in the dark with its lights off until it was a car-length away. The cruiser then sped past them to a distance of about fifty yards and did a hard spin forcing Tom to slam on his breaks as the cruiser came to a complete stop in a diagonal position facing the Preston's SUV on the road. The deputy inside the cruiser ran out pointing his shotgun directly at Tom's windshield yelling "Get out! Get the fuck out right now! Get the fuck out you monsters!"

Tom and Katie instinctively held up their hands while they slowly opened their doors and exited. As frightening as the scene was, they welcomed the law and the chance that the help they were seeking had arrived.

"Officer please, we need your help," Katie started.

"Do not say another word ma'am," came the hostile response.

"Please officer, our children were kidnapped and two people were murdered," Tom tried to get his attention and show that they were the ones in need of help.

"You need to shut your mouth right now. You're in a stolen vehicle with the lights off fleeing a murder scene!"

"Please officer, you must understand sir. This is our car. Our children were kidnapped and we were heading to Marquette to get help and find them. We were trapped in Manchineel and we escaped to McIntosh but the people who helped us were murdered by the people in Manchineel."

The officer took a long hard look at Tom and Katie after that. He then paced over to them still clutching his shotgun tightly and pointing it back and forth between them in deliberate spurts. Tom was able to glimpse the officer's silver nametag which had "DEP. MAYBIN" engraved in black. Tom guessed that Deputy Maybin was either attached to the county sheriff or one of the local towns.

"What drugs are you on folks?" Deputy Maybin sternly asked.

"None sir," they both replied.

"This vehicle is registered to one Oliver Gustafson, a resident of McIntosh and a friend of mine. He just purchased it and showed it to me yesterday morning. If you were in Manchineel then you would have passed my police station on this road and yet you never stopped there seeking any help. And the only murders are the nineteen folks in McIntosh – my neighbors! Kids! Kids for Christ's sake! Including my kin – all here in McIntosh." Deputy Maybin tried to continue before his emotions overcame him. He quickly wiped his eyes with his right shirtsleeve while pointing his gun in the Prestons' direction with his finger moving close to the trigger. "Now both of you get on the ground and put your hands behind your backs or I'll let my emotions take over!"

Tom and Katie saw how unstable the deputy was becoming. At the same time, the deputy shouting that kids had been murdered sent chills throughout their bodies.

"Kids were murdered, officer?" Tom asked choking up.

"Shut up!" Deputy Maybin shot back before stumbling on whatever other words he was trying to spit at Tom. He was too choked-up to articulate anything else.

"Officer, please, our kids were taken. We don't know what happened to them." Katie was in tears and just broke down crying after managing to get the words out.

Fortunately for the Prestons, Deputy Maybin saw that they genuinely appeared to be terrified and shaken-up. He slowed down his breathing and was able to control himself as he lowered his shotgun. "Nineteen kids aged seventeen to twenty-one were just murdered in McIntosh, my hometown. One of them was my cousin Cliff," he said while tears flowed down his right cheek.

Even more fortunate for the Prestons was the fact that Deputy Maybin couldn't read their minds at the moment. In horrific irony, all the Prestons could think about was that their children were not among those murdered in McIntosh. That comfort, however, was shallow since the murders did not bode well for their children, especially because Tom and Katie hadn't found them and were now stuck in the middle of a worsening situation where the police officer whom they had been seeking was now walking over to arrest them with his own cousin murdered.

Following a brief pause to wipe his tears, Deputy Maybin cautiously approached the Prestons while reaching for his handcuffs. Tom noticed that he was young, maybe in his mid- to late-twenties with an athletic build and, once the deputy was standing over him, Tom looked away towards the pavement so that the deputy would not think that Tom was staring at him as some form of challenge. Deputy Maybin then quickly reached down and harshly handcuffed Tom's hands tightly behind his back. He then cuffed Katie in the same manner before straightening up and reading the Prestons their *Miranda* rights: "You have the right to remain silent. Anything you say can and will be used against you in a court of law. You have the right to an attorney. If you can't afford an attorney, an attorney will be provided to you at no cost to you. Do you understand your rights as I have stated them?"

"Yes sir," Tom said in an effort to try and start winning the deputy over knowing full well that they would be in his custody for some time.

Deputy Maybin forcefully helped lift Tom and Katie off the ground and escorted them towards his cruiser. He then opened the rear door closest to them and ordered them to get inside.

"Officer, please take my wallet and check

inside for my vehicle registration," Tom pleaded as he stuck his right hand in his right rear pocket and produced his wallet. "You'll see that the vehicle belongs to me. I'll sit locked in here with my wife Katie and you can verify that we're no thieves. Officer, I swear to God I am telling you the truth."

Deputy Maybin studied Tom's mannerisms and eyes and grabbed the wallet out of Tom's hand still afraid that he was in the midst of two crazed strangers who were mass murderers. He flipped through the wallet and found Tom's registration inside one of the inner card pockets. Next, Deputy Maybin motioned for Tom to join Katie in the backseat. He then shut the door and walked over to the SUV pulling a small LED flashlight out of his utility belt. Tom watched as Deputy Maybin shined his flashlight over the SUV's vehicle identification number while cross-referencing it with Tom's State of Michigan registration.

After he was done comparing the vehicle identification number with the registration, the deputy seemed to pause by the SUV for a few seconds. He then briskly walked back to the cruiser and got on his computer. Tom could not see the screen, but he saw the deputy holding his license and automatically assumed that the deputy was checking to see if Tom had a criminal record or warrants out for his arrest. Tom twiddled his fingers behind his back to keep circulation in his hands while listening to the deputy's keystrokes on his computer. Roughly five minutes later, Deputy Maybin gave a deep sigh and hopped out. He then ran around the front of the car and opened the rear door by Katie.

"Ma'am, sir," he began looking at both of them in a mixture of contrition and confusion, "your registration and license both check out. I heard your name Mrs. Preston and didn't need a license to check you out since I had your husband's information to cross-reference. Anyway, as you can tell, it's been an emotional night for me. And I have no idea how Ollie came into possession of this car since the VIN checks out to your registration. Mr. Preston, I saw your State of Michigan Bar Association card in your wallet so I know you understand the law. I have nineteen murder victims, kids working the farms in McIntosh, my cousin Cliff," he then trailed off and covered his face with his right arm for a few seconds before continuing. "You are strangers from Metro Detroit driving up here at 4:15 a.m. You say you came from Manchineel, so how is it that you passed my police station without stopping if your children were kidnapped and two people in Manchineel were murdered as you were telling me in the beginning?"

"We were being held prisoner in Manchineel," Tom began "and a couple told us that we would find help in McIntosh. They secretly gave us the keys to their car and we drove it to

McIntosh. They were murdered for helping us by our captors." Tom paused as he noticed the cynical look in the deputy's eyes. "Look, I know it sounds crazy bu-"

"You're damn right it sounds crazy Mr. Preston. It's 4:15 in the morning. They gave you keys and you drove to McIntosh sometime after midnight? That's what you want me to believe on top of kidnapping murderers?"

Tom closed his eyes for a second to gather himself then straightened up and continued, "We had to leave after midnight because we couldn't escape Manchineel until our captors fell asleep. We got into McIntosh and found that Ollie has a secret truck that he used to hack into our SUV which is how he got our vehicle to shut down and then he towed it to a separate garage behind his garage."

"That big storage building behind his garage where he keeps his fishing boat and snowmobiles?" Deputy Maybin asked incredulously.

"I swear to you there's a big rig in there," Tom replied. "There's computer equipment and a camcorder with our family on it."

"Then how is it that you left McIntosh without passing by my police station?" the deputy asked again trying to investigate and test the veracity of what Tom was telling him.

"There's a secret road behind that separate building that goes out of McIntosh and leads to this road."

"Ollie told me that it was just a shortcut he had paved to get to this main road so he didn't have to keep turning around his fishing boat."

"I promise you, the big rig is there with the equipment. I can show you."

"Well, you're gonna have to. We're heading back to McIntosh because I've got a lot to tend to now. The whole town's going to be buzzing and flustered and scared out of their minds when they wake up. Our police chief should be back at the scene by now along with the State Police. We'll probably have news crews show up at some point as well." He choked up momentarily and rubbed his right arm across his forehead. "My family's gonna have to plan a funera-" he began before choking up and leaning over with his hands on his knees.

"The Chief woke me up screaming frantically into my phone barely more than an hour ago. It's just the two of us up here and we take turns doing a late shift periodically, maybe once or twice a week. It was his turn to do the late shift, and he called screaming about the murder scene. We've never had anything like this happen up here. It's quiet, neighborly. The Chief couldn't make out all the details; he was choking on his words. He told me he had to get our forensics kit back at the station and that he was bringing in the State Police and sent me out here in case the perpetrators were on the road.

"Look, I'm gonna have to keep you in

custody and leave your vehicle here until we get everything sorted out. In the meantime, let me get those cuffs off you so you can be more comfortable and I'll check out your story. If it matches up with what we find at Ollie's, you're free to go. If not, you best hope that you had nothing to do with what happened tonight."

*Of course hotshot cop, always end with a threat. Wait 'til you see Ollie's second garage.*

With that, Deputy Maybin removed the Prestons' handcuffs while keeping them locked in the backseat of his cruiser. He then tore off down the road back to McIntosh which took barely fifteen minutes since he wasn't driving without headlights and hadn't taken Ollie's secret detour. Also, being a cop had its perks like driving without a speed limit and a state-of-the-art grille guard to protect against deer which posed the only real potential threat on the empty road.

When Deputy Maybin pulled into McIntosh, they didn't see any police vehicles or sirens. Just the same four street lamps and nothing else.

"Huh? That's odd. The Chief told me he'd be back here by now with a State Police unit to seal off and search the town, and tracking dogs." He grabbed his walkie talkie off his shoulder strap, "Chief, where'r you at, sir?"

"I'm still at the station talking with the State Police," came the response through some white noise. “It’s taking a while to get the dogs up here and all of their unit together. None of us have ever dealt with anything like this. I should be ready to leave in about fifteen minutes. The State Police are about a half-hour away.”

“Roger. I’ll meet you in town,” the deputy responded.

“Officer, would you mind if we could show you Ollie’s second garage real quick,” Katie pleaded.

“Yeah, I said I would look and check out your story. You’re one-for-one so far. It better be two-for-two when we get in there.”

“It will be,” Katie assured.

The deputy carefully climbed out of the cruiser and opened the back door by Katie to let the Prestons out.

“I’ve got keys,” Tom volunteered.

“You stole them or received them from the couple that you said helped you?” Deputy Maybin asked now suddenly on high alert.

“The couple,” Tom replied quickly. “I didn’t steal anything.”

“I’ll tell you what,” Deputy Maybin bluntly instructed Tom, “walk up ahead, open the door and turn on the lights. If the truck is not in there, just the fishing boat and snowmobiles that I’ve seen, you’re going straight to my jail. Got it?”

“Yes sir.”

Tom shuffled over to the door with the

keys and fumbled around with them until he found the right one. Deputy Maybin approached him with Katie as Tom opened the door. Tom felt around the wall inside briefly trying to locate the light switch and then flicked the lights on. After everything they had been through, he was practically expecting for the big rig to have vanished. But, sure enough, the big rig was still in position taking up the garage space. Tom and Katie both breathed sighs of relief.

"Well I'll be eating crow for breakfast," Deputy Maybin said confounded. "I've never seen this before. This is the freakiest-looking truck I've ever seen in my life. Let's see about that equipment inside now."

One by one, the three of them climbed into the cabin and, yet again, Tom and Katie breathed another round of relief sighs staring at the computers, camcorder, and camera which were exactly where they'd left them. Katie reached for the camcorder and held it up for the deputy to inspect. She turned it on and played the video of the children being taken. The deputy rubbed his head in bewilderment as the night was getting more complex by the minute.

"Those are your children, Mrs. Preston?"

"They are," Katie said choking up. After everything that she had been through, it felt as if her throat was swollen to the point of almost being sealed.

Tom leaned over to the deputy holding

the digital camera screen up and showing the deputy the pictures that had been taken of their family. "See Officer, this is all of us together. They hacked into our phones and erased everything but they stalked and targeted our family. It's all on their own equipment. You see? I swear to God we were telling you the truth the whole time. Do you believe us now? Do you see?"

Deputy Maybin humbly nodded in concerned understanding and then reached up to his shoulder and grabbed his walkie talkie. "Chief, we've got a new situation here. Amber alert. Repeat, amber alert. We have three kidnapped children. What are their names?"

"Dawn, Tommy, and Jake," Katie quickly answered.

"Dawn, Tommy, and Jake Preston, Chief. Do you copy? We're going to need more assistance with this investigation at the farm and now this amber alert. I'm currently behind Ollie's garage. Whatever is going on here is now beyond out of control. Please advise, over."

"Over!"

The bedspread in the twin bed loft of the truck suddenly sprung to life. In an instant, what looked like a crumpled blanket, sheet, and pillows came out of its camouflaged state and took the form of a scaly human-like creature, although its eyes seemed almost human. As the creature leaned in towards them with a swinging arm, the scales on its body were changing color to complement the changing background. The arm continued right into the deputy's throat sending blood splatters all over the cabin hitting Tom and Katie as they looked on in shock. The deputy instinctively grabbed the creature's arm but his body quickly went limp. The creature's hand was entirely covered by the deputy's throat and, after a slight pause, retracted with a huge chunk of the deputy's larynx and esophagus in its grasp. Tom could see that its hands had slightly elongated dark nails that came to fine points, almost like claws.

Whether out of hunger or desire to taunt Tom and Katie, the creature raised the deputy's flesh to its mouth and took it all in in one gigantic gulp leaving tracks of blood across its chin and mouth. In taking down the food, it slowly rolled its eyes back as it raised its head to the ceiling. And in that brief second of pause, Tom and Katie both saw their only chance to try and escape.

Putting himself between Katie and the creature, Tom followed Katie out of the truck and slammed the door. They ran out of the garage and into the alleyway between Ollie's Garage. Suddenly, they saw blue and red flickering lights from over by the town's entrance. Without hesitating, they ran towards the lights and, although expected, were grateful to find a police cruiser with a special "Chief" decal on the side. Fortunately, they made sure to run towards the direction that the cruiser was heading so that they would be seen in its headlights.

Inside the cruiser, the police chief spotted them and the blood splatters on their clothes and skin. He grabbed the cruiser's microphone and shouted "Get in!" as he sped up to them and angled the car sideways with the doors unlocked. Tom opened the backseat door for Katie to get in first and he hurried in behind her with a slam of the door.

"Thank you! There's something out there!" Tom half-hollered through the holes in the squad car cage separating the front from the back. "It just got the deputy and then went for us!"

"We have to get out of here now!" Katie joined in the panic.

"I hear you," the Chief said as he swung the car around and headed out of McIntosh. "I take it you're the Prestons that Deputy Maybin just called in about?"

"Yes sir," Tom panted.

"There's a lot more going on here than either of you knows. That's why the State Police team hasn't made it out here yet. I'm gonna get you to safety. Just stay calm, okay? By the way, I'm Chief Tiebolt, and I also serve as the town reeve of McIntosh."

# BLOODY SUNRISE

## *Chapter Seventeen*

As the Chief tore out of McIntosh, Tom and Katie took special notice when he stayed on the road towards Manchineel instead of turning the other way at the fork in the road. Based on what they had learned from the departed Deputy Maybin, the police station was the other way and should have been close by since it had to be somewhere in between the fork and Ollie's secret road.

"Why are you heading towards Manchineel?" Katie uttered with deep concern.

No answer came from the Chief.

"Chief, why are we heading towards Manchineel?" Tom tried.

This time, the Chief responded only it was not a verbal response. He simply held up his right hand to the cage with a clawed index finger slightly extended as if to say 'calm down and be quiet.' The hand was just like the creature in Ollie's truck, gray and scaly and subtly changing tones to camouflage itself amid its surroundings.

Tom and Katie both shouted reflexively. The creature just laughed in hissing spurts. Tom and Katie tried opening their doors but they were locked.

"There's no way to unlock a police car's rear door from the inside," the creature said while continuing its hissing-laugh.

Tom then swiveled his body resting his back on the seat with his legs up in the air. He kicked at the window with all his might. Katie leaned into the back of his neck to brace him so that he could maximize the force of his kicks without the window sliding him backwards along the seats.

"Those are shatter-proof windows," the creature said hiss-laughing even harder. It removed its police hat revealing its scaly head which it scratched with its clawed fingers. "Everyone will be so glad that I found you. They were worried sick when you snuck out. Naughty, naughty. I hope Edward Stanton hasn't found out yet. Have you been in his basement? I wouldn't wish that on anyone."

At that point, Tom sat up in silent defeat and moved over so that he was directly behind the Chief and could avoid the Chief's stares in the rearview mirror. It was just past five o'clock and the moonlight had been replaced by the light of the rising sun although it was still mostly dark outside. Fittingly, the incoming light was a dark red.

In his mind, Tom continued to rehash the night and try to think of things that they should have done differently. He could not think of anything. These creatures, the townsfolk, whatever the link between them, they were always multiple steps ahead of the Prestons. This was their home turf and they knew everything. The Prestons were outsiders and they knew nothing – nothing of their hosts, nothing of what they were facing, and nothing of where their children were or what was happening to them. Tom leaned into the door and wept. He no longer had the ability or desire to look for clues or hash things out. Gazing into the blood-red incoming light, he couldn't help but recall his grandfather, a U.S. Navy veteran, teach him the famous saying "Red sky at night, sailor delight. Red sky in morning, sailor take warning." He also recalled his grandmother, a former Sunday school teacher, telling him that "Hell is the loss of all hope."

Tom went into a catatonic state for a few minutes until the cruiser rounded the bend to the Manchineel entrance. *Home sweet hell.* He looked over at Katie who was also in a catatonic state and had been for quite some time. She looked pale. Her skin appeared dry and her hair seemed frizzed. As strong as Tom's bond was with their children, her deteriorated look reminded him just how strong the maternal bond is between mother and child. And while that might have given him a little bit of a recharge for his paternal instinct to protect his family, he definitively felt in his heart that he had lost.

The squad car pulled up right to the end of the main road where the closest part of the lake was about twenty yards away. Three black-robed and hooded figures stood just past the end of the road waiting for the car. Tom looked over to the center of the squad car's console through the cage to check the time. The clock read 5:20. Outside, the sunrise had proceeded in earnest. The dark red gave way to bright red accentuated by the brightening yellow of the rising sun. Gazing around the car, Tom noticed about another dozen figures wearing black robes with black hoods walking towards the car. One of them seemed to be favoring its ribs as if it had been injured. Tom's heart began racing again and he looked over at Katie. She noticed the closing figures too although she gave no visible signs of worry as if she was resigned to whatever their fate would be.

With the approaching figures at about ten yards away, one of the three figures that had been waiting for the car walked over to the rear door by Katie and opened it. To everyone's surprise, Katie bolted out of the car like a gazelle fleeing a pack of lions. The approaching figures moved to flank Katie and cut her off from everything but the water. Katie didn't flinch and she continued running right towards the lake and into it to avoid them at all costs. Tom got out of the car to watch Katie and one of the hooded figures made sure to put a hand on Tom's shoulder as a warning gesture for Tom to remain where he was.

When Katie's feet hit the water, Tom noticed that something seemed off. The lake was magnificently pristine and blue and yet the splash produced reddish beads of water spraying up. The further into the lake that Katie ran, the more Tom noticed that the splashing water looked red. Eventually, Katie was chest-deep in the lake. Blood-red water was in her hair, dripping from her face, arms, and neck, and stained into her clothes. Katie looked at her hands and used them to scoop up the lake water. It looked like a pool of blood and yet, the rest of the lake had the perfect blue appearance of always. Katie flung the blood-water from her hands and shrieked looking around at the hooded and robed figures standing around the lakeshore gazing at her. Her whole body was shaking. Tom then weighed what might happen to them if he ran to her. Just then, one of the figures walked over to the edge of the lake and removed its hood to reveal the face of Maryanna Forsythe.

"Katie, please come over to me," Maryanna pleaded in a sweet voice. "I promise that no harm will come to you."

"You have my word as well," came a

nearby voice. It was Deacon Forsythe himself walking over to everyone with his hood down.

"No! You're monsters!" Katie shouted back. "I won't go anywhere near you ever again, you fucking monsters!"

Tom glanced around weighing possible courses of action. Unfortunately, there didn't seem to be any and, when the hooded figure holding onto his shoulder noticed what Tom was doing, he gave Tom a deadly stare as if to say "Move and you die." By that point, however, Tom didn't care that much. In fact, that was just one more threat in nearly thirty-six hours of threats. They were backed into a corner without their children so why back down? Maybe the Manchineelians would give something away, or maybe he could piss them off. Just that alone at this point would be one little victory for them and that would be good enough.

"Oh fuck all of you! You already said you were going to kill us! You stole our children! You lied about it! What the fuck is wrong with you! We've had enough you motherfuckers!"

"Tom, is that any way to talk? You were so much better dealing with conflict on Friday."

Those words echoed from the Chief who had just gotten out of his squad car. He walked over to Tom and Tom could see his golden nameplate with the word TIEBOLT etched across the middle. The Chief removed his hat and Tom noticed a necklace protruding from between the buttons on the Chief's shirt revealing a charm of a tree with two circles carved in its trunk. Tom also glanced at the belt buckle containing the same symbol that was visible just beneath the Chief's utility belt.

"It's you? What the fuck is going on here?" Tom was beyond confused as Gerald Tiebolt, owner and operator of the clifftop tourist stop on I-75 was standing before him.

"Tom, I need you and Katie to relax. Your children are nearby. They are safe, for now, but their safety from here on out depends entirely upon you. Katie, did you hear that?"

Katie had stopped flailing in the bleeding water and just stood in place staring at Tiebolt and his cadre of murderous morphing creatures. Tom likewise stood in place staring.

"You must have a lot of questions besides the obvious ones about your children," Tiebolt began. "If you live long enough, you may get the answers. You haven't slept in almost twenty-four hours. You must be exhausted. You're going to go back to the Forsythes to clean yourselves and get some rest. I'm sure the Reverend explained that we have an important service this morning. We'll come retrieve you when we are finished and you will speak with the Reverend."

"We're not going back to the Forsythes'!" Katie yelled in protest.

"What is your other choice?" Tiebolt called smugly back. "You do want to know about your children, don't you?"

"Only a monster would give a fake choice to its victim," Tom said bluntly to let Tiebolt and the others know that he and Katie were not some ignorant fools waiting to be victimized further.

"I won't disagree with you as to the word 'victim,'" Tiebolt retorted heightening Tom's fear level to its maximum. "But the word 'monster' is one of perspective. In war, opposing sides are monsters to each other. To prey, hunters are monsters. We're on former Native American land and, to them, every non-Native American is a monster for stealing their land and acting indifferent to their plight and former existence every time they try to reclaim their land or protect its resources. So don't pretend that the word monster makes a person inherently bad, unless he or she is bad."

"Like kidnapping, murder, false imprisonment," Tom said vengefully.

"I would be very careful treading in your shoes," Tiebolt spat back. "Our courtesy, as you know, only extends to a point, pun intended." With that, Tiebolt let out a hissing laugh of self-amusement before continuing. "I suggest you go back with the Forsythes. I'll accompany you to make sure there are no further issues. That's the only way you can ensure your childrens' safety. Come on now."

Tom slowly walked over to the shoreline

and assisted Katie out of the water. She was dripping wet drenched in blood-water which poured around Tom's hand and shoulder as he helped her up to shore. Their midnight run to McIntosh had ended in mealy defeat as their jailers were taking them back. And, in the cruelest of twists, they were being forced to do whatever their jailers demanded under threat of harm to their children whom they had not seen in over a day – the longest day of their lives and it only looked downhill as the sun rose up towards the trees.

The crowd of robed Manchineelians surrounded the Prestons on their second march of defeat back to the Forsythes' home, and the fourth march to the front door in total. On the way back, Tom grabbed a branch from a trumpet vine that was growing up around a white trellis in the front yard of the Forsythes' neighbors' home. The trumpet vine was among Tom's favorite plants in the world for two reasons. One, the vines grew bright orange-red flowers that were large and protruded like trumpets adding a beautiful ambience to any landscape. Second, the flowers were a favorite of hummingbirds which were Tom's favorite type of bird. About five years earlier, he had planted a trumpet vine in his backyard around a twelve-foot tree stump from a dead tree that he had a crew cut down leaving only the heightened stump. The vine had grown thick around the stump and, at least twice a week, Tom would sit on his deck early in the morning to watch the hummingbirds feed on the flowers' nectar. Occasionally, he would be able to watch the hummingbirds come feed in the late afternoon on a Sunday if they weren't running around like crazy between the childrens' sports teams, family events, or some work that Tom had to catch up on at the office.

In this instance, Tom grabbed a small branch out of curiosity and broke it off from the rest of the plant about six inches from the ground. He lifted the broken end up to his eyes and looked at it briefly. Nothing seemed unusual until he rubbed the broken end across his empty palm. The water that had been traveling through the vine left a bloody red streak across his palm. He raised his hand up to show Katie and then dropped the broken branch on the ground.

"I guess the Garden of Eden is made of blood," Tom said in a sarcastic and accusatory tone.

"The whole world runs on blood and you know that," Tiebolt responded sharply.

*It does, but is it supposed to?*

# A FEAST OF FLESH AND DUST

## *Chapter Eighteen*

The group arrived at the Forsythes' front porch and Maryanna held them there while she went inside to fetch some towels. When she returned, she asked Tom and Katie to remove their stained socks and shoes and wipe themselves down so they wouldn't track blood in her house.

*What fucking nerve. 'Don't track the blood we drew into our house.' How righteous of you to make that request.*

It seemed that Deacon Forsythe was making, or at least forced to make, an effort to appear less intimidating as he held back in the rear of the group allowing Maryanna and Tiebolt to escort the Prestons upstairs yet again. By the time Tom and Katie reached their room, there seemed to be a calmness surrounding them. Maybe everyone was just tired from lack of sleep, but the calm felt foreboding amid an abyss of dead hope.

"You know that our sinks and showers are broken," Maryanna said quietly. "You know to use the water bottles to wash up with. I trust that you will or else someone will be forced to clean you. Understand?"

Tom and Katie nodded half-heartedly as Tom thought *of course your plumbing's broken. It's full of blood water. This whole fucking town is on blood water.*

"Someone will come get you when our service has concluded and you can have your time with the Reverend," Maryanna continued. "I will leave a meal for you on the dining room table. You know where it is and you can have the run of the house. The Reeve will explain everything else while the Deacon and I get ready for the service. As officers of the Sacrarium, it wouldn't do for us of all people to be late. Gerald, can you take care of the rest?"

"Yes, of course I can," the Reeve said escorting Tom and Katie into their room as Maryanna took her leave.

"I thought you were the police chief of McIntosh?" Tom asked.

"I am. I'm also the Reeve of Manchineel. I'm also the Reeve of McIntosh and I work in the county clerk's office and own my own business as you know from your visit. I'm like the eyes, ears, and paperwork of this area."

"You're an intelligence officer," Tom said

shrewdly. "And Ollie is your internet-slash-electronics guy I suppose."

"You continue to reinforce my taking a liking to you Tom. You're a smart man. And, you know, you could have made all kinds of nasty threats to me when the safety rail broke and again for when your son was stung. You could have thrown a fit and you could have asked for a hell of a lot more than the medical expenses, drinks, food, and the souvenirs that I offered. But you didn't. You acted like a gentleman. I mean, I did too, but most people would have flown off the deep end or at least allowed their anger and emotions to make them irrational and vindictive."

"So no good deed goes unpunished by you?" Tom challenged.

"You're right to think that way for now. It'll soon change for you."

"How so? I mean, what is the meaning of all of this and what is going on here?"

"Isn't that what you lawyers would object to as a compound question?" the Reeve said with a laugh. He then gazed and pointed at the ghost story book on the nightstand by Tom's side of the bed. "I see you've been reading the book that I persuaded Dawn to take."

"Why did you do that? Why did you persuade Dawn to take that over everything else in your store?" Katie was now becoming more interested in the conversation.

"I figured it would be fun to see if anyone, Tom in particular with his lawyerly investigative skills, might find the needle-in-a-haystack of a clue. I see that you have been reading the book Tom. Did you find the clue?"

"No, nothing seemed relevant," Tom replied throwing his hands out in front and to his sides.

"Maybe I had you pegged all wrong," the Reeve said tightening up the pleasant expression on his face. "What is it that you looked for before you, shall we say, took a detour to McIntosh?"

"I looked for stories about disappearances."

"That's it? Well, I guess you were pressed for time. What about now, anything stand out to you?"

"Well, our children were stolen from us in the middle of the night and we have been put through a game of your townsfolk pretending that we had no children. We ended up being offered help by Marjorie and Herman Stanton only to end up in torture devices and watch them murdered by your constituents or friends or whatever your relationship is with them. We fled to McIntosh to find help only to find out that Ollie is the one who broke our car down by hacking into its computer system and then a deputy tried to save us while dealing with nineteen murders in McIntosh. He had his throat ripped out and eaten by a snake-like creature that turns humanoid in the daylight and is in fact all of you."

"I ran into that answer with asking an open-ended question to a lawyer," the Reeve snickered. "You've got facts entangled with clues and you left a whole slew of them out. I'll tell you what, it's getting on six a.m. You guys need to wash, rest, and eat. Ollie's got cameras watching every inch of the outside of the house so we'll know it if you leave. And, if you leave just one more time without permission, you will not be seeing your children again I'm afraid to say. So take that warning seriously. We have a rather lengthy service at the Sacrarium but you know that it is not far away at all. We'll come get you later this afternoon." As the Reeve took his leave, he turned to Tom and said "I always liked the story 'The Parchment'" before walking out of the room and closing the door behind him.

Katie refused to be alone in the bathroom without Tom so he sat on the toilet seat cover while she took off her wet and bloodstained clothes and heaped them in a pile in the back of the bathtub. She used two water bottles to rinse her body and another two to rinse her hair. She then quickly rubbed shampoo in her hair and soaped her body before using five more water bottles to rinse off. Katie remained in the bathroom wrapped in a towel while Tom followed suit. He hadn't realized just how much blood sprayed on him from the deputy's neck until he removed his shirt and shorts and piled them on top of Katie's clothes heap. He quickly rinsed off and dried himself before grabbing a towel and heading back to the room with Katie to put on some warm and dry clothes.

Had their vacation gone as planned, they would have been waking up with the children in another hour or two and cooked pancakes on their camping stove in a park overlooking Lake Superior complemented by some fresh cherries or blueberries. Instead, they were each putting on sweatpants, t-shirts, and zip-up sweatshirts preparing to sleep in the fancy dungeon that their hosts and childrens' kidnappers had made for them. They were ravaged with guilt and failure.

Katie laid down on the bed despondent. Tom hoped that she just needed to recharge her batteries but he sensed that she could really be on the verge of being broken. He watched as she fought off sleep and then seemed to be fighting it even as she slipped out of consciousness. He would have been the same way but for the Reeve's parting words. Tom reached over to his nightstand and picked up Dawn's book. He quickly flipped to the table of contents page which listed all of the stories with a one-sentence summary beneath each one. He scrolled down the list until he found the one that the Reeve had referenced.

**The Parchment**
A Native American parchment curses all those who hold it to death.

Tom ignored the story when he was reading through the book and looking for potential leads and clues. It seemed like a typical horror genre: cursed object brings death to all who touch it. That was the furthest thing from what they were dealing with. Maybe the Reeve was trying a new way to mess with his head. Or maybe the Reeve was telling him where to look for more clues to start putting things together. Either way, Tom's curiosity slightly re-energized him and he realized that he could not sleep until he read the story. Taking a deep breath, he flipped to the story and began.

**The Parchment**

In the early spring of 1675, a French and Algonquin fur trade expedition from Sault Sainte Marie headed west. While setting up traps among a hilled forest in the mid-Upper Peninsula, the traders came upon the thawing yet still frozen body of a Native American girl. The Algonquins recognized her wardrobe as belonging to the Korbani tribe, the remnants of which had last been observed traveling with a group from western Europe, long believed by the French to have been a British expeditionary force sent by King Charles II to secretly fortify and colonize the area in the prior years. Based upon the girl's solitary position and death from apparent exposure, the expedition assumed that she had died fleeing from some sort of attack, perhaps by the Chippewa tribe. The expedition desired to give the girl a proper burial and, in moving her body, discovered that she died clutching a parchment containing a drawing of a tree with two horizontal circles etched in its trunk.

The head of the expedition, figuring that the drawing might have some clue as to the fate of the Korbani tribe and potential whereabouts of a British force in the area, retained the parchment to provide to the commanding officer upon their return to Sault Sainte Marie. Unbeknownst to the expedition, the commander, Jean Carierre, had already dispatched a company of scouts and French regulars to search for the British. Later that night, a dense fog enveloped the area and, for reasons that remain unclear, the incoming French company mistook the fur trade expedition for members of the British force that they had been sent to locate. The French company fired upon the traders and a chaotic battle ensued with heavy casualties suffered until the company commander and expedition leader engaged each other in combat and realized that they were both French and on the same side. Although they were able to call of their men and cease the hostilities, it was not before nine traders and six soldiers had been killed with a total of twelve more wounded on both sides.

In their weakened and wounded conditions, both groups worked their way back to Sault Sainte Marie. Commander Carierre then sent two companies accompanied by a reformed fur trading expedition to the area with strict orders to maintain contact to avoid friendly casualties. He demoted the first company commander and put the second company commander in charge giving him the parchment as a reference. On the fifth week of their new expedition, a massive blizzard struck the area and, in the aftermath, many of the men succumbed to pneumonia.

The new company commander divided the remaining healthy men into units of seven and had them scout in all directions looking for signs of the British with strict instructions to return to their base camp in one week's time. Every unit returned on time and reported no signs of the British or any non-Native persons in the area.

On their way back to Sault Sainte Marie, the company commander caught his leg in one of the traps left behind by the first fur expedition. His foot was amputated upon arrival in Sault Sainte Marie and he died of infection shortly thereafter but not before returning the parchment to Commander Carierre who died of pneumonia three weeks later. It was not, however, until months later that the parchment became known in infamy when word that the ship carrying Commander Carierre's body back to France had sunk in the Atlantic during a storm. At that point, those in Sault Sainte Marie believed the parchment to be cursed and left it in the commanding officer's office which was then sealed and locked.

As the years passed and new soldiers rotated in, the parchment went from a real horror story of a mystery to a fictional scary bedtime story to nothingness. The parchment was not even referenced when a war nearly erupted between the French and Ojibwe tribe after an entire Ojibwe village disappeared in the 1740s without so much as a trace other than the fact that other Ojibwe in the area had known of its existence. Only after sincere apologies from the French elite inn conjunction with substantial gift offerings were the Ojibwe placated into believing that the French had nothing to do with the disappearance.

During the Seven-Years' War, the French force at Sault Sainte Marie was significantly increased necessitating the unlocking and use of the former commanding officer's office. The new commanding officer, Major Stefan LaPont, who had no knowledge of the history of the office, noticed the parchment among his predecessor's papers as well as some shorthand notes about the parchment. Unfortunately, those notes were written prior to the parchment's infamy and the multiple references to the British led the new commanding officer to misinterpret the notes and suspect that the British had a secret corridor in the Upper Peninsula from which to attack the city. In order to dispense with the threat, he dispatched 75% of his fighting force to the west in the direction where the notes said the parchment had been found. While his force was away, a message came to send them to Fort Frontenac as reinforcements. Without those reinforcements, Fort Frontenac fell to the British in 1758.

LaPont was chastised and reassigned by his superiors to return to Montreal along with the majority of his force. The night before LaPont departed, he met with his replacement and the remaining military officers to discuss the Sault Sainte Marie operations during which time LaPont showed them the parchment and accompanying notes. At the exit ceremony the next day, an accidental discharge of a cannon that was being repositioned caused several powder kegs to explode by LaPont and the officers killing him and many of them.

The remaining officers

were perplexed by the incredible bad luck of the accidental cannon discharge and LaPont's inability to assist Fort Frontenac due to his decision to send his force west. Rather than blaming LaPont who had a stellar reputation up to Sault Sainte Marie, they blamed the parchment as a cursed object. Its infamy was reborn at that moment and confirmed when the officer who had placed the parchment in a desk drawer was killed in a wolf attack while on a scouting patrol outside of the city. Yet again, the parchment was lost to time as the desk went unused. The British eventually came to control the land following the Seven-Years' War.

One event that has long vexed historians is the so-called "Bloodiest Battle Never Fought." During the war of 1812, the British had sent two large expeditionary forces out of Sault Sainte Marie, one west and one south, to secure the Upper Peninsula and prevent the city from attack. The western force, smaller than the southern force and estimated at 300 soldiers, was led by Captain Wesley Chambers. Chambers had taken over the old military command office in Sault Sainte

Marie as the British had built a far better office for its superior commanders. It was rumored that Chambers had seen the parchment and believed it to be a lost British expedition such that he volunteered to lead the western expedition out of his great sense of adventure.

The British had correctly prepared for the possibility of an attack as a force of 250 militia men from Michigan, Ohio, and Kentucky, had crossed Lake Michigan to attack Sault Sainte Marie from the west. The last known dispatch from the British force was an update from a rider that the British had made camp and believed that there was a colony of people nearby. The rider then rode back to the camp but never returned after that and there were no signs of any camp. Neither the British soldiers nor the militia were ever seen or heard from again.

In the spring of 1880, oil baron Tipton Welles arrived in Sault Sainte Marie looking for oil in the Upper Peninsula. While in the city, he discovered the parchment being auctioned off and took a liking to it. After purchasing the parchment, he headed west and discovered some hilled lands that looked promising. Welles hired about 100 men to help him set up operations and the workers arrived with their families and set up a temporary city for their work. While they were engaged in exploring for oil, Welles received word that one of his foremen had struck oil in central Michigan. He left the Upper Peninsula to check on the oil find and died of a heart attack while in transit. In the meantime, Welles' company had made arrangements to relocate the Upper Peninsula workers to the Lower Peninsula to assist with the new oil find that summer. The workers and their families, however, had disappeared without a trace leaving Welles' son to find replacements as he assumed control of his father's business.

The parchment ultimately came into the possession of Welles' sole living heir, his great-grandson Alexander, who had planned to look for his great-grandfather's long lost oil field in the Upper Peninsula after returning from the Korean War. Alexander returned to Michigan prematurely after suffering shrapnel wounds to his legs when a mortar hit a supply truck near his unit. He used the last of his family's fortune to pursue oil in the Upper Peninsula. Alexander, who needed surgery on his wounded legs, hired a foreman to purchase equipment and hire a crew of 100 men to prepare his great-grandfather's oil-find site for drilling while he recovered from surgery. When Alexander returned to the site following his surgery and rehabilitation, the site was completely empty without any trace of the men or their families. Alexander believed that the foreman had stolen his money and absconded. Like his great-grandfather, he died of an apparent heart attack.

When Alexander's estate went up for auction, a small historic museum in Mavett purchased the parchment. Shortly after the parchment was put on display, the museum burned down with the curator-owner, Mildred Towson, inside. The parchment had been placed in a frame and, although the museum was entirely destroyed by the fire, no ashes or remnants from the frame were found in the rubble, only the remnants of the other items and poor Ms. Towson.

By the time that Tom finished reading the story, his renewed energy had dissipated. Although interesting in its own right, Tom had no idea how the story tied into Gerald Tiebolt, Manchineel, or anything else that had happened to the Prestons over the last roughly thirty-six hours. Perhaps Tiebolt had sent Tom on a snipe hunt. Or perhaps the series of unfortunate coincidences, tragedies, and disappearances or whatever they collectively or independently were had something to do with Tiebolt and Manchineel. But, if there was a connection to be made, Tom's exhaustion had peaked and his mind could no longer function on even the most basic level, let alone the investigative level required to attempt to connect dots, if any dots even really existed.

The comfort from the warmth and softness of the bed overcame Tom. His eyes closed involuntarily as he nodded off into something resembling sleep. At first, he was cloaked in peace and warmth surrounded by the sensation of floating among clouds in the warmth of his clean clothes and comforter. As the time passed, however, the warmth turned into feelings of angst, fear, confinement, and failure. Sweat began forming in Tom's pores as he saw flashes of Herman Stanton being spiked in the iron maiden, Marjorie placing keys in his pocket before being shot, escaping Manchineel with Katie, the old big rig in Ollie's Garage, Deputy Maybin, the snake-man creature ripping out and eating the Deputy Maybin's throat as the deputy could do nothing but let his eyes bulge while witnessing his own horrific demise, the video of the children, the pictures of Tom's entire family on his phone, the Reeve starting as a creature and then becoming a man again, and Deacon Forsythe staring him down threatening to rip Katie's head off if he disobeyed the huge man-like creature again.

Tom began tossing and turning as the sweat leaked out all over his body. He couldn't help but feel that he had forgotten to do something. There was a feeling of emptiness. Something was missing beyond the children. No, it was a mission that he needed to accomplish. He had to save his children but there was something he needed to do first. With the angst and stress building up inside of him and the wetness from his sweat-soaked clothes, Tom forced himself into consciousness opening his eyes in a panic. He had sweated so much that, for a second, he thought that he had pissed himself. Bolting upright, he looked at his watch which read 11:38. The Deacon and the others would still be in the Sacrarium for some time so Tom sprung out of bed and began to change into some dry clothes, this time a pair of jeans with an undershirt and an open flannel shirt on top. Katie had not been sleeping well either and she mirrored Tom getting out of bed although she did not need to change.

"Just follow me," Tom said quietly. "I need to check on something." Before leaving the room, he grabbed his pocket knife along with the Stantons' keyring and placed them in his front-right pocket.

"Does it matter if we leave the cellphones?" Katie asked.

"Probably not, but let's just leave them anyway."

Tom hustled down the hallway and the stairwell and into the dining room. He stared up at the painting over the mantle for a good thirty seconds focusing on the trunk area.

"What're you thinking, Tom?"

"Hold on a second. I need to concentrate. Holy shit, Katie! Oh my gosh, how did we miss it?"

"What?"

"Look up at the tree trunk?"

"It's the tree of life with the apple of life. The Reverend told us. We knew that."

"No. Look at the tree's trunk. Focus on the tree's trunk."

The painting was not only expertly done, but it was painted with an excellent hidden picture inside, like an optical illusion. The curves and lines on the bark of the trunk formed another image. Actually, two images. By staring at the trunk long enough, Tom and Katie could see that there was a snake wrapped around the trunk pressing an apple to its mouth. The snake's head and apple also were shaped almost like two horizontal ovals forming an infinity sign.

"That's remarkable," Katie exclaimed, "but what does it mean?"

"I'm not sure yet, but this is the same symbol that was on the Reeve's necklace. I noticed it back at the store but there was no reason to think anything of it. I also noticed it on the Reeve's belt buckle this morning. It's in this picture, and it was also on the Forsythes' pins, Edward Stanton's shield in his room where he executed Marjorie, and obviously on the window with Herman and Marjorie's bodies. They're a cult of some kind."

"We know that. And they turn into snake creatures."

"Right. But why? We need to keep searching. Maybe that will help us find the kids before those asshole Manchineelians come back for us."

Tom led Katie out of the room and, as they left, they noticed that the design in the middle of the sconces was a snake wrapping itself around an apple. Tom guessed that all of the sconces throughout the Forsythes' house were the same and Katie agreed that it was probably the case. They were so enthralled with the painting and sconces and what might come of their findings that they paid no attention to the meal that Maryanna had left on the table for them.

Tom stopped outside of the dining room and, on a hopeful hunch which was something more than a whim, grabbed the Stantons' keyring from his pocket. He had successfully used four of the keys and now grabbed the fifth key. Back in McIntosh, Tom and Katie were so pressed for time and worrying about being caught that he never gave much notice to the fact that the fifth key was a tad larger than the others and looked rather old-fashioned. At the time, he was more concerned with finding keys that would fit a house door and car. Now, he was trying to break into rooms in an old house for which the fifth key seemed like a potential fit, especially given the older-looking locks on the doors. As he began to slip the key into the lock of the door closest to the dining room, he knew it would work. The key easily moved into place and, with a twist, Tom heard the bolt unlock and he proceeded to open the door.

The room inside was an utter letdown. It was mostly empty with about a dozen extra chairs for the dining room. There were also some shelves along two of the walls that held serving trays, pots, pans, bowls, and other items for feeding and entertaining. In another lifetime, the Prestons might have enjoyed perusing through the items as they seemed to be antiques and of exquisite quality.

Disappointed but not discouraged, Tom and Katie exited the room and Tom remembered to lock the door. He then went to the next door and, using the same key, managed to unlock it. Just as he had hoped and thought of as a possibility, Marjorie Stanton had left them a master key for the inside of the Forsythes' home. Unfortunately, the room was also a dead end as it served as a coat closet. It was interesting to note, however, that the Forsythes had a number of leather and fur coats hanging up that looked themselves to be antiques. It was almost like items that one would wear to a local Renaissance festival. Again, they were items that the Prestons might have enjoyed viewing and even trying on under different circumstances. They promptly left the room with Tom again remembering to lock the door.

It was almost noon and Tom didn't know how much time they had before being fetched. He ran across the front hall to the hall leading to the parlor. He quickly took note of the locked doors and began to go through them. The first one, which was on their right, was a large room that contained knitting equipment, knit pillows, and several quilts and afghans. Interestingly, there were also some bejeweled tiaras and antique jewelry encased in a wooden antique cabinet along the far wall.

Without taking the time to truly appreciate the beauty or value in the room, Tom and Katie left and again locked the door behind them. The next two rooms were on the left side of the hallway. The first room contained what appeared to be a series of paintings neatly stored in a custom crate. Several more paintings were hanging on the walls. The next room was essentially a medieval armory that reminded them of the Stantons' home. There was an old suit of armor along with other pieces of armor propped up on stands in the middle of the room with a large sword and shield hung together in the middle of the far wall with other swords hanging on the other two walls. In a corner, Tom noticed a bow as well as a set of two crossbows. He thought of picking them up to use against their captors but he could not find any arrows. It was also interesting that he could not find any daggers among all of the swords and there was no point in taking a sword. It would be impossible to conceal with its long and heavy blade, and the Manchineelians seemed to be far more skilled with weaponry than he could learn to be in however many minutes they might have left.

There was one room left on the right side of the hallway. Tom locked the door behind them as they left the armory room and headed to that lone remaining room. Walking across the hall, they both glanced through the entranceway to the parlor to look out the window at the lake and Sacrarium. The good news was that they saw no one outside meaning that they still had time. They also looked at the sconces lining the hallway and at the far but visible end of the parlor and confirmed that they were in fact the same snake-around-the-apple design.

Tom reached for the last lock with the master key and opened the door which led to a room that looked like the Deacon's study complete with a library and reading couch. Many of the books on the shelf looked old and were bound in leather. The Deacon's desk was an enormous carved wooden piece that had a large wooden chair behind it with padded leather on the seat, back, and armrests. Behind the chair is where Tom saw it hanging on the wall. A large glass frame with a parchment inside displaying a drawing of a tree with two circles that, upon closer view, had some washed-out details that at one time had clearly been a snake coiled around the trunk with an apple pressed to its mouth. Tom was sure of this based on the Forsythes' painting, service pins, and sconces, the Reeve's belt buckle and necklace, Edward Stanton's shield, and the other Stantons' blood-stained window.

"The Parchment," Tom muttered with slight awe.

"How do you know about this?" Katie inquired.

"It's in the story that the Reeve suggested before he left."

"Did you read it?"

"Yes," Tom nodded and proceeded to summarize the story. For as tired as he had been, he was somewhat surprised that he was able to retain most of what he had read a few short hours ago. Katie listened intently and, just like Tom was doing as he rehashed the story, she was trying to figure out what the symbol on the parchment had to do with the matching symbols in Manchineel.

"She was the daughter of the last chieftain of the Korbani tribe." The voice from behind them scared them half to death as they involuntarily shrugged their shoulders and flinched forward reigniting the pain and soreness in Tom's back from the muscle he had pulled the day before. Turning slowly, they noticed the Reeve staring up at the parchment with a look of awe and admiration combined with a subtle undertone of contempt. He barely took notice of Tom and Katie staring at him and continued. "She was only about thirteen years old so I suspect that one of her parents drew the symbol on the parchment and gave it to her, but I actually have no idea who drew it."

"Why would she have drawn or be given this parchment?" Tom's curiosity gave him a convenient excuse to prolong being taken to the Reverend, something for which he was not mentally prepared.

"All I can do is guess, Tom, but I think that it was to show the symbol to anyone that she found who could help her."

"Why would she need help?"

"The Korbani were being attacked."

"Who was attacking them?"

"To fully understand the situation, like any event, you have to take a step back and up. The Korbani were lousy fighters. That's why there were so few of them remaining when they helped found Manchineel. They practically had no choice but to help found this town. They were no match for the Algonquins and Iroquois or any of the other indigenous tribes. They were certainly no match for the more heavily armed French. And they were definitely no match for us. But they were very clever. It was a hot and dry month that year and the chief ordered the remaining male and female warriors to set a brush fire. He then ordered the non-warriors to run away and get help from anyone under cover of the smoke from the fire. We eventually caught everyone except for the girl. We heard stories passed around the area that she had traveled and hid in a hollowed-out tree trunk that she found to avoid detection until she was overcome by the elements or got sick. In fairness, we carried many foreign diseases with us from Europe."

"*We* and *us*?" Katie said. "Why are you speaking in the first person?"

"Son of a bitch!" Tom exclaimed. "You aren't descendants!"

"Oh my God!" Katie realized. "That's why

you have no cemetery in Manchineel."

"I practically spoon-fed it to you," the Reeve said nonchalantly.

"So you're what? Manchineelians?"

"I like you. I like you both. This is quite a thing to go through and yet you're still standing and you still have some moxie to you. Manchineelians. It has all these connotations to it, doesn't it Tom? Like 'eel' for snake and 'ians' as a pseudo-homage to aliens. You're a one-man lawyer and marketing firm. Let's see how much longer you both can last. On that note, I noticed on the way in that you hadn't touched the meal that Maryanna prepared. If you're in any way hungry or thirsty, now is probably your last opportunity for a long while."

Tom and Katie both acknowledged their hunger, if for no other reason to buy some extra minutes before being taken to the Reverend for whatever that meant. Tom didn't want to say it but it felt like they were death row prisoners being offered a last meal before execution.

The steak, eggs, and toast that Maryanna had left for them stayed relatively warm in their insulated serving plates and plate covers, although the toast was of course soggy by the time that Tom and Katie sat down to eat. Neither one of them could stare away from the painting. Their heads were cluttered and dizzy with everything that they had learned and figured out up to that point, however the most important point was the only one for which there were no clues or leads as their children were still missing with no recovery in sight. In their immediate future there was only the unpleasant prospect of meeting with the Reverend and finding out their fate. Learning about the true history of the Manchineelians was a distant third on their thought list at the moment.

When they finished eating, the Reeve escorted them to the Sacrarium. Secretly, Tom and Katie had hoped to take a tour of it when they arrived in Manchineel. Now, however, they feared that it would be anything but holy on the inside.

Walking up the hill, Manchineel looked as Eden-esque as ever. The sky was royal blue with scant clouds and the water reflected vibrant shades of blue, like a shimmering sapphire, mixed with shades of teal almost like the Caribbean Sea. The trees and bushes were lush as was the grass beneath them, and flowers were in bloom in the gardens and plants all around. As they approached the Sacrarium, the giant glass windows forming a semicircle in the center of the wall overlooking the lake came into focus. The building was much bigger than it appeared from the Forsythes' parlor and was roughly the size of a small museum. Through the windows, Tom and Katie could see what appeared to be a barren tree. They could not see much of the trunk from their vantage point but there were large skylights overhead that clearly illuminated the tree and bathed it in sunlight.

To their left, there was water flowing out from beneath the Sacrarium and into the lake like a tame waterfall. Tom and Katie both walked over to get a closer look since there did not seem to be a river on the other side of the Sacrarium. Although the water appeared to be shallow from a distance, up close they saw that it was actually several feet deep with tree roots curving through it in all directions, almost as if there was no gravity between the lake and the tree. Tom could not resist the urge to investigate it. He knelt down at the water's edge and took a scoop with his hand. Just as it had the night before, the water turned blood red as it formed a puddle in his palm.

"It's blood, isn't it?" he asked the Reeve.

"All knowledge in good time," the Reeve responded.

Tom reached down again to take another scoop. As his hand swept through the water, it was snagged roughly by one of the roots. Tom flailed and threw himself backwards to rip his hand from its grip. Bloody red drops from his hand leaving the water flew up splashing small blood dots on his arms, legs and cheeks. The back and palm of his hand bore fresh stinging cuts from the root.

"Maybe look but don't touch would be a good motto for you both from here on out," the Reeve said enigmatically.

The Sacrarium's entrance was on the side opposite the lake. The Reeve walked Tom and Katie around to the entranceway which was comprised of a stone platform with a set of stone stairs rising up to an elevated stone platform between two marble columns that complemented the stone exterior of the building. At the end of the elevated platform, there was a giant metal door displaying the sign of the tree and snake holding the apple around its trunk to form an infinity sign. The Reeve grabbed the handle and pulled the door open with a bit of a grunt signifying its substantial weight which Tom assumed was meant to keep all manner of weather and unwanted guests from breaking in.

The interior of the Sacrarium had a majestic yet ancient feel to it. It was set up like a church with five rows of wooden pews divided into three columns – one on the left, one in the center, and one on the right – that formed a semicircle around a podium with the tree symbol carved three-dimensionally into the front and made of pure gold. Each of the pews had the tree symbol carved in the back center. The floor was a dark marble that, during the daytime, seemed somewhat neutralized by the sunlight beaming through the windows. Behind the podium was the tree and the roof above the tree was simply convex glass panels with curved wooden beams running between them for support forming a giant personal greenhouse for the tree. For all of the natural sunlight that the tree was receiving, it was indeed barren as it had appeared to the Prestons from the outside. In fact, it looked almost dead. It was a dull gray color without leaves and hardly any grooves or knots of bark. To Katie, it reminded her of a life-sized version of the tree models that elementary school students annually made from clay in art class before giving them any details, let alone leaves.

Tom could not see the base of the trunk but he could hear people below leading him to assume that there was a level beneath them and that the base of the tree was there. The walls of the Sacrarium contained some ornately carved wooden shelves and a few small display tables with various artifacts on them. There were seals, rings, necklaces, crowns, and books. In addition, there were large golden tools on several shelves about two feet in length that looked like giant melon scoopers.

On the far right, there was a stone archway above a stairwell that led to the lower level. The noise from people below was echoing through it as well as from the back by the tree. Within seconds of them arriving, Reverend Jacobson appeared in the archway at the top of the stairs wearing a white three-piece suit, white dress shirt, white tie, white shoes, and a white religious skull-cap to top off the ensemble. Tom and Katie froze in trepidation.

"Reeve, we got a late start as you can imagine from all of the recent events. Why don't you go get dressed and then join us below. I'll escort our guests of honor."

"Thank you kindly Reverend," the Reeve said as he turned to the left and walked away.

The Reverend took a long hard stare at Tom and Katie and, despite the unpleasant scowl emanating from his eyes, wore an amiable grin across his face. "It's my privilege to welcome you Tom and Katie to one of our more important pre-Grand Jubilee rituals. I assume that, given your concern for the welfare of your children, we won't have to shackle and gag you to prevent you from running away or disturbing our ceremony do we?"

Tom and Katie just stared back at him completely unsure of how to respond to their new surroundings in the Sacrarium and whatever ceremony they were going into as "honored guests."

"Say that you understand and will behave so that we don't have to worry about our ceremony and you won't have to worry about your children."

"We understand."

"We'll behave."

"Good. Now let's make our entrance," the Reverend said as he began to lead them down the stairs.

"Reverend, what is this ceremony called," Tom asked out of curiosity stemming from his fear of what might happen to them as honored guests.

"That's a good question Tom. All in time my friend. All in time."

The stairwell had a platform two-thirds of the way down where it wound to the left and opened into a large Victorian-looking room that spanned the length of the floor above it. The walls consisted of large boards of dark brown paneled wood with wooden columns in between at about fifteen feet apart with the same sconces that the Forsythes had throughout their home, but these sconces were made of gold as opposed to the iron-colored metal at the Forsythes' home. The ceiling was comprised of carved wooden panels painted white from which a dozen gold and crystal chandeliers hung scattered around the room. Between the sunlight from the windows surrounding the tree and the light from the sconces and chandeliers, the room emitted a glow that seemed almost futuresque and starkly contrasted with the antique, Victorian décor of the Sacrarium and town as a whole. It was certainly an odd combination, but not nearly as bizarre as the scene within the room.

To their right, there were two tables spanning approximately eighteen feet in length covered in white cotton tablecloths stationed against the wall next to the stairwell. In the center, there were two humongous silver serving trays with covers that were easily two feet in height covering them. A total of eight more silver trays, four on each side of the trays in the middle, filled out the remaining space on the tables. The trays were huge in their own right and each tray had a cover that looked to be about a foot-and-a-half tall.

The floor of the room was made of refurbished shiplap except, starting from about fifteen feet away from the tree, the floor was made of smoothed stones which encircled the tree except for leaving a five-foot barrier of soil between the stone floor and the tree trunk. Five boulders had been placed equidistantly around the trunk at the edge of the stone floor and it appeared that tree roots had circled themselves around the boulders as if to further anchor the tree.

To the right of the tree stretching from the shiplap flooring to the edge of where it met the stone flooring, there was a long and tall table covered in white fabric. Tom could not make out what was beneath the fabric cover, although he assumed that he probably did not want to know.

As for the people, they were seated on wooden chairs on the outside and inside of white clothed tables that had been set up like a circle around the perimeter of the room with narrow gaps at either end for ingress and egress. Tom instantly recognized the people as the townsfolk of Manchineel, although he was having trouble considering them to be people any longer. Like the Reverend, they were all dressed in pure white. The men were all dressed in white suits with white buttons, white vests, white shirts, white ties – although several of the men were wearing ascots instead, – and white shoes. The women were all wearing white dresses with white gloves. The dresses, all different, had the commonality of being conservative. They were floor-length and covered the shoulders, chest and upper arms. The gloves, however, ranged from arm-length to hand-length. The women also seemed to have their hair pulled back with various white ribbons as did a few of the men who had long hair.

The Reverend escorted Tom and Katie to two empty seats that had been placed just beside the two tables with the covered serving pieces where they had walked in from the upper level. He then took his place by his wife Molly on the outside of the table closest to the tree in the circle so that his back was to the tree and he was facing his constituents from the middle looking out around at them. The Jacobsons were flanked by the Forsythes and the Thornhills and then Tom noticed some of the other familiar faces, Edward Stanton and Oliver Gustafson in particular.

Still standing, the Reverend raised his arms to which the townsfolk quieted in response. "The cycle has come to its end and it is time yet again for a new beginning. We reflect on the past and we prepare for the future. Let us now take a few minutes in silent reflection of what was, what is, and what can be."

The demeanor and body language of everyone suggested to Tom that there would genuinely be a few minutes of silence unlike the typical 'moment of silence' requested at sporting events or functions to commemorate something important, usually tragic, that lasted maybe all of ten seconds. He decided to quickly scan the room and was able to count 68 places around the tables circling the room.

*That's impossible. Count again. How can there be 68? It should be 66.*

"My friends, my dear lifetime friends, colleagues, confidants, kin, we embarked on an expedition and are now enduring the ultimate adventure of ascendancy. Born to mortality, now there is only us, the angels, and the Divine. Let the Feast of Flesh and Dust commence."

Before being able to follow through on his train of thought, Tom noticed that the tables around the room held large silver serving trays with shiny silver covers. However, there were no utensils for eating – no silverware, cutlery, serving pieces, plates, napkins, or glasses. Katie had picked up on that fact long before he did and Tom caught her staring with worried intrigue at the silver trays on the tables just as he was now about to do. As the Reverend finished with his words, everyone waited for him to take his seat. When he did, the trays were removed revealing heaping piles of raw meat and entrails glistening from the wetness of blood which had not been washed off. In fact, the pooling of blood along the tray bottoms revealed that no washing had occurred; only cutting and removal.

Without hesitating, the Manchineelians reached into the trays with their bare or gloved hands grabbing pieces of meat and placing them in their mouths, scarfing the morsels down almost instantly. Some of the pieces were much longer than morsels in which case the diner would hold the end of the piece while taking it in with slow gulps. The meat and entrails dripped with blood as they were grabbed and consumed, and as Tom and Katie looked closer, they could make out whole organs like spleens, kidneys, intestines, liver, brains, and even tongues stacked amidst the meat on the platters. Tom had specifically noticed the organs after observing one of the men gulp down what appeared to be several inches of a large intestine while the woman next to him was picking chunks off a liver. Around the room, white gloves turned bright crimson with the blood from the feast and the townsfolks' clothes were increasingly stained with the blood splatters from their food. Chins dripped blood from bloody lips bearing bloody mouths and teeth and yet none of the townsfolk seemed remotely fazed by the gore.

Several minutes into the feast, the group's hunger seemed to be getting satiated to the point that conversations began again in earnest like before the Reverend had arrived with Tom and Katie from the upper level. Under the cover of their noise, a thoroughly nauseated and horrified Katie turned to Tom and whispered "we forgot a clue in the car. They hardly ate any of the cooked food they made for us. And when they did, it was like they were choking it down."

"You're right. They only eat their food raw, and only meat and organs at that."

"Hey, I also counted 68 seats and they're all taken."

"Are you including us?"

"Of course not. Come on."

"How is that possible?"

"I have no idea."

They continued to watch in loathsome disgust as their hosts-slash-jailors-slash-kidnappers who were also some sort of creatures-turned-humans or vice versa scarfed and slurped down all of the raw bloodied meat and entrails, down to the last shred. The feast had lasted for nearly twenty minutes and yet Tom and Katie could not adjust or become accustomed to the gruesome spectacle of the townsfolk eating flesh. It was as loathsome as it was creepy and, by the end of the feast, Tom's and Katie's nausea was exacerbated by the loud chorus of satisfied belches that rang around the table from the blood-soaked participants. There were also a few hiccups and, at one point, Deacon Thornhill sneezed so hard that blood from his mouth spat in a streak across the tablecloth in front of him. Tom and Katie both looked around hoping that there was a garbage can or bag nearby because they desperately wanted to vomit. Finding none, they simply turned in their chairs with their heads down trying to breathe in short controlled spurts while drowning out the surrounding noise by placing their hands over their ears.

Several minutes later, Reverend Jacobson rose up again and uttered the following: "We have fulfilled the first formal step of our renewal. With the feast of flesh, we have nourished ourselves for the days to come. Now, it is time to consecrate our oaths and replenish that which brings us replenishment; sustain that which sustains us; revive that which revives us. God's ultimate creation came to us and we to it by the most remote of circumstances and chances such that it was our fate and destiny. Tonight marks the first night of the full moon lasting through Wednesday, the summer solstice and our Grand Jubilee. Let us now commence the ceremony of dust to begin the awakening and the dawn of our future. Will the Deacons please assume your positions."

Deacon Forsythe and Deacon Thornhill

dutifully rose from their chairs and walked over to the large table by the tree. They took spots on opposite sides of the table and stood in the middle facing each other. At the same time, they extended their hands towards the cloth covering the table and removed it in unison as they began to fold it evenly until it was small enough for Deacon Thornhill, who was on the side closest to the Reverend, to walk over with it and hand it to the Reverend for safekeeping. Beneath the cloth, there was a giant machine that, to Tom, looked like some sort of grinding contraption. The table itself was black metal and looked like a conveyor belt held up by a strong steel frame with black steel panels extending outwards in 60-degree angles to prevent items from falling over the sides. At the end of the conveyor belt, there was a large enclosed area in the shape of a smoothed box and Tom could see several jagged steel rollers lined up together to crush whatever was sent through the conveyor belt. He was unable to see the back of the table where whatever was sent to be crushed would presumably come out.

"Let us now have the designated officers come forth to commence the awakening," the Reverend instructed.

Five of the women and five of the men rose up from their seats and walked over to the far end of the room. They paired off into groups of two and each pair reached down and together lifted up on opposite ends of what looked like ten-gallon silver soup pots, except with pointed fronts like spouts. Each pair proceeded to one of the five rooted boulders anchoring the tree and, when each pair was positioned, they began pouring out the contents - blood - all over the boulders and the soil surrounding the tree. When they finished, the pairs each took several steps back and everyone in the room stood at attention. The roots wrapped around the boulders began to soak in all of the blood on them, and they somehow even drew in the blood from the boulders as well as the blood that had dripped ono the stone floor. At the same time, the blood that had been glistening on top of the soil sank into the ground leaving no trace of itself.

Half a minute later, there was a loud gurgling sound emanating from the tree and echoing throughout the Sacrarium. The Manchineelians began smiling and pumping their fists triumphantly, but the Reverend stood before them and raised his arms up with his hands out and motioned them to calm down. "It certainly has been a while friends, but we are not there yet. Reeve, please come forward with our Captains. It is time for the final step."

The Reeve and a woman appearing to be his wife rose up from their seats close to the Prestons and walked over towards the tables against the wall behind the Prestons. They were joined by the Reverend and Molly Jacobson,

Patricia Thornhill, and Maryanna Forsythe. Oliver Gustafson and his wife walked over from the far side of the table and behind them were Edward Stanton with his wife Lucinda and another couple who, as they got closer, appeared to be none other than Marjorie and Herman Stanton.

*No fucking way!*

Tom wanted to jump out of his chair and yell "you're dead, they killed you" but the flesh-eating and blood-pouring combined with their bloody mouths and bloodstained white dress-clothes served as intimidating deterrents. He saw that Katie's eyes were bulging and knew that she was feeling the same way. After the group had fully converged towards the tables behind the Prestons, they stood in a semicircle around Tom and Katie followed by a silent eerie pause.

*They're going to throw us in the grinders. They're going to fucking throw us in the grinders. We're man-snake food. Or snake-man food. Either way we are so fucked. What happened to our kids? That wasn't them at the feast? That wasn't them at the feast! Dear God no! Please. No!*

Rage, horror, and panic built up inside of Tom and he was ready to jump up and gouge out the eyes of one of the group. Reverend Jacobson was conveniently the closest to him and also physically the weakest looking of the group. *Yeah, if they're going to kill us, I'm taking their leader out,* Tom thought.

Reverend Jacobson took notice of the

wild look in Tom's eyes and, for a split second, Tom thought he observed the Reverend reveal a look of concern. For Tom it was empowering to at least see that he could make his tormentor feel something other than what the tormentor wanted to feel.

"Are you not enjoying our feast Tom?" the Reverend asked defiantly as he composed himself.

"I thought it was rather different," Tom said in a lawyerly politican-esque way after realizing that the Reverend's dislike for his facial expression could prompt a very bad response for Katie and the children.

"Well, thus sayeth the lawman," the Reverend mocked. "Katie, give me the truth. What do you think about our feast?"

"It's repulsive, repugnant," Katie said as she began to weep.

"I don't see what's so gross about it," Patricia Thornhill piped in. "You and Tom just had the same thing only yours was cooked."

With that, the Stanton brothers each lifted the lids off of the huge serving trays in the middle of the tables revealing ten human skulls stacked in two layers on each ovular tray, seven on the bottom and three on top (twenty total between the two trays). Of everything that Tom and Katie had seen in the last two days, this was the most haunting image and one that would never fade from their minds. It was made worse by Patricia's words which made Tom and Katie realize that they had not eaten steak from a cow. Katie bent over to the ground and wretched as she fell out of her chair. Tom swung off his chair and likewise vomited against the wall. He was not a vegetarian but he never ate meat from a bone and he never ate meat other than from the big three: chicken, pig, cow. The thought of venison never appealed to him and the one exotic food he had tried, a bite of alligator in Florida in his youth, was a far cry from human flesh.

"Tell me we didn't just eat our children!" Katie shrieked.

"Oh my God!" Tom screamed realizing the implication.

"Fair question under the circumstances," the calm version of the Reverend responded. "The answer is no you did not. Your children will be fine as long as you behave. That was the deal. Now sit back down and shut your mouths."

The Prestons did as they were told and watched in horror as the others lifted the lids off the other serving trays revealing stacks and piles of human bones. From the skull count, Tom assumed that those were the murdered people in McIntosh. The Jacobsons led the procession of the other ten individuals who each carried the trays over to the table with the Deacons. The Stanton brothers, both thick and strong, each carried a tray of skulls with the others following behind them with the other trays. Deacon Forsythe pushed the power switch on the conveyor belt and flipped the switch to turn it on in the forward direction toward the grinders. Herman arrived first and dumped the skulls onto the belt. Tom watched them bob and roll down the conveyor belt and then he witnessed and heard the sickening crunches as the skulls were quickly broken apart while being pressed into the rest of the machine through the grinders. Katie covered her mouth with her hand. Mere seconds after disappearing, thick clouds of dust blew out of the back of the machine. It was the powder remnant of the skulls.

Edward followed suit and dumped his tray of skulls onto the conveyor belt and they, too, were crushed apart and blown out the back. Each of the other eight individuals waited his and her turn to dump their serving trays of bones onto the conveyor belt and watch as the bones were crushed into a fine dust. With each tray of bones, Tom and Katie grew more sensitive to the sounds of the bones being crushed. It was almost like torture having to wait to endure the next round of crunching knowing that it would seem louder and longer than the previous one despite the grinders' roar. At the end, there were ten empty serving trays and a thick cloud of dust which, instead of settling all over the floor or circulating with the air floating around the Sacrarium, seemed to be drawn towards the tree.

As the machine spat out the dust in clouds, the dust seemed to be lifted towards the tree at all angles. Tom and Katie could see dust float up towards the branches but their view was cut off by the ceiling. They also saw dust floating towards the trunk but their view of the lower trunk was obstructed by the bloody white Manchineelians. They could, however, see the dust that floated towards the middle of the trunk. When it touched the trunk, the wood incredulously bent inwards and then, seconds later, took a more lively form with its perfectly rounded dormant grayness transforming into a bark-like layer with ridges and a rich gray-brown color.

The Manchineelians, who had been standing for the entirety of the bone crushing ceremony, began to clap and cheer as the tree sucked in every last speck of dust.

"Come friends, let us marvel in the awakening," the Reverend invited.

Several of the Manchineelians hurried over to the stone path to look up at the tree. The rest of them, including the Reverend and Deacons, headed up the stairwell to observe from the upper level. Deacon Forsythe grabbed Tom's and Katie's arms and said "come on and watch" in a tone that, despite being an order for them to follow, was said with glee. Tom and Katie joined the knot of Manchineelians running up the stairwell and then to the area behind the podium to stare in awe at the tree. As they arrived, the trunk and branches began flashing the bark-like layer with ridges and rich gray-brown color while leaves began forming along the branches. At first the leaves seemed to pop up like dark green pine needles but they unfolded into perfectly symmetrical egg-like shapes with pointed ends about four inches long and flashing a vibrant bright green color. Once several hundred leaves had unfolded with more forming every second, a low humming rang out from the tree and echoed throughout the Sacrarium.

"The Feast of Flesh and Dust has been consummated!" the Reverend cried out triumphantly to the sounds of more clapping and cheers from the Manchineelians. They joyfully watched and cheered as the leaves filled out the tree and danced in rhythm to the tree's humming. Minutes later, the branches were filled with leaves and the humming stopped. The Manchineelians correspondingly broke off from their cheers and dances, although their mood remained festive and they continued to socialize with each other.

Tom and Katie moved to a pew away from the podium and the Manchineelians. Other than being the "guests of honor" with whatever horrible fate that bestowed, they certainly weren't part of the ceremonies that had just taken place. Frankly, they had no understanding of the meaning for what had just taken place.

"Is there a word other than surreal for this moment," Tom began to ask Katie "or is it simply that humans have been misapplying the word surreal to lesser moments than this?"

Katie gave a tired shrug and a quick smirk. She could not imagine anything more surreal than what they were witnessing and just sat back against the pew looking out into the scene as Tom did the same. The warm summer sun illuminated the building and the freshly revived tree reflected golden rays off its leaves while the Manchineelians joyfully socialized in their white blood-stained dress clothes. It was almost like they were completely aloof to the fact that they had cannibalized twenty humans (likely the nineteen murder victims in McIntosh plus the deputy, also a murder victim) and then fed their blood and bones to fertilize the tree. Neither Tom nor Katie had any desire of finding out the meaning of being the "guests of honor" but for the fact that they needed to find out about their children and how, if possible, to get them back safely.

"It is surreal indeed," a voice called out behind them.

Tom and Katie turned their heads to see Marjorie and Herman Stanton walking over to them.

"No need to get up, just stay as you were," Marjorie said politely. "You must be exhausted. We'll just stand over here," she said as she and

Herman walked over to the pew two rows in front of Tom and Katie so that they wouldn't have to move or crane their necks looking up to speak with the Stantons.

"You both did well," Herman said approvingly. "Marjorie gave you some major help, but few people could have pulled off as much as you did."

"Are you immortal?" Tom asked bluntly. He was in fact exhausted and getting tired of the gamesmanship and threats followed by more gamesmanship and threats.

"That's a question for the Reverend. You'll have your time with him soon enough. I'll just tell you that the iron maiden has a secret door behind it and the spikes just pierced some bags of deer blood."

"I'm also good at special effects, plus makeup and fake props," Marjorie added referencing the gun and her fake execution.

"Why did you go through all of that? Why did you put us through all of that?" Katie asked in disbelief.

"Well, to start at the beginning," Herman said, "my parents named me after the Greek god Hermes who was known as the 'divine trickster.' It's even more appropriate now since Hermes could travel between the mortal and divine realms. I was always playing off people and Marjorie was much the same way. That's how we were drawn together. Anyway, we need to keep this short because this isn't our place. Suffice it to say that we needed to get a better understanding of each other. Us of you, and you of us. I know you don't understand, but you will soon enough."

With that strange exchange, perhaps the Stantons' attempt at ameliorating whatever relationship they believed they had with the Prestons while they were in a festive mood, the Stantons took their leave and headed towards their fellow Manchineelians. As they walked away, Tom suddenly had the urge to feel the outside of his pockets and realized that someone had taken back the keyring at some point during the ceremony. As always in Manchineel, he and Katie were at least one step behind in action and multiple steps behind in comprehension.

# THE DEVIL'S JOKE

## *Chapter Ninteen*

Sitting back against the pew, Tom and Katie succumbed to their physical and emotional exhaustion nodding off to sleep while the Manchineelians continued their joyous post-ceremonial celebrations. All manner of time was lost on them as they were adrift in an oasis of happy sounds surrounded by the warmth of the sun overhead. The air itself felt fresher and seemed to cleanse their bodies as they peacefully rested.

The festive noises eventually ceased leaving silence in their place. It was this silence, sudden and empty, that caused Tom and Katie to stir as sleep gave way to consciousness. Indeed, the silence acted like a void reminding them of the void in their lives without their beloved children and they slowly awoke to the same scene that they had left only with fewer of the Manchineelians remaining in the room. The good news was that the sleep, a true power nap, had reenergized them, however long it had lasted. The bad news of course was that their status quo was markedly worse since their purpose as guests of honor was probably next on the Manchineelian agenda.

The Jacobsons, Tiebolts, Forsythes, Thornhills, Stantons (all four of them), and Gustafsons were all standing together on the upper level looking over the tree. Several of them looked over at Tom and Katie taking notice that they were awake and exchanged a few quick words with each other.

“Welcome back Prestons,” the Reverend called out to them, “I hope you had a pleasant rest.” He gave a brief pause then continued, “Please come up and join us. Now.”

Tom and Katie rose up and slowly walked over, both wondering if the final step of the service was for the Reverend and his crew to throw them off the overhang and into the tree. It would make no sense logically if their children were still alive but, if they were not, it made all the strategic and logical sense in the world.

“There’s no reason to be hesitant,” the Reverend said in a reassuring voice that rang hollow to the Prestons. He could tell that neither Tom nor Katie was going to speak under the circumstances so he started the conversation. “Before we jump into the meat of our situation, no pun intended, I don’t believe you’ve met Pamela Tiebolt or Shelley Gustafson,” the Reverend continued while pointing at Gerald's and Oliver's respective wives. Pamela Tiebolt and Shelley Gustafson each said a courteous hello while exchanging brief nods with the Prestons before the Reverend began again.

"We did not mean to ignore you for the last hour or so. It has been several years since we have seen the tree this lush. Wouldn't you agree that this is a beautiful tree?" He looked deeply into Tom's and Katie's eyes demanding an answer.

"Honestly, not after what we witnessed," Tom finally blurted out.

"Not at all," Katie said in support.

"There's that word again, honestly," the Reverend scoffed to which his cohorts snickered. "Here's the honest truth Tom and Katie: in your hearts you both knew the beauty of the tree as it sprung to life from its dormancy. Watching the bark rejuvenate and the leaves grow and spread was a thing of beauty and wonder. You are both avid outdoors folk. We could tell from your vacation destination and how you packed. You are not pretentious people, at least no more than any other honest folk working to get by in life. And here is your conflict: you witnessed cannibalism – true cannibalism. I'm sure you picked up on the fact that we consumed the flesh of the twenty souls taken in McIntosh last night. And when I say we, I mean all of us: us, the tree, and you."

Tom and Katie openly cringed at that remark.

"Yes, you did," the Reverend continued. "Now, you of course will take the position that you ate a steak without knowledge as to what it was. But that is only a partial truth, like your answer to my question a few seconds ago. The whole truth is that you enjoyed the steak when you ate it. Similar to the fact that a part of you enjoyed watching the tree awaken. It is truly a thing of beauty. And you can smell and even taste the freshness of the air from its foliage. You've barely slept the last day-and-a-half and, in just an hour, you feel energized and rejuvenated from the fresh air gifted by the tree and our ceremony which brought it back to full life."

Tom wanted to protest in earnest given the twenty murder victims and their kidnapped children which was objectively inexcusable. The Reverend noticed Tom's eyes and staved off his forthcoming protest.

"Before you say anything Tom," the Reverend said piercing him with the gaze of his steel blue eyes, "I have another question for you both. What is missing from the tree?"

Tom and Katie immediately grabbed for each other's hands and tensed up.

"Oh no, no, no," the Reverend said laughing waiving his hands in the negative. "We aren't here to throw you into it. For all my years and studies, I failed to make that connection when I asked. That being said, what is missing from the tree?"

"The apple," Katie answered.

"Right you are. Excellent job Katie."

"So this is the tree of life," Tom said incredulously. "The tree of life is in the Upper Peninsula of Michigan? Forget all of the biblical references to its location, it was an apple tree in the Upper Peninsula? This is the bed of human civilization? This is Mesopotamia?"

"I forgive you for the snark and sarcasm Tom," the Reverend said "because at least you are somewhat intelligently relying on the biblical references. I assume you are referring to Genesis Chapter 2 and the rivers of Pishon, Gihon, Tigris, and Euphrates?"

"Yes, I am – although I only remembered the Tigris and Euphrates."

"To answer your compound question, Tom," the Reverend said with a wink to the lawyer, "this tree is in fact part of the tree of life. It was grown from a cutting of the tree of life and ultimately brought here by us when we left Europe over 340 years ago. I'll give you a second to take that in."

The Reverend's statement had already made the undivided attention that he was receiving from Tom and Katie all the more focused. He paused momentarily before continuing. "As for the biblical references Tom, you are either misreading or misinterpreting Genesis 2.

The language is: 'A river issues from Eden to water the garden, and then it divides and becomes four branches.' Most people, like you, in fact everybody, misinterprets the four rivers to be the borders of Eden. The language, however, says the opposite. It says that those four rivers come from the one river that feeds Eden.

"If you look at a map, this is the only logical conclusion. Based on what we know from Genesis 2 and geography, the Pishon river, while never specifically located, was in a land where there is gold and lapis lazuli and bdellium. This is confusing because gold and lapis are found in abundance in Afghanistan while bdellium is found in Eritrea. Then you have the Gihon river which also has never been specifically located but is said to wind through the whole land of Cush. Cush is a reference to Africa and is often thought to include the Nile. The other two rivers, which most people know, are the Tigris and Euphrates which form in Turkey and meet in Iraq. There is no way these rivers form borders for anything because only the Tirgis and Euhprates intersect. The source of the rivers, therefore, had to be somewhere north of what is now known as the Middle East and not in the so-called Mesopotamia region in Iraq."

With that, the Reeve and Deacons stared at the Reverend with foreboding looks of concern. The Reverend acknowledged them and waived them off. "I know. I know, friends. The

King and the Chamberlain forbid disclosing its location. As do I. As do we all. Fear not. That shall always remain our secret."

"There's a King and Chamberlain in Manchineel too?" Tom asked.

"Not here, no."

"Are they with others like you?"

"They are. Alas, I cannot disclose our numbers or the locations of our brethren. However, I can tell you that there are more like us out in the world. So now, the first of the million-dollar questions, so to speak: how did we find the tree of life? The short answer is mostly luck and no small amount of skill."

"Well that clears it up."

"Tom, I like you. I have told you this several times already, but I am a busy man and we have a lot to do to prepare for our Grand Jubilee tonight. If I have to endure your *snarcasm* or impatience any longer, I am prone to lose mine. Once that happens, it will be the endgame for you and yours.

"Anyways, the group of us whom you see before you are the descendants of an ancient and secret society aptly known as The Eternal Quest. The society's symbol has been slightly modified over the centuries to our present symbol which you have now seen many times: the tree of life with the serpent of Eden clutching the apple of eternal life where the snake's head and the apple are deliberately combined to form the infinity symbol. During the first crusade, our ancestors were a combination of knights and clergy. When they sacked Jerusalem, the clergymen were highly educated in the full bible, Old and New Testaments, and therefore fully understood the significance of the Jewish Temple and the mandates of God that they housed. The clergymen shared that knowledge with the knights who were assigned to escort them and, as Jerusalem fell, headed straight to the location of the Temple where they observed the Israeli priests desperately preparing to seal off an ancient passage which currently remains beneath the Temple Mount. Our ancestors agreed to provide the Israeli priests with safety for themselves and their families as well as conceal the ancient passage in exchange for a tour through the tunnel that it led to after the battle had ceased. Both sides lived up to this agreement and the priests took our ancestors into the tunnel which, to this day, has been sealed off from the public. Inside, our ancestors saw the Ark of the Covenant between God and the Jewish people.

"Rather than taking the Ark or disclosing its location, our ancestors were smart enough to realize that the Ark's existence would have led to death at the hands of the Church which had based its existence on competing with Judaism and used the destruction of the Second Temple as a rallying cry to maintain power in the ashes of the Roman Empire. The Knights Templar are often rumored to have seen the Ark but they were wiped out because they grew too wealthy and powerful for the tastes of the Church and certain monarchs who were indebted to them.

"At any rate, our ancestors formed The Eternal Quest because the Ark confirmed to them that God is real. Think about that Tom and Katie. Really, sincerely, think about that. The Ark of the Covenant was the first tangible confirmation to mankind as a whole of God's existence. It was not just a sign to individual prophets, like a voice or burning bush. The Ark was the first physical confirmation to us all of God's true existence. And, by extension, the Ark's very existence is tangible confirmation that the Old Testament is real. With that being the case, the true prize for mankind is immortality by eating from the tree of life. Faith is certainly important, but most important is the beginning of human history and there is nothing in Genesis prohibiting us from eating the fruit of eternal life. Nothing. That was The Eternal Quest, the ultimate quest for humankind: immortality! That is the true power of divinity!

"For nearly 200 years since discovering the Ark, our ancestors secretly held meetings where they brought in the most knowledgeable rabbis from Europe to translate the Hebrew language in the Old Testament. Once they had consensus on the translations, or at least a consensus on alternative translations for certain sentences, they, and then we, began the other lengthy process of trying to figure out the tree's location. Again, I can't tell you where it is, but let's just say that the Old Testament is the most ancient script in the world. Modern science would have helped us tremendously at the time by telling us that the land on Earth was all one continent called Pangea at its creation. That makes finding the Garden of Eden vastly clearer than it was over 700 years ago.

"Under the pretense of going to assist the crusader strongholds near modern day Israel, we headed significantly north. In total, we had over 4,000 strong, which included over 3,000 mercenaries since we anticipated difficulties, and the continent was, as always, ravaged by war and corruption. Frankly, our chances of success were slim. We had Mongol hordes to the north and Muslim armies to the south. Also, the Christian armies would not be friendly knowing that we were not crusaders or there to support them in combat. The long months of travel, especially when winter arrived, took its toll and several of us and a few hundred mercenaries died of illness or absconded.

"Eventually, we arrived at what appeared to be our final resting place during the spring and right before summer. We had managed our way through a mountain pass and were in a valley by a body of water. Again, I have to be vague on the precise location. Food was scarce. There was little in the way of vegetation, let alone edible vegetation, and, strangely, no wildlife to hunt. By the water's edge, we noticed an enormous tree easily over 50 feet tall. Despite being by the water and not having any other trees in the immediate area to compete with, it looked dead like much of the surrounding landscape. We took that as a further sign that we were soon going to be dead as well.

"That night, we saw campfires in the distance to the north of the valley and to the south. We also saw fire light coming from the mountain pass. We knew that we had been spotted and surrounded by a retreating Mongol horde to the north looking to loot and ravage on their way out of Europe. To the south were Turks believing that we were crusaders encroaching from the north. The Georgians were at the mountain pass having followed us on suspicion that we were enemy mercenaries. We spent the night and early the next day preparing our defenses. By midday, the three armies were upon us in the valley and a four-way battle ensued where we were heavily outnumbered five to one but had the benefit of the three attacking armies fighting each other as well.

"We prevailed by nightfall but less than 1,000 of us remained. We were starving and exposed to the elements and further attack so we banded together and stood watch all that night.

Come morning, we were greeted with a major surprise. The valley, which had been strewn with dead bodies and dyed in blood, was overgrown with dense green vegetation and without any traces of the bodies or bloodstains from the previous day. The gigantic tree, however, remained in its deadened state sticking out like a long skeletal hand protruding from a grave in the middle of the freshly grown valley.

"With our enemies vanquished, our lone remaining problem was food because there was none. We sent hunting groups out in all directions but they returned with nothing. A week's time passed by and we had finished all of our emergency rations and were starving to death. A group of several dozen of the remaining mercenaries essentially began a mutiny demanding more money than what we had paid them and threatening to take their pay in our flesh due to their hunger. They finally drew swords, we drew ours, and we killed them all within minutes."

Tom looked over to the Stanton brothers who responded to the Reverend's words with an exchange of smiles, some audible laughs and a quick old-fashioned handshake of hands around each other's wrists. The other Manchineelian officers took notice and began smiling and softly laughing to themselves.

"Yes, yes," Reverend Jacobson acknowledged, "I'm sure you saw the Stantons' coats of arms. They are among the greatest warriors to come out of Europe. Herman with the rare aptitude for cunning and culling the enemy, and Edward with an insatiable desire to destroy his enemies in battle.

"Well, back to our beginnings. By nightfall, our hunger had overtaken us. We ended up consuming the mutineers and burning their remains under the first night of the full moon for the month. It just so happened that it was also before the arrival of the summer solstice. When we woke up the following morning, the skeletal remains of the mutineers were crumbling into dust amidst the dying flames. It was at that point that, without so much as a breeze, the dust rose up from the ashes and was consumed by the tree just like what you observed a short time ago. It went from what must have been dormancy to a rich lushness in a matter of minutes.

"It was then that we of The Eternal Quest were convinced that we had found the tree of life. However, we were then stuck with the one question that had never dawned on us: when or how does the fruit grow so that we can eat it? Everyone looked to me and the other clergy members for the answer and we spent the next three days trying to figure out the riddle of the fruit. On the fourth day, which coincided with the last day of the full moon and the summer solstice, a thought occurred to me that Adam and Eve were effectively sacrificed for eating from the tree of knowledge and perhaps such a sacrifice would be needed to eat from the tree of life. Bishop Foley and Abbess Margaret, two of our seniors who seemed more indoctrinated in Church teachings than in The Eternal Quest, volunteered to offer themselves as a final act of service before hoping to join God. They walked over to the tree in a grand procession surrounded by all of us as soon as the moon became visible and, as they touched the tree, a blinding light protruded from its trunk and consumed them on the spot. When the light ceased, there was just the tree, still lush, and the moonlight.

"None of us could sleep that night. We waited until morning and, when the sun shined brightly on the tree as it rose over the valley, flowers started to bloom immediately followed by apples. Hundreds of apples. Everyone took at least one apple and ate (we learned then and later that the quantity eaten was irrelevant). Immediately, we felt a change in our bodies. Those who had wounds watched as their wounds healed. Those who were sick felt their illnesses disappear. Body parts that ached felt brand new. Our energy was like that of a young adult. We found the tree of life! The Eternal Quest succeeded!"

The Manchineelian officers all nodded and gave the Reverend a reverent round of applause after which the Stantons and Gustafsons proceeded out of the Sacrarium. As they left, the Reeve turned to Tom and Katie and said, "That's the shortest amount of time the Reverend has ever told that story," to which the Reverend gave a smirk of mock annoyance while the others laughed.

Tom and Katie were then alone with the Jacobsons, Forsythes, Thornhills and Tiebolts. The Reverend gave them a long look-over and said, "I'm sure that cleared a great many things up for you."

"It did and it didn't," Tom replied.

"Don't be shy now Tom and Katie. Now's our chance for dialogue. You'll have earned it by the end so ask away."

"So, based on your story and the story of the parchment, there is a massacre, a feast of flesh, and a ceremony of dust to awaken the tree of life at every full moon summer solstice?" Tom asked.

"Yes."

"Roughly every seventy years give or take?"

"Yes."

"Are you always snakes at night?" Katie asked.

"No, on both counts," the Reverend answered thoughtfully. "First of all, our bodies take the form of serpents in the biblical sense. If you recall from Genesis Chapter 3, it was a serpent who tricked Eve into eating from the tree of knowledge. God punished the serpent and made it a snake taking away its limbs. Myself and the other clergy, along with the rabbis with whom we collaborated in the early years, wondered about the fact that the serpent could speak to Eve. Combine that with Genesis Chapter 10 in which God, in response to the Tower of Babel being erected to reach the heavens, 'confounded the speech of the whole earth; and from there God scattered them over the face of the whole earth.' With the benefit of modern science, we know all living things are made of the same building blocks: DNA. We also know that the embryos of humans, mammals, birds, reptiles, and fish look alike at certain stages. All of this suggests one common ancestry where living things, like the serpent, were at one time all very similar, almost one and the same. We only become like the serpent during the new lunar month on the full-moon summer solstice every seventyish years and it disappears once we consume the fruit of life."

"So the tree of life is not really eternal?" Tom asked.

"Actually it is. The ceremonies are performed so that we persist as our human selves. Without the rituals, we would permanently become our serpent selves."

"How did The Eternal Quest manage to conceal its existence for all these years?" Katie asked.

"We used our available resources to fortify the valley in case anyone else attacked.

After that, we extended our borders into the surrounding mountains which sourced the body of water. Once we did that, we had our stronghold and concealed it to the best of our ability from the outside world maintaining constant security and scouting patrols. There was no point in immediately returning to our homes because, once the crusader-held city of Acre fell, which we pretended that we would reinforce when we left our homes, we would have been labeled traitors and killed. Or at least killed after not being willing to account for where we had been. We waited until about fifty years had passed before returning to our homes as the heirs to ourselves and then, over time, sold our homes and moved our assets to our stronghold. As you can probably extrapolate from the tale of the parchment, we used our wealth to bribe nearby leaders into sending us labor to build up and improve our domain. Then the help disappeared."

"No one ever caught onto you from the massacres or the longevity of your stay in the stronghold?" Tom asked.

"Not until the Enlightenment. We have a Scrivener. He doesn't live among us in Manchineel. He serves as our historian to ensure that we have a record of our past to guide our future. He is also a very clever and creative man who devised a series of ruses to facilitate our secrecy. Knowing that people succumb to their fears, he suggested that we prey upon such fears to counteract peoples' desires to explore new places. Following our second summer solstice Grand Jubilee, the Scrivener began writing stories and telling tales of werewolves preying upon peoples' fears of wolves and bears in the forest. When Vlad the Impaler emerged, the Scrivener added to his infamy by creating the word vampire so that people would remember the tale and spread it in perpetuity. He came up with all kinds of horror stories about monsters in scary forests and mountains which all helped to divert attention from The Eternal Quest's existence. As for massacres, there were always massacres in Europe so our lesser scale of killings went unnoticed, especially given the infrequency of them."

"So what happened during the Enlightenment?" Tom asked.

"The context is important. The world has always been getting smaller, but it became substantially smaller when the Enlightenment brought a new level of self-awareness and sophistication to the people across Europe. At the same time, weapons and warfare were modernizing at a breakneck pace. Our existence and need for modern weapons was drawing attention from the expanding neighboring countries -"

"Forgive my interruption Reverend, but why do you need weapons if you're immortal?" Tom was genuinely curious about this seeming paradox.

"It's a good question Tom. We are immortal, but an instantly fatal blow will kill us. One of our scouting patrols was attacked and captured in Poland-Lithuania during a full moon summer solstice year. Several of them were killed and the rest became their serpent selves wreaking havoc on their captors and their captors' kin after they could not eat from the fruit of life. That is how we know what happens if we don't eat the fruit of life on the full moon-summer solstice anniversary. They were hunted down but it took years and they inflicted hundreds of casualties on the Polish and Lithuanians. Once in serpent form, they took on a much different disposition that was all about cunning, violence, and chaos which seemed to get worse with the passage of time. Stories of the serpent men carried across Europe and our leader, the King, decided that it was time for The Eternal Quest to branch out in order to maintain our anonymity. One thing I neglected to mention is that our numbers had nearly doubled over the centuries due to our unmarried members taking spouses, and to children, and to children taking spouses, although conception for us is rare.

"The 68 of us in Manchineel chose this location because the idea of the New World appealed to us. We are all northerners at heart and this location just seemed to call to us."

"So why are we here? Why were our children taken?" Katie finally asked the most important question for her and Tom.

"Katie, you and Tom are going to be the sacrifice." Despite the gravity of his statement, the Reverend showed no emotion whatsoever, let alone compassion.

"Sacrifice?" Katie was incredulous. "Why? We have children! We never did anything to you. We never did anything against you. Please--" Katie paused in helpless sorrow. "Please don't do this to us. We beg you."

"You're all out of your God-damned, God-forsaken minds!" Tom had enough of the Reverend for the moment. He could tell from the Reverend's tone that there was no way in the world that the Manchineelians were going to change their minds about forcing he and Katie to sacrifice themselves. Tom also realized that their only leverage against the Manchineelians was that he and Katie were needed alive in order to be the sacrifice which meant that he could get away with a certain amount of insults and rude language, but only to a shallow degree given that he, Katie, and their children could still be physically hurt by their captors. To avoid that end, Tom refrained from continuing with his insults.

The Reverend closed his eyes in irritation but, before he could address Tom, Katie reiterated the all-important question: "Where are our children?"

"Your children are safe and happy," the Reverend surprisingly responded in a pleasant tone. Neither Katie nor Tom could tell whether the Reverend was genuinely happy that Katie had moved on from Tom's insults or whether the Reverend was just acting manic. "Dr. Arbour and several others have been taking care of them and we have been looking in on them as well. They have all the electronics, shows, and movies that they could possibly want, and they think that you have been forced to go to Marquette to deal with the car. Tonight marks the beginning of our Grand Jubilee with the first night of the full moon and, on Wednesday night with the last night of the full moon and the summer solstice, you will sacrifice yourselves to the tree of life."

"So tonight, at the Grand Jubilee, you are going to wipe out McIntosh and then force us to orphan our children on Wednesday?" Tom asked.

"That is the plan Tom. The world continues to get smaller. McIntosh is very close in proximity to us and it is on the verge of breaking out in affluence due to its burgeoning success in farming and soon-to-be mastery of the Internet both in attracting tourists and online sales. In seventy years, there could be people everywhere here and we need to prevent this area from attracting attention.

"As for you and your family, I have been honest with you. I like you. I like your family.

The same goes for everyone here. Frankly, we could use greater numbers here. Though we do travel and get around, we 68 have been together for the better part of a millennium. We will take good care of your children and, when the time is right, they will become one of us. Your sacrifice must be made willingly and you were chosen by us for our own selfish purposes."

"No. No way. There is no way that we were just randomly chosen by you. Why us?"

"Because you forced our hand Tom when fate intervened," Gerald Tiebolt entered the conversation.

"We did not! There was nothing we did to warrant this. Nothing at all and you damn well know it!"

"Look, the sacrifice isn't something that can be planned far in advance," Tiebolt responded. "Imagine if the sacrifices had time to think through their actions enough to change their minds as they continuously pondered their faith versus the certainty of the moment. We can't afford to miss the full-moon summer solstice. That is absolutely not an option for us."

"How could we, or fate, possibly have forced your hand?"

"Because, quite honestly, we had other sacrificial targets from McIntosh lined up until your family mishaps at my cliff-top attraction. It was almost like a sign that your family was marked. At the same time, we couldn't risk the chance of your sons' injuries coming back to haunt us. You seemed like nice, educated, and reasonable people. But we couldn't take the chance of a lawsuit or investigation sniffing around my business, especially now."

"So you effectively murder us and steal our children? That's your safety net? That's your plan for eternal life?"

Neither Tiebolt nor the Reverend immediately responded.

"No, that's you plan for eternal damnation," Tom continued seeing that his captors were momentarily speechless, and his words dripped with accusatory venom.

"We are liberated from damnation, mortal," the Reverend smugly retorted.

*My words stung you, you son-of-a-bitch. You went right to the immortality card because you have nothing else. I fucking hurt you.* At that point, Tom felt emboldened by his taunt and the Reverend's witless response. He allowed the rage simmering within him to take control as he threw all caution to the wind. "So, oh great Reverend, title of a man of God, recipient of the benefits of the tree of knowledge and of the tree of life, you commit unspeakable evils to perpetuate yourselves. There is no reconciliation for that. That is damnation!"

"Tom, I get your anger. But that is the divine joke. People took from God the knowledge to know good from evil and, being created in

God's image, people on the whole chose and still choose evil. That is what we are. It is how we were created."

"You're wrong unless you think God is a monster. Everything here is soaked in blood and evil. You think that's God?" Katie spat out incredulously.

Tom then burst into uproarious laughter which took everyone, even himself, by surprise with the volume at which it projected. With eyes all on him, he tried to explain. "You have eternal life but are faced with becoming the snake-man without a massacre and willing sacrifice. You have been alive for what, over eight hundred years? You are no closer today than you were at birth to understanding the meaning of life or the universe while you must hide from the world before preying on it. It sounds like the Devil's joke to me."

The Reverend and the others froze. Among their scowls, finger-stretching and neck spinning, Tom could see that he had finally really gotten to them. The Reverend gave Tom a long hard stare before speaking again. "You take it any way you wish Tom. The same for you Katie. At the end of the day, the fact is that this here is part of the tree of life. The tree's existence confirms creation and God and the Book of Genesis. Humans are dust in the beginning and dust at the end. So we can either blindly believe in an afterlife which is not in the Book of Genesis, the Torah, the Old Testament, or anywhere else from God's mouth, or we can believe in no afterlife but simply returning to dust which is what is written from God's mouth."

"But God tests us. That is the ultimate test of faith," Katie added.

"And it is now that your ultimate test begins," the Reverend responded. "Think of it like this. If your only hope leads to hell but hell is eternal life, then hell is heaven. We take our leave to prepare for the Grand Jubilee and allow you to discuss that which neither of you will admit to anyone but perhaps each other." With that, the Reverend and the Manchineelians exited the Sacrarium. Much of Tom wanted to punch their serpentine noses through their brains for the smug smirks on their faces and kidnapping their children but it was the part of him that shamed him which kept him in silent contemplation while he and Katie were left alone before the tree of life with only the darkest of options before them.

Outside the Sacrarium, Manchineel was bustling with the townsfolk setting up for the Grand Jubilee. All of them had washed themselves and changed back into their regular clothes. Two large tents were set up on opposite sides of the lake with clusters of small tents set up around them. People were busy hauling tables and chairs over while others set them up underneath the large tents. The Reeve was glued to his cellphone presumably talking to various people in McIntosh as he organized their arrival for the Grand Jubilee.

A short time later, trucks and cars from McIntosh began to arrive. The Manchineelians had set up a drop-off area by the lake for convenient unloading and a large 20-acre grass field in front of the town for parking afterwards. As the trucks and cars rolled in to Manchineel, they pulled up by the lake and their occupants got out and unloaded their wares which they carried over to the various tents before parking their cars and returning to set up within the tents. Several of the Manchineel residents were simultaneously carting their own items to the tents.

The tents were set up almost like an art fair where each tent had one theme or type of item. The Haverhills and Maybins filled the Haverhill Honeybee Farm tent by placing jars of honey, beeswax, honeycombs, and royal jelly on a heavy wooden stand on one side of the tent with beehives on stands on the other side. Next to them, Nathaniel Stein was hanging oil paintings of landscapes and Upper Peninsula landmarks on the walls of his tent and placing his best works on easels by a chair that he placed in the back-center for himself. The Stantons proudly displayed several swords and shields that they had forged and, behind their tent, they had set up an axe-throwing game where residents could try to throw axes at various wooden sculptures that the Stantons had placed about ten yards away.

The DeWeis family had filled their tent with fresh blueberries and cherries and homemade pies for everyone to sample – they wanted the whole of McInstosh and Manchineel to experience Pie Time. Debra Kozlowski lined the walls of her tent with her best-looking quilts with other ones folded on a small table in the back. Next to her tent, Samuel Borden was taking his time laying out his wooden recorders and pan flutes in between playing various tunes on his own recorder. Dorothy Schlotten, in contrast, was having a difficult time unpacking her wind chimes and birdhouses. They kept getting stuck in their packing boxes or falling down as the sweat dripped from her forehead and the profanities slipped from her lips until she finally had her tent in order for which Maisy Dorbert was grateful since Dorothy kept bumping into the sides of her tent and knocking over her display of products that she was offering at her market.

Several of the small farms from McIntosh brought woodcarvings, fresh vegetables, fresh berries, jams, jellies, and syrups, and Carlota Libum had outdone herself bringing one dozen of her special carrot cakes. In between them, the Denissons had set out their rare and expensive antiques fully expecting to be sold out by sunset. Their hopes were somewhat dashed when the Marshes of Manchineel set up their tent of glass vases, goblets, platters, pitchers, and even a chandelier that they had blown in their basement workshop.

Another cluster of tents, mainly operated by Manchineel townsfolk, offered various craft projects such as making custom picture frames and birdfeeders. In addition, Lilith Townsend was offering instructional painting (she graciously opted not to display her oil paintings as she was a far superior painter to Nathaniel Stein). Amid that cluster, the odd Sweeneys had set up their tent with last year's leftover pumpkin cans and pumpkin butter which, compared to the Sweeneys, looked brand new and clean. Behind them, the Clovis family filled their tent with a lush display of dozens of flowering perennials and Ted Husker had lined his tent with the colorful new rabbits-feet keychains.

The lone tent that remained unoccupied after all of the other tents had been set up was the one traditionally used by the Burles that always proudly displayed the U.P. Organic Tea banner with its letters in huge bold font. The Burles had not been seen all day and their absence would have been conspicuous because they had always participated in Manchineel's annual Jubilee. The Reeve, however, had been telling the people of McIntosh, including the families of the kids at the warehouse, that the Burles had a small fire in their warehouse the night before due to the kids partying and that, after the kids had fixed the damage and helped the Burles prepare several dozen orders for shipping, Deputy Maybin would escort them with the Burles to the Grand Jubilee, no charges pressed. That story, their trust in the Reeve, and their desire to keep their town's dirty laundry private to make a good impression in Manchineel were more than sufficient to placate the townsfolk of McIntosh and they continued with preparations and plans to attend the Grand Jubilee unaware of the previous night's horrors or the morning's feast.

*This is madness. Unbridled, unequivocal madness.*

Tom and Katie were completely and thoroughly mortified. They were mortified by the fact that their initial conversation amongst themselves inside the Sacrarium had flowed so naturally between them. They were mortified by the fact that their ensuing conversation with the Reverend and the Reeve felt like the first genuine conversation that they were having with them as the foursome stood together on the platform outside of the Sacrarium door. And Tom and Katie were mortified by the fact that they were agreeing to a sacrifice that, no matter its ends for their children, served as both an immediate and eternal condemnation of their souls. Sacrifice in this sense was absolutely synonymous with suicide and murder.

For such a blunt and serious topic, the meeting barely lasted twenty minutes. When it concluded, the Reverend and Reeve triumphantly returned to the final Grand Jubilee preparations. Tom and Katie solemnly opened the door to the Sacrarium and slowly walked back inside. As always seemed to be the case after dealing with their captors, their heads were slumped in defeat with their fates now all but sealed.

Once the tents were set up and the trucks and cars had cleared the drop-off area, Oliver Gustafson drove into Manchineel in the beat-up brown big rig to which he attached a flatbed that was hauling five enormous barbeques, a refrigeration unit, a freezer unit, a large box containing microphones and speakers, and another large box containing fireworks. He pulled the truck right into the drop-off area and then hopped out and directed others in offloading his cargo.

The barbeques were immediately put to work and, within fifteen minutes, they were fully heated and cleaned. A team of Manchineelian chefs then began cooking the main meal of beef ribs, hamburgers, hot dogs, and grilled vegetables. Another team of Manchineelians was busy covering the tables with cloths and lining up caterer-quality stainless steel buffet sets for heating and serving the food along with plates, napkins, eating utensils, and beverages that included lemonade, iced tea, and sodas. Oliver Gustafson led a team with the freezer unit over to the empty organic tea tent and set it up as an ice cream tent. A fireworks team moved the fireworks to the far end of the lake near the Sacrarium and set them up while Reverend Jacobson and the Deacons set up the microphones and speaker system in front of the big rig flatbed so that, while near the lakeshore, they still allowed a ten-yard gap for people to comfortably pass through to get to the tents on either side of the lake.

When the residents of McIntosh began arriving in earnest, the Grand Jubilee was all set and ready to get started with food, ice cream, crafts, and a Manchineel band playing combinations of folk, country, and classic rock tunes in the background. The band played continuously throughout the evening with various townsfolk subbing in every half hour or so to relieve each other.

The mood could not have been more festive or congenial with the exceptions of the Clovis family, who had yet to have a visitor from Manchineel come to their tent to look at their plants, and Kristie Dorbert who hadn't seen Curt Maybin all night. Unlike the parents of the kids at the Burles' farm who assumed that the fire damage and repair work were greater than the

Chief had originally let on, Kristie was frustrated and irritated with Curt being assigned to watch over everyone while missing the Grand Jubilee. Amid Kristie's incessant walking around the perimeter looking for Curt to finally arrive and hoping to have a meaningful kiss and long embrace with him before the night ended, well-fed and happy mouths engaged in conversations with each other as they mingled throughout the evening.

Just before sunset, the band stopped playing as Reverend Jacobson and Gerald Tiebolt stood side-by-side at the microphones. Tiebolt asked for everyone's attention for a few minutes to which many from McIntosh cheered for him with shouts of "Reeve!" demonstrating his popularity among them.

"On behalf of the wonderful people of McIntosh, I want to thank our most excellent friends, neighbors, and hosts in Manchineel for another successful summer Jubilee. When Reverend Jacobson and I started this five years ago, we had no idea how well it might have been received and I am just so pleased that it has become tradition. Living up here in the jewel of the Upper Peninsula, it is the ultimate treat to be able to enjoy each other and the fruits of our labor in a genuine and non-touristy manner. That's really what living up here is all about."

A round of polite and appreciative applause broke out as Tiebolt stepped back from the microphone and gestured to the Reverend that it was his turn to speak.

"What a privilege it is to have such fine neighbors," Reverend Jacobson began. "You know, this isn't just the fifth anniversary of our Jubilee. We here in Manchineel have been referring to it as the Grand Jubilee because it falls on the beginning of the full moon just before the summer solstice. I had asked the Reeve about perhaps moving this to Wednesday on the last day of the full moon and the actual summer solstice but he indicated that, unlike us folks here in Manchineel, the great people of McIntosh are up at the crack of dawn farming and working hard during the week."

A round of laughs broke out among the crowd before the Reverend continued. "There is a special significance though to this celebration. We in Manchineel have a story that has been passed down to us from our ancestors who settled here and founded our beautiful town in 1674. When our ancestors arrived in the Upper Peninsula, they came across a long-abandoned village where the remnants of a Native American tribe known as the Korbani had last been spotted before it was thought that they had become extinct. In the relics of the village, our ancestors came across a parchment which they translated to mean that the daughter of the chief had scouted the area and located the most beautiful piece of land off to the east that she had ever seen or imagined. She led the tribe's remaining people there.

"Where the parchment ended, our ancestors filled in the blank when they arrived at the land of Manchineel on which we are now standing. They saw it as their Garden of Eden and felt the history here, almost as if the Korbani had never left. In fact, even a man of God like me can admit that this beautiful land which we share in Manchineel and McIntosh is truly like the Garden of Eden while we can also feel the spirituality of our history here. I know we, from Manchineel, will always be a part of this land. And I hope that all of our friends and neighbors will become part of this land from tonight on as well."

The residents of McIntosh gave the Reverend a warm round of applause along with a few approving whistles. The residents of Manchineel gave their Reverend a round of applause for the undetectable foreshadowing of his fictitious story while the Reeve gave him a sideways glance and subtle smirk as if to say "You always outdo yourself Caleb." The two community leaders stepped away from the microphones together as the band began playing again in earnest.

Tom and Katie had remained inside the Sacrarium while the Grand Jubilee proceeded as part of their agreement with the Reeve and the Reverend before the festivities commenced.

Their whirlwind weekend defied description and truth being stranger than fiction was certainly apropos to their situation. It was an eclectic collection of words that involved horror, wickedness, and irony.

Watching the dusk through the windows, they heard low hums coming from the tree as if it was expecting the coming onslaught. It was almost like the tree was a pet knowing that it was nearing feeding time. They clutched each other's hands as they moved to the wall by the door fearful that the tree might reach out for them while, at the same time, fearful that one of the serpents would barge through the doors and come after them. The words that they had exchanged only hours earlier with the Reeve and the Reverend from which they had ironically drawn comfort now seemed hollow and empty.

The dusk began fading as the bright light of the full moon and hundreds of surrounding stars began to fill the blackening blue expanse of the sky. With nighttime arriving so late in northern Michigan and the Grand Jubilee falling on a Sunday, the residents of McIntosh began to say their farewells and head towards the parking area since it was already well past their normal Sunday bedtime. The band was playing slow and soft farewell music to complement the departing residents of McIntosh as the residents of each town were exchanging their goodbyes.

At the entrance to Manchineel, Oliver Gustafson pulled up in his tow truck. There were two Manchineel residents in the front seat with him and four others sitting on the tow bed. It was no coincidence that the number of Manchineel residents driving with Gustafson equaled the number of people who had booked and arrived at the McIntosh bed-and-breakfasts earlier that day. Behind the truck was an oversized trailer covered on top and across the back by a black canvass cloth. Gustafson drove the truck towards the lakeshore and pulled past his brown big rig. He then put the truck in reverse and swung the trailer perfectly in a wide arc so that it cleared the front of the big rig and then went straight to the very edge of the water. The six people in and on the tow truck hopped off and headed towards the tents.

Suddenly, the band switched into playing music which was fast, heavy, and loud. It sounded like Ludwig van Beethoven and Johann Sebastian Bach were simultaneously engaging each other in a battle of the bands. The music caught the McIntosh residents by surprise and, as they reflexively turned to the band to figure out why they were playing such music, they were further caught off guard by fireworks being launched at the far side of the lake next to the Sacrarium seemingly timed to shoot off every five seconds or so. Distracted by the commotion of the band and fireworks, the McIntosh residents hardly noticed their hosts transforming under the moonlight into their serpent humanoid forms. The music and fireworks signaled the attack, the likes of which had not been seen anywhere in the world for nearly seventy years.

Gustafson raised the crane on his tow truck to its maximum height which caused it to lift the trailer up from the truck side and, as it rose, dozens of bodies tumbled out into the lake and disappeared into the water. The bed-and-breakfast owners and residents who had chosen to remain in McIntosh and abstain from the Grand Jubilee due to age, illness, or disinterest had all been cleared out as the first victims of the night's massacre.

Everywhere, McIntosh residents were freezing in place trying to simultaneously process one or more of seeing bodies being dropped from the trailer behind Ollie's tow truck, the frantic music being blasted by the band, the explosions and flashing lights of the fireworks, and the serpentine faces of the Manchineelians coming at them from all angles with spiked teeth and outstretched scaly claws. By the time the McIntosh residents had processed enough to know that they were in mortal danger, the first couple dozen of their townspeople had already been felled with a series of throat slashes, broken necks, or all-out attacks on their bodies with biting teeth and stabbing claws.

Panic quickly spread among the surviving McIntosh residents running in all directions to escape the much quicker Manchineelians who easily tracked them down. With each passing second, the Manchineelians became more aggressive. It was almost as if their lack of weapons made them want to tear into their victims with more violence and less mercy. Bodies were soon being decapitated, limbs ripped out of sockets, and chunks of flesh were bitten off in a massacre-turned-frenzy. In less than fifteen minutes, the entire town of McIntosh was strewn across Manchineel in bloody stumps and heaps or deposited into the lake.

# THE AFTER

## *Chapter Twenty*

The night was almost as sleepless as the last. The pillows and blankets were more than sufficient, and the leather sofas that had been pulled out after the lower level had been cleaned and cleared following the Manchineelians' cannibalistic feast were extremely comfortable allowing Tom and Katie to nestle right into the cushions. But there is no rest for a disturbed mind, especially in the very location of the feast. All night long, Tom's head pounded with the shrieks of over four hundred men, women, and children, in choir with the tree's humming, and fireworks exploding in the shapes of cymbals with the embers morphing into bloody flesh. Those thoughts were part of a loop in Tom's mind followed by Mrs. Stevenson, Tom's favorite Sunday School teacher, giving a lesson on the Bible's ethical laws: "When given the choice to die or have another killed in your place, you must choose death." That quote was followed by flashes of hell, eternity in a casket, and the empty black void of death. Finally, Tom thought of Dawn, Tommy, Jake, and their futures, complete with spouses and grandchildren. Then the thoughts cycled around right back to the shrieks.

Tom sat up morosely just at the crack of dawn and stared silently at the tree. Katie was already doing the same, sharing Tom's look of grief, guilt, trauma, bewilderment, and shame. Ironically, there was no time for Tom or Katie to add emptiness to their list of bad feelings in the present. They had chosen. All that was left was to play it off to the children so that they could move on and lead normal lives like all children should.

Shortly after eight o'clock, Tom and Katie heard the Sacrarium door opening followed by metallic clanking and footsteps. The Reverend and Molly Jacobson arrived with Deacon Forsythe and Maryanna carrying trays of breakfast and a carafe of fresh hot coffee. Despite being stuck in the aftermath of a massacre which no rational person would believe, let alone comprehend, Tom and Katie were truly grateful for the warm sustenance of the food and coffee. It was the first calm moment, a relative term under the circumstances, that they had shared in the last twenty-four hours without worrying about their children or enduring physical threats from their captors, notwithstanding their impending sacrifice. The parties had reached an agreement the previous afternoon before the Grand Jubilee, and the Prestons needed to get their affairs in order. Tom specifically had a number of arrangements to make in order for the Manchineelians to keep their end of the bargain.

"How are the children?" Katie asked in a dry and scratchy voice, the remains of what was left from the previous day's terror. The trauma had been so harsh that Tom wondered whether the Manchineelians had caused permanent damage to her vocal cords.

"Oh, they're fine. They've been doing great," Molly answered. "Dr. Arbour gave them a special fruit punch-flavored drink last night so they should be sleeping until later this morning. They don't know about anything other than you having been driven to Marquette by one of our neighbors because there was an auto shop that was open and had the part that you needed while our neighbor was coincidentally visiting his mother but staying the night at her house. Your children are very smart, as you know, and they grilled us on the details to see if there was any way that you could have returned to Manchineel yesterday, but that's the story they were told and finally accepted. At any rate, I'd wager that you will have missed them much more than they missed you."

Tom thought about calling bullshit on

that line but it was not a good time. The balance of power being what it was, there was no reason to upset the plan for the next three days and ruin the time that they had left. Besides, there was a chance that Molly's perception was correct and Tom sincerely hoped that was the case.

Tom and Katie took their time eating breakfast in the relative peace of the moment and got their much-needed boost from the coffee. Caffeine was going to have to be their substitute for sleep for the remainder of their time together in Manchineel. The group engaged in small talk and, slightly after nine o'clock, the Forsythes escorted Tom and Katie back to their home past an unsurprisingly green and pristine landscape as if nothing but the morning dew had fallen overnight. Unlike the other times that they were forcefully returned to the Forsythes' home, Tom and Katie were greeted with their fully restored and repaired SUV parked in the Forsythes' driveway. Upstairs, their cellphones were fully charged and getting decent reception. As an added bonus, their files had all been returned to them – photographs, documents, emails, applications, everything.

Katie, dry of tears by that time, sat quietly on the edge of the bed poring through all of the pictures both on her phone and in her files. The children would be brought to her soon enough, but she could not wait to see their young shining faces and smiles.

Tom, in the meantime, gave Katie a warm hug around her shoulders as he headed into Deacon Forsythe's study to make the necessary phone calls and arrangements. Even with his phone and files back in working order, he was terrified by the thought of how easily the Manchineelians, or anyone for that matter, could seemingly wipe out and later replace a person's existence. In many ways, the restoration of his phone made Tom feel even less secure than he had felt when his phone was deleted because now the Manchineelians could seemingly track the Prestons at will. Tom wasn't a technology guy by any means, but he was fairly certain that the Manchineelians had loaded his phone and files with Trojan horses or whatever applications or malware they desired in order to keep an eye on him and his family.

Dr. Arbour and his wife Ginnifer eventually brought Dawn, Tommie, and Jake over to the Forsythes' house just past eleven o'clock after the children had woken from their drink-induced slumber and had a chance to brush their teeth and dress for the day. Tom and Katie put on their best acting job in trying not to cry, speak loudly, or hug and kiss the children too much in order to downplay their day apart. Fortunately, the children seemed more excited about having the car back. Maryanna had graciously prepared a lunch for the Prestons, and the Forsythes and Arbours kept them company while they ate.

Tom finished quickly and headed back to the Deacon's study to continue with his work while his family remained with their hosts talking and, eventually, retreating to the parlor to play some old board games.

Two hours later, the Prestons were hiking around a peaceful lake guided by the Arbours. Neither Tom nor Katie went anywhere near the water at first, and they both cringed and held their collective breath when Tommie and Jake put their hands in trying to catch a frog. It was only when the boys excitedly caught the frog and the water on their hands showed no signs of blood that Tom and Katie exhaled.

Later that afternoon, the Prestons were joined at the lake by the Gustafsons and the Stanton brothers who relieved the Arbours to take the Prestons fishing on a pontoon boat. Yet again, the word surreal failed in Tom's mind to describe how he and his family were having such a fun day with their captors. Watching the children's faces marvel with excitement as they caught thirteen fish between them while Ollie and Herman taught them how to quickly grab and unhook the fish defied the word surreal. Edward Stanton seemed to be reading Tom's mind or thinking along those lines as he looked directly at Tom and winked after Jake caught the first fish, a one-pound largemouth bass, and Ollie taught the young boy how to hold and unhook it.

At eight o'clock in the evening, as had been agreed, the Prestons returned to the Forsythes' house where a supper awaited them in the dining room. To please Jake, Maryanna made sure to set the table with her silver and gold silverware that he loved. Afterwards, the Prestons retired to their rooms where televisions and DVD players had been set up for their entertainment. Tom and Katie made sure that the children never saw the Deacon or Maryanna after dusk and, when the children fell asleep, Tom quietly walked downstairs to the Deacon's office to continue with his work.

Tom's journey down the hall and to the office was not for the faint of heart. Although the Forsythes knew that Tom would be working in the office, they never discussed with Tom where they would be or what they would be doing while Katie and the children were asleep. As Tom walked down the darkened hallway to the stairwell entrance, the only light came from the entryway on the main level below. Tom was having visions of the Forsythes in their serpentine forms creeping up on him in the dark to feast on his flesh, and he repeatedly had to shut his eyes and steady himself against the wall before being able to slowly proceed to the Deacon's office. Once he safely reached the office, however, Tom was able to engross himself in his work which absolutely had to be finished to perfection as time was running out.

Hours into his work, Tom was exhausted and craving his holding-cell bed upstairs. He quickly took a mental inventory of all the work that he had completed and all the work that remained for him to complete. Satisfied that he was ahead of the game and would have more than enough time to finish the remaining work, he closed his files on the laptop computer that Oliver had lent him, closed the screen, and prepared to head to sleep.

"I hope your work product is as good as your focus."

Tom bolted upright as sharp bolts of pain raced through his back where he reaggravated his pulled muscle yet again. The serpentine form of Deacon Forsythe had appeared sideways through the office doorframe just as quietly as the suddenness of the giant man's hissing words.

"I hope it is too, for your sake." Tom instantly recognized the voice, despite the hiss, as Deacon Thornhill although he could not see him. The man-serpent never had a pleasant thing to say, let alone a pleasant demeanor.

Deacon Forsythe's claws scratched against the doorframe as he slowly moved into his office. In response, Tom leaned into the Deacon's heavy desk for support and slowly pushed himself up into a standing position shooting more bolts of pain through his back. Upon gaining his balance, Tom steadily moved backwards, a combination of surprise and fear at the Deacon's arrival and entry into the office which effectively cornered Tom behind the desk area. In the office's lighting, Tom could clearly see the Deacon's olive-gray serpentine eyes, scales and claws. With his heart rate increasing, Tom also noticed the Deacon's sharp teeth beneath his snout and the fact that he was now effectively cornered by the monster who, having no need to conceal himself, stood before Tom in the office's electrical light free of any camouflage to match the surroundings.

Before Tom could speak again to determine what intentions, if any, the Deacon had, Maryanna entered the room followed by the Thornhills and the Tiebolts. Facing six serpentine Manchineelians was more than Tom could bear and he quickly stepped backwards until his throbbing back bumped into the wall.

"Pity we can't do the sacrifice now," Patricia Thornhill hissed as her husband moved alongside her to flank Tom while giving an approving hiss-laugh.

"Pity we can't eat any more until after the sacrifice," Maryanna hissed.

It was at that point that Tom panicked given that Maryanna had been among the kinder, again a relative term, of the Prestons' captors to that point. Hearing her serpentine form speak those evil words, Tom shouted "Get away from me now! All of you! Or you'll have no sacrifice." Tom then began looking around for any objects he could use and grabbed the only thing in his view that made any modicum of sense: a dagger-shaped letter opener.

"Relax Tom," the Reeve hissed at the back of the group as Deacon Forsythe effortlessly ripped the letter opener from Tom's hand. "Maryanna didn't mean anything by it other than the fact that we all hunger at night during this period. We came here for your protection just in case any of our brothers and sisters lack our self-control. Please, go up to bed and you may continue in the morning."

"Your sacrifice will be well worth it in the end Thomas," the Reverend hissed. "Take solace and assurance in that. This is God's plan for you and for us."

"I- it will be, I hope" Tom replied in a wavering voice as he put up his hands in a feeble attempt to hold off the knot of serpent people closing in on him as he exited the office. The entire way back to his room, Tom walked at a brisk pace while looking from side to side even though the constant twisting wreaked havoc on his back. He refused, however, to turn around for fear of seeing the Manchineelians lurking behind him in ambush position and, instead, he merely listened for their footsteps or claws which, luckily, he never heard.

*No fucking way that just happened* was all Tom could think as he briskly and fearfully walked the main level hallway back to the entry way, then up the darkened stairs, and then down the darkened hallway to his room. Of all the horrors that he and Katie had endured on their trip, he didn't think he could ever be alone in the dark again without running in fear of the images of six serpentine Manchineelians cornering him in the office. *No fucking way that just happened!*

When Tom arrived at his room, he panicked all over again at noticing that Katie was missing. He spun around and ran to the children's room where he noticed Katie sleeping in the bed with Tommie and Jake.

*Thank God! Well, of course she would be with our children. Why would we ever go to sleep without our children in Manchineel? Why would we ever let our children out of our sight ever again? Why the hell did I even assume that Katie and I would sleep in a separate room?*

With the images of the six Manchineelians cornering him in the office continuing to race through his head, Tom leaned against the doorframe of the children's room until his back stopped throbbing enough for him to walk again. He then returned to his room to retrieve his pillow and comforter which he gingerly carried across the hallway and placed next to Dawn's mattress on the floor before lying down and falling into some semblance of sleep. As with the previous night, it was a restless and distressed form of sleep. In between dreams of Manchineelians, his children missing, and all of the other weekend horrors, Tom woke up at periodic intervals to make sure his family was all there. In the background of his dreams and sleep-like haze, he could hear Katie doing the same from the boys' bed. In two days' time, all of this would come to an end if they even made it to that point.

Tuesday was another good family day. It began that way by Tom making the smart decision to not tell Katie about the previous night. He merely told her a half-truth in that he had accomplished a great deal while working late as they were washing up and getting dressed for the day.

Following a French toast and fresh fruit breakfast prepared by Maryanna, the Prestons and the Tiebolts drove to Tahquamenon Falls where they enjoyed the entire package of watching the Upper Falls (50 feet in height and 200 feet in width) and hiking in the streams around the Lower Falls (a series of five smaller waterfalls surrounding an island). Known for their beauty and brown color due to the tannins from the cedar swamps that the Tahquamenon River drains, Tom always felt that the rusty color gave them a rustic and somewhat creepy look. Now, however, Tom saw only natural beauty and took comfort in knowing that such beauty could endure for millennia. At the same time, Tom reflected on the uncomfortable contrast in the ancient brown falls' beauty and the menace of the ancient Manchineelians in their white homes amidst the Garden of Eden.

Upon returning to the Forsythes' in the late afternoon, Tom spent the next several hours completing his work and getting all of his other affairs in order while Katie and the children hiked around Manchineel and received warm greetings from the townsfolk who happened to be outside as well. When Katie and the children returned, the children ran to their room to watch a movie while Katie walked in on Tom kneeling in prayer at the side of the bed in their room. Neither of them had ever been religious practitioners, but Katie fully understood. She joined Tom, and the two of them engaged in a second prayer session after putting the children to sleep a few hours later. Just before dusk, Deacon Forsythe knocked on their door and told them "I'll come get you in the morning."

Tom and Katie cringed at the Deacon's words and reflexively lifted their comforter up like children trying to cover themselves from the boogeyman in the closet. For all of their emotional preparation over the previous days and hours, the Deacon's words gave life to the finality of their path. There was no getting out of their agreement or going back on their word. Their decision was made and set in stone. Their discomfort and dread of spending the night in their room in Manchineel without their children was only surpassed by the dread of what was to come.

The private jet, flown by Ansel Marsh of the Manchineel faithful and wearing the seal of The Eternal Quest on his pilot's cap, landed in Marquette shortly after two o'clock in the afternoon. Tom and Katie, wearing borrowed casual business clothing from Herman and Marjorie Stanton, were accompanied on the roundtrip flight to Metro Airport and back by Gerald and Pamela Tiebolt along with two other men from Manchineel, brothers Jamison and Willem Chrysopelea. All of the Manchineel contingent posed as business partners and Tom's new clients looking for a private investment in their oil drilling project. As the jet parked in its private hangar, the Prestons and the Manchineelians escorted the two passengers out to a waiting stretch limousine driven by one Oliver Gustafson.

Tom had spent his working time on Monday and Tuesday scanning and forwarding the late nineteenth century documents of one Tipton Welles, former owner of the parchment, that had been lent to Tom by Gerald Tiebolt to effectuate his plan. Tiebolt, in his position at the clerk's office, had made sure to transfer all of Tipton Welles' land to himself decades earlier in his attempt to conceal Manchineel and its secrets. The thought of Tiebolt's acts, whether out of foresight or simply setting the stage for future massacres, was simply too much for Tom to ponder or worry about under the circumstances so he ignored the subject throughout his remaining time in Manchineel. Instead, Tom had spent his time preparing title documents and exclusive rights agreements for their primary passenger to review along with a pro forma, corporate documents, and an investment agreement.

The primary passenger, one Stellan Bandik, had initially been annoyed with Tom for calling him on a Sunday afternoon while he was out golfing. Bandik, however, quickly changed his tune when Tom informed him that he and Katie had befriended a small business group in the Upper Peninsula who had obtained exclusive drilling rights on land believed to hold nearly two hundred million dollars' worth of oil in an untapped well. Tom explained to Bandik that the group needed approximately ten million dollars in investment capital to hire workers and purchase the necessary equipment and, in exchange for said investment, would be willing to grant Bandik a twenty percent stake in the venture. Tom further explained that another five million dollars was needed for a top-secret project that would revolutionize the oil industry but that the project could only be discussed in person. Tom then invited Bandik to come up and meet with the business group and tour the site on Wednesday with his secretary with whom he could stay at the group's exclusive five-star hotel. The only thing that Tom demanded of Bandik was that Bandik sign a non-disclosure agreement so that no one would know about the investment deal or Bandik's whereabouts in connection with the deal.

Following his greed and trusting in Tom based on the masterful legal representation that Tom had provided to him in the courts, Bandik signed the non-disclosure agreement and agreed to be flown up on Wednesday with his secretary-slash-mistress Robin. The two of them enjoyed their champagne and caviar flight as well as the stretch limousine greeting them at the airport which provided comfort during the long drive to the Manchineel region. At their first destination, the empty downtown of McIntosh followed by a tour of the crop fields towards the back end of town, Gerald Tiebolt gave an award-worthy performance describing each and every step of how and where their company was going to drill out the oil.

Tom and Katie both felt that they also gave exceptional acting performances by remaining stoic while Tiebolt continued his spiel by telling Bandik how lucky they were because the land of McIntosh was completely vacant. Even as Tiebolt fabricated tales of economic hardship in McIntosh and the last remaining properties being foreclosed upon more than one year ago with his "company" now owning all of the land outright, another legal item fabricated by Tom, Tom and Katie did not flinch. Tom even chimed in by representing to Bandik that he had spent the previous day at the county clerk's office going through the title records of each of the McIntosh properties and that such properties were in fact legitimately owned by Tiebolt's "company."

Tiebolt then proceeded to talk about his plans to clear the land for drilling, noting to Bandik that most drilling activities would be performed on the farmland without having to spend any of Bandik's investment funds on removing existing houses and buildings. Bandik, of course, seemed pleased with the prospect of not having any of his investment wasted on demolition work in order to focus entirely on production and profits. To that end, Tiebolt began his wrap-up by discussing all of the prospective purchasers and purchasing arrangements that he had reached for the oil once it was drilled. To reinforce his manufactured arrangements, Tielbolt provided Bandik with significantly more optimistic numbers than Tom had provided on his pro forma while Tom represented to Bandik that he had looked into the prospective purchasers who were tremendously large and profitable operations. As the time passed, Bandik grew from receptive to unabashedly eager to invest in the oil-drilling venture. Bandik was chomping at the proverbial bit to sign the investment agreements that Tom had prepared for him while speaking to his Manchineelian hosts as if they were already business partners.

Tom, for his part, maintained his role as the dutiful lawyer refusing to allow Bandik to sign anything until Bandik was presented with the top-secret component of the deal at dinner. In taking this tact with Bandik, Tom was reinforcing to his client that Tom was only looking out for his best interests in order to maintain the impression with Bandik that Tom was on Bandik's side and that this was a business deal into which prudent people should never rush until they properly review and analyze all of the details. It was a tremendous and profitable deal as far as Bandik was concerned, but Tom wanted to make sure that Bandik did not become too enraptured in it only to suddenly back out if he felt that the deal seemed too good to be true. At the same time, Tom knew that Bandik was not worried about him in any way. More precisely, Tom knew that Bandik would never suspect Tom of engineering a sham deal or getting Bandik involved in a business venture that would lose him money. As far as Bandik was concerned, Tom was owned by Bandik's good friend and Tom's boss, Dean Strickland, such that Tom could never do anything adverse to his interests. Tom was merely playing the game using his knowledge of Bandik against him in order to keep him on board and in the haze of greed and promise of financial paradise.

What pained Tom throughout the process was the undeniable fact that this whole charade was Tom's idea. It was Tom, not the Manchineelians, who devised this evil ruse. He and Katie had agreed to this path to preserve their family and it would be their judgment. For all the horror inflicted upon them by the Manchineelians, Tom and Katie were now partnered with the Manchineelians in this game of death with the purported justification of preserving life.

Sensing Bandik's impatience and eagerness to move things along and finish the deal, Tom asked Gerald Tiebolt to drive them to dinner and the final phase of the trip. As much as Tom wished for his game to conclude, he knew that there would never be any real conclusion as long as he lived, but he refused to accept another way or dwell on the subject, at least at that moment or anytime in the near future. Tiebolt whistled over to Oliver Gustafson who then drove everyone to Manchineel.

Gustafson pulled up to the very edge of the lake where Katie had bolted into the water and the Manchineelians had committed their fifth grand massacre a mere three days beforehand.

"This place is gorgeous!" Robin's astonishment was palpable.

"Is there going to be a real estate component with this deal?" Bandik asked as Tom subtly rolled his eyes at Bandik's insatiable greed and nerve asking about real estate in front of Tom after Tom defended him throughout his own real estate scandal.

"There could be," Tiebolt responded. "If you join up, we can bring you into the real estate side of the business. I can even see you having a residence of your own up here. We'd love to have you."

"Tom, look into that for me as soon as possible," Bandik commanded.

At that point, Tom lost what little sense of remorse and compassion for Bandik that he had. He also took a second to appreciate Tiebolt's wit at Bandik's unknowing expense.

"Mr. Bandik, Robin, please come on up with us to the Greenhouse, as we call it," Tiebolt said pointing to the Sacrarium.

The group walked up the hill towards the Sacrarium, all the while Robin remarked about the unparalleled beauty of Manchineel while Bandik kept stating how many millions the land could be worth. By the time they reached the Sacrarium's enormous gothic entrance, the Manchineel contingent hated Bandik as much as Tom and fully understood why Tom had devised the plan and Katie agreed to it. Oddly enough, Bandik finally said something that everyone agreed with while marveling at the structure and its marble columns as the gigantic door was pushed open from the inside: "This place defies economics."

“You have no idea Mr. Bandik,” Reverend Jacobson said while approaching him with Herman Stanton at his side. Tom almost burst into laughter at the sight of them pretending to be scientists in white lab coats bearing The Eternal Quest symbols on the chest pockets.

“This is the top-secret component of the deal,” Tom said to an anxious Bandik.

“That it is Tom,” the Reverend acknowledged. He then leaned forward to shake Bandik’s hand and said “Welcome Mr. Bandik. Welcome Robin. Tom has told us great things about you, and we look forward to having you on board as partners. My name is Caleb Jacobson and this is my research partner Herman Stanton. Normally in business deals, this is the part where the seller says something cheesy or quirky to the investor to spur more interest in the deal and get it done. The reality here is that this is not something that we can undersell. Why don’t you follow me into the Greenhouse so you can actually see what we’re here for. Words won’t do it justice, and the oil investment will pale in comparison to what we have here.”

With that, the Reverend motioned everyone forward as he walked them towards the tree of life. The main level had been cleared of its pews, lectern, and sacred objects leaving only a large empty space overlooking the tree. Despite its emptiness, the room felt grand in its size as it was illuminated by the fading sunlight reflecting off the leaves of the lush tree.

Robin walked over to the balcony continuing with her praise of the beauty of Manchineel. Bandik, on the other hand, only walked halfway to the balcony before stopping to stare at the tree in bewilderment. Tom suspected that Bandik could not grasp the concept of raw natural beauty free from materiality. At the same time, Tom circled back to the word surreal in the fact that Bandik and Robin had no clue that they were standing before the single greatest object on Earth known to mankind.

Like Tom, the Reverend noticed Bandik's confusion and took that as his cue to continue with the presentation. "About five years ago, we located a cluster of trees that were unlike trees anywhere else in Michigan or North America, or anywhere else in the world for that matter. We actually discovered them about ten miles from where you were today on land that we had drilled and where oil had spilled. We kept the spill under wraps from the environmental agencies as we tried to determine what happened with our drilling equipment which appeared to have had some sort of malfunction. We need to upgrade our equipment and, as you know from your discussions with Mr. Preston and Mr. Tiebolt, that is where you and your investment come into play.

"Fortunately for all of us, no one ever discovered the oil spill or we might have some competition for what is about to happen here. You see, weeks after the spill, we noticed that the oil was virtually gone and, although the vegetation that had been touched by the oil was dead or dying, the trees were still thriving. We uprooted this tree and have been conducting tests on it. It appears to essentially transform oil into several organic compounds which are healthy for the tree and the environment. It is, effectively, the key to getting rid of pollution which benefits the world and, frankly, could save the world. Even more frankly, these trees are worth billions!"

"We're talking tens of billions," Tiebolt echoed.

Robin gave an audible gasp and Bandik excitedly twiddled his hands together.

"Come on with us to the tree so you can see it up close for yourselves."

The Manchineelians then escorted Bandik and Robin to the stairwell and walked down to the ground level giving them a quick tour of the area that had somehow been superficially remodeled to look like a laboratory and conference room. Both Tom and Katie had noticed some of the equipment from Oliver Gustafson's office being used as props and managed to contain their amusement. A long table had been formally set along with a piping hot meal and bottles of wine. As a nice touch, the Manchineelians had placed the investment agreements that Tom prepared on a silver platter in the middle of the table for Bandik to sign with a gold and pearl pen.

"Mr. Bandik, the deal is on the table for you to sign at your pleasure," Tiebolt invited.

"Tom, this deal seems to be in order. Everything I could want, right?" Bandik's tone showed no hint of seeking or needing Tom's guidance.

"Absolutely right sir," Tom responded in his formal voice.

Bandik leaned over putting the pen to paper as he signed the documents. He then stood up feeling all-important as Gerald Tiebolt quickly congratulated him with a handshake and gesture to keep the pen while the rest of the Manchineel contingent, and Robin, clapped in a circle around them as the summer solstice sun began setting.

"Before we get started on this magnificent meal," Reverend Jacobson announced, "let's have our new partners come and feel this tree. You will be amazed. There is no other tree in the world that feels like this."

Bandik and Robin excitedly walked over to the tree while the Reverend explained that they would feel that it had a different texture and bark structure than other trees. With all of the dollar signs on their minds, Bandik and Robin failed to notice that all of the remaining Manchineel townsfolk had quietly entered the Sacrarium and were eagerly watching from the main level balcony. The Arbours had given the Preston children the same fruit punch drink following their day of babysitting after telling them that a new problem was found with the family car. With the darkness from the setting sun making its way into the Sacrarium, Tom and Katie both noticed the Manchineelians starting to bear their serpentine forms. They slowly moved together forming a knot while Tom wrapped his arms around Katie.

Oblivious to the tension and anticipation surrounding them in the Sacrarium, Bandik and Robin placed their hands side-by-side on the tree's trunk. The building was dead-silent.

Suddenly, Bandik began to speak. "I think I can actually feel something."

"Wow, I can feel it too. What's that--" Robin began in an unidentifiable tone before cutting out.

While all of the Manchineelians watched the spectacle in silent reverence, Tom observed the Reverend giving a bewildered and curious glance towards Bandik and Robin just as a bright light emerged from the tree's trunk and completely enveloped them.

*He didn't see that coming, whatever Bandik and Robin meant. The great know-it-all didn't see that coming, whatever "that" was.*

For everything that had occurred in Manchineel, Tom added this new layer of intrigue and mystery in that, of all the things that he would remember and carry with him for the rest of his life, he would never be able to forget or stop thinking about the look on the Reverend's face following Stellan Bandik's and Robin's last words at the tree. No matter what happened or what the Prestons wanted to believe, Tom knew that they had just been firsthand witnesses to the fact that life, history, and reality on Earth existed in an exponentially broader sense than they and virtually everyone else in the world had previously known.

The children piled out of the car exhausted from the long trip home and eager to go through the comforts of their possessions that had remained at the house during their two-week vacation in the Upper Peninsula. Tom and Katie reminded them to take in all of their bags but to leave their bags with clothes in the laundry room. Later that evening, Dawn made popcorn and the family enjoyed a quiet evening in front of the television.

The next day, Tom noticed an express delivery box at their front door when he went to get the mail. Whatever was inside of it felt smaller than the shipping box, although it weighed about ten pounds. Tom called Katie over and opened the shipping box. Inside, surrounded by bubble wrap, was a cherry wood box that was roughly the size of a shoe box. Engraved on top was the symbol of The Eternal Quest. Tom opened the box and inside were five lustrous green fruits resembling apples, each one set in its own soft holding compartment lined with smooth golden silk. Attached to the inside of the box was a note.

*My Dear Tom and Katie,*

*You have truly left a profound mark upon us. As you can surmise, our gratitude is eternal. You only need one fruit apiece should that be your decision and, when your children are of age, they can make that decision for themselves. Should you choose to join your path with ours, we bid you welcome. There is so much more for you to know.*

*Fondly,*
*Reverend Caleb Jacobson*

After pulling the Reeve and Reverend Jacobson aside at the Sacrarium prior to the Grand Jubilee, Tom presented the master plan that he had discussed and agreed upon with Katie: concoct the scheme to trick Stellan Bandik and his mistress into unknowingly taking their place as the sacrifice so that Tom and Katie could live out their lives with their children. The reward for this cruelty and deceit, for complicity in the murders of two human beings, however bad or flawed, was before them in the form of immortality wrapped in silk in a cherry wood box.

Tom and Katie placed the box in their secret bedroom safe. They were mentally exhausted, in fact drained, from the longest two weeks of their lives. They knew that their decision required a great deal of time and the utmost consideration as they were again facing the ultimate choice between life and death. The promise of immortality was as frightening as it was liberating. Indeed, no matter how much immortality immunized them from the pressures of every-day life, there would always be the questions of whether an immortal human existence was some form of eternal damnation replacing a heavenly afterlife and whether their actions in Manchineel precluded them from Heaven in any event. Exhausted and wanting to avoid the weight of their decision and the consequences for all of their actions, Tom and Katie closed and locked the safe. Their test of faith would have to wait for another day.